SPELLSHOCK

Also by W. V. Fitz-Simon

THE WITCH OF CHEYNE HEATH:
Book 1: Waking the Witch
Book 2: Craftwork
Book 4: Paint it Black

THE WITCH OF CHEYNE HEATH
BOOK 3

W. V. Fitz-Simon

Dedo Press
New York

For inquiries regarding this book, please contact:
witold@wvfitzsimon.com

www.wvfitzsimon.com

Cover Design: Curtis Wallin
www.curtiswallin.com
Interior Illustrations: Barbara Hulanicki
www.barbarahulanickidesign.com

ISBN: 978-0-9771733-7-2

Published 2020

For my mother,
Barbara Hulanicki

1

"DO COME IN," SAID THE woman, her long face obscured by a large and bizarre pair of glasses: two thick pink circles joined by a white squiggly line, and a bright blue fleck in the corner of each eye that suggested an upturned eyelash. "I'll put the kettle on and you can tell me all about it."

That's my line, thought Gosha, taken aback.

Małgorzata Mierzejewska Armitage had dreaded the prospect that this woman might be another witch, an inconvenience that would have created no end of problems, but she was in luck. The iridescent ropey vines of Influence, the magical force emanating from all human beings, that swirled around the woman's pink, red, and blue colorblock cocktail dress in Gosha's second sight told her this was an oath-bearer, most likely an acolyte of Abundance.

The acolyte's house was in the only truly posh part of Cheyne Heath, right at the edge where the King's Road cut across the borough on its path from Chelsea to Fulham. From where she stood, Gosha could see the street that marked the border wall of the wards that held her husband, George, at bay. Half a mile away on the other side of the boundary was World's End and her favorite boutique that she hadn't visited in four years, not since George had murdered his father and she'd been forced to embrace her heritage and become a witch.

Alfie squeezed her hand, bringing her back to the present.

"How is dear Bessie Walpole?" said the acolyte as she led them into the house.

"Remember." Gosha leaned in to whisper in Alfie's ear. "Newlyweds trying to find the money to buy a new house."

He pecked her on the lips and waggled his eyebrows, a mischievous dimple creasing his cheek. His smile caused her heart to beat faster and somewhere further south to tingle. He knew about Craft and Influence, and had proved sturdy enough to take the secret world of the spheres in his stride, but she'd never enlisted his help on behalf of a client before. She hoped his experience working as a bouncer in the nightclubs of Cheyne Heath had trained him to think on his feet.

"She's doing very well, Mrs. Ogilvy." Gosha lied in response to the acolyte's question. Bessie Walpole was a writhing bundle of regret for falling prey to the pitch of this sorcerous con woman. "She has such wonderful things to say about your techniques."

That much was true. No matter how much Gosha and Belinda, Bessie's daughter, tried to convince Bessie that her sudden inability to pay her electricity bill was the fault of this fraudulent spiritual advisor and not her own inability to manifest prosperity by force of will alone, Bessie refused to say a bad word about her.

"Ah," said the acolyte. "Bless."

As they stepped across the threshold, Gosha shuddered. Most of her work as a witch was mundane stuff. She spent her days preparing potions and poultices, blending teas and crafting candles, with the occasional augury thrown in to make the passage of days more interesting. She had yet to master the art of fortune-telling, her telling deck still only half done, but most of a reading was telling the querent what they didn't know or refused to see about the present, and her skill in clairvoyance was more than proficient enough to satisfy any client who visited her kitchen. Once in a while, resolving a visitor's problem required direct intervention of a more physical nature, for which she was grateful to have Alfie.

The switchblade he had given her and taught her to use weighed comfortingly in the pocket of her red felt bolero jacket, a steal of a find in Morel Market that only cost her a charm against erectile dysfunction and a cure for migraines.

Most man-made threats to the health and wellbeing of her visitors could be taken care of with a flash of steel, an occasional Doc Martens boot to the groin, and a well-placed spell of intimidation. Only twice before had she been forced to deal with oath-bearers. Both times had been near-catastrophic, with the lives of hundreds of innocents threatened, the trouble only averted by the skin of her teeth. In the aftermath, her life had been transformed for the worse.

A dense and cloying scent of potpourri wafted at her from somewhere within the living room and made her sneeze.

"Sit, sit," said the acolyte gesturing to two sofas and an armchair arranged at crisp right angles around a long coffee table. "Make yourself comfortable."

That will be a challenge, thought Gosha.

The color scheme of the living room was an eye-watering visual cacophony of bright and contrasting color. Blue, peach, pink, yellow, green, and red furniture pieces fought for dominance against a background of stark white walls. The furniture was all hard lines and nonsensical asymmetrical shapes with crisp flat surfaces better designed for looking at than sitting on. The overall effect was of a children's playhouse designed by a demented architect.

Memphis design, thought Gosha, the style-obsessed part of her brain salivating even as her senses reeled from the avant garde absurdity of it all. *Not cheap.*

"Not there, you gorgeous creature," said the acolyte with a flirtatious widening of the eyes as Alfie made for the armchair. Alfie was an effortlessly handsome charmer that men and women of all orientations warmed to quickly, but few of his admirers acted as brazen as this woman. "That's my chair. You may sit here."

She patted the space at the end of one sofa by the armchair. Gosha had introduced Alfie and herself as husband and wife, but realized neither was wearing a ring. Her own wedding ring sat on a shelf in her studio, out of sight but not forgotten, no matter how hard she tried. She kicked herself for overlooking such a simple detail. Details were important when you were putting on a show.

"I'll get the tea," said the acolyte and disappeared into the back of the house.

With the second sight gifted her by the touch of her talisman of power, a treasured tube of lipstick that nestled against her breast in the folds of her bra, she could see thick currents of Influence sweeping through the room, much denser than what normally flowed through the world. It swirled around the armchair at the head of the coffee table.

"So," whispered Alfie. "Is she a witch?"

"Thank god, no," said Gosha as she wandered around the room inspecting the furniture. "But she is an oath-bearer. Keep her talking, but be careful. You saw what she did to Bessie Walpole."

Photographs in irregular geometric designs and primary colors lined all the display surfaces in the room. As Alfie slid into the sofa and crossed a long leg over a shapely thigh, she tore her eyes away from him and turned to the nearest collection of shots. To her surprise, there was no sign of the acolyte herself in any of the pictures. All featured a middle-aged woman in a variety of over-designed business suits with massive shoulder pads, pencil skirts, and far too many ruffles. At first, Gosha thought they were production stills of Joan Collins from that show, 'Dynasty,' on the telly, but closer inspection revealed much less attractive features beaten into shape by a serious application of cosmetics. Flawless on camera, Gosha suspected in person she would look like an over-made-up clown.

"Do you recognize the woman in all these pictures?" she asked Alfie.

He leaned over to pick up a picture frame from the coffee table.

"Never seen her before." He shrugged.

"That," said the acolyte, returning far too quickly for the tea to have been made conventionally, "is Portia Twill-Quimby herself."

She placed the tea set on the coffee table in front of her armchair. At the center of the red lacquer tray was a jumble of cylinders, balls, and tubes that must have been the teapot. Her mother and Elsie would have recoiled from it in horror, but it was an object of such strong and radical design that it made Gosha breathless with desire. She'd been stuck making potions in her kitchen for so long without even a glossy magazine to keep her company, she'd fallen completely behind the times. The world had moved on without her.

A sly smirk fluttered across the corner of the acolyte's lips when she saw the expression of unbridled lust on Gosha's face. Gosha began to rearrange her features back to a less naked expression, but decided she could make it work for her and sat on the sofa next to Alfie, hugging his arm and openly admiring the tea set as the acolyte poured.

"Who is Portia Twill-Quimby?" asked Alfie, cheerfully playing along.

"A truly great woman," said the acolyte. "She's an award-winning entrepreneur and philanthropist and, I'm proud to say, she is my mentor. Many of the techniques I use to help my clients come from her. She's a national treasure."

Must be the saint, thought Gosha as she eyed the teacups, three blue-gray inverted pyramids with giant pink circular handles. *I must ask the ladies if they know anything about her.*

Gosha froze the muscles of her face to stop the expression of disgust that threatened to consume it as the hot tea poured out of the black tubular spout. Translucent tentacles of Influence coiled around the liquid, pulsing and questing from the surface of the cup. The acolyte handed it to Alfie with an inviting smile.

Gosha snapped her hand out and gently wrapped her long fingers around Alfie's wrist before he touched the saucer. Even accepting the cup from the acolyte might bind him to her in some unknown way.

"Oh, no tea, darling," she said. "Remember the diet."

He looked at her, eyebrows raised in a question. Understanding flickered behind those pretty blue eyes, and his gaze flickered to the offered cup in alarm.

"Oh yes, the diet," he said and pulled his hand back. He sat on his hands with a sheepish grin and looked like a schoolboy caught with his fingers in the cookie jar.

A scowl rippled across the acolyte's face for the briefest instant as she replaced the cup on the tray. Gosha noticed she didn't partake of the tea herself.

"What diet is that?" she said with an inquiring smile. Gosha would have loved to play poker with this woman. Her inner monologue was as clear on her face as if written in thick black marker.

"No tea, no chocolate," said Gosha. More tentacles of Influence sprouted from the pile of cookies on a lime green square plate on the tray. "No biscuits or sweet things. Basically nothing brown, yellow, or orange. Only green and red foods. It's called the Huddersfield Diet."

She pursed her lips shut and inwardly rolled her eyes. She was babbling.

"The Huddersfield Diet," repeated the acolyte. "I've never heard of it."

"It's the latest thing." Gosha couldn't help herself. After decades of lying to everyone around her about coming from a long line of witches, now that she'd accepted the truth, she could lie about as effectively as her two boys. "From America. I read about it in a magazine."

"Is it good?" said the acolyte, her face an oval of curiosity.

"Amazing," said Gosha. "We've never been better. It completely changed the way I feel about Communist China and Top of the Pops."

Oh my god, thought Gosha, watching herself yammer as if from a great distance. *Make it stop.*

Alfie cleared his throat loudly and shot her a worried glance.

"Bessie Walpole said you might be able to help us," he cut in, to Gosha's relief. "We're trying to buy a house. I work in the city and my wife is an amazing fashion designer." He put a hand on her back, helping her steady her nerves. "We want to start a business together, but we're having trouble raising the capital."

Not bad, thought Gosha. *Not what we planned, but not bad at all.*

The acolyte nodded. "Did Bessie tell you what I do?"

"She said you were a spiritual advisor," said Gosha. "She said you helped her manifest wealth and prosperity."

The acolyte sat back in her chair and steepled her fingers in a mockery of wise counsel.

"Portia Twill-Quimby has taught us that the human mind is like a magnet of desire. Every thought, every hope, every wish you put out into the world draws toward you its like. If you think thoughts of beauty and prosperity, beauty and prosperity will be brought back to you a thousand fold. If you are unable to raise the capital you need, it must be because you are sending signals to the universe that you are unworthy of it."

She spread her hands in the gesture of a magician at the completion of an impressive trick, as if her point were proved beyond a doubt.

"What I will help you do is cleanse your aura at the quantum level and seed your consciousness with affirmations and visualizations that will guarantee you the success you desire."

"That sounds brilliant. Doesn't it darling," said Alfie, turning toward her.

If she didn't know him well, she would have thought he had completely fallen for all the acolyte's drivel, but she'd seen that same look on his face at work, humoring chatty drunks away from the bar and into a taxi, a job at which he was very good.

Gosha would have happily wiped the smug look off the acolyte's face with the back of her hand. Bessie Walpole, Midge Beadon, Tessa Chapman, and heavens knew how many others had all drained their savings and spent their pensions attempting to fulfill this Ogilvy woman's outlandish requirements. She couldn't sit here and listen to the idiot woman blather on. Alfie seemed like he had the situation under control.

"I'm terribly sorry, but do you mind if I use your loo?" she asked.

"Yes, of course." The acolyte dismissed her with a wave, her focus entirely on Alfie. "Go back out to the *foyer.*" She said it with a pretentious French accent. "It's the second door on the left."

Alfie watched her as she rose. She winked back at him on her way out the door.

The rest of the house was decorated in the same avant-garde playhouse style as the living room, everything new and nothing distracting from the complete look.

It must have cost her a fortune, thought Gosha, knowing full well where the money came from.

She found the loo, opened the door and looked inside a tiny cubicle that contained a toilet, a sink, and a red and tangerine linens cabinet with squiggly legs ripped from a demented Disney cartoon. Were it Gosha's, she would have displayed it in pride of place in her studio between her shelves of equipment and the cabinets filled with her archive of photos which now served no other purpose than to be a storehouse for dust.

She closed the door without going in, shutting it from the outside with a confident click just shy of a slam.

"Rorgatisk," she said, and the door locked from the inside.

"Pezhvatek," she said, and the vibrant colors around her dimmed to gray as the sound of voices from the living room muted. Anyone who

looked at her would see nothing other than the room around her. As long as she didn't interact with the environment, she was effectively invisible.

She looked up and down the hall. The stairs were to her right. She needed to get a move on if she was going to find Bessie Walpole's heirlooms before the acolyte realized something was up.

2

SHE CLIMBED THE STAIRS SLOWLY, unsure if putting weight on a creaky step would break the spell of concealment, but she made it to the second floor without giving herself away.

A long corridor stretched the length of the house. The only open door was at the end, leading to another bathroom. She stood outside the nearest and pressed her ear against the wood, hoping to make out if there was anyone on the other side, but the spell of concealment muted her senses. Four closed doors on this floor and likely the same upstairs. She would have to risk exposing herself to cast a finding spell.

From an inner pocket of her bolero jacket, its four outer and two inner pockets a rarity in a woman's garment, and another reason she was happy to indulge in something so frivolous, she withdrew a large leather wallet. Clicking open the silver clasp, she folded it open and rummaged through its contents: fifteen buttons, five silk, five taffeta, and five canvas; four small glass vials of various potions; three twigs harvested in the dark of the moon from a copse of trees at the center of the heath; seven or eight swatches of different kinds of cloth; a piece of card holding five dressmaker's pins; a small envelope containing talcum powder, and a feather from a wild duck. Each item had been processed to act as a carrier of Influence to be used in spells, charms, and potions. Buttons were always useful. She fished them out of the wallet and dropped them in one of the outer pockets in her jacket just in case, but what she really needed was the feather.

From the rear pocket of her black jeans, she took a photo of Bessie Walpole in her younger years, when her husband was still alive. Dressed up for some important occasion, she wore the ring, necklace, and bracelet Gosha was here to retrieve, poor Bessie's only real possessions of value.

She held the feather in one hand and the picture in the other and spoke one of the first spell words her mother had given her.

"Sutturah."

The spell of concealment popped like a bubble, the careful shroud of Influence masking her from the world around her dissipating as the finding spell created a twisting opening within her. Influence flowed from her talisman pressing against her skin through the opening of the spell to be shaped into a drifting, winding twist of power that plucked the feather from her fingers and wafted it past her up the stairs to the top floor.

"Pezhvatek," she said, and the spell of concealment enveloped her once again in its shroud of security.

She rounded the stairwell to climb the next flight in pursuit of the lazily drifting feather as it bobbed toward the last of two doors on the right and stopped.

Got you, thought Gosha.

Still concealed, with one hand on the doorknob, she pressed her ear against the door as hard as she could. She was almost certain no sound came from the other side, even through the muting of the concealment spell. With a wince of anticipation, she turned the doorknob as quietly as she could and eased the door open to let the enchanted feather through. Her shroud of Influence dissipated.

Once inside the empty bedroom, she breathed a sigh of relief and clicked the door shut. The feather flitted across to a giant wardrobe made of irregular boxes, each of a different shade of red or orange with giant black globes for door knobs, bumped against it and stopped. Gosha opened the doors and stood back, surprised by what she found within.

Inside the wardrobe was what she could only describe as an altar. A large oil painting of Portia Twill-Quimby dressed in another frilly power suit with mammoth shoulder pads stared down beatifically at her. Five large porcelain bowls stood beneath, each filled to the lip with a magpie's trove of jewelry: bracelets, necklaces, rings of every kind of precious metal and gem glittered in the afternoon light that flooded through the bedroom window. In Gosha's second sight, thick vines of translucent blue-tinged Influence grew from the bowls to twine and weave around each other in an ethereal thicket that grew up and around the painting. The portrait itself glowed with the blue of Influence, and the image of Portia Twill-Quimby was crowned in a coronet of ghostly blue vines to her inner eye.

"What the hell," she whispered.

The enchanted feather hovered over the bowls, buffeted by the rising Influence. Gosha peered into the cupboard at the hoard of treasure, loathe to get too close to the vines for fear of what they might do. If Bessie's jewels were in there, she would have to dig to find them.

She took out her field kit and selected one of the vials. Fathom's bane. It had taken months for Iron Jenny, her supplier of magical paraphernalia in Morel Market, to procure this tiny sample. A powerful dampener of Influence, the substance was created from the blood of someone who had been celibate for a year, drawn by a silver dagger within a stone circle under the full moon, the blood to be seasoned for another year in a specially Crafted chestnut box. She kept her sample with her at all times, but thankfully had never needed to use it before today. It would be a devil to replace.

She popped the cap and squirted two short sprays at the altar. The effect was immediate, the vines freezing. She reached out to pluck the feather back and wrapped it delicately in her hand to protect it, and opened the bedroom window with the other.

"Collusetoire."

A sudden and violent gust of wind blew through the room disintegrating the vines and clearing the air of all ambient Influence. She pushed the window shut and released the feather which bobbed happily over to one of the bowls and spun above it.

"Who in unholy hell are you?" said a voice behind her.

In the door stood a lanky middle-aged man dressed for a long hike in the country in his white oxford, green jumper, and a pair of corduroys. His aura was a gentle glow around him, no vines. He wasn't an oath-bearer.

"Denise asked me to come up and get something for her," she stammered.

"No she didn't," said the man. "DENISE!" He shouted down the corridor. "Get up here! One of your cretins is in the..."

Gosha leaped across the four feet between them to put a hand on his shoulder.

"Falethta," she said, and the man's eyelids fluttered as he crumpled to the floor, asleep.

It was too late. Gosha could hear the sound of feet clattering up the stairs. She turned back to the altar and brushed the feather aside. She rummaged through the contents of the bowl and found Bessie Walpole's jewelry.

"Sebastian!" shrieked the acolyte from the corridor, Alfie behind her. "Back." She pointed a manicured finger at Alfie who was yanked away by an invisible force. She stepped over her sleeping companion into the room and saw, with horror, the altar.

"What have you done?"

She pointed a finger at Gosha and her tentacular aura whipped out at her, driving Gosha back against the wall. Gosha struggled against the ethereal tentacles that held her in place, but couldn't break free.

"You ruined it." The acolyte wrung her hands as she hovered over the altar. "You ruined it."

She turned on Gosha and began to move her hands in the air as if sliding beads on a giant abacus. Her aura intensified, the tentacles writhing tight against her.

"Gyerzhat," said Gosha, her mother's favorite all-purpose hex, doled out liberally on those ordinary people who offended her in the market.

The word created within her a tight and chaotic opening that spun knotted Influence out at the acolyte. Ogilvy's companion mumbled and shifted in his sleep, tangling his legs between the acolyte's feet, knocking her off balance to tumble to the lurid green carpet. The vines of Influence holding Gosha in place disappeared. She pushed away from the wall, jewelry in hand, and made a dash for it, stepping over the jumble of limbs spreadeagled across the floor. The acolyte grabbed at her boot, but Gosha's Doc Martens were large and slick. A good tug and Gosha was out in the corridor and down the stairs as Alfie picked himself up off the landing.

"Go, go, go," she shouted, grabbing his hand as she ran, pulling him down with her to the front door.

As she reached to turn the deadbolt, the entire house lurched like a boat in a sudden gale throwing her and Alfie to one side. They hit the wall hard enough to knock the breath out of their lungs and leave them writhing, winded on the floor.

Ogilvy and Sebastian ran down the stairs. Denise raised her palm toward them, tentacle vines writhing around her, and the world went dark.

3

GOSHA AWOKE TO THE SHARP pain of her lipstick talisman digging into her ribs and found herself lying on a sofa in the living room restrained by a tangle of solid vines sprouting leaves and berries, her mouth gagged by a great fibrous knot of plant material. Alfie lay on the sofa across from her, still unconscious, his arms and legs twisted back and held behind him by his own tangle of plant matter. She tried to speak, but all she could do was make indistinct muffled sounds and drool.

"What are you going to do?" said Sebastian, his raised voice chiming in from another room.

"What am I going to do?" screeched Denise. "This is all your fault. You're supposed to vet these people."

"They were a referral from that idiot Walpole woman. She's sent you countless rubes. How was I supposed to know she knew someone like that? What is she, anyway? One of your lot?"

"No. I don't know. I don't think so. I don't know how she disrupted the offering. A proper acolyte shouldn't be able to do that. Oh, Lady Empress! The offering! I have to get it back up and running. If Portia finds out, she'll do terrible things to us. Keep an eye on them."

Footsteps stamped up the stairs.

Gosha's field kit and switchblade were both in the pockets of her bolero jacket, but she couldn't free her arms to get to them. The double-headed serpent ring on her right hand that was her connection to the Shadowlands was only useful under the light of the full moon, and her handbag in which she kept various other bits and bobs of Craft was on the floor where she had left it by the sofa on which the acolyte had trussed up Alfie.

Alfie's eyes flickered and opened, his body tensing up as he realized his situation and he fought against the vines that bound him. She struggled too, but the more she pulled against the vines, the more they cinched in around her. With her limbs so restricted, her muscles cramped with sharp pain.

Alfie flicked his eyes up to the door behind her, closed them and went limp. She shut her eyes and did her best to copy him.

"Bloody hocus pocus," Sebastian muttered.

Gosha heard the legs of his corduroys scuff against each other. The light from the window darkened beyond her eyelids as he paced around the room.

"Denise," he called, heading back out to the stairs. "What's happening up there?"

After all the trouble she'd been through since taking the Witch's Betrayal and embracing her heritage of Craft, Gosha had used the gift of the serpent ring to forge a few specific spells for occasions like this. She had memorized the exact word she needed that would free her from the tangled vines, but what good was it if she couldn't speak it? She would have to improvise and create an impromptu spell to get herself out. Such spells were always risky. Influence was always ready to obey the will of a witch, but it had all the subtlety of an over-enthusiastic puppy. She needed exactly the right image to guide it or she might find herself in even more trouble.

It wasn't enough to simply visualize herself speaking. She needed a strong imperative, a powerful image that could evoke emotion deep within her. She needed to see herself speaking, singing, shouting, free to express herself without restriction. She wracked her brain trying to summon the right memory, her panic mounting until she remembered the David Bowie tribute show she had been to six months ago. Johnny had been performing and had got her in for free as his plus one. She hadn't been out since before Christmas and, that night, had sung her throat raw. She imagined herself singing along to Let's Dance with a hundred other people, felt the push of her lungs and the exhilaration of being one with the crowd.

There was more than enough Influence left in the house after her little banishing upstairs to power the spell. The drifts of power that circulated around her froze, startled by the call of her will, and rushed toward her, summoned by the lipstick to pour through her body. She opened her mouth and imagined herself singing until she had no more breath. Influence flowed through her throat and into her mouth, pushing into the vines. Whatever acolyte's equivalent to a spell Denise Ogilvy had used to imprison them resisted, but the rush of power cut through it. The gag shattered, the splinters flying out of her mouth and knocking the tea set off the coffee table where it had sat, neglected, since Gosha had given herself away upstairs.

"Cathlathet," she said.

The shaping of High Influence that the acolyte had used to create the vines was no match for Gosha's spell. Gosha had been meticulous and relentless in her Crafting. She studied all manner of knots, chains, and manacles for months, and meditated for days upon the nature of being bound and restrained before summoning the power of the jasper ring one moonlit night to forge her spell. The vines loosened and unraveled like slippery eels, leaving her free in a heap of dead vegetation.

As she picked herself up off the sofa, Alfie squealed through his gag. A hand reached down from behind her, grabbed her hair and yanked her head back. Sebastian hooked his free arm around her neck.

"Denise," he shouted. "They're getting away."

"Tatlet."

She gasped and reached out with one hand as she pulled at the arm pressing across her throat with the other.

The switchblade in her pocket lurched and hurled itself into her open palm. She clicked it open and swung her arm up and back behind her, hoping to cause enough damage to make Sebastian release her.

Sebastian shrieked and pushed her away, knocking her to the floor between the sofa and the coffee table.

"She cut me," he whined. "She cut me."

She swung her free hand up and pushed her open palm toward him.

"Puthut."

A barrage of Influence surged through her and thrust Sebastian back to crash with a thud into the wall. He slid to the floor, unconscious.

"She's ruined it," wailed Denise as she trotted down the stairs. "I can't get the transference back up. It's a disaster."

She stood in the doorway, stunned at the sight of Gosha free and Sebastian once again unconscious on the floor.

"Pirit," said Gosha, swatting her hand at the door which slammed shut in Denise Ogilvy's face.

She pointed at the lock—

"Rorgatisk."

—and it clicked loudly shut.

She scooted around the coffee table and put a hand on Alfie's vines.

"Cathlathet."

The vines writhed, unraveled, and disintegrated around him. He rolled off the sofa.

Before Gosha could even offer her hand to help him up, the locked door began to crackle and split as thorny vines consumed it, plump pink roses unfurling until the entire doorway was replaced with a lush blooming rosebush that divided and coiled itself up into an arch that allowed the acolyte to step through.

"Puthut," said Gosha, extending a palm toward her, but with a screech of frustration, the acolyte made a series of sharp gestures with her hands, and ripped Gosha's spell apart.

"No," said Ogilvy with all the indignation of a kindergarten teacher who has lost control of her class, and twisted and swatted her hands in the air as if wrestling with a particularly complex hot water boiler, charging up the Influence around her.

"Vezhramak," said Gosha, the spell her mother used when Gosha was a child to freeze her in place when she refused to behave.

"I said no," snapped the acolyte and, with a gesture, ripped the spell apart, continuing with her elaborate pantomime. The floor underneath Gosha began to vibrate in deep, low waves that liquefied her gut and made her teeth rattle.

Gosha aimed the tip of her switchblade at the acolyte's shoulder.

"Pakkat," said Gosha, and the knife flew from her hand as if she had thrown it with all her might, but the acolyte swatted it aside and it embedded itself in the wall.

"Stop it, stop it, stop it," screamed the acolyte with the petulance of a child.

The furniture shook, a coating of dust rising off the bright egg yellow carpet. The low shag turned into a green lawn. Furniture around them warped and twisted, sprouting branches lush with fruit and flowers. Vines climbed up around Gosha and Alfie's legs.

"Tatlet," said Gosha, and the switchblade flew back into her hand. She touched the tip to the vines as they crawled up her legs.

"Bataraja," she said, and the vines burst into dust.

She dropped the blade, confident she could recall it if she needed it, vaulted over the crumbling sofa, landed in a fighting crouch and punched with all her might. Her fist connected hard with the acolyte's temple and she went down, crumbling into a heap on the floor.

The throbbing beneath them stopped, Gosha's ears ringing in the sudden quiet, and the rising woodland that threatened to overtake the room subsided, leaving behind the chicer-than-chic living room, though the clean edges and bright colors were now battered and worn.

She walked back to Alfie as he pulled himself up off the floor and offered him a hand.

"You okay?" she asked.

4

"ALL THAT WORK YOU'VE PUT in at the gym really paid off," said Alfie as they maneuvered the stunned bodies of the acolyte and her crony onto the nearest sofa and Gosha used her mother's immobilization spell on them.

"Wake them up, will you?" she said, touching Alfie's arm affectionately.

As he set about reviving them, she retrieved her handbag and took out her notebook, a palm-sized booklet filled with written notes, each page bearing a word of gibberish carefully spelled out with emphasis clearly marked and a brief description of what the word, each a spell she had forged herself with the Shadowlands ring, would do if she spoke it aloud while in contact with her lipstick talisman. Ever since Pauline Sutton, the Saint of Shadow, had shown her how to use it to forge spells, she had thought long and hard about what she would need if ever she found herself facing an oath-bearer again. There was much she could do with a witch's Craft and spells, but it all paled in comparison to the damage an oath-bearer could accomplish with their control of High Influence. She had prepared for the next time she faced an oath-bearer with as much imagination as she could muster.

She found the spell she was looking for. It was risky, a bluff that relied mostly on a threat of retribution she could never back up. She mouthed its syllables to herself a handful of times to fix it in her memory. The spells of her mother, Agnieszka, and Agnieszka's friends were all words in secret languages spoken only by women handed down across generations. Agnieszka had never taught Gosha hers, mostly because Gosha had been willful and rebellious as a child, and had wanted nothing to do with Craft. Now, when she Crafted her own spells, a skill lost for generations, she had to use nonsense words that sounded nothing like anything she might say in normal conversation, lest she accidentally cast a spell she never intended. It made remembering them all a challenge

"Alfie." She took out her field kit and removed from it a square of white muslin. "Take my handbag upstairs and get all the loot these two con artists have stolen." She handed him the piece of cloth. "Wave this in the air for a few seconds before you enter the room. If it doesn't change color, you're good to go."

Unlike her, Alfie had no second sight. The treated swatch of cloth would tell him if there were active Influence in the room.

He took the bag and the swatch and went upstairs. Afraid he would also be affected by the spell she intended to use on Ogilvy and her partner, she needed him at a safe distance when she cast it.

She pushed the coffee table out of the way to better loom over Ogilvy. Their eyes, the only thing the spell would allow them to move, darted about frantically. She knew how they felt. For your body to no longer obey you was not a pleasant experience.

She planted one hand on her hip and pointed the switchblade at them with the other.

"Alutroyd."

An eerie cry, part wolf, part demonic bird, echoed through the house and the sky outside darkened. The eyes of the two con artists grew wide and locked on her. Her face, she knew from practicing the spell in front of a mirror, elongated and turned the pale of death, her teeth appearing to sharpen to angry points, her eyes deepening to dark coals. The stench of carrion filled the room.

"Your little scheme ends now," she said, her voice grating and cracking like shattering glass. She put her feet up on the sofa between them and leaned in close. "You're ruining people's lives and I won't have it. Cheyne Heath is mine. The people who live here are under my protection. If you continue to run your con, I will be back, do you understand?"

She ran the tip of her switchblade across the cheek of the acolyte, careful not to draw blood. A bead of sweat pooled on the acolyte's brow and dripped down the side of her face.

"Blink if you understand me."

They both blinked furiously, fluttering their eyes like coquettes in a silent film.

She rose up to her full height.

"In fact, you would do well to pack up and leave Cheyne Heath entirely."

Out in the foyer, Alfie came down with her handbag. He held it up and nodded at her.

She folded the switchblade shut and walked to the door.

"It's a nice house," she said, looking around. It really was. "You shouldn't have trouble finding a buyer. You have until the end of the week. I'll be back to make sure you're gone." It was a Tuesday, which gave them more than enough time to clear out. If they didn't, Gosha wasn't sure what she would do.

She left them blinking furiously, took Alfie by the arm and walked outside.

"Patastis," she said, looking back toward the house as they slipped into her black Mini Cooper. A light diffusion of Influence rippled away from her to wipe clean the lingering effects of the intimidation spell and the spell that restrained Denise Ogilvy and her partner inside the house.

Alfie reached across the gearstick to pull her toward him and kiss her on the lips.

"You were amazing," he said.

His eyes glittered with the charge of what they'd done, reflecting back at her the giddy buzz she felt from casting so many spells in such a short time. She grinned and caressed his cheek. Outside, a shadow moved across the window of the house.

"We'd better get a move on." She turned the key in the ignition. "It won't do us much good if they come out and catch us snogging in the car."

"You were so slick," he raved on. "And those things you did with the knife. I had no idea you could do that."

She listened to him babble as she drove them back to Canterbury Gardens, her buzz souring the further she drove, the buoyant high of spell-casting draining away, leaving her feeling tired, fuzzy-headed, and depressed. Her path home took her to a part of Cheyne Heath she knew well, the traffic pattern leading her toward Miranda's mews house. When she reached the next intersection, she turned left rather than right to avoid it.

"Aren't we going home?" asked Alfie, breaking from his excited monologue.

"I thought we'd go this way for a change."

"But we'll hit traffic on Riley Avenue."

"I want to go this way," she said, snapping at him.

He blinked at her, silenced by worry at her outburst.

"You okay, luv?" He reached across the gearstick and put a hand on her thigh.

She sighed, leaned one elbow against the window, and ran her fingers through her hair.

"I'm sorry," she said. "Miranda lives down that way."

She untangled her fingers from her fringe and switched hands on the wheel so she could squeeze his. She'd told him the whole story of her relationship with Miranda, including the trouble with George and Emerson Margrave, Saint of Desire, which had almost killed them both. Johnny and Alfie had been able to roll with learning about the hidden world of witches, Influence, and the Spheres, but Miranda, who had experienced so much trouble and grief in her life, had not. Gosha hadn't seen her dearest friend in two years. The last time was a random encounter at an art gallery on a rare occasion when Gosha had been able to tear herself away from the endless stream of visitors to her kitchen. Miranda had recoiled when she saw her across the room, fear and disgust etched on her face. Gosha smiled, waved, and left.

"You should try calling her," said Alfie.

"I don't know what good that would do. If you could have seen the look on her face. She's terrified of me."

"She just doesn't understand. You were trying to help her. I know you, you'd never harm her."

Miranda's absence in her life hurt as if a physical part of Gosha somewhere deep within had been cut away, the hole it had left filling with poison and regret. It was easier to bury all thought of Miranda than to push for something that would only cause more pain. Lords and Ladies knew she had enough waiting in her kitchen at home to distract her. She patted his hand and gripped the steering wheel. He took the hint with his usual good nature.

"What about all this stuff?" he said, pulling a handful of rings and bracelets from her handbag.

"It'll take a while, but I can use Craft to locate all the owners. Then I'll have to figure out a way to get everything back to them that doesn't require witchcraft as an explanation."

She glanced over at the jewelry.

There could be thousands of pounds in there, she thought.

Cash was hard to come by in her line of work. People were happy to trade for the services of a woman who could get results when licensed professionals failed them. She always had enough clothes for the boys and food for the larder. There was always someone ready to fix the roof or the plumbing, but paying for the mortgage, taxes, and the gas bill were another matter. Liquid funds were hard to come by. George was relentless. Whenever she rustled up someone who might pay her on the books for a photo shoot, or a gig as a makeup artist, George somehow discovered and found a way to sour the deal. It had been four years since she had kicked him out and created the wards that barred him from all of Cheyne Heath. All his control over Influence as Saint of Authority was useless within the boundary, but still he managed to force his presence on her.

She missed the turn to Canterbury Gardens.

Mustn't dwell on what can't be changed.

"I hope what we did will be enough," she said.

"We'll keep an eye on them. I can send some mates round to keep watch."

Sometimes she thought she would drown without his relentless optimism. Today, though, it wasn't enough to keep her uplifted. Too many spells. She was going to have a hangover in the morning.

5

"GOGA." HER MOTHER MET THEM at the door, a rare look of worry on her face. "You have a visitor," she whispered. "It's the police."

A West Indian woman in her late twenties dressed in a somber work suit and carrying an oversized leather satchel stuffed to burst with files came up behind her.

"Mrs. Armitage?" she said, taking from her pocket an ID card which she opened to show Gosha and reached out a hand for her to shake. "My name's Esther Stuart. I'm with the council, Child Protection Services."

Gosha passed her handbag containing all the jewelry back to Alfie as she shook the young woman's hand.

"I'll see you later," he mumbled and turned to leave.

"Is this your boyfriend?" said the CPS worker.

"Yes," said Gosha.

"I'd like to talk to all of you, please."

Alfie looked to Gosha, who nodded back. He shut the front door and lowered the handbag gently down among the sneakers and wellies.

"What about?" asked Gosha.

"Why don't we go into the kitchen and have a cup of tea," said the social worker.

"Okay." Gosha raised an eyebrow as she led them back into the kitchen. This was a day of having her own lines fed back at her.

"Alfie Lester." Alfie shook the CPS worker's hand and gave her his best high-wattage smile.

"Mother, why don't you put the kettle on?" suggested Gosha as she invited the social worker to sit at the kitchen table. It was a beautiful June afternoon, sunlight shining through the large conservatory windows around them.

Agnieszka made a bee-line for the cupboard where they stored all the ingredients of Craft, kept padlocked now that the boys were old enough to allow their curiosity to overcome their sense of obedience. Keeping the world of Craft and Influence a secret from them was a huge challenge, but Gosha was determined to allow them their innocence for as long as she could.

"Mamusha, no," she said as Agnieszka put her key in the padlock. "Use the tea from the other cabinet. Do you like Earl Grey?" she asked the social worker.

"Lovely, thank you."

Agnieszka ignored her and clicked the padlock open.

"Mamusha," said Gosha firmly. "Earl Grey."

Agnieszka frowned, clicked the padlock shut, and took out a packet of Twinings from the real pantry.

"What's this about?" said Gosha to the social worker who took out a notebook from her satchel.

"Does Mr. Lester live here?" she asked.

"He stays here sometimes."

The social worker made a note in her book.

"And he has contact with the children?"

"Yes," said Gosha, alarmed. "Has something happened with the boys?"

"This is just a routine check. I'm here to follow up on a report."

"A report? From whom?"

"I'm afraid I can't disclose that information."

Gosha didn't need confirmation to know. This was another ploy by George to force her back to him.

"There's nothing to be alarmed about," said the social worker. "We only want to make sure your sons are safe and doing well. Are they here?"

"Mamusha," said Gosha. Agnieszka was boiling the tea the mundane way, the special pot that boiled water in under a minute when you rapped it three times sitting unused on the back hob of the stove. "Are the boys in their room?"

Agnieszka grunted with a nod.

"We can start with a tour of the house," said the social worker. "Then I'll need to talk to the boys. Shall we?"

"Yes, of course," said Gosha and rose from the table.

"What's in the basement?" asked the social worker as they passed the stairs to Johnny's flat.

"I have a tenant who lives down there."

"And do they have access to the rest of the house?"

"Yes, they do."

"Are they here, now?"

"No." Gosha could say that with confidence. If Johnny were home, the most current pop hits would be blaring up through the floorboards.

Alfie rose to join her, but she shook her head to tell him to stay, and followed the social worker upstairs.

The young woman was thorough in her inspection, going into each room and eyeing it with an appraising gaze that would impress any competent real estate agent. Gosha surprised herself at the glow of house-pride she felt overcome her anxiety as they made their way from the top of the house down to the boys' room. That very morning, spurred on by nervous anticipation at the impending encounter with Denise Ogilvy, Gosha had awoken at dawn and tidied the entire house.

The boys were entertaining themselves quietly in their room, unusual for them on a weekday afternoon in the school year. Most days, after their tea, they'd be tearing around the house. Timothy sat quietly on his bed reading one of his beloved Hardy Boys books while Edmund struggled with three bean bags trying to teach himself to juggle. Now eight and ten, the boys could be unholy terrors when it suited them.

"Hello, Mummy," said Timothy without looking up from his book. He was always a polite little boy when Edmund wasn't egging him on.

"Hello, boys. This nice lady would like to speak with you."

Edmund dropped his bean bags.

"Why?" he asked, walking over and standing in front of them, his hands on his hips, a far too severe expression on his face for a ten-year-old. He looked just like his father.

Timothy put his book down and sat up on the edge of the bed.

"I'd like to hear how you're doing at school," said the social worker with the soft kindness of a kindergarten teacher.

"I haven't done anything wrong," said Edmund, cutting to the heart of the matter as he usually did. "Did someone tell you I did?"

"Edmund, don't be rude. I'm so sorry," said Gosha to the social worker, hugging Edmund with one arm as she ruffled his hair, but he wasn't to be deterred from his outrage. If the situation hadn't been so fraught, Gosha would have thought his behavior funny. And if he hadn't looked so much like George.

"It's not a bother," said the social worker. "I must speak to them alone. And then I'd like to talk to you and the others."

Both boys looked worried. Given their propensity for mischief, this was their usual response to authority. All it would take was a word from Gosha and she could put the social worker to sleep. Agnieszka was sure to know some recipe that would have her out of the house happy that the boys were fine, but experience had shown Gosha that Craft could create as much trouble as it solved.

"I'll be right downstairs, boys," she said. "Answer the lady's questions."

"Thank you, Mrs. Armitage," said the social worker as Gosha turned to leave.

"This is your husband's doing," said Agnieszka, stabbing a sharp finger at Gosha as she entered the kitchen, as if Gosha were complicit in this intrusion into their lives.

"Yes, Mamusha. Obviously."

Alfie rose and hugged her. She kissed him on the cheek and sat where she could see the stairs.

"Immoral bastard," said Agnieszka as she brought the tea tray over to the kitchen table.

To her mother, everyone's faults boiled down to immorality, though it was never clear to Gosha what standard Agnieszka used as her yardstick. Whatever it was, no one could possibly live up to them.

"What's all that gaudy tat in your handbag?" Her mother placed a well-worn mug of Earl Grey tea in front of her.

The social worker doesn't rate the good china, then, thought Gosha.

"The woman we went to see was an acolyte, not a witch."

Her mother hissed between her teeth.

"Why must you bring ruin down upon us?"

Gosha did her best to ignore the comment. The first thing out of her mother's mouth was usually a snipe against someone. Gosha took it as a mental clearing of the throat her mother used to arrange her thoughts. Somehow her mother's friends allowed it to roll over them. Perhaps because they didn't have to live with her.

"She was using all that gold as some sort of offering to her saint. She had a whole altar set up to the woman."

"Which sphere?" asked Agnieszka as she ladled four teaspoons of sugar into her tea.

"Abundance. Do you know why she would have been doing that?" Gosha blew on the hot liquid in her mug and took a sip. She never liked the fragrance of Earl Grey, too flowery, but it tasted so good going down.

"No idea. You can ask Elsie when she comes over for your lesson."

Her mother poured a third mug for Alfie, but tapped it with her fingernails and didn't pass it. She tolerated him, but refused to make any extra effort to welcome him into the household.

He puts up with so much to be with me.

Her relationship with her mother had settled over the past few years. Agnieszka's attempts at controlling Gosha's every thought and deed had dwindled to sharp comments and judgemental looks. She hadn't tried to use Craft against Gosha since that awful fight three years ago when the Sphere of Shadow had threatened to consume the neighborhood, and they hadn't had an argument in months. Gosha still had hopes they might one day find real closeness between them.

"It's a good thing that creature downstairs isn't here," said her mother, squashing that hope before it could take root. "That police would never stand for it. She'd have the boys out of here before the moon rose."

Her mother had got the message from Gosha and from her friends that her miserable attitude toward gay people like Johnny wasn't acceptable. Now she projected her feelings onto others.

"She's not the police, Mamusha. She's a social worker from the council."

Gosha heard the click of the boys' door opening and the social worker's footsteps on the stairs. She rose to greet her from the bottom of the staircase as she descended.

"Everything go okay?"

The social worker smiled as she passed, not giving anything away. Alfie and Agnieszka stood politely as she entered the kitchen and Agnieszka placed a mug on the table in front of her.

"Your tea."

"Please, have a seat everyone," said the social worker as she put her mug to one side so she could spread open her notebook on the table.

She took her time flicking back a few pages to review her notes. When she was satisfied with whatever she was reviewing, she laid the notebook flat, crossed her hands over it, her pen tucked between two fingers ready to be deployed, looked up, and smiled. Gosha, Agnieszka, and Alfie waited frozen for her to speak.

"I just have a few questions. They're quite routine. The boys are doing very well in school, I hear."

"You do?" asked Gosha.

"Yes, I went to their primary school at the end of last week to talk to their teachers."

Gosha's heart hammered in her chest. How long had they been under investigation?

The social worker looked around the kitchen, rose and went to the fridge, opened it and peered inside.

"What's this?" she asked, pointing at something on the bottom shelf.

Gosha leaped up to see what it was: the two vats of Gosha's homemade makeup. She had been to the market for groceries the day before, so the fridge was well-stocked. If the social worker had come before then, she would have found it almost empty.

"It's cosmetics," she said.

"And you keep them in the fridge?"

"They need to be refrigerated or they'll spoil."

The social worker raised an eyebrow.

"They're taped shut," Gosha stammered. "The boys can't get at them."

The social worker nodded and closed the door, turning to the nearest cabinet, which she opened to find boxes of the boys' breakfast cereal.

"What's in there?" she asked, pointing to the padlocked cabinet.

"That's where we keep the booze," said Gosha with a laugh, but the social worker frowned.

An image of the rows and rows of glass jars containing all manner of oddities that filled the cabinet popped into Gosha's mind. She tried desperately to change it, suddenly terrified that the social worker would somehow be able to see what she was thinking. Was telepathy a real thing? She had never thought to ask.

"It's only a couple of bottles of wine and some rum for cooking."

This was the truth. There was wine and rum in there, though she would never dare drink it for pleasure. They'd been specially treated to be rich in Influence. She had no idea what would happen if someone took a sip.

She tried to smile, but her face froze in a rictus that must have been something to behold. The social worker looked at her oddly for a moment, then returned to the table and her notes. Gosha joined her back at the table.

"So Mister..." The social worker looked at her notes. "Lester and, I'm sorry," she said to Agnieszka, "I didn't get your name."

"Agnieszka Mierzejewska."

The social worker jotted the name down, but when she got to her mother's last name she paused.

"Myeji—?"

"Mierzejewska."

The social worker frowned and scribbled something down that had far too few letters to properly spell Agnieszka's name. Agnieszka grinned at Gosha with a look of triumph.

"Mr. Lester and your mother have regular contact with Edmund and Timothy?"

"Yes," said Gosha. "You've seen my mother's room, and Alfie stays here—"

"About four or five times a week," he chimed in. "If I'm working nights, I go back to my flat so as not to wake anyone."

"And where is your place of employment?" asked the social worker, pen poised.

"I work security at a few clubs and bars around the neighborhood. And some other places when they need an extra hand to keep an eye on things."

"Can you name the establishments, please?"

"Back Door, Drudges, and the Quick, mostly. And there are a few caterers I muck in for."

The social worker's face was a blank mask as she noted this down, not giving away if Alfie's job was a good thing or not.

"You have a lovely house, Mrs. Armitage," she said when she was finished.

The clock on the wall ticked loudly. It felt to Gosha like they had been here for hours.

"Thank you." Gosha gripped her mug with both hands for fear they'd shake with nerves.

"It must take a lot to keep up. What kind of work do you do?"

"Um," she stammered as a memory of struggling with Denise Ogilvy sprung into her mind. "I'm a photographer and a makeup artist."

"So, freelance?"

Gosha nodded.

"That must pay well."

"Yes, it does."

When I can get someone to give me a job, she thought.

"How many times a month would you say you work?"

"Well, um." She couldn't lie. Something about the woman's manner told Gosha she knew exactly how much she had worked in the past year. "I haven't worked in a while."

"Mm-hm. So how do you make ends meet?"

Gosha looked at Alfie and her mother, desperate for rescue, but she was on her own.

"We have my mother's pension and rent from the tenant. I sell my cosmetics in the market. And I do odd jobs for people."

The social worker made a note. "What kind of odd jobs?"

Gosha opened her mouth, but her mind skipped a gear and spun in neutral.

"I clean up other people's messes." The words came out without her thinking. Inside, she cringed.

"You work as a cleaner?"

"Yes," said Gosha. "Yes, a cleaner. Everyone needs a hard-working woman to clean their house once in a while."

Agnieszka smirked and nodded at Gosha's words, coded language from Witches' Cant, the secret argot that allowed witches to speak in the open about affairs of Craft without fear of persecution.

"How often do you clean for people?"

Gosha brightened to find herself on firmer ground.

"Most days," she said. "Six or seven times a week."

The social worker pursed her lips and made a note. Did that mean she approved or not?

"The calls never stop," Gosha yammered. "You'd be surprised how much of a mess people can make. Or perhaps you wouldn't." She laughed.

The social worker's eyes softened. Perhaps that was a good thing.

"Can you give me references? People you clean for regularly."

Again, Gosha's mind went blank. She looked at her mother in a panic. Who could they send the social worker to who would corroborate her story?

"Tracey Dobbs," said Agnieszka. "You've been cleaning for her since the baby was born."

Tracey was one of the first visitors to Gosha's kitchen. She understood that the help Gosha provided was of an unconventional nature. If questioned, she would know to go along with the charade. Gosha had several other regulars like that: Polly Stanton, Michael Delargy, Stephen Berger. She rattled off their names for the social worker and where she could find them.

"Thank you for answering all my questions," said the social worker when she had finished writing everything down. She capped her pen, closed her notebook and stuffed it into her satchel.

"That's it?" said Gosha, surprised.

"For now." The social worker rose and Gosha led her to the front door. "I'll submit my report in a few days, once I've finished my inquiry," she said on the front steps. "You'll get a letter from the council within thirty days. Have a good day, Mrs. Armitage."

Gosha went back inside, pushed the door shut, and burst into tears, her hands trembling. Alfie rushed over to her and wrapped his arms around her as she sobbed.

"It's going to be okay," he whispered as he stroked her hair. "You were brilliant. Everything's going to be fine."

She looked up over his shoulder to see her mother in the kitchen door, watching and judging.

6

GOSHA SPENT THE NEXT HOUR with Alfie running up and down Morel Road in search of the people whose names she'd given to the social worker. All understood what it meant to have the council come round asking questions, and all were grateful enough for the help Gosha had been to them over the years to bend the truth in her favor. The only person she didn't track down was Polly Stanton. For such a quiet, mousy woman, she got about a lot. She was never where you thought she would be. Gosha left word with a few stallholders in case she stopped by.

Gosha and Alfie returned home to find Elsie and her mother nattering in the kitchen over a cup of tea. Elsie's niece, Margie, sat on the other side of the kitchen table poring over an exercise book filled with notes. In one hand she held a deck of cards, her telling deck. Each time she turned to a new page of the exercise book, she held up the top card of the deck and compared the image on it with her notes. Elsie was training the young woman in the ways of Craft in preparation for her Betrayal, the ritual that would give her all the powers of a witch, training Gosha had never received herself. As a girl, Gosha had been a terrible student, more interested in dreaming about glamorous movie stars than paying attention. As an adult, when she needed it desperately, it turned out her mother was a terrible teacher, incapable of imparting more than the most rudimentary techniques. Now, Gosha was sitting in on Margie's lessons.

"There you are, my dear," said Elsie, rising to enfold Gosha in her ample embrace. The smell of lavender, cedarwood, and lambswool wafted up from her hand-knit cardigan. "What a trying day you've had. That awful, awful man."

She held Gosha at arms length so she could look up at her, her round face wrinkled with smile lines offering her more sympathy than her mother ever had.

"We don't have to do this now if you don't want," she said, her voice a high-pitched singsong. "We can come back tomorrow."

"No, you're here. Let's do it. I've been looking forward to it."

They were in the middle of creating their own telling decks. If George had stooped to calling the local council on her, she needed all the help she could get. And besides, left to herself she would only fret.

"What do you think?" asked Margie, stepping back from the worktable upon which she had laid out all the cards she had finished. She was a bright girl, recently turned nineteen, who looked like she could have stepped out of a Constable painting with stalks of wheat in her hair. With high marks in her exams, she could have studied art history or gone to St. Martin's School of Art, but had instead decided to learn Craft from her aunt.

The cards were a little larger than a standard deck of playing cards, each cut from textured art paper and featuring hand-painted watercolors that took Gosha's breath away.

"They're gorgeous," said Gosha. "You have a real talent."

A witch created her own deck of cards for fortune-telling herself with whatever skills and materials she had available. Gosha had used old negatives from her archive of past work and found objects to create photograms, exposing the negatives and objects directly onto photographic paper which she then processed with chemicals to fix the image. Margie's cards were bright and beautiful, pastoral scenes and compositions of trees and flowers that would make any professional botanist jealous. Gosha's were more somber, ghost-like images against dark backgrounds. Photographic paper and chemicals were expensive, but she'd found an owner of a local photo lab afflicted with the shakes from a life of heavy drinking who paid her with all the materials she could want for a potion that steadied his hands. Making the cards was more fun than she'd had in years.

"Stupendous, girls," said Elsie, standing between them and hugging them close as she looked over their work. With Elsie as a teacher, Gosha would have made very different choices about her life.

Gosha had let Elsie teach them in her studio, a room she guarded jealously, but it was quiet and open, and the one room in the house where her mother wouldn't come in to snoop and make comments.

"You've made your Major Arcana with representations of the known spheres and the other cardinal cards, and you've created the four conventional suits. Margie, dear, what are they, and what do they signify?"

Margie reached for her exercise book.

"Ah-ah-ah," Elsie trilled. "Come on, dear. You know these by now."

"Buttons for wealth and health," she said, putting the book down and counting off on her fingers. "Brushes for art and passion. Cups for love and emotion. Needles for thoughts and deeds."

"There you are," said Elsie and gave her niece a squeeze. "Now we get to the fun part. What you've made so far are your own interpretations of a conventional tarot deck. A witch's telling deck is different. You will also need to make a suit for family, a card to represent each important relative, by blood or marriage."

Gosha grimaced. Would she have to make one for George? Perhaps a card made of solid black.

"And then the best bit," Elsie continued. "A witch's telling deck has an additional suit that's yours to choose. We call it the suit of wilds, but each of us names her own for herself. My suit of wilds I call leaves. This is what I want you to start thinking about next. It should express in some way your own inner spirit. I want you both to make a list of the things that are most important to you. What are the images you might associate with them, and what objects around you resonate the most?" She clapped her hands. "And now, we practice. Shuffle your decks and we'll try a simple three-card spread."

Not only had Gosha never had formal training in Craft, she'd had no formal training in anything else. Everything she knew about photography and makeup she'd figured out for herself. Elsie was a great teacher. This was heaven.

Gosha and the others sat around the worktable. She shuffled her deck, cut it with her left hand, and dealt herself three cards.

"What did you get?" asked Elsie.

The first card showed an image of George wearing a ghostly crown, the second a woman standing alone in a forest, the third a tower silhouetted by a giant moon. The cards had no label, but even though at this point she had made eighty cards for her deck, she remembered what they all were.

"Authority, the Witch, and Shadow," she said.

Elsie raised her eyebrows and grimaced.

"Oh dear." She reached into her handbag, an old-fashioned wedge of peach-colored leather with a metal clip and a matching handle. The kind worn by the Queen.

Elizabeth II, not the Queen of Secrets, Saint of Mystery, Gosha thought, still finding it strange to live in a world where referring to the Queen required clarification.

From the handbag, Elsie removed a bundle of herbs. She snapped her fingers near the end of the bundle and the dried leaves and stems began to smolder, giving off a richly scented smoke. She waved the bundle in a circle above the table and the gray clouds that billowed off it spread out to envelop them.

"There you go," she chirped. "That'll take care of the interference. I should have realized it would be a problem. That can happen when you get too close to saints. Now you should be able to see the wood through the trees. Try again."

In the first card a gray fog obscured a trio of figures that could be animals, people, or a monstrous combination of both. In the second, the white silhouette of a nail spiked up against a dark background with a simple crown like the paper ones you get from a Christmas cracker ringed around its tip. In the third, an open hand nestled a blooming flower. Superimposed upon it was a young woman with her arms raised and her head thrown back, mouth open in a scream of defiance.

"The Unknown, the King of Needles, and Liberation," said Gosha.

"Oh," exclaimed Margie, always as bright and cheerful as her aunt. "That's a coincidence. I have the same thing, but my Liberation card is upside down."

"Mine is, too," said Gosha.

Elsie stood and walked around the table to peer over Gosha and Margie's shoulders at their spreads.

"With the cards, there are no coincidences," she said, her usual upbeat manner gone, replaced by an uncharacteristic frown. "Shuffle your cards and try again."

Gosha and Margie did as they were told, watching each other as they turned over their cards. Once again, they both drew the Unknown, the King of Needles, and Liberation reversed.

"That shouldn't be possible," said Elsie as she went back to her side of the table and pulled out her own deck, a collection of hand-drawn inked and colored cards. "Again, please."

She shuffled, cut and dealt along with them. Again, the Unknown, the King of Needles, Liberation reversed.

"Agnieszka," she called at the top of her lungs as she got up and went out on the landing. "Can you come up here, please? And bring your deck. Something's happening."

"What?" grumbled Gosha's mother as she came into the studio, looking around at the photographs that lined the walls.

"Would you deal a three-card spread please?" asked Elsie as she shuffled her deck. "Freeform, no focus. You too, girls," she said to Gosha and Margie.

The Unknown, the King of Needles, Liberation reversed.

"Hmm," said Agnieszka as she peered at the array of spreads on the table. "That shouldn't be."

"Again, ladies," said Elsie.

The Unknown, the King of Needles, Liberation reversed.

All four stared at their spreads in silence, Gosha's dark and ominous, Elsie and Margie's bright and colorful, her mother's a jumble of chopped up images from magazines with thick lines in marker scrawled upon them.

"We need a party line," said Elsie and Agnieszka in unison.

They leaped to their feet and ran to the door.

"I'll get the candles, saucers, and rum," said Elsie, disappearing downstairs.

"Goga," said her mother from the doorway. "Go through every room in the house, turn off any lights and cover all the windows. I'll get the mirrors."

"What's happening?" squealed Margie, frightened by the sudden turn of events.

"It's for a party line. They want to talk to the others," said Gosha. "Hang out here. I'll be right back."

It took ten minutes to check every room for lights and to close all the blinds. By the time she returned to the studio out of breath, her mother and Elsie had propped up three wall mirrors on the worktable with a saucer full of rum and an unlit candle balanced on the middle of it in front of each.

"Johnny's not home," she said. "I couldn't get into the flat."

"Never mind," said Agnieszka, waving her in. "Close the door and turn out the lights."

With the blackout curtains drawn across the windows and the door shut, the room was plunged into darkness. Gosha heard fingers snap and all three candles ignited at once. Elsie muttered a word in her secret language that sounded like Gaelic but wasn't. The surfaces of the three mirrors rippled and changed to reveal one of the other witches—Mei, Eleanor, and Shreya—in each.

"I was in the middle of a consultation," snapped Mei, her dark hair pulled back with three red lacquer chopsticks sticking out of her bun, a pair of jade chandelier earrings dangling down from her lobes. She usually dressed like any suburban granny. If she was in her full Chinese regalia, she must have been putting on a show for a visitor.

With short-cropped brown hair and a green blouse, Eleanor in the next mirror could have been a contemporary of Margie, though her true age was a mystery only hinted at by the strange historical references she constantly made. As far as anyone could tell, she might be a thousand years old. The third witch in the last mirror, the final member of her mother's group of friends, was Shreya, an older Indian woman with white hair tied back and wearing a pink and gold sari.

"What is so important that you must interrupt my chai?" said Shreya sipping from a cup of fine bone china.

"Do you have your telling decks on hand?" said Elsie. "We need a three-card spread from each of you, freeform and no focus, please." She turned to Gosha and Margie. "Freeform means the positions of the spread have no predetermined meaning. No focus means there was no question asked when the deck was cut. It's like free-association. It gives you a general idea of what's in the air. Try again."

All six witches and one witch-in-training shuffled, cut, and dealt.

"The Unknown," said Mei, "the King of Needles, and Liberation reversed."

"That's what I have," said Eleanor.

"Also me," said Shreya.

"One more time, everyone," said Elsie.

The results were the same.

"Can't be," said Mei.

"Eleanor, dear," said Shreya. "Have you ever heard of such a thing before?"

Eleanor's memory for anything further back than last Tuesday was always iffy, but sometimes she unearthed a useful insight or two.

"Snow in summer," she said as matter-of-factly as if she were reading a recipe, "and winter blooms are oft desired but rarely do they bless."

"Eleanor, drink your tea," shouted Mei.

Eleanor's mysterious age made her a little spacey and hard to comprehend if she didn't drink the tea of a special blend of herbs regularly. And even then, you often didn't know what to do with the information you got from her.

"Hush, dear," said Shreya. "She means no."

"Fire up any other oracle you have, ladies," said Elsie. "We need to get to the bottom of this."

The heads in the three mirrors disappeared leaving only the image of the respective kitchens of each witch.

Agnieszka and Elsie rose once again to head downstairs.

"I'll use a scrying bowl," said her mother.

"Tea leaves for me," said Elsie. "Girls, keep re-dealing and shout if anything changes."

"I'm so confused," said Margie as she shuffled her deck.

"I wish I could say you get used to it," said Gosha.

Five more times they shuffled, cut, and dealt, each to the same result, before the three heads popped back into their frames and Agnieszka and Elsie returned, her mother carrying a small bowl of water, Elsie a teacup.

"Smoke and death, rubble and clouds," said Eleanor.

"Me, too," said Shreya. "A lot of confusion."

"I have people walking," said Mei. "They're all covered in dust and heading in the same direction."

"I get the same thing," said Agnieszka.

"Something terrible must be coming," said Elsie. "Keep dealing, girls."

Gosha's spread read the Unknown, the King of Needles, and Chaos.

"Something changed," she said. "Liberation was replaced by Chaos."

"I have that, too," said Margie.

"Chaos?" squeaked Elsie. The card represented the first sphere, the sphere that existed before all the other spheres were formed. "Deal again."

"The Knight of Cups, the Seven of Needles, and Devotion," said Gosha.

"Mine's different," said Margie. "The Three of Wands, the Two of Cups, and the Ace of Hearts."

The others all re-dealt. All reported different results.

"Whatever it was has passed," said Agnieszka.

"What did it mean?" asked Margie.

"Nothing good," said Agnieszka.

The phone on the worktable rang.

Everybody, even the witches behind the mirrors, jumped.

7

"MAY I SPEAK TO MAL..." the man on the other end of the line stammered as he tried to pronounce her full name.

"Małgorzata Armitage," she cut in, putting him out of his misery. "Yes, this is she."

"Who is it?" whispered Agnieszka, reaching for the receiver.

The extension in the studio was on a long cable. Gosha picked the phone up and walked over to the window to get some space so she could think.

"Oh, wonderful," said the man. His voice was deep, resonant even over the telephone line. "My name's Joel Adair. I'm calling from the firm of Waterford, Wakefield, Winston, and Whorl. You've probably never heard of us, but we're a boutique agency that caters to a select roster of clients. Much of what we do is public relations and legal representation."

Five witches and one trainee stared at her with wide and expectant eyes, making it hard to concentrate.

"How can I help you, Mr. Adair?"

The ladies all whispered the name to themselves and started quiet conversations. Margie remained confused.

"We've heard good things about your work," said Adair, "and wondered if you would be interested in coming in for a meeting."

Gosha's heart leaped in her chest.

"A meeting?"

"Yes, we have a very high-profile account we need a fresh eye on, and I think your creative approach would be just the thing. Would you be interested in coming in?"

"Yes. Yes, absolutely." She knew she should be playing it cool, but she hadn't had a call for a real job in months.

"Um, we're on a bit of a timetable," he said. "Do you think you could come in first thing tomorrow? Say 9 o'clock?"

"Yes, 9 o'clock is fine. I can be there."

"Excellent. Let me give you the address."

He rattled off a street on the east end of Cheyne Heath, almost across the border into Kensington. In her former life she was down that way all the time, but she couldn't recall ever hearing of a big PR firm with offices there.

"I'll see you first thing, then," he said. "Give my name at the front desk. Joel Adair."

She put the phone down and turned to the assembled women awaiting her news.

"I have a job interview."

She beamed.

"A job interview," said Agnieszka, none too pleased with her announcement.

"A PR firm wants me for one of their accounts."

Where did I leave my portfolio? she wondered as she looked around the room. She hadn't been through it in over a year, not since she patched up her misunderstanding over competing clients with Millie Hargreaves, and had struck up a bartering agreement between them, regular photo shoots of the witch-turned-hairdresser's work for regular haircuts Gosha could never have afforded otherwise.

"You can't," said Agnieszka. "There's work to do."

"This is about work, Mamusha."

There it was, up on the shelf with all her reference books. She wove past Elsie and Margie to get it down.

"I forbid it," said Agnieszka, crossing her arms as of her word were final.

"Why don't you and I gather up our cards and go and make some tea," Elsie twittered at Margie as she reached for her telling deck and purse with a nervous eye on the other two.

"Something important has happened and you're going to turn your back on it?" said Agnieszka.

Margie wasn't getting Elsie's message about clearing out ahead of the row that was brewing around her, so she led her niece from the room by the arm. The three candles on the worktable winked out all at once. The mirrors rippled, returning to reflecting the studio in the light coming in from the landing through as Elsie and Margie fled to the safety of the kitchen.

"There were five witches in here with me," said Gosha taking down the zippered leather portfolio, determined not to allow her mother to steamroll over her. "I think you can all handle the situation."

"You are so very cavalier in the face of trouble, aren't you? You think because you have brought down saints you are above it all."

Gosha slammed the portfolio on the worktable and made the mirrors and saucers rattle.

"I think nothing of the sort, Mother," she said, locking eyes with Agnieszka. "I take this all very seriously. I take this house seriously, and the electricity bill, and the water bill, and the food bill. This job is money. Actual money, not gray market goods and bartered services. If we don't have enough of it, this all goes away, and four of us can't live off your pension."

Agnieszka looked about to say something, but instead she harrumphed, pursed her lips and walked away, leaving Gosha to the elation of a rare victory over her mother and an out-of-date portfolio in desperate need of freshening up.

At five minutes to nine the following morning, Gosha pushed through the glass doors to the lobby of Waterford, Wakefield, Winston, and Whorl, her portfolio tucked under one arm. Up till two in the morning, she had re-worked it three times, settling on a selection of shots that might not have been her most current but which gave the best impression of her technical skills. After five hours of sleep, she'd awoken to the realization that she hadn't planned what to wear and dove into her closet, pulling out every last stitch of clothing that suggested she was loaded and wasn't desperate for the job. She settled on a pair of lace-up black leather stiletto boots styled like a pair of Doc Martens, her best black jeans, a dark burgundy turtleneck to highlight the oxblood shade of her lipstick, a pair of black suspenders, and a vintage men's tuxedo jacket. After half an hour working on her makeup, she had descended the stairs to be met by the widened eyes of the boys and a look of disapproval from her mother.

The girl behind the front desk at the offices of Waterford, Wakefield, Winston, and Whorl barely glanced at her.

"I have an appointment with Joel Adair," said Gosha. "The name's Armitage. Małgorzata Armitage."

She had thought of going back to her maiden name, even though she and George were still married, but her Polish surname was even more of a mouthful than her first name, and everyone knew her professionally as Armitage. She was buggered if she was going to slink off into anonymity, no matter how badly George tried to slander her.

The receptionist, a young West Indian woman in a fuchsia business jacket with the largest shoulder pads Gosha had ever seen, and earrings that dangled from her lobes like a pair of complex kinetic sculptures, tapped at a giant computer keyboard. Whatever she saw on her screen confirmed Gosha's story, though it did nothing to soften her unimpressed expression.

"You can have a seat," she said, gesturing to a white puffed sectional sofa that undulated across the glass and concrete lobby. "Mister Adair will be with you shortly."

Gosha perched on the edge of the sofa, her portfolio across her knees. She remembered the last time she'd been down this way: to a restaurant opening five years ago with George and Miranda, three short months before her life fell to pieces. The street had changed radically since then, half of it knocked down to be replaced by shining architectural marvels like this one. Waterford, Wakefield, Winston, and Whorl occupied the entire five-story building. Gosha had wracked her brain to recall anyone who might have been their client, but to no avail. If she could have, she would have called Miranda to ask if she knew them, but that wasn't an option anymore. With no one else to call, she was going in blind.

Beyond the glass lobby, the office was alive with young, hip people bustling about with armfuls of files and mugs of morning coffee, clustering together for impromptu meetings and shared jokes, rising and descending the vast spiral staircase that swept up the center of the building. The buzz of energy in the office was palpable even from the glass fishbowl of the lobby. She wondered what the flow of Influence would look like in a place like this where so much important work was obviously going on. Her lipstick talisman was in the pocket of her jeans along with her car keys. Without it touching her skin, she had no reliable second sight. She could slip it out and take a peek, but she didn't need to see Influence to know she wanted desperately whatever job they could offer.

A burly man with broad, rugby player shoulders that required no shoulder pads, and close-cropped hair that masked a prematurely receding hairline, pushed through a door to her left and strode toward her. Dressed in a brown pinstripe bespoke three-piece suit with shiny brown leather oxford brogues, bright pink socks, and a matching pink pocket square, he reached out a large hand.

"Mrs. Armitage." He smiled, his eyes warm, his face open and kind. "I'm so glad you could come in." His hand dwarfed hers, but he squeezed it gently as she rose. "Why don't we go upstairs and have a chat."

He led her back through the doors into the office and up the spiral staircase to the third floor.

"Forgive me," she said as he led her to a glass-walled conference room that looked out over Kensington. She wondered how much it had changed in the four years since she trapped herself in Cheyne Heath. "I'm not familiar with your firm."

He opened the door and gestured for her to enter.

"Yes, we do like to keep it that way." He closed the door behind him. "Please have a seat."

She unzipped her portfolio and opened it up on the conference table between them.

"You didn't say who your client was," she said, launching into the pitch she had been running in her head since the night before, "so I brought a broad selection of my work: some portraits, some fashion photography, some promotional work."

She turned the pages one at a time, looking to read his reaction as she gave a quick explanation of each shot before moving on to the next, working her way toward the last photo, her favorite, the portrait of Miranda that had launched her as a photographer, an image that had recently become famous again as Miranda's singing career reignited in the years since Emerson Margrave almost consumed her. Adair looked and listened quietly, a growing quizzical expression on his face.

"I'm sorry, Mrs. Armitage," he said, laying a hand on the page she was about to turn to reveal Miranda staring winsomely out over Cheyne Heath. "It's my fault. I wasn't clear over the phone. These are all wonderful, but it's your other set of skills we're interested in."

She sat back in her chair and tried to process what he had said.

"My other... Oh, I see. The makeup."

She cleared her mind and shifted gears. Not as exciting, and a bit of a professional step back, but still the kind of work into which she would be happy to launch herself. A job was a job. She flipped the page to the portrait of Miranda.

"I did the makeup in several of the earlier shots, like this one of Miranda Lovelock."

"Ah, no," he said. "Your other set of skills."

Now she was confused. If he didn't want her as a makeup artist...

"Oh," she said, understanding his meaning.

Of course, she thought, suddenly on edge. *Witchcraft. How foolish of me to think it could be anything else.*

The hairs on the back of her neck stood to attention. She flicked her eyes around the room to scope out the exits. Where Adair sat, he partially blocked her escape through the door they had entered by, but there was another door behind her. The spiral staircase would be an awkward getaway route to manage in her stilettos, but she spotted a bank of elevators at the other side of the building and a fire escape door beside them.

This might all be nothing. She might be completely overreacting. Some of the boys' school teachers were acolytes and were perfectly harmless. Pauline Sutton, Saint of Shadow, had turned out to be benign, but they were in a small minority. All the other oath-bearers she had encountered so far had either tried to manipulate her or kill her.

"My other skills," she said, and slipped her hand into the pocket of her jeans. "I don't know what you mean."

As her fingers grazed the black plastic tube of her lipstick talisman, the room lit up with Influence. Under normal circumstances Influence meandered and flowed like a lazy river. In here it was thick and vibrant as it swirled around the room in a steady spiral, emanating outward from a column at the center of the table over a high-tech office phone, and spread to the glass walls. The hairs on the back of her neck grew rigid like the bristles of a brush as the heavy flow buffeted against her like wind off the ocean. Around Joel Adair it wrapped and curled, enveloping him in a series of concentric wheels. At first she thought the effect was the aura of an oath-bearer, but the Influence that coalesced around him was a product of the room. His own delicate, ordinary aura radiated off him to be picked up by the spinning wheels.

Adair glanced around to take in what she might be looking at, his smile soft and open.

"Yes," he said. "We understand you're a witch."

"A witch?"

She laughed, a harsh and unconvincing bark.

"I think you're mistaken. I've been to a few Bauhaus concerts and burned some incense in my time, but that doesn't make me a witch, does it?"

She made her face a blank mask. Now was not the time to give anything away. Were these people allies of George? If Adair had been an oath-bearer, a saint or an acolyte, she might have cast her spell of concealment on the spot and fled. He was neither, although the spinning wheels around him seemed to mark his affiliation, if only she knew what they represented. She had only ever seen the auras of five spheres, and the other witches thought there could be upwards of twenty.

He interlaced his fingers and leaned across the table toward her.

"I'm sorry to be so abrupt, Mrs. Armitage." His expression turned serious. "I understand it must be alarming to be confronted in this way by a stranger. I imagine the etiquette involved in hiring the services of someone such as yourself is highly nuanced. Normally, we would have made more delicate overtures, and we would ask you to sign a non-disclosure agreement, but I'm afraid we're dreadfully pressed for time. Are you familiar with Sir Wilfred Stepney, the painter?"

She knew Sir Wilfred well enough. He was a member of the Cheyne Arts Club. She'd spent many a happy drunken night there surrounded by famous artists like Sir Wilfred, and Johnny had told her a few stories of debauchery involving the old misanthrope from back when Johnny worked for him as a life model.

"We've crossed paths."

"He's in a spot of trouble. We need someone to find him."

"Why not hire a private investigator?"

"If only it were that easy. We suspect Influence was involved in his disappearance. A commonplace solution like a private investigator would complicate matters. We require specialized talent."

"Influence?" asked Gosha, determined to hold her ground.

Adair sighed and ran a hand over his scalp.

"Mrs. Armitage, we mean you no harm. We're not affiliated with your husband or the Queen of Secrets. The partners took note of the excellent work you did three years ago in the matter of Vivien Drake and Roy Merton. Sir Wilfred is extremely important to us, but the politics of the situation severely limit what we can do directly. We need someone who understands what they're dealing with outside the norms and conventions of the Convocation."

She had heard the same pitch from Euphemia Graham, the self-styled Queen of Secrets, Saint of the Sphere of Mystery. Gosha remembered well the greedy look in her eye when she'd tried to convince Gosha to join her. But this Joel Adair seemed genuinely worried about Sir Wilfred. She'd inherited a black and white view of the politics of the spheres from her mother, but she'd seen enough to know not everyone associated with Influence was a murderous schemer.

The phone on the table trilled. Adair rose and walked around to pick it up.

"Adair speaking," he said into the receiver and turned his back to Gosha. "I don't— Yes. Yes, of course."

He placed the phone back on the cradle.

"Mrs. Armitage, perhaps if you talked to the partners, they could give you the assurances you need to help us."

Sir Wilfred was a miserable old sod, but he was also a genius, with work in the Tate and the National Portrait Gallery. Since her mother had placed the witch mark on their front door to attract those in need, Gosha had tracked down four missing family members, six absconded fathers who owed child support, and three beloved family pets. A finding was an easy spell to cast, and perhaps she could make a new connection out of it. At the very least, she'd get a better sense of who these people were and what they wanted.

"Very well," she said.

8

ADAIR LED HER FROM THE conference room to the bank of lifts on the other floor. Two of the three lifts had the usual light-up buttons and overhead numbers you would expect. The third had only a keypad where the call buttons should be and a single light above the door. He tapped in a string of numbers on the keypad, and the light turned on. The door slid open a few seconds later.

"After you," he said.

The walls, ceiling, and floor of the lift were shiny chrome. She looked at the reflection of herself iterating off into infinity.

The doors opened again to lead them to a dark expanse, the only light four overhead spots shining down a few feet away. The room might have been the size of a football field or no bigger than the pools of light that interlocked on the matt black flooring, for all she could tell.

"Do have a seat," said Adair, leading her to a plush office chair and chrome side table at the edge of the pools of light.

In the light were four desks, simple office workstations arranged at right angles like spokes on a wheel. On each stood two large white computer terminals, the green-on-black monitors and chunky white keyboards facing away from each other. At the center of the pool, the hub of the wheel, stood a man-sized tower of black mesh behind which a shifting array of lights winked on and off. At each workstation stood a woman typing away at one of the keyboards. The four women were each a different age: the youngest in her twenties, small and mousy in a skirt, blouse, and cardigan combo; the oldest in her fifties, a tall and slender woman of African descent wearing a sleek gray business suit. The other two were both blond-haired, blue-eyed and fresh-faced English girls in conservative business wear.

With her lipstick nestled in her palm to show her, the Influence in the room flowed thick and powerful, the computer tower at the center the still-point of a great spiraling whirlpool. Each of the women, like Adair who stood to one side of her chair, had their own mundane auras enveloped by concentric spinning wheels of power, as if they were at once oath-bearers and not.

"Małgorzata Mierzejewska Armitage," the dark-skinned woman read off her screen, pronouncing the name perfectly with a BBC newscaster's plummy accent. "Thank you for accepting our invitation."

The small, mousy woman walked to the other side of her desk and began typing at her second terminal.

"Time is of the essence," she read. The hands of all four women fell still. "The disappearance of Sir Wilfred Stepney has caused alarming repercussions in the ecology. He must be found immediately if poise is to be maintained and stagnation avoided."

Out of the corner of her eye she saw Adair cross his arms and frown.

"He is integral to the prophecy of the Fall," read the older of the two blonde women, "in ways we have yet to determine."

"Not only," read the younger blonde, "has he been removed from the event sequence of his life, he is gone from the roster of our oversight. Something blocks him from us. This we have never experienced."

"Excuse me, but who are you?" Gosha asked.

The fingers of all four women clattered in a brief flurry across their keys to record her words and then fell still.

Gosha had walked the nightmare landscape of the Shadowlands and had felt less disoriented.

"We are the Lords of Fate and Fortune," read the African woman.

"We are the wheel of karma," read the mousy girl.

"We churn the cosmos and maintain balance," read the older blonde.

"Without us the world will stagnate and die," read the younger.

"You're the lords of a sphere?" she asked. "I'm speaking to supernatural beings? Where's your saint? Where are your acolytes?"

The women typed and were still.

"We have needed neither saint nor acolytes since we first awoke in the dawn of this era," read the African woman.

Rarely did a day go by that her mother didn't issue some murky warning about High Influence and the Spheres. Most Gosha took with a pinch of salt, but Agnieszka was always very clear about the Lords and Ladies, and nothing Gosha had witnessed in her four years of witchcraft led her to doubt it: avoid them at all costs.

Perhaps her mother was right. Perhaps she was reckless. She'd let her curiosity get the better of her. She had to get out of here as quickly as possible.

"I think you have the wrong person," she said, the four women typing her words. "I'm not the woman you think I am."

The mousy girl left her workstation and disappeared into the gloom beyond the lights, returning a moment later with a thick file of papers which she handed to Gosha before going back to her terminals. Gosha opened the file and looked through it with horror. On the top was a black and white shot of her taken at a distance with a telephoto lens. She glanced at the typed sheets of paper beneath. They were all detailed reports about her daily movements, about her family history stretching back to their first arrival in the UK, about all the people who had come to her kitchen for help. In the back was a stack of photos of her mother, the ladies, the boys, even George.

"We have an exhaustive assessment of your capabilities and your character," read the mousy girl.

Whatever apprehension Gosha was feeling burned away in anger at this invasion of privacy.

"If you know so much about me, you know I'm unable to leave Cheyne Heath. You know my husband is the saint of Authority. You know he tracks everything I do. I'm hardly in a position to be your secret agent."

"That is incorrect, Mrs. Armitage," read the older blond. "He only conjectures in regard to your activities, and he acts impulsively. To divert him or to focus him would be a simple thing to arrange."

Behind her, Adair buried his face in one hand.

"To focus him," she said, alarmed. Was that a threat?

Adair stepped forward into the light.

"My Lords, may I speak?"

Four sets of fingers clacked furiously on their keyboards and stopped.

For a long while there was silence.

"A witch is an aberration," read the younger blonde. "She wields Influence and yet answers to no higher power. She is anathema to the celestial pantheon and the Convocation of Saints. She traffics in base favors, consorts with dark powers, divides the foul from the fair—"

"I think I've had enough of this," said Gosha, hot under the collar as the woman read on. She dropped the file loudly on the floor, its contents slipping out in an unruly mess, picked up her portfolio, and rose to leave. The lord at the other end of the computer wasn't accusing her of anything she hadn't done, but the underlying tone was an insult.

"My Lords, please!" said Adair, raising his voice as he addressed the tower, his outburst stopping Gosha in her tracks.

The women's fingers tapped and again there was silence.

"You may speak," read the African woman.

"I'm so sorry, Mrs. Armitage," said Adair in a low voice, almost a whisper. The women lifted their hands, poised to type, but they couldn't make out what he was saying. "They mean well, but this is the disadvantage of not having a saint to act as an intermediary. We have to deal with it all the time downstairs. It creates so many problems. They don't think like you and I. They don't understand the way the human mind works, which is rich, given where they come from."

The Lords and Ladies of the Spheres emerged out of formlessness, Eleanor had told her, once Influence had been tamed and could be controlled. Influence came from humans, and the Lords and Ladies emerged from Influence like gods of the human psyche.

"Please sit," he said, gesturing to the chair. "I think I can make a better pitch for your help. Will you let me?"

A thread of flame ignited within her whenever someone talked down to her, but Adair was sincere and her tiny furnace was cold. She walked back to the chair and sat.

"Have you seen the portents?" he asked, crouching before her, keeping his voice low so the four women couldn't hear. "There was a big one yesterday, the largest yet recorded."

"Yes," she said in a normal tone of voice and the women typed the three letters, making Gosha jump. "Yes," she repeated, pitching her voice low to match Adair's.

"According to our departments of research and statistics," he said, "it's a prophecy of doom. The Fall, everyone's calling it. Predictive Analysis has nothing to say about the scope of the prophecy, when it will hit or what its triggers may be, but Modeling has given us some pretty convincing strange attractors, people or places that are in some way key to the whole affair, even if we don't know why. Sir Wilfred is one of them, perhaps the strongest in play at the moment."

"I can't even pretend to understand what you're saying."

Gosha looked nervously at the women, but they didn't react.

"Forgive me." He shook his head with a smile. "It's so easy to fall into jargon. Something big is going to happen and it's going to be bad. Sir Wilfred is, in some way, crucial to it all. Six days ago he went missing. He's been a client of the firm's PR division for some time, but his account got bumped to upper management when Modeling gave us a heads up."

"Are you saying you actually do PR?"

She had seen many strange things since her Betrayal, but a Sphere of Influence handling celebrity public relations topped them all.

"Oh yes. It's an excellent cover for our real work."

"Which is?"

He exhaled deeply.

"It's hard to explain. For the ecology of the realm to be healthy, Influence must be allowed to flow freely, but it tends to get bunged up around the Spheres. Blockages occur. When they do, it's very bad for everyone. Disease, civil unrest, bigotry, nationalism, the whole realm could fall into disaster if any one sphere amasses too much control. The job the partners have tasked us with is to keep it all flowing. It's subtle work that has to be done without the Convocation knowing. We're not supposed to meddle in each other's affairs, but, honestly, that's all we do here. If we show too much interest in Sir Wilfred beyond our capacity as PR agents, the Convocation will ask questions, and questions will lead to conflict. We haven't had a war between the Spheres in the British Isles since 1066. With the Fall coming, we need to keep it that way. You're in a unique position to help us. You have access to Influence but have no affiliation to complicate matters. Plus, no one cares about witches."

He realized what he said and grimaced.

"I'm so sorry. That was terribly offensive. I've read your file. It's very impressive."

Her head swam whenever she had to deal with the intricacies of High Influence and the politics of the Spheres. She'd take casting a fertility rite or a charm against shingles any day.

"If you've read my file," she said, "you know I'm the worst person to turn to. My husband does everything he can to spoil anything important I get involved in, and the Queen of Secrets hates me. I can't even leave the borough. I haven't been out of Cheyne Heath in four years. I appreciate the offer, Mr. Adair, and the vote of confidence, I really do, but I'm not the woman to help you."

She got up to leave.

"I can refer you to another witch, if you like, but I think I should be going."

He pushed himself up out of his squat and rose to his full height, towering over her.

"Could you at least take a gander at the case? Come with me to Sir Wilfred's house and take a look around. Any light you can shed on what happened to him would make a huge difference. We ask for one day of your time. Nothing more. We'll pay, of course."

He removed a folded slip of paper from the inside pocket of his jacket and handed it to her.

"Would this be sufficient for your time?"

She unfolded the paper and nearly dropped it in surprise. Five thousand pounds. Her mind reeled at the thought of the relief that amount of money could bring her.

"I suppose I could take a look," she said and the women's fingers clattered across their keyboards.

9

THEY TOOK THE COMPANY CAR, a giant black American town car converted to right-hand drive, an ostentatious choice for an organization that said they wanted to operate behind the scenes. The interior of the car churned with its own microcosm of Influence that swirled in concentric circles around both Adair and the driver. Her lipstick was tucked into the cuff of her sleeve to hold it against her skin. Not ideal, but an opportunity to secrete it in her bra somewhere secluded had yet to present itself.

"Do you have a picture of Sir Wilfred in that file of yours?" she asked.

Adair flicked through a thick sheath of papers and photographic prints and pulled out a black and white shot of Sir Wilfred with an outstretched brush scowling at a canvas.

"And I need a street atlas."

"Ashton, do you have one up there?" said Adair, leaning forward in his seat.

The driver reached across to the glove compartment without taking his eye off the road and took out a large A to Z atlas that he offered back. Gosha opened it to a spread of Cheyne Heath and laid it across her lap. From her bag she removed her makeup kit and took out her powder brush and compact, dabbed the brush into the powder and took another look at the photo. She hadn't seen Sir Wilfred in years. In her memory he had become a caricature of himself: wild bushy eyebrows atop a long nose and thin, pouting lips. This must have been a recent photo. His hair was grayer, wrinkles etched deeper into his face, and bags hung under his eyes.

"Sutturah."

She blew the powder off the brush over the map. The contented high that came with casting a spell eased up a portion of the lingering apprehension she felt from being in the presence of the Lords of Fate and Fortune.

To her surprise, the swirling Influence in the car picked up the spell-charged powder and whipped it away into nothingness. She'd never seen the spell behave this way before. If Sir Wilfred had simply not been in Cheyne Heath, it would have turned the pages until it found the map it needed to fulfill its purpose, and if someone was using Influence to mask his location, the powder would have burned away.

Adair watched her with wide eyes.

"Could he have left London?" she asked.

He shook his head.

"We've conducted extensive inquiries. He hasn't been in plain sight of another human being since last Tuesday. If he had left London, we'd have found out. He seems to have, quite literally, vanished."

"Were those shots of his paintings I saw in there?" She nodded toward Adair's file. "May I have them?"

Sir Wilfred was famous for his portraits, raw and unadorned evocations of his subjects' inner selves. Sometimes naturalistic, sometimes stylized, they all shared the same encapsulation of humanity in all its light and intensity distilled onto canvas. Of the seven pictures Adair handed her, she selected the three that evoked the most emotion in her and returned the rest.

From the pocket of her tuxedo jacket, she took out her field kit, astonished at how deep her training in Craft had taken hold that she had brought it and her unfinished telling deck with her to what she thought would be a normal job interview. She took out a small, white candle she had stolen from the votive stands in Repton Oratory and a cheap plastic lighter. She kept meaning to ask Elsie to teach her the trick of igniting a flame with a finger snap.

She spread the photos across the atlas on her lap and lit the candle.

"We might have to change course abruptly," she warned the driver and held up the photos to look at them.

"Pelletethaneras."

The serpentine finding spell lifted the flame off the candle wick. The flicker of light floated, suspended in mid-air and winked out.

"Any luck?" asked Adair.

"No. It's as if he doesn't exist."

A mechanical chattering crunched at them from a small dot matrix printer set in the dashboard. The driver pulled the wide ribbon of paper toward him to read what had been printed.

"It's Event Management, sir. They say I need to park here. I'm sorry. It'll be a bit of a walk to the house."

"Not to worry, Ashton."

The driver pulled in to the nearest parking space and out they got. They were back in the posh part of Cheyne Heath. Large, gorgeous, well-kept houses lined the street. Her own house was big, but she and George had reclaimed the entire building from complete disrepair. These houses had never fallen on hard times.

"Do you use spells?" she asked as they walked. "I don't know how High Influence works."

"High Influence?" Adair smiled. "Like High Church? Is that what you call it? Does that mean there's Low Influence as well?"

Offense prickled at her cheeks. Gosha would never have thought of herself as taking pride in witchcraft, but this was the second time Adair and his Lords had managed to get her back up.

"No, only Craft."

He must have realized he'd put his foot in it again and looked sheepish, a strange expression on such a large man.

"No, we don't have spells. We have access to Influence, but it's very labor intensive. We have whole floors of people devoted to research, prediction, and execution. My understanding is it's much easier in the other spheres, but the partners have their reasons to do it this way. They just don't tell us what they are."

They reached their destination after a ten-minute walk, only two streets away from Denise Ogilvy's house. She made a mental note she needed to check with Alfie for news from his mates that were keeping an eye on her.

Sir Wilfred's house was the last on a row of Victorian behemoths. Large white bay windows looked down at them on either side of a filigree and glass awning over the front steps. The interior of the house was dark. She leaned over the balustrade to peer inside, but couldn't see much through the gloom.

"Do you have keys?" she asked.

"I'm afraid I can't interact directly with your investigation, only observe and advise." He carried with him the file on Sir Wilfred and a large leather suitcase which he lifted to show her and beamed her as if she would know what it was. "We have the full resources of the office available to us as well. Just ask. If I can make it happen, I will."

Great, she thought. *Now I'm breaking and entering. Not how I thought today would go.*

"Heckatisk," she said with a hand on the doorknob. The lock mechanism clicked.

"Amazing," whispered Adair.

She pushed the door open and stood on the threshold. Inside, a thin but powerful current of Influence whipped through the house, looping from room to room, up the stairs and down again in an endless current. She thought she saw a figure moving somewhere deeper inside and reached a hand back to Adair.

"Stay there for a moment."

She stuck her head further in through the doorway.

"Hello?" she called. "Wilfred? It's Gosha Armitage."

No response came. She waited and listened, but there was no further sign of movement.

The current of Influence worried her. It was too purposeful to be a simple product of the environment. She took out her field kit and ran her fingers across its contents. She had nothing in it that could diagnose the intent of the current. Her telling deck might have been able to help if she knew how to use it properly, but she only knew a few tricks she could do with it. She'd have to do something more direct and hope for the best.

From the kit she took out a white feather, goose down harvested from the reeds that surrounded the big pond on the heath. Holding it before her, she blew on it gently as she released it to float into the house. It drifted slowly for a few feet until it was swept up by the current and wafted away at a fair clip. It disappeared to the left, through the dining room and into the back of the house, only to re-emerge in the rear foyer and whip up the stairs. It came down again a few minutes later and swung back into the dining room to continue its loop.

So far so good, she thought and reached a hand out to dip her fingertips into the current, but it left her alone, flowing around her without interruption. She took a deep breath and stepped into the house.

Nothing.

"I think it's safe," she said beckoning Adair in behind her, though she kept an eye on the not-aura of wheels that spun around him, ready to push him back with a spell if the current interfered with them.

He put the briefcase and file down just inside the front door and stepped in. The current distorted around him, spinning his translucent wheels faster, but otherwise he was left untouched.

"It's chilly in here," he said with a shiver.

It didn't feel chilly to Gosha. Must be from the interaction of his wheels with the current.

"Careful," she said as the feather looped back toward them and she pulled him out of its path. "Let's go this way."

She led him into the dining room, following the current.

Sir Wilfred's house was decorated with expensive antiques, the historical grandeur leavened by modernizing touches. To Gosha's surprise, the walls of the dining room were lined with modern paintings from Sir Wilfred's contemporaries. A rampant egotist, she half expected to find one of his giant nude self-portraits suspended above the fireplace to torment his guests.

Everything in the room was where it should be, stowed away between social engagements, but something in the house was off, and not only the unusual pattern of Influence. She couldn't put her finger on it, but it nagged at her from the edges of her perception.

They went through to the kitchen, a pristine white-tiled showroom, a stark contrast to the lived-in jumble of her own, though she had heard stories of Sir Wilfred's dinner parties. He fancied himself a chef and was known for his many-course meals of exotic delights.

The feather swept by once more, leading them through the kitchen to the rear foyer and the living room, where giant, overstuffed couches sat next to Louis XVI French armchairs arranged beneath a giant crystal chandelier.

There. In the corner of her eye.

"Did you see that?" she asked.

"No." Adair looked around, startled. "What was it?"

"Something moved in here."

"Maybe a cat?"

There again. Too large to be a cat. A shifting of shadows in the mirror as if someone had walked through the room. A ripple of thrill spread across her shoulders and was gone.

"Here, kitty," said Adair in a high-pitched singsong at odds with his sturdy frame as he stooped to look around for his imagined moggy.

"It's not a cat," she said.

The figure had moved toward the foyer. She wished she had her camera with her. She'd become much better at using it as a focus for scrying.

"Let's go upstairs."

On their way up they passed bedrooms, a study, a library filled with art books. At the top, the entire upper floor was knocked through for Sir Wilfred's atelier. With gables on one side and a skylight on the other, the sparse, whitewashed room glowed with morning light. An empty easel stood in one corner, to its side a glass-doored cabinet containing all his pigments carefully arranged on the shelves by shade, the only shock of color in this sterile and ascetic workroom. She had been in many painter's studios in her time before her Betrayal. None of them looked this clean and empty.

Since her Betrayal and the awakening of second sight that allowed her to sense Influence when her lipstick touched her bare skin, she had been in the workspaces of one or two creative people: Johnny's living room where he kept his keyboards and guitars; the developing room of the lab technician with whom she traded for materials; the rehearsal studio under the flyover at the top of Morel Road where a young choreographer with chronic knee problems created her pieces. They all shared the same characteristic, an explosion of Influence that suffused the space and radiated out into the world around them. Not only was Sir Wilfred's atelier visually sterile, but the only Influence within was the thin current that whipped through it.

There. There it was. In the trifold mirror standing in the corner.

She walked over and stood before it, her image reflected back at her three times, the black and burgundy of her outfit leaping out against the pale background of the studio.

"What is it?" asked Adair, walking over to her.

"Don't move," she said, and he froze.

She softened her gaze as she might when taking a picture or scrying for hints of what lay hidden. There was definitely movement in the room behind her, but nothing she could see, exactly. She fingered the red carved jasper ring in the shape of a two-headed serpent on her index finger. Tonight was the first night of the full moon. She'd be able to use the ring to forge a new spell specially designed to help her see, but she didn't think the firm's partners could wait. Elsie had taught her a trick with the aces of her telling deck that could help focus a freeform manipulation of Influence.

She took out her deck and shuffled through it to take out the Aces of Cups, Brushes, and Buttons. Needles wouldn't do her any good. They were too brainy, too certain. She needed a foundation of openness and curiosity for what she had in mind.

She fanned out the three aces and held them at arm's length: the silhouette of a makeup brush for the Ace of Brushes; the refracted angles of a gem-cut crystal button for the Ace of Buttons, and a thimble for the Ace of Cups. She slipped the lipstick from her sleeve into her palm and concentrated, searching her imagination for an image that might guide the Influence that, even in this strangely attenuated environment, flowed through it.

It came to her quickly. She imagined herself walking through a series of curtains, one after the other, parting them and stepping through in an endless unveiling. The Influence flowing through the lipstick in her right hand responded to her thought, flowing around her and bringing the three cards to life, giving them awareness and intelligence, albeit crude, that received the image and gave it detail, weight, and depth. When the image in her mind was as well-developed as she could make it, she released it. The Influence of her impromptu spell spun around her and flashed into the mirror, and what she saw behind her in the reflection changed.

She and Adair became hazy and opaque. On the floor at the other side of the room kneeled Sir Wilfred with a bucket and brush scrubbing at a patch of color on the floor until it was clean. When he was satisfied, he dumped the brush in the bucket, picked himself up off the floor and turned to leave. He stopped at the mirror to look at himself. His eyes were hollow, his sockets ringed in darkness, his irises and the whites of his eyes tinted an unnatural brown amber. He opened his mouth and moved his lips, but the spell only allowed her to see and not to hear. She tried to read his lips, but his mouth made shapes that seemed like gibberish. He dropped his head and sobbed, slouching as he lugged the bucket of filthy water with him to the stairs.

She leaned in to watch him go and was about to head downstairs when he re-entered the room. She thought perhaps time had passed, as his gray and white hair was now lank and unkempt as if it hadn't been washed for several days. He was naked, his soft aging body splattered with paint. He dragged with him a large canvas tarpaulin which he carried across the room, walking out of her sightline. She looked into the other side of the mirror to see where he went. The easel.

He came back into view with the tarpaulin wrapped around a large painting, his brown amber eyes wide and glowing. He ranted, spitting what could only be curses as he carried the painting to the door and shifted sideways to maneuver the canvas through and down the stairs.

"Come on," she said to Adair, waving at him to follow with her fan of cards.

As she ran down the stairs, a mirror on the wall showed Sir Wilfred shouting his curses as he carried the painting down. She stopped and pressed her face into its surface to watch him for as long as she could. He passed the floor below them and kept going down through the house. She pushed away from the wall and trotted down the stairs in pursuit.

Thankfully there were mirrors everywhere. She followed his disembodied reflection from mirror to mirror downstairs to the foyer and the back of the house. In the surface of a chrome vase filled with dead, stinking lilies, she watched him manhandle the painting through the cellar door. A naked overhead bulb switched on casting a stark light that showed a hint of plastered walls, and then the spell broke, the image vanishing to be replaced by the closed door. Adair pulled up short behind her.

"What's in there?" he said.

"Sir Wilfred stashed a painting down there."

She turned the knob, and the door clicked open. Stairs led down into the gloom. She flicked the light on.

"Let's take a look," she said and headed down.

The cellar was large and damp, not what Gosha would have thought of as a good place to store a painting. What little Influence there was in the air was weak and sluggish. Metal shelves lined the walls filled with the usual bits and bobs you would expect in a cellar. On the far side from the stairs was a large wine rack filled with bottles, Sir Wilfred's wine collection another legend from his dinner parties. Propped up against the wall was the tarp-covered painting.

"That's it," said Gosha, walking over to inspect it.

As she pulled at the tarp, a sudden fluttering of tiny wings burst out from the canvas. She threw up her hands to protect her face and stumbled, falling back and dropping her lipstick, her second sight immediately fading.

"Are you okay?"

Adair rushed over to help her up.

"I'm fine."

She winced as her grazed elbow brushed against the inside of her sleeve.

"Rajequist," she whispered and then realized she had dropped her lipstick and cards. Her healing spell wouldn't work without the talisman.

Adair stopped to pick them up for her. Not another soul had touched the black plastic tube since she had imbued it with power during the ritual of the Betrayal that had turned her into a witch, but Adair gave no indication that touching it had any effect on him.

"Here."

He passed her belongings back to her.

"Thanks."

She did her best not to snatch them off him.

As she curled her fingers around the lipstick and second sight returned to her, she recoiled in horror. A swarm of tiny beating wings spewed from the solid black surface of the painting, fluttering about the room, beating at her face. A great cloud had settled around Adair's concentric wheels, the wings so thick, even in their translucence, they obscured him. The wings burrowed into the wheels, eating at them, dissolving them into a dark and twisting effervescence. Gosha had seen the effect before. Left unchecked, it would end in corruption so profound to the aura of the person afflicted, they were plucked from reality by the Lords and Ladies.

She pointed the lipstick at him.

"Puthut."

A wave of Influence rushed out at him, lifting him off his feet and propelling him up the stairs and out the cellar door, but the beating wings still clung to him.

"Puthut," she said again, aiming the wave so it carried him out the open front door and into the street where he crashed into the trunk of a giant beech outside the front gate.

She ran to catch up with him, finding him slumped on the ground, stunned. She took out the bottle of fathom's bane from her field kit and sprayed him until it was empty. The wings, the wheels, and the twists of corruption froze.

"Collusetoire."

A powerful blast of wind blew across him wiping away all the Influence that clung to him, good and bad. She knelt and placed a hand on his shoulder.

"Rajequist."

A gentle fizz of Influence bubbled through her.

Adair's eyes snapped open. He pushed himself up the trunk of the tree and stepped away from her, stammering.

"What— What the hell!"

"I'm sorry. There's something very wrong with that painting. It would have killed you. I had to get you outside so I could clear away what it was doing to you."

He patted the pockets of his suit jacket, took out a four-inch square of tinted glass in a silver frame, and held it up in front of him, inspecting himself.

"My sheath is gone. What did you do to it?"

"Your sheath? Do you mean the wheels?"

"Yes, the wheels," he snapped. "What did you do to them?"

The ambient Influence in the street had begun to coalesce around him in a steady, circular drift.

"I had to dispel them, but they're starting to reform."

He checked himself again through the square of glass.

"Thank the Lords," he said and sat heavily down on the low stone wall that stretched across the front of the property. "Are you okay?"

She smiled and sat next to him.

"I'm fine, but that thing downstairs is dangerous. We have to do something about it."

He craned his neck to peer over the front hedge.

"I need my briefcase."

The fluttering wings and their corruption were gone.

"It's safe," she said.

He stood and edged cautiously toward the door, reached across the threshold, and grabbed the briefcase. Returning to the pavement, he perched on the wall once more, placed the briefcase across his knees, and clicked it open. Inside was a large, blocky telephone handset nestled in a cradle embedded in the surface of a black plastic box that filled the briefcase. Next to the handset was a large green button set into the plastic. He held the handset to his ear and pressed the button.

"Joel Adair," he said. "Event Management. Yes. Priority one. I need a hazard team at the Stepney residence. Yes, an unregistered artifact. High-risk extraction."

He replaced the receiver in its cradle and clicked the briefcase shut.

"It will take a few moments for the lads in Event Management to calculate a free causality path," he said.

"A what?"

"They need to find a sequence of events that will allow the hazard team to contain the painting safely without alerting the Convocation, something that seems random and won't alert watchful eyes. It's a tricky job. Not that I need to tell you. You've dealt with the Queen of Secrets. What's she like?"

"Dangerous," said Gosha, sitting back down next to him on the wall. "If you have workarounds available to you, I don't understand why you need me."

"We tried on our own, but our methods are too indirect. The slightest hint of another sphere cottoning on to what we're doing and we have to change tack."

"So there are other spheres involved in all this?"

All the more reason for her to take the money and walk away at the end of the day.

"Possibly. We can't be sure. There's too much activity in the realm right now because of the prophecy. Everyone is stepping on everyone else's toes as they try to figure out how it will affect them."

"Do you know about auras?"

"Yes," he said, taking out the square of glass. "That's what this is for."

"Did you see the aura that came off the painting?"

He shook his head.

"It was like fluttering wings, swarms of them. Any idea what sphere that could be?"

"No," he said with widening eyes. He took out a notebook and pen from his jacket to jot down the information.

"What's your sheath?" she asked, looking over his shoulder as he scrawled his notes.

"Sort of an artificial aura," he said without looking up, "gifted upon us by the partners. It keeps a lot of what we do under the radar."

An unmarked blue van drove up and a crew of six men and women in hooded white paper suits and surgeon's masks emerged from the back carrying large silver equipment cases. The lead figure stopped at the front gate.

"Basement," said Adair. "It's a painting. Highly toxic. Contain and remove. Send it to Analysis for a report. Research can get in on it as well, if they want."

10

THEY STOOD AT THE THRESHOLD watching in silence until one of the hazard team stuck their head out from the back of the house to give them the okay signal. As they brought out the painting enmeshed in a cocoon of plastic sheeting and foam, she noticed a datebook next to the telephone on the side table by the stairs.

"Tuesday was the last day Sir Wilfred was seen?" she asked as she thumbed through the pages.

"Yes," said Adair coming to look with her.

She found the page for last Tuesday.

"He had an appointment with a Dr. Dropnick at one in the afternoon," she read. "And a party in the evening."

Dropnick, she thought. *I've heard that name before. But where?*

"A party? Where?"

"Doesn't say."

Propped up on a silver tray was a stack of cards and letters.

"Here you go."

She took out a square white card with embossed lettering, an invitation to an engagement party at the Cheyne Arts Club.

"We'll go there next," said Adair.

A rush of panic made her heart beat faster. The Cheyne Arts Club was the last place she wanted to go.

"That's not a good idea. I'm persona non grata there thanks to my husband. And I'm not a member anymore. They won't let me in."

"Oh, that's not a problem," he said cheerfully and clicked open his briefcase to use the phone.

"Joel Adair," he spoke into the handset. "Event Management. Yes. Priority one. Reputation adjustment and membership renewal at CAC-6842 for GMC-347."

He hung up and closed the briefcase.

"We should be able to clear up your standing enough with the club itself that they'll let you back in. And we'll pay for your membership, of course. I wish I could do more, but it will take time."

"No, you don't understand. George has gone to great lengths to turn everyone there against me." The last time she'd been to the Club, before her membership dues had run out a few months after George had become Saint of Authority and she had banished him from the neighborhood, an old friend had spat in her face, but refused to say why. After that she never went back. "No one will talk to me."

"But you know most of the people there?"

"Yes, that's what I'm trying to explain. They all hate me."

"Mrs. Armitage, analysis of the painting could take days. This," he tapped the invitation with a well-manicured fingernail, "is our most pressing lead. All I'm asking is that you help me find where he went. You must surely have some tricks of persuasion up your sleeve. Sir Wilfred's life could depend on it."

Every nerve in her body screamed at her to say no.

"All right."

She surprised herself.

"Let's go."

She looked at her watch. Noon.

"Lunch service will be starting in a minute. It's as good a time as any."

They sat in the town car across the street from the club waiting for the go-ahead from Adair's portable phone. The club's ongoing war with the gentrifying neighbors must have reached a detente, as the front of the building, normally covered in vibrant, artistic, and usually obscene murals, was now a stark and conforming white.

The Cheyne Arts Club was once Gosha's favorite place in all of London, somewhere she could relax around others like her, somewhere she could drink and talk and exchange ideas. A meeting place for many of the friends she loved most in the world, it represented the epitome of the kind of life she wanted to live, and thanks to the poison George had spread among her friends, she had been rejected by it. She knew whatever slander George had spread was false, but she still felt guilt, still felt shame. The idea of going back in there filled her with dread.

An electronic trill came from within Adair's briefcase. He clicked it open and took the receiver.

"Adair, yes. Yes. Great job." He returned the phone to its cradle and clicked the briefcase shut. "We're all set. Management is waiting for us."

Gosha hesitated as she put her hand on the door handle and squeezed the chrome.

"Forgive me, Ma'am," said the driver, mistaking her hesitation for the expectation that he would open the door for her. He unfastened his seat belt and made to get out of the car.

"No, no," she stammered, feeling even worse about herself. "I'm fine. I have it."

She opened the door and slid out to follow Adair across the street. He rang the doorbell, a large brass button. She had never had to ring the bell before. Members were given a key.

The large black front door opened to reveal a face she'd never seen before, a young man in gray pinstripe trousers, a crisp white shirt, and black suspenders.

"Joel Adair and Gosha Armitage to see the manager," said Adair. "He's expecting us."

"Gosha Armitage?" The young man furrowed his brow in confusion, but then the penny dropped. Disgust flashed across his face before he was able to contain it.

Great, she thought, her heart sinking. *My scandalous reputation precedes me, and I don't even know what I'm supposed to have done.*

The young man ushered them in and led them to the manager's office at the back of the building. An older couple whose names she couldn't remember came out of the dining room headed for the bar. She smiled as they passed, but the woman leaned in to whisper something to her husband, who grimaced and looked away.

She had known the day manager, Peter Stanger, for years, had even been to his daughter's wedding, but he looked at her with cold eyes that betrayed no emotion.

"Joel Adair from Waterfield, Wakeford, Winston, and Whorl." Adair thrust his hand across the manager's desk. Stanger rose and reluctantly shook it. "I believe you have a new membership package for Mrs. Armitage."

"No," said Stanger. "I have nothing of the sort."

"Really?" said Adair with unflappable cheer. "An arrangement was made between my firm and your board of directors. Perhaps they haven't contacted you..."

The phone on Stanger's desk rang.

"Ah," said Adair. "I bet that's them now."

He smiled, revealing a row of perfect white teeth as Stanger answered the phone.

"Hello?" The manager's eyes glazed over as he listened to the voice on the other end. "But—"

He turned his back on them as he spoke, as if that gave him privacy.

"Yeah, she's here."

He turned back and looked Adair up and down.

"Okay, okay. I'll do it."

Stanger frowned at them and put the handset back on the cradle.

"Dean," he shouted to the young man who had shown them in and who now hovered in the doorway. "Get Mrs. Armitage a key. I'll need you to fill out the forms again," he said to Gosha. "But you're fully reinstated as a member."

"Thank you so much," said Adair. "We'll be in the bar?" he addressed the question to Gosha.

"Yes," she croaked, her throat tight, and coughed. "Yes, the bar."

"After you," said Adair.

Her hands shook with nerves, so she stuffed them in the pockets of her tuxedo jacket. As they walked through to the bar, she glanced at the ceiling and walls for signs of the destruction she and George had caused when he first assumed the sainthood of Authority and tried to use his power to bend her to his will. The one thing the club didn't lack was money. They had the holes patched up and the club open to members within a month.

The barroom, also used for performances, banquets, and the annual summer ball, made up half the floor plan of the building. With twenty-foot ceilings, a small stage, a skylight, and French windows facing out on the garden, a full snooker table, and a carved wooden bar that stretched the length of one wall, the room was the heart of both the club and the arts scene of Cheyne Heath. At twelve-thirty in the afternoon, most of the club's members would just be rolling out of bed, but a handful of the more industrious ones, and some of the heavier drinkers still going from the night before, were scattered around the room.

"Over there," said Gosha, pointing to a face she recognized sipping a beer and chatting to a friend at the bar. "That's Mark Sims. He's a close friend of Sir Wilfred."

"Let's talk to him," said Adair.

She took a deep breath and walked over to the bar, doing her best to ignore the elderly couple that had recognized her earlier and was now, judging by the looks of fascinated horror on their faces, regaling a group of people gathered round the snooker table with the stories George had been spreading about her.

"Excuse me, Mark?" she said, approaching Sims from behind and placing a hand on his shoulder.

A renowned journalist turned celebrity biographer, Mark Sims had always been the wise and gentle counselor of the club, always willing to lend an ear and generous with advice, contacts, and hard cash.

"Hello," he said as he turned with a smile that fell from his face the moment he realized who Gosha was. "Oh, it's you. The whore of Canterbury Gardens. I thought they kicked you out. Ralphy," he said to the bartender. "Get this riffraff out of here, would you?"

"I'm sorry miss," said Ralphy. His round face and curly blonde hair made him look too young to be tending a bar. "This is a members-only club."

"You can check with your manager," said Adair. "She's just been made a member."

"And who the fuck are you," asked Sims. "Her pimp?"

"Joel Adair, sir," he said, unfazed by the insult as he handed Sims a business card. "Waterford, Wakefield, Winston, and Whorl. I believe we handle the PR for your publisher."

Sims squinted at the card with distaste.

"I wouldn't believe a word of what this woman has to say." He tossed the card on the bar and turned to Ralphy. "Check with Stanger."

Ralphy scuttled away.

"I need to ask you about Sir Wilfred," said Gosha.

Sims groaned with disgust, took his drink and turned to his companion, a woman Gosha remembered was a textile designer who watched the exchange with avid interest.

"Come on, Melissa. Let's go out to the garden. The stench in here has suddenly turned my stomach."

He took her by the elbow and led her outside.

Gosha couldn't move, couldn't turn her head or even raise her eyes. Every muscle in her body constricted as if to pull away from the humiliation.

Money be damned, she thought. *I have to get out of here.*

"I'm sorry," she said to Adair as she turned on her heel and fled for the door. "I told you this was a huge mistake."

"Mrs. Armitage." Adair rushed to catch up. "Wait. Let me put in another call to Event Management—"

"Gosha." A familiar voice stopped her in her tracks as Gosha reached the front door. "What are you doing here?"

A rough voice, harsh and cracked by years of abuse, but still filled with warmth and emotion. Her oldest friend in the world, Miranda.

She looked well, had regained some of the fire in her bearing she'd lost after her guru had turned out to be a murderous sorcerer and her best friend a witch. It was a relief to see her, to hear her voice. Despite herself, Gosha rushed over to and wrapped her arms around her in a hug, but Miranda stood rigid and didn't return the gesture.

"You shouldn't be here," said Miranda. "After all you've done."

Gosha pulled back.

"What has George told you?"

"He told me everything, about the lies and the affairs. About how you stole all his money and threatened the boys to kick him out of his own home. He told me about—"

She looked around to see if anyone else was nearby.

"—the evil things you and your mother did to trap him," she whispered. "Why on earth would you show your face here? These are decent people."

Miranda knew all about George, about how he murdered his father and how he'd been involved with Emerson Margrave who would have consumed her life to slake his thirst for power. How could Miranda have believed him and turned her back on Gosha, the one who saved her life?

"Sir Wilfred Stepney has disappeared," said Gosha, her voice clipped of all emotion lest she scream with frustration or dissolve in tears. "He was here last Tuesday evening at the party. Were you there? Did you see him?"

Miranda blinked, processing Gosha's unexpected response.

"He was drinking with Dougie Barber. I saw them leave together before the party was over."

Dougie Barber was another fixture of the Cheyne Arts scene. He and Wilfred were notorious carousers and denizens of the night.

"There you are," she said to Adair who had watched the whole exchange with an appalled look on his face. "Dougie Barber. I think he lives near here."

She turned her back on Miranda and walked out of the club.

11

GOSHA FLED ACROSS THE STREET to the town car and the driver standing by, ready to open the door for her.

Great, she thought, her humiliation driven deeper by the act of kindness. *He thinks I'm a prima donna.*

She slumped into her car seat wanting nothing more than to bury her head in her hands and weep, but Adair got in beside her.

"I am so sorry, Mrs. Armitage." She glanced up at his stricken face and turned away, desperate to be anywhere but in the car with him. "That was entirely my fault. I should have realized the delicate situation you were in. I have your cashier's check on me. If you can just see this through to Mr. Barber, I'll hand it off to you and you can be on your way."

She nodded.

"Ashton: Douglas Barber, member of the club, lives locally."

"Yes, sir," said the driver and punched a series of pink buttons on a black plastic box next to the steering wheel.

His dot matrix printer chattered to life and spat out a few lines. He tore the paper off to read what was written, turned the key in the ignition, and drove off.

They arrived at Dougie Barber's house, a much less grand row house, within five minutes. The lights were off and three bottles of milk sat on the front step by the door. All business, she didn't wait for Adair or the driver to get out of the car. She ran up the front steps to the front door, unlocked it with a spell, and pushed it open. Inside, she found the same attenuated flow of Influence cycling round the modest house.

"It's exactly like Sir Wilfred's." She took another down feather from her kit and released it to be carried along by the flow. "Don't touch anything in case there's something else like the painting."

They followed the feather up three flights of stairs, ghost images flickering in reflective surfaces as she passed. On the second floor was Dougie Barber's studio. Dougie was a successful graphic designer. The walls of the house were covered with poster art, but his studio was empty, the built-in bookcases stripped bare, the walls cleared and everything painted the same whitewash as Sir Wilfred's atelier. The only thing that remained in the room was his drafting table and stool. On the table an envelope lay face down. A red wax seal held it closed. Pressed into the seal was a pair of moth wings that shimmered with dark Influence in her second sight, giving the impression the moth was alive.

"That's it," she said, pushing Adair out of the room. "Get your hazard team in here."

As he ran back down to the front door where he had left his briefcase phone, she pulled the door to the studio closed and stood before a vintage concert poster for Miles Davis at the Fillmore East framed behind glass. A shadow passed behind her reflection and headed up the stairs. She followed it from poster to poster to the top floor and the master bedroom.

Lying on the bed was the body of Dougie Barber, his skin dessicated and mummified, his mouth open as if to scream. In one hand, the corpse held a knife he had used to slice his wrists the way you did if you were serious. The skin of his forearm was parted from elbow to wrist, but no blood stained the white bedspread.

She remembered a late night at the club at Christmas time one year shortly after Timothy was born. She remembered a rare dusting of snow over the grass and bushes of the garden at the club. She remembered lying on the overstuffed sofa with a glass of whiskey in one hand and a cigar in the other as Dougie regaled them with a story about David Bowie, a juggler, and a tame alpaca. She remembered the gleam in his eye as he delivered the punchline and fifteen people roared with laughter. She remembered the look of devotion on his partner's face, only a year before the poor man died of cancer.

All her shame and humiliation suddenly felt small and meaningless.

She went back down to find Adair closing his briefcase.

"They'll be here soon," he said.

"You should call the police as well. Dougie Barber's body is in the bedroom."

"His body?"

"Do you have my check?"

He glanced between her and the upper landing, a frown on his face.

"Um, yes. Of course."

He took an envelope from his inside pocket and gave it to her.

"Consider this a down payment on my retainer," she said without opening it. "I'm taking the case."

12

"WILLY'S DEAD?" SAID JOHNNY, SQUINTING the creamy-brown skin across his cheekbones and brow as if to protect his eyes from the sun, or from tears.

"No," said Gosha, his hands in hers, and sighed. "I don't know."

"Oh, thank god."

He collapsed into the futon sofa.

"I hope not. Only Dougie Barber. But Willy's been missing since last Tuesday. He and Dougie left the Arts Club together, and no one's seen them since. Any idea where they might have gone?"

An enormous poster of Kate Bush, sepia-toned in Victorian costume about to pass a key in a kiss to a chained Houdini, stared down at Gosha from Johnny's living room wall. One of Sir Wilfred's go-to life models for years, Johnny's relationship with Sir Wilfred had been intermittent and stormy, until Johnny had decided he needed to stop being someone else's muse and find a muse of his own, but even then they still saw each other around town, at bars where Johnny had scrounged drink tickets, at dinners where he paid his share of the bill in charm, at shows where a mate had got him on the list. Johnny struggled with his career, a little too ahead of the curve, a little too creative, a little too outrageous. But he was good, really good. His big moment would surely come soon if the thick waves of Influence that always sloughed off him could be believed.

"He and Dougie always go to Uncle Jacky's together on Tuesdays. Tuesday night's the Docks. Crappy rock music and lots of working-class men. They like their bit of rough. Want a puff?"

He took an antique metal biscuit tin off the side table and began to roll a joint with his long elegant fingers and navy blue varnished nails.

"Uncle Jacky's? I've never heard of it," she said.

"It's down the end of Garter Street. Grotty little place. You wouldn't have." He sprinkled a healthy handful of weed on the rolling paper. "It's more my kind of place than yours."

He winked at her as he licked the edge of the paper and sealed the roll.

"Someone's paying me to find Willy," said Gosha, catching the familiarity off Johnny. Sir Wilfred hated it when Johnny called him that.

"Paying? Actual dosh?"

"Yes, his PR firm."

The non-disclosure agreement Adair had made her sign was in her pocket. She needed to give it a once-over and figure out how much it would allow her to tell Johnny. He knew all about Craft and Influence, so that part wouldn't be an issue, but Gosha couldn't be sure how much she'd compromised herself by entering into a formal agreement with a sphere. There hadn't been any notable Influence around the document, and she didn't sense anything change when she signed, but you never knew.

He lit the joint, took a drag, and passed it over. She took a small hit. The boys were asleep. It couldn't do any harm.

"Wow," he said as he breathed out a lungful of smoke. "Can you get me in with them?"

"If I can, of course."

The effect of the weed hit her quickly, mellowing her out and opening up her second sight without the need of her lipstick. Influence flowed thick and strong around Johnny. She wasn't worried his big break had yet to come. It would happen.

"I need to go down there and ask around if anyone saw them."

Johnny took another hit and shook his head.

"You won't get in. It's men only."

"That seems rude," she said, not getting it for a moment, but he raised a long, tapered eyebrow at her. "Oh, I see. Would you go down there for me?"

When he had said it was more one of his places than hers, she thought he meant another one of his out there avant garde performance art spaces he had dragged her to where people froze their feet in blocks of ice and played glowing violins, or hung naked from the ceiling and recited the ingredients off packets of digestive biscuits. He meant it was a gay bar. God, she could be dense sometimes.

He offered her another toke, but she turned it down with a wave and a smile.

"Not my scene," he said. "Just a bunch of butch queens sniffing each other out. Alfie would have better luck than me."

"I'll ask him if he'll go."

"Oh, honey, no," he said with an exaggerated American accent as he carefully knocked the burning tip of the joint into an ashtray to preserve the rest. "They'll eat him for breakfast. I wouldn't do that to him."

He slumped back on the futon couch and took a long look at her through squinted eyes.

"Stand up, deary," he asked.

"What?"

"Indulge me."

She got up and stood in front of him.

"Stand with your feet a bit wider."

She did.

"Shove your hands in your pockets."

"Why?"

"Just do it. And slouch."

She twisted her face into the leer of an old lech and rounded her back.

"Ugh. Not like that," he said. "The wind will change and you'll be stuck that way. Yeah, I can work with this."

"Work what?" She straightened up and arched her back to undo the knot the slouch had put into her muscles.

"Yeah, you can't be doing that," he waved a finger in the direction of her breasts. "And we need to get all that makeup off you."

An hour later she didn't recognize herself in the mirror. A thin young man with slicked-back hair and a hint of stubble stared back at her. Johnny had put her in the battered old hobnailed boots she only wore when she was building sets for a shoot, rolled up the cuffs of her jeans, traded her burgundy top for a plain black t-shirt with her most restrictive sports bra underneath compressing what little bust she had almost to nothing, and a cheap men's jacket with sleeves rolled up to the elbows to reveal the ropey forearms she'd developed in the past couple of years of training with Alfie in the boxing ring.

"Let me see?" said Johnny.

She turned around and posed, shifting her weight onto one leg and giving her best James Dean pout.

"Don't push it," chided Johnny, shaking his head. "For Uncle Jacky's you need to stay firmly on the butch side of gender bender."

She shifted to a wider stance and slouched like he had shown her.

"Yeah," he said. "You're ready. Let's go downstairs and debut your new look."

Alfie didn't recognize her at first as she walked into the kitchen where he pored over the crossword puzzle in the evening paper. It was only when her mother saw her, made a guttural sound of disgust and stamped upstairs to her room that his eyes widened with realization.

"What is going on?" he said, a broad smile spreading across his perfect mug, and spun her around. "You look mad."

"I need to go out for a job," she said. "Will you come with us?"

"You're going outside dressed like that?" He frowned and smiled at the same time. "Yes. Yes, I wouldn't miss it for the world."

He pulled her toward him and hugged her close.

"WHAT is THAT?"

He pushed her away to look down at her crotch.

"A pair of your socks."

She smiled and blushed.

"Talk lower," said Johnny as he went to the cupboards and brought back a jar of instant coffee.

He poured out a small amount into his palm and began to rub it into her fingers.

"The interview I went on today?" she pitched her voice as low as she could. "Not a photography job. They want me to find this famous painter Johnny knows. Ow!"

A grain of dried coffee wedged painfully under her fingernails.

"Why are you doing that?" she asked in her normal voice.

"Alfie, show us your fingernails."

He stuck a hand out. He had done a poor job of clipping his nails, with bits of dirt still clinging under the ravaged tips.

"Details are important," said Johnny. "You know that."

"Which painter?" asked Alfie.

"Sir Wilfred Stepney," said Gosha, not expecting him to know who that was.

"Oh yeah. I went to an exhibition of his work at the Royal Academy."

"You did?" said Gosha. "When?"

“It was before we met. I had a life before you, you know.”

“Aren’t you a man of surprises.”

She pulled him close to kiss him.

“None of that,” said Johny, brushing the mess he’d made with the coffee into the bin.

“What, two attractive gay men can’t show affection for each other?” She winked at Alfie.

“Yeah, not like that. I told you. Go butch or go home. And you,” he bore down on Alfie, a slender brown finger pointed at his chest. “Are you going to be able to handle this?”

“I’ve worked gay bars,” he said, waggling his eyebrows. “I know how to behave around the boys.”

13

THE ARCHITECTURE OF GARTER STREET was an odd mish-mash of periods of expansion from Cheyne Heath's varied history. On one side of the street stood rows of two-story brick houses with shops at street level, such as you might see in country villages across the south of England. On the other side, nineteen-sixties warehouses loomed menacingly over their quaint neighbors. At one end was a Victorian church, on the other an old Art Deco movie house that had been renovated into a cut-price jeans emporium. The door to Uncle Jacky's was tucked away down a narrow alley between two warehouses, the only indication it was there the single lighting sconce above an industrial door, and a large man with a buzz cut and muscles bulging out of a white t-shirt and jeans two sizes too small for him.

"When we get there," said Johnny as they crossed the street, "look bored and scratch your package."

"Do you know the bouncer?" asked Gosha.

Alfie shook his head.

"Darling," said Johnny to the enormous man as they approached, camping it up more than Gosha had ever seen him. "Is this it? Can we come in?"

He flashed his eyes and cocked his hips at the bouncer who looked around uncomfortably and grunted with a nod of his head as he opened the door for them.

"There you go," whispered Johnny as they went in. "Simple misdirection. He didn't even look at you."

Behind the door was a short, narrow corridor lit only by a red light above the entrance. At the far end, on a stool behind a rickety podium sat an old biker with a classic handlebar mustache in jeans, t-shirt, and leather vest, his pale skin glowing against black walls in the dim light. He was reading a dog-eared copy of a Jean Genet novel, a blindfolded man's naked back across its cover.

"No birds," he said when he saw them.

Gosha cleared her throat and scratched at the bulge of socks stuffed down the front of her jeans.

"Fuck off, mate," said Alfie with exactly the right balance of offense and playfulness. "He's not a bird. Can we come in or not?"

He wrapped his arm possessively around her neck and pulled her close. She stared at the doorman with every ounce of bored nonchalance she could muster, crossed her arms and flexed her muscles as hard as she could.

"He's a fella?" said the doorman with surprise, taking Alfie at his word. He put his book down to take their money. "Sorry, mate. Fiver each."

Alfie took his roll of cash out of his pocket, peeled off fifteen quid and handed it to the doorman.

"For all three of us."

The doorman took the money, grunted and went back to his book.

"Nicely done," said Johnny once they were out of earshot.

"I told you I know how to behave," Alfie grinned.

The space was filled with men of all ages, all dressed in variations of a common uniform of jeans, white t-shirts, and leather accessories. Seventies glam rock crunched out of the speakers and a handful of patrons shuffled about and bobbed their heads in the square pit surrounded by a railing in the middle of the room that served as a dancefloor.

"Ugh," said Johnny, cringing at the music. "Slade. You owe me for this, love. Let me see if I can find out anything at the bar. See that doorway in the back?"

A black curtain hung across an opening in the far wall. Two men put their beers down on a tall bar table covered in half-full glasses and went in.

"Whatever you do, do not go in there. Either of you."

"Why?" she asked. "What's in there?"

Alfie coughed loudly and Johnny stared at her hard with one eyebrow arched.

"Oh." She felt her face flush as she realized what he was getting at.

Alfie tittered beside her. She punched him hard in the arm as Johnny disappeared into the crush.

"Are you okay," Alfie asked, leaning in to talk in her ear over the music. "It must have been hard finding that body."

She thought back over the past few hours, calling back into her mind the sight of Dougie Barber's dessicated corpse. It hadn't seemed real. If she hadn't been standing in his bedroom, she might not have known it was him. The memory of him and the knowledge he was gone affected her more than the sight of his deformed body.

"I can handle it."

"I know you can," he said.

He squeezed her arm and curled his fingers around hers in a clandestine grip.

"Fucking bitches," fumed Johnny as he pushed back through the crowd toward them. "I hate places like this. I couldn't even catch the bartender's eye. There's no sisterhood anymore. You're up, pal."

He slapped Alfie on the shoulder and pushed him toward the bar. "Don't come back without vodka tonics and answers."

Alfie grinned, kissed Gosha on the neck and pushed into the throng.

"You really lucked out with that one," said Johnny as he watched Alfie disappear. "Sweet, strong, and about as far from uptight as you can get in a straight boy."

He pushed at her playfully with a shoulder.

"Yeah, he's a keeper," she said.

"Careful," he smirked. "Even gay men don't smile like that."

Alfie returned within ten minutes carrying a handful of drinks and with a young man in his mid-twenties in tow.

"This is Jerry," said Alfie as he passed out the drinks. "Jerry, this is Johnny and..."

He suddenly looked stricken. They hadn't agreed on a name for her.

"Tomasz," she blurted out, her father's name.

Jerry nodded hello to them all and sipped his drink. He had the same slicked-back hair she did, his bony chest pale under his leather waistcoat.

"You're looking for Wilfred and Dougie?" he said leaning in and shouting to be heard above the din. "They usually go to Dorothy Gale's on a Monday night."

"No one..." She tried shouting over the music in her deeper register, but it made her throat hurt, so she gave up the charade. "No one's seen them since last Tuesday. We're friends of theirs. I'm worried about them. Were you here then?"

"Yeah, they were with some posh git I'd never seen before. Young guy. Looked like trade to me. New around here. Very flirty. Always up in everyone's business. Made a bee-line for them when they came in. He was really working them. I took a piss next to him and he kept bragging they were taking him to Bar de Bauche."

"Where's that?" Gosha asked, looking at Johnny.

"No idea."

"It's a drag club down by Well Street tube station," said Jerry. "Invitation only. I went with my lover once. He works in the City. Got one through his job."

"Any good?" asked Johnny.

The boy wrinkled his nose.

"Not my thing. Too poufy."

"The bar or your lover?" said Johnny with a bitchy sneer.

"The bar," Jerry snapped back. He began to lose interest in the conversation, his eyes drifting toward the back room. "Try asking that guy."

"What was his name?" asked Gosha.

"Something weird and old-fashioned, from a kid's book. Caspian. That was it." He turned to Alfie and winked. "Thanks for the drink."

He made his way over to the back room, threading through the crowd. He paused at the black curtain and looked back at Alfie before slipping through.

"You made an impression there," said Johnny.

"Nah," said Alfie. "Not my type. I like my fellas with less—"

He pinched his fingers together and sniffed the air as if he were a connoisseur of fine things struggling to find the right word.

"—cock."

14

IT WAS MIDNIGHT BEFORE THEY found the club. A hastily cast finding spell in the car yielded nothing more than smoldering ash of face powder drifting across her street atlas, which at least told them the club was masked with Influence, both a good sign that they were onto something and a bad sign for what they might find when they got there. Gosha drove them around the immediate vicinity of Well Street tube station, road by road, eliminating bars and clubs they came across with Alfie and Johnny's combined knowledge of Cheyne Heath nightlife and a copy of Time Out to fill in the gaps. They found the entrance to Bar de Bauche down the side of a sixties brutalist mountain of stepped concrete, its glass doors and a velvet rope guarded by two imposing bouncers in all-black suits.

Gosha parked the car a street away, took her lipstick out of her pocket, and tucked it into her shirt, the plastic digging painfully into her ribs beneath the binding elastic of her sports bra.

"Plan of attack?" she said, turning to Johnny in the back seat, his long legs pulled up at an awkward angle in the cramped space of the Mini.

"No idea," he shrugged. "We're well beyond my manor."

"I can do the talking," said Alfie. "I'll chat up the bouncers. We might get what we need from them."

They approached the club slowly. The nighttime Influence drifted around them more strongly than it would have on other nights, whipped up by the full moon that shone down upon them. Her nerves on edge as she scanned her awareness for any adverse side effects of the Influence-fueled masking of the club, it occurred to her this might all be a colossal waste of time. The moon was full. She could have spent the evening in her studio working out the perfect spell that would give her the information she wanted with the jasper ring that gave her access to the power of the Shadowlands.

"We're underdressed," said Johnny. "Take a gander at those two."

A middle-aged couple stepped out of a limousine and approached the velvet rope, the man in a full tuxedo, the woman in a draped sheath of strawberry satin wearing jewels that glittered in the light that hung over the club door, a fur stole draped across her shoulders. The man presented an invitation to one of the bouncers, who looked it over, nodded, and unclipped the velvet rope to let them through.

"Mac," said Alfie as they approached, recognizing the older of the two bouncers.

"Alfie-me-lad," said the bouncer, reaching across the rope so they could clasp hands and clap each other on the back in a half-hug. "What're you doing up this way?"

"Any chance we can come in?"

"Ah, sorry mate," said Mac with an expression of genuine disappointment. "Invitation only."

"Any leeway for friends?"

"Can't, brother. They're serious here. Members and quotas and shit. I'd be out of a job."

Alfie nodded, a look of wise understanding on his face.

“You met my lady, Gosha?” he said, putting a hand on her shoulder.

Mac’s eyes flickered between the two of them quizzically as he shook her hand.

“Fancy dress party,” said Gosha, and Mac relaxed.

“Looks good,” he said, holding onto her hand with a firm grip longer than appropriate for a casual greeting. “Wow. Alfie said you’d been training. Want a job on my crew?”

He released her hand and laughed, Alfie pretending to join in on the joke.

“Hey, Mac.” He leaned in to talk to him quietly. “We’re looking for a friend of ours. He’s gone walkabout and we’re trying to track him down. We’re worried he might have done himself a mischief. Drugs and stuff. Apparently he was here last Tuesday. Were you on the door then?”

“Nah, but Pat was.” He turned to the other bouncer. “You was here Tuesday, right?”

“Yeah,” said Pat from the other side of the roped enclosure. “What did your friend look like?”

The only distinguishing feature between Pat and Mac was age and haircut, Pat ten years Mac’s junior and sporting a poorly trimmed flat-top.

“Mid-fifties,” said Gosha. “Salt and pepper hair, long nose. He was with friends, a man his age and a younger one.”

“Oh yeah. I saw them. Came in late, right before the show started.”

“Did you see them leave?” asked Gosha.

Pat shook his head. “That was the night after Cathy had the sprog. I only worked a half shift.”

“That was Tuesday?” said Mac, chuckling. “You poor bastard. The first eighteen years are the worst.”

“Fuck you, old man.”

“Do you think there’s anyone else on tonight that might have seen them?” asked Gosha.

“Probably,” said Mac.

"Do you think we could ask them? Maybe a manager?"

Mac looked awkwardly between her and Alfie.

"No, I'm sorry. It's a tight ship back there. They've got no time for faffing around."

Another well-dressed couple stepped up to the ropes. Mac took their invitations and let them through.

"Look," he said once they had gone in. "It's great to see you. Catch you at the Barkley on Saturday."

His body language made it clear they should move on.

"Yeah, yeah," said Alfie. "Cheers, mate. Nice to meet you." He exchanged a nod with Pat as they turned to go.

"Sorry I couldn't get us in," said Alfie as they walked back toward the car.

"Not to worry," said Gosha. "We'll see what Adair can do."

She pushed a coin into the slot of the public phone as the receiver beeped in her ear. Joel Adair had given her a number he could be reached at after hours, insisting she call whenever she needed it.

"Night line," said a woman's voice at the other end.

"This is Gosha Armitage. I need to speak to Joel Adair, please."

"Yes, Mrs. Armitage. You can hang up. He will call you back momentarily."

"Don't you need the number?"

"The system has it."

The line went dead. She replaced the handset on its cradle and the phone rang.

"Mrs. Armitage," came Adair's voice down the line, bright and cheerful. "What can I do for you?"

"I need help with a lead. Sir Wilfred went to a club called Bar de Bauche. I need to get in to talk to the staff."

"Bar...? Oh dear. Did you attempt to enter the location?"

"Yes, but they turned us back at the door. We need an invitation to get in. Can you help?"

"Possibly, but it's tricky. Are you absolutely sure you need to speak to them?"

"Yes, this is the next place Sir Wilfred and Dougie Barber went after the arts club."

"Okay. Wait there. Do not attempt anything without me. I'm coming to you."

"You don't have to come down here. Can't you call your people and get them to put us on the list?"

"It's not that simple, Mrs. Armitage. Don't do anything. I'll be right there."

Ten minutes later, the town car rolled up to the phone box and Adair stepped out, dressed in perfectly creased dusty blue wool trousers and a tailored tweed jacket over a white shirt. A floral print cravat covered a hint of hairy chest.

"Mrs. Armitage," he said, throwing a worried look at the others without a second glance at her gender-bending appearance. "The terms of the non-disclosure agreement were explicit."

"These are my associates, Mr. Adair," she said with bravado to cover the sudden fear that she had screwed herself out of a job and into a lawsuit by involving Johnny and Alfie. "Alfie Lester and John Suharto. Contrary to what you might believe, witchcraft is rarely a solitary endeavor. I need them to do my job effectively."

He frowned.

"This is highly irregular."

"Do you want results? Sir Wilfred was seen entering Bar de Bauche, but we need to find out when he left and with whom if we're to track him down."

"Yes. Yes, you're quite right. Very well. We'll proceed, but I would appreciate being notified if you choose to involve any others in your search. It will affect our calculations. The boys in Analysis will be most upset. Please let me do all the talking. This is a very delicate situation. We'll have to come to terms with management before we can enter."

"Why all the formality?" whispered Alfie as they walked back to the club.

She shrugged.

"It must be an etiquette thing. These spheres seem to operate like kings and queens in a period drama."

"This is going to be awkward," he grimaced as they approached the velvet rope and Mac gave them an unhappy look.

"Good evening," said Adair. "My name's Joel Adair. I'm with Waterford, Wakefield, Winston, and Whorl. We represent your establishment. We should be on your private list."

Mac squinted and frowned at the card and shot an accusatory glance at Alfie who mouthed "sorry mate" at him in return.

"Yes," he said. "I have you on our list."

He reached for the velvet rope.

"No, no, no," said Adair. "That's not necessary. I just need to speak to your manager. I believe Mr. Bowie Blades should be working tonight. Could I trouble you to bring him out here? If you give him my card, it shouldn't be a problem."

Mac scowled at Alfie and turned to Pat as he went inside.

"You okay here?"

"Yeah, yeah. I'm fine."

They stood in awkward silence before the rope as Pat stared them down, unimpressed.

"Nice cravat," Johnny said to Adair.

"Oh, thank you." Adair smiled. "I just got it. I think it's a bit of a reach for me, though."

"No, it looks good on you." Johnny leaned in and adjusted the bright fabric of the cravat, patting down Adair's chest in an extremely intimate gesture for two people who had only met five minutes ago, though Adair didn't seem to mind. "There you go."

They were an odd pair standing next to each other, Johnny tall and slender, Adair tall and sturdy, both with their own innate grace.

The door to the club swung open and out stepped a broad-shouldered man with close-cropped light blond hair in the kind of tuxedo James Bond might wear to emerge from the sea: an off-white jacket and gleaming white shirt with a tight black bar of a bowtie across the collar beneath a faint dusting of stubble. He carried in one hand a long, black brick of a walkie-talkie with a rubberized antenna. Around him swirled the aura of an acolyte, strong, distinct and close to the skin: a radiant glow circled by a burning comet. Gosha had seen the aura before, on some of the teachers at the boys' primary school, but she'd never learned which sphere it belonged to.

"Mr. Blades," said Adair. "I am very sorry to interrupt your proceedings, but we've come up against a bit of an emergency—"

Blades cut him off with a gesture and waved them all to one side of the velvet rope so that Mac, who had emerged behind him, could admit another glamorous couple.

"You can't waltz down here and demand admission. I know we have an alliance, but—" The voice that came out of Blade's mouth was surprising, lighter and more musical than Gosha might have expected, with a slight German accent.

"That's not what's going on, I assure you," said Adair. "It's the matter of the open account."

Blades grunted, the sweeping comet of his aura strong and vibrant compared to the tight, sedate wheels of the sheath of Influence that spun around Adair.

"The client in question was last seen entering your hallow. We request your permission to inquire of your number if anyone saw or spoke to him. Any information your people could provide might help to close the account."

“I can’t let you in,” said Blades. “Your presence would be too disruptive. Her Holiness La Davina is present. She won’t stand for an intrusion.”

“La Davina?” said Johnny.

“I don’t need to enter.” Adair, gestured to the others. “These are representatives of the firm. They aren’t oath-bearers. They can pass unnoticed.”

Blades looked at them for the first time, his eyes dismissing Alfie and resting longer on Johnny and Gosha, taking time to size them up.

“Very well,” he nodded. “Your proxies may enter. But,” he turned to address the others. “You will not be allowed on the floor, only in the back of the house. I’ll decide with whom you may speak.”

“That’s wonderful,” gushed Adair. “The partners thank you for your generous consideration. I’ll be off and leave you to it.” He turned to Gosha. “Call me the second you leave. And, please, for the Lords’ sakes, don’t ruffle any feathers. These people are our allies.”

“I’ll be the soul of discretion,” said Gosha.

Blades unclipped the rope and held it to one side to allow them through.

“Your first time in drag?” he said as Gosha passed.

“Yes, is it okay?”

“Not bad. Your binding could be better.”

The penny dropped for Gosha. Mr. Bowie Blades was a woman in male drag.

15

INSIDE THE CLUB, INFLUENCE FLOWED thick and strong, a layer of hazy scintillation in Gosha's second sight, superimposed over the glitzy-glamorous decor. The front doors let in on a wide staircase carpeted in navy blue with the club's logo—an ornate, crowned 'B'—woven into it in a repeating pattern, that led down to a low reception area. The walls were lined with gold flocking that shimmered in the light of a crystal chandelier suspended above them and a giant mirrorball that gently turned, spreading a gentle vortex of glitter around them.

"Follow me," said Bowie Blades, leading them down to the reception area below. At the bottom he gestured with his walkie-talkie for them to wait by the desk. "Bhatia, sweetie," he said to a dark-eyed, slender beauty in a pink sequined gown with a daring neckline who sat behind the desk. "Call down to Ron and find out who's here that was on last Tuesday. He can get me on the walkie."

Bhatia picked up a multi-line phone, hit one of the buttons and covered her mouth with one hand as she spoke into the receiver.

"You can use my office. I'll bring the people to you," said Bowie Blades, looking between the three of them, unsure who was boss.

"That's wonderful," said Gosha. "Thank you so much."

He grunted and waved them to follow with his walkie-talkie as he stepped through blue velvet curtains into the club proper. A grand staircase led down to a main floor filled with cafe tables. A crowd of buzzing glitterati drank cocktails and champagne awaiting the show that was about to start. A red velvet ruched curtain hung from the large proscenium arch. Music filled the room, the deep and throaty warble of Edith Piaf regretting nothing. Influence washed over everyone in great currents that flowed through the crowd, punctuated by the vibrant comet-auras of acolytes sprinkled throughout the throng. Gosha counted a dozen before she lost track.

"This way," said Bowie Blades, leading them around the balcony that circled the bar.

"Oh my god," said Johnny, pointing down at a raised enclosure to one side of the floor where the most glamorous of all the crowd sat and caroused. "That's Delilah Davina. I saw her on the telly hosting the Royal Variety Show. She's amazing."

At the center of the revelry sat in state a statuesque older woman, jet-black hair piled high atop her head in the style of a flamenco dancer, a veil of black lace across her eyes, her dress of black sequins glittering in the light. The burning comet that swept around her in Gosha's second sight was more powerful than any other in the club, its orbit large enough to encompass all those that sat around her. Without doubt, this was the saint.

Gosha didn't have much time to observe Delilah Davina. Blades pulled a curtain to one side revealing the door to his office.

"In here," he said.

The room beyond was a let-down after the glamor of the club, as was the way of all backstage areas. The walls were lined with metal shelves filled with restaurant supplies and cases of expensive champagne. A desk sat in the corner with a metal chair behind it and two in front.

Bowie Blades' walkie-talkie barked, garbled squawking coming across the speaker.

"Got it," said Blade, though Gosha hadn't understood a word. "Ask her if she can spare time to come up to the office. She's going on first, so don't bother her about it if she doesn't want to."

He sat at his desk and placed the walkie-talkie on its end in front of him. He didn't invite them to sit.

"I only have one person who was on last Tuesday. Bonita Fascinante."

The walkie-talkie barked and chattered. Blades snatched it up and thumbed the talk button.

"Got it." He put the walkie-talkie back down. "You're in luck. She's on her way."

The knock came almost immediately. The door opened to reveal a diminutive dark-skinned woman in a white beaded sheath with a white feather boa draped across her shoulders. An enormous diamond necklace hung across her chest to match her giant diamond chandelier earrings that draped from her earlobes down to her shoulders. She reached up a white satin-gloved arm, leaned seductively against the door frame, and patted her short, tight curls revealing a hand covered in huge, glistening rings. Her comet-aura spun around her.

"Bowie, darling," she said with a kitten's purr and a faint Jamaican accent. "How may I help you?"

A bell of familiarity tinkled in Gosha's memory at the sound of her voice, but if she had met this woman before, Gosha couldn't place her.

Bowie stood, walked round the desk and, with exaggerated chivalry, pulled back a chair so Bonita Fascinante could sit.

"Mademoiselle, these people have a few questions to ask you."

"Questions?" She fluttered her long false eyelashes. "How delightful. I adore answering questions, especially if they're about me."

She perched on the edge of the seat and crossed her legs, tucking her white patent leather heels beneath the chair.

"It's about the matter with the PR firm," said Bowie, who leaned against the edge of his desk and crossed his arms.

They both turned to look at Gosha and the others, their spinning auras intertwining in the small office.

"Oh," said Bonita, her manner turning sober. "Have they found Sir Wilfred and Mr. Barber?"

"They found Dougie Barber," said Gosha. "He..." She couldn't think how to say it. Everything that came to mind sounded so brutal, so out of place in the presence of this soft-spoken beauty. "He died."

Both Bonita and Bowie stiffened.

"I am sorry," Bonita said. "He was a kind and talented man. Such a gentleman."

"They came here on Tuesday with a young man," said Gosha. "Did you see them?"

"Oh, yes. I wasn't performing that night, just enjoying the show with everyone else. Wilfred and Dougie were here with their friends. Andrew Mills, Joseph Hobbs, and Richard Howell."

Gosha knew all three men from the Cheyne Arts Club. Mills was an illustrator, Hobbs a painter, and Howell a sculptor. She made a mental note, wishing she had thought to bring pen and paper, to check in on them the next day and see if they were all where they ought to be. She had a horrible suspicion they wouldn't be.

"The young man they came in with, can you tell me about him? I believe his name was Caspian."

"Oh yes, Caspian Dudley. A charming fellow, though a bit mercenary. He's had quite the debut on the scene. No one had heard of him before Christmas, and then suddenly he was in here at least twice a week. And on the arm of a new beau every time, as if he were auditioning."

"Yes," said Bowie. "An impressive feat that put many a mind to wonder. Our guest list is quite exclusive."

"And then," said Bonita, "he found the man to whom he was willing to give his favor: Sir Wilfred. Although, I'm not sure they were well suited to each other. There was always friction between them."

"That's how Willy likes it," said Johnny. "He loves a good row now and then. Keeps him interested. Sounds like this guy knew just how to play it."

"I sat with them for a time on Tuesday," said Bonita. "It didn't seem like all was going that well. Sir Wilfred was being a bit of a boor. Very handsy, and young Caspian playing hard-to-get. Not the kind of company a lady likes to find herself in."

"Did they leave together?" asked Gosha.

"Mm." Bonita nodded. "All of them, as a matter of fact. The whole table left right after the first show."

"Do you know where they went?"

"No. As I said, I wasn't too interested in all that hanky-panky. They're lovely, talented men, but a girl has a reputation to keep, and boys do like their japes."

She rested both hands on her beaded knee and fluttered her eyelids with a coy smile.

Something about that smile, thought Gosha.

"Have we met before?" she asked.

"Why, yes, Mrs. Armitage," said Bonita. "Clever of you to notice. I always suspected there was more to you than met the eye. In my other life. How are Edmund and Timothy? I do miss having them in my classroom."

Her small hands and slender hips, the curl of her smile and the lilt of her accent all coalesced in Gosha's memory. Bonita Fascinante had been the boys' primary school teacher.

"Mr. Granger," said Gosha. "You look fabulous."

"Aren't you sweet. Please call me Bonita. When I'm wearing a gown like this, I prefer to have a name to match. And you, what should I call you in this alluring specimen of manhood you've become?"

Despite the lipstick digging into her ribs under her sports bra, she had forgotten she was in drag herself.

"Oh, Gosha. You can call me Gosha."

Bonita pursed her lips in a smile and raised her eyebrows as if to say "really."

"The boys are doing great," said Gosha. "You were hands down their favorite teacher at Stibbington Primary School."

"They're sweet boys. Edmund was always a terror, but he has a good heart."

"Have you seen Caspian Dudley since that night?"

"He came in on Thursday and again on Saturday, each time with a different gentleman. I thought he had his fill with Sir Wilfred and they had parted ways. We were only informed about the disappearance on Sunday."

She looked to Bowie Blades for corroboration.

"Our goals and those of your firm coincide in many areas," said Blades. "We are happy to ally ourselves with you, but we have our hands full with our own business. We don't have time to pursue every fear or suspicion your partners may have about what may or may not come. We must always be practical, or those we care for will surely suffer. We regret what has happened to your client, but we cannot jump every time you call."

"Oh, Bowie," said Bonita, reaching across to squeeze his hand, "they're only trying to do their jobs." She released it and turned back to Gosha. "Mr. Dudley only ever comes when there's an early show. I'm going on in about ten minutes. He might come tonight and then you can talk to him yourself. Can they stay, Bowie? They can have my table."

"Tonight is not for them, Bonita. Tonight, in our hallow, is for us. Only us."

She swiveled in her seat to face him.

"They came to us on a mission of mercy. It's our duty to help any who come to our doors, without question. All we have to do is let them stay. It couldn't be more simple, could it? I know Gosha. I'll vouch for her."

Blades frowned, thinking, his hand reaching out for his walkie-talkie.

"Very well. Because you vouch for them."

Bonita rose to leave.

"Boys," she said to Alfie and Johnny with a wink as she opened the door, "close your mouths. You're drooling."

Bowie led them out of the office and grabbed a bus boy as he walked past.

"Jerry, show these people to Miss Fascinante's table, please."

"Yes, Mr. Blades," said the boy. "Follow me, please."

"That was a fella?" said Alfie. "She had tits and everything."

"Don't be rude," said Gosha.

"No, he's right," said Johnny. "I've been around drag queens up close before. She's not just doing drag. There's more going on there to make her look like that."

The busboy led them to a small, round cafe table right at the edge of the stage. As they took their seats, the house lights went down and the full moon circle of a follow spot opened up on the curtains as they rose. A smattering of applause rippled around the room as the crowd grew silent in anticipation of the show.

Bonita stepped into the spotlight. No longer in her beaded gown, now she wore a white wool pant suit cut large and flowing, with a men's shirt with white-on-black polka dot tie and a white beret.

"How could she have changed so quickly?" said Johnny.

She walked to the front of the thrust stage to violin strings playing the intro to "La Vie En Rose." When Marlene Dietrich began to sing, she followed along in a perfect lip synch, enrapturing the audience with her serenade. She stepped down into the audience to weave her way in a circle through the crowd and back to the stage for the end of the song. As she mounted the stage once more, guitars and percussion struck up a lilting phrase to be joined in by the bright chords of a piano. Bonita danced a simple shuffle as she walked the stage and lip synched to the gently discofied version of the same song by Grace Jones. As the music reached its crescendo, she strode to the front of the thrust and began to spin in a perfect pirouette. When the middle eight began, and the song released into abandon, the spiral flow of her aura contracted about her and, with an audible crack and shimmer of lighting, her outfit transformed yet again. The crowd went wild, jumping to their feet in rapturous applause.

"What the fuck," said Johnny, mouth agape.

The billowing white pantsuit metamorphosed into a tight black shark-skin bodysuit with leggings that merged into impossibly high platform boots with stiletto heels. Over it she wore a black ringleader's coat and a mirrored top hat. As she spun, the spotlight caught the tiny squares of mirror and threw a myriad beams of light about the club. As Grace Jones sang her final roar, Bonita broke from her spin and placed her long boot on the center of their little table and leaned forward in a bow of mock exhaustion.

"He's here," she whispered as the crowd roared. "Over by the bar."

16

THERE WAS NO MISTAKING CASPIAN Dudley: five-foot-ten, dark blond hair in unruly curls tamed by an expensive haircut, blue eyes that caught the reflection of the lights around him. He sipped a tumbler of whiskey, cool and confident among the crowd. An older man stood next to him, sharing a joke with a woman in a little black dress, one possessive hand on Dudley's shoulder that the young man only tolerated, his eyes scanning the crowd.

"I know him," said Johnny. "I remember him from the Comet Club. He was just a punk back then. Short hair, eyeliner, and a mass of safety pins."

"You sure?" said Alfie. "That was years ago."

"You don't forget a pair of eyes like that. And we shagged in the men's room a couple of times."

Dudley reached behind him and placed his glass on the bar. He leaned in to whisper something in his companion's ear. His companion's hand slid up to the back of Dudley's head and pulled him close for a greedy kiss, but Dudley pushed him away and headed for the staircase up to the balcony.

The lights shifted as Bonita waved to the crowd and disappeared behind the curtain. Heavy synthesized beats and the throaty wail of Annie Lennox replaced the disco confection of "La Vie En Rose" as a second performer took the stage.

"Let's go," said Gosha.

They rose from their seats and stooped as they cut across the crowd, threading between the tables, and made their way to the back of the club. By the time they reached the stairs, Dudley was at the top and heading along the mezzanine. They scuttled up the steps to find him disappearing into the gents.

"We can't all go in there," said Alfie as they approached the door to the men's room.

"Let me take a crack at him," said Johnny as he ducked inside.

"Wait here," said Gosha to Alfie.

She pushed through the door—

"Pezhvatek."

—and vanished, concealed from the world by the spell. Behind her Alfie swore.

"That's the one thing you do I hate," she heard him say as the door closed behind her.

The bathroom was all black marble and white tile. Empty except for Johnny and Caspian Dudley, the sounds they made echoed off the hard porcelain walls. Johnny took his time at the sink primping in the mirror as Caspian stepped back from the urinal, zipped himself up and walked over to wash his hands.

"Hey," said Johnny with a perfect facsimile of surprise. "I remember you. Comet Club, yeah? Those were the days, weren't they?"

Dudley glanced at Johnny, didn't like what he saw, and kept rinsing.

"Were you there when it went up in flames?" Johnny continued, undeterred. "What a mess. I was outside waiting for my mates. I saw the whole thing. So disturbing. Had nightmares that night, I can tell you."

The night of the fire the entire population of Cheyne Heath had been sucked into the Shadowlands to fuel a mad acolyte's lust for power. The acolyte would have succeeded had it not been for Gosha, Johnny, Alfie, Agnieszka, and the ladies. Everyone affected had woken up the next morning harmed by nothing more than a bad hangover and several hours of lost memory. The witches of Cheyne Heath worked hard for weeks to smooth over the rough edges left by that incident.

Dudley ripped off a length of paper towel from the dispenser and dried his hands without responding.

"Hey," said Johnny, refusing to give up. "Weren't you in here with Willy Stepney? I used to model for him, you know."

Dudley crumpled up the paper towel, tossed it in the bin and pushed past him and out the door with Johnny on his heels, but the door closed before Gosha could get to it. As she leaned into it, the spell of concealment broke. Out on the mezzanine, Dudley almost ran into Alfie.

"He's gone missing," said Johnny, catching up. "I think you were the last person to see him."

Dudley took one look at the three of them and bolted for the stairs to the street.

"Fuck," said Alfie as they took off after him.

Dudley was fast and strong, taking the stairs two at a time without slowing. He barreled through the front doors and leaped over the velvet rope with the grace of a hurdler. Closest to the stairs when Dudley pegged it, Alfie reached the ropes first and stumbled through them, pulling down the stanchions as he passed.

"Sorry Mac," he shouted as he followed Dudley down the street.

Of the three of them, Gosha was the strongest runner, having run three miles every day for the last four years. Once they were on level ground she soon caught up with Alfie, Johnny trailing behind, but

Dudley kept ahead of them by a dozen yards. He wove through the streets without any clear destination, and turned a corner down a side street where several buildings on either side were under construction, tarps, dumpsters, and chain-link fences lining the street. When Gosha reached the corner, Dudley was nowhere to be seen.

Alfie and Gosha stopped dead, huffing and puffing to catch their breath as Johnny caught up. Gosha took out her field kit and unscrewed a bottle of sea salt, pouring the entire thing into her palm.

"Sutturah," she said when finally she could catch enough breath.

The Influence from the finding spell blew the salt off her hand in a winding trail that spiraled into the air as it searched for its quarry. It lashed out, throwing itself against the rusted metal of a rubble-filled dumpster to their right, and fell to the grimy street, spent.

"Caspian," said Gosha, easing her way toward the dumpster. "We just want to know where Sir Wilfred is. We think he's in danger. Can you help us?"

As she reached the skip, Dudley fled from his hiding place heading back the way they had come.

"Dammit," she shouted as she took off after him, her legs pounding, sprinting her forward as fast as she could.

The gap between them narrowed to an arm's length. As he broke right toward the main road where traffic and pedestrians would make it hard for them to follow, she reached out and grazed his arm with her fingertips.

"Falethta."

She barely managed to huff the word out, but Dudley crumpled under the effects of the sleeping spell, his body slack, momentum throwing him into a line of rubbish bins that broke his fall.

"Bugger," said Johnny as he came up panting behind her. "I haven't run this much since cross-country at school."

"Why did he run?" asked Alfie. "Is he a wizard?"

"An acolyte? No," said Gosha looking around in case anyone saw them. "I'm going to wake him up. Don't let him run again."

The sleeping spell was an easy one to break. She stooped and rubbed her knuckles briskly across his chest as Alfie and Johnny crowded in on either side.

"Mr. Dudley, wake up."

He opened his eyes, saw where he was and tensed, his eyes darting around, terrified.

"Who the fuck are you?"

"Calm down, Mr. Dudley. We just want to ask you a few questions."

He drew his feet up under him and attempted to get up, but lost his balance and clattered back against the rubbish bins.

"Careful, mate," said Alfie.

"Fuck off. I'm not your mate," Dudley snapped back.

"Easy." Gosha squatted down on her haunches beside him. "You were the last person to see Wilfred Stepney and Dougie Barber last week. Where did you all go when you left the club?"

"I went home. Had to work the next day."

Gosha exchanged glances with Alfie. She knew what a bad lie looked like.

"Mr. Dudley. Caspian. Dougie Barber is dead. We're worried Sir Wilfred might be next."

"I don't know anything about that. We left the club and I went home. Who the fuck are you? You're not coppers. I don't have to tell you anything."

She looked up at Alfie and caught a glimpse of her reflection in the door of a car parked behind him. They didn't look remotely intimidating. Above her the full moon glowed in the cloudless night sky. She could try the spell she'd used on Denise Ogilvy the other day, or she could take advantage of the moon and Craft a spell that would force him to speak to them.

She stood and turned to Alfie.

"Watch him a moment," she said and walked a few steps away.

She looked up at the moon and held the red jasper ring on her right hand.

"Lady Moon, I stand beneath your light and beg admittance to your Shadowlands."

An eerie peacock screech echoed from afar and the small disk of moon grew and grew until it filled the sky, the power of its glare as strong as the sun. The ring grew soft and slithered around her finger, unraveling and falling to the floor. She'd done this many times in the three years since Pauline Sutton, Saint of Shadow, had gifted her the ring, but it still gave her the willies.

The ring expanded, lengthening and widening across the ground until it became a vast serpent with coils that wrapped around parked cars and draped from lampposts, a giant dragon head at either end that towered above her.

"Well, well, brother Aloysius," said the head to her left in a camp and plummy voice that could have played Shakespeare. "If it isn't our favorite witch."

17

"DEAR MAŁGORZATA," SAID ALOYSIUS, THE other head, pronouncing the full Polish version of her name flawlessly. Though this dragon guardian of the Shadowlands no longer terrified her, she still couldn't tell one head from the other. Only when they referred to each other by name could she keep track of which was which. "Aren't you a vision of dark and surly masculinity. Look, brother. She has the aspect of a man. Have you ever seen such a thing?"

Murgatroyd, the first head to speak, ducked close and flickered its forked tongue at her.

"Oh yes," it said. "I do approve. So fetching, so handsome, such a delightful change. Your company is always a delight in the dark and murky landscape. We have only the lady in the tower to keep us company, and as radiant as she may be, she is so often preoccupied with her prayers."

The lady in the tower was Pauline, who Gosha had hidden from everyone, including herself, with the first spell she had forged in this strange intersection between the waking world and the shifting dream of the Shadowlands.

"How is your lady?" she asked.

"As well as ever," said Aloysius, rippling his scales. She watched the fluttering wave work its way along the loops of the serpent's body until they reached the head of its brother, who blinked and narrowed its eyes, an expression she had come to understand was their equivalent of a smile. "She sends her regards and wishes health and happiness upon you and your loved ones."

"Please send her my best in return."

"And to what do we owe the pleasure of your company on this night when the veil between our worlds is so thin?" said Murgatroyd. "Have you come to create mystery? Have you come to shape your reality? We do so enjoy it when you do. The monotony of this endless landscape crushes our souls."

"Yes, Murgatroyd. I have come to forge a new spell."

"You never disappoint us," said Aloysius. "Your last visit beguiled us for a decade."

Time flowed differently in the Shadowlands. Sometimes the dragon heads claimed she hadn't visited them in years. Other times, only days had passed for them. For her, in this intersection between waking reality and dream, time always passed slowly. When she returned to the waking world, she knew only seconds would have elapsed.

"I'm happy to entertain you," she said, with a bow. Pauline had instructed them to act as a barrier between Gosha and the shifting confusion of the Shadowlands, but they remained a strange creature that stood on protocol and decorum.

"And will you require our help this time?" said Murgatroyd. "It's been many decades since we have been called upon to be more than sentries."

Simple spells that manipulated the physical world—lockings and unlockings, pushes and pulls, even basic healings—she could forge by herself, but spells that sought to change human behavior required the help of these two.

"Yes, I will need your help."

Their heads swayed and spun above her and the coils of their shared body shifted and rolled.

"What is our task?" asked Aloysius.

"What feat of creative cunning must we help you achieve?" asked Murgatroyd.

She thought for a second. Clarity was essential with the dragon heads. She only had one chance. Muck it up and she'd be left with a spell that did no one any good. She had three pages of useless gibberish words in the back of her notebook with the effect she had intended and the unfortunate results she'd actually achieved.

"I have a young man who's keeping secrets. I need to know the truth."

"Ah yes," said Aloysius, rearing up above her, its ears twitching, its crest fanning out behind its head. "An enchantment to lay him bare. A conjuration to rip the truth from his lips. An incantation to burn his falsehoods away."

"No, no, no," she said. "No ripping, no burning, and certainly no laying bare. I just need to convince him I mean him no harm and that telling the truth will help us."

"Oh, brother," said Murgatroyd with a low, rumbling chuckle. "Such melodrama. Such excessive gusto. As always, I know what the witch needs. You're far too emotional. I love you for it, but it's so impractical. All that tearing around and gnashing of jaws. Exhausting!"

Gosha stopped herself from rolling her eyes. These two seemed to think they had distinct personalities when, as far as she could tell, they were two peas in a pod, two dragon heads on a snake.

"I can be reasonable," said Aloysius, lowering his head to look her in the eye. "I can be subtle and devious. I can charm as well as you, brother."

"Oh, really? You think you have the wile and guile to trick a man to reveal his all? Very well. Go ahead. I await with pleasure your certain failure."

"Stand back, brother. Prepare to be amazed. Prepare to be struck dumb. Prepare for perfect art. Małgorzata, darling. Where shall we begin?"

The witches had taught her to cobble together impromptu enchantments from images of power that tapped into the human subconscious, adding detail the way you would add spices to a stew to develop a robust and rich flavor. When the stew was complex enough, the energy of the spell was ready to be released. The serpent heads required a different way of thinking, one that was sterile and analytical, a series of commands to bind and direct Influence. As she mastered this new approach, she'd come to wonder if this was the way of High Influence, a cold and harsh domination of the layered opulence of Influence compared to the majestic celebration of it that was Craft.

The serpent heads required three elements to forge a spell: a cornerstone, a column and a spire. The cornerstone laid the foundation, dictating the nature of the work, the column defined its intent, and the spire laid out the way it was to be achieved. With no time to prepare and mull over what she wanted of the spell, she needed to think clearly and quickly about what it meant to encourage someone to give up a secret they didn't want to tell. The dragon head Aloysius' outburst had been a great help to tell her what she didn't want her spell to achieve. She needed to know what Dudley was concealing, but she didn't want to force it out of him against his will. She needed him to want to tell her. If the cornerstone was to be truth, the column had to be comfort and safety, and the spire trust.

She took out her telling deck in the silk pouch she'd found for it at a sweet, if misguided, new age shop on the other side of Morel Market, and shuffled through the cards. She only had a few of the meanings memorized, but the power in the cards lay in the pictures. As she searched for images that might suggest truth, she realized what an impossible task it was.

If not truth, then perhaps history. She found three cards: one that depicted a stack of open books in a library; one a contact print from a series of photos she had taken at a dinner party at the Cheyne Arts Club long before the children were born and she was still happy; one a hand holding a fountain pen, a teardrop of ink dangling from the shiny nib as it prepared to write; one a portrait she had taken of a young poet with her first book clutched to her breast.

"For the cornerstone," she said to the dragon head and held the cards up so that it could see.

Both heads inhaled sharply with the delight of connoisseurs.

"Magnificent," said Aloysius.

A great coil of its body rolled out from behind a lamppost and flopped to the ground in front of her. Its eyelids flickered and waves of color rippled across its scales until they reached the coil where they became a shifting billow of shape and shade.

She returned the cards to her deck and shuffled through them again, finding a photograph of herself hugging the boys tight, their faces contorted by squeals of delight, a photograph of Edmund asleep in bed with one arm wrapped around his favorite stuffed toy and a thumb in his mouth, and a photograph of her home, the front door open to reveal, in the kitchen at the back, Alfie, her mother and the boys enjoying their tea.

"For the column," she said, showing Aloysius the three cards.

"Exceptional," it said, rippling colors down the length of its body into the coil before her.

For trust, she only needed one card: a shot she'd taken of Edmund aged four holding her hand and looking up at her into the camera.

"For the spire," she said, showing it to the dragon.

"Breathtaking," it said as it sent another ripple down its length.

The shifting shimmer of scales upon its skin evoked within Gosha a complex mix of emotions.

"Such a delight to work with a witch," said Aloysius. "Such a fresh and unexpected approach."

"And now," said Murgatroyd, hovering above her. "Payment."

The dragon heads always required of her some form of sacrifice, something of value to her, something important that would hold their attention and add richness, they claimed, to the monotony of their existence. There was a strange ritual to this negotiation. Often they turned down her first two offerings out of hand, no matter how treasured the gift, but offering something up of real value in the first and second proffer expecting it to be rejected had backfired in the past. Everything she offered had to be important enough to catch their fancy, but not so important that she would regret its loss.

Though she hadn't thought she would need to forge a spell, she'd known she would be out and about during the full moon and had prepared, bringing with her three offerings. She patted her telling deck into order and slipped it into its pouch.

"What about that?" said Murgatroyd, dipping his head toward her, his tongue slithering out from between his lips to savor the air. "That is an amusing implement. It would bring us days and days of interest."

Both heads froze in the air, all movement restrained as if they held their breath. It was a rare negotiation in which they didn't make a play for some object of power she had on her. Usually it was her lipstick. A product of the Witch's Betrayal, the ritual that had given her access to Craft, she could never make another. In this half-world, as in the Shadowlands themselves, objects had significance. Whatever she gave them would be more than just the thing itself. Some essential part of her would leave her, never to return. She had once made the mistake of offering up a silk button Crafted to be the seed of a recipe to help determine the perfect day for a planned outdoor wedding, and now no spell or recipe that forecast the weather would work for her. If she surrendered her telling deck, who knew what she would be trading away.

“This?” she said with mock surprise. If she denied them too strongly, they could become fixated on it as the only payment they’d accept. She’d learned that the hard way as well. Now she couldn’t sew on a button without spiking her thumb and drawing blood all because of a Crafted needle left out where they could see. “Oh, you don’t want this. It’s just foolishness, pictures and cuttings that caught my fancy. What about these?”

Keeping it hidden inside her jacket for good measure, she removed from her field kit a trio of photos she’d taken, each representing a cherished memory. They had responded well to such things in the past. She would lose the memory along with the picture, so she always took care to select the sort of recollections she knew she had plenty of, or ones that would be easy to replace.

“This one,” said Murgatroyd the moment she presented the three snapshots. His tongue lanced out to pierce a photo of Miranda, a candid shot from the nineteen-sixties taken in their favorite boutique on Kensington Church Street. Miranda was posing in the mirror trying on a purple felt hat with giant circles cut out of it, her lips pursed in a mockery of a Brigitte Bardot come-hither pose.

“Joy and sorrow fermented into a heady brew. This. We will take this.”

The tongue and the snapshot disappeared into its maw and Gosha felt a brief tinge of loss, though suddenly she couldn’t recall of what.

“And now,” said Aloysius, “the sign. What shall you use to summon this symphony of emotion and control?”

Working with the dragon heads, Gosha had come to understand the wisdom of a secret language to mine for the use of spells. She had never learned her mother’s and now struggled to make up gibberish words for each new spell she forged.

“Are you ready?” asked Aloysius. She nodded. “Then perform the sign three times.”

“Actalet, actalet, actalet,” she said.

In the distance a shadow wraith screeched its peacock cry, and a wolf howled. A wave of red and black swept across the scales of the coil that contained the essence of the spell wiping them clean.

"Applause, applause, my brother," said Murgatroyd. "A magnificent display, a feat of glorious skill. Never have I—"

A discordant chorus of screeches and howls cut through the night air, the feral denizens of this bizarre half-world stirred to frenzy. The dragon heads froze as a stain of rusty brown spread across the vast moon above them. What Gosha first thought was fog rolled in around them, white clouds turning the air opaque, but as the billow reached her lips, she realized it wasn't fog, but dust, a fine powder with a bitter taste and an acrid smell.

"To the tower!" cried Aloysius.

The serpent coils slithered and whipped around her, the heads looming out of the dust as they gathered up their shared body and skimmed away.

"Protect our Lady from the prophecy of doom," cried Murgatroyd, and the serpent was gone.

18

A COLD WIND BLEW THE dust away and the moon returned to its usual size, a bright hole in the night sky of Cheyne Heath. The demented chorus of wolves and wraiths stilled to silence.

A prophecy of doom, she thought and slipped her telling deck out of its silk bag.

She gave it a quick shuffle and cut it with her left hand. The top three cards she drew were the Unknown, the King of Needles, and Liberation reversed.

What could it mean? she wondered. A prophecy so powerful it shook the Shadowlands.

She returned the deck to its bag and its place in her pocket. She could only perform one investigation at a time.

"I thought you needed to do some, you know..." said Alfie as she approached him.

"I got what I needed," she said and stood over Dudley, offering him a hand to get up out of the rubbish bins.

"Actalet," she said as he took her hand.

The word of a spell would usually create an opening within her that shaped the Influence that flowed through the lipstick, molding it into a command that could change the world in some small way. This new spell she'd forged created two matched openings, one within herself, one within Dudley. A short gush of warmth flowed between them, connecting them for a fraction of a second before the spell completed its work and the openings sealed themselves as if they had never been there.

"What?" said Dudley, not understanding the spell word.

"Nothing." Gosha smiled. "I'm so sorry about the confusion." She wiped a patch of grime off the sleeve of his jacket with one hand. "I didn't mean to make so much trouble. I do apologize."

He looked at her and the others and the hostile set of his eyes softened.

"Yeah, no bother," he said, relaxing.

"Caspian, can you tell us anything about where Wilfred Stepney went after you left Bar de Bauche?"

"Sure. We all went to Andrew Mills' house. He just bought this giant wreck of a place on Cornwall Road he wanted to show us."

He slipped his hands into the pockets of his pants and smiled at her, but didn't volunteer anything else.

"So you went to Andrew Mills' house. Did you stay long?"

"Couple of hours."

"What time did you leave?"

"Probably one in the morning."

"Was Wilfred with you?"

"No, the police had taken him by then."

"The police?" she said, surprised.

"What the fuck?" said Johnny behind her.

"Johnny," she snapped, fearful that the effects of the spell might be dispersed by his outburst, but Dudley's relaxed manner remained unchanged. "The police took Wilfred?" she asked him. "Why?

"The house was raided."

"For what?"

"Sexual offenses."

"What on earth...?"

"He means the Sexual Offences Act," chimed in Johnny. "*Homo*-sexual offences."

"But it's not illegal to be gay," said Gosha.

"Only technically," said Johnny with a scowl. "It is illegal to do anything gay in public."

"In public?" She found it hard to believe that prim and stuffy Sir Wilfred was an exhibitionist. "He was caught having sex outside?"

"In public means if there's anyone else around," said Johnny. "Doesn't have to be outside."

"I don't understand."

"The fuzz can arrest you if you're having sex while someone else is in the house," said Johnny. "If they want you, they're going to get you. Doesn't take much under the law to make up an excuse."

"That's right," said Dudley. "I got Wilfred alone and let him kiss me, let him feel me up. Then I excused myself, found the phone and called the station. The task force were waiting."

"What," hissed Johnny, seething. "The fuck. You stitched him up."

Johnny took a step toward Dudley, but Alfie got in his way.

"Easy, mate."

"Why would you do such a thing?" asked Gosha.

"The task force wanted him," said Dudley with a shrug. "They wanted all of them."

"What task force?"

"They operate out of Herbert Road Station."

Herbert Road. That was on the other side of Cheyne Heath.

"Are you a policeman?" she asked, and he snorted.

"No way."

"Why were you working for them?"

"I got busted for having sex in a public bathroom on the heath. They said I had to help them or they'd prosecute and ruin me." He shrugged again, as if it were no big deal.

"You fucking wanker," said Johnny, his voice growing louder with anger as Alfie held him back, though his outburst had no effect on Dudley. If it were because of the spell or because he was just heartless, Gosha couldn't tell. "Willy's a good man. He's never done anything bad to anyone. He doesn't deserve this."

"Why did they want all five men?" she asked.

"Dunno. They told me they wanted to pick up a group of blokes and pointed me at Bar de Bauche. I gave them a bunch of names. When I told them about Wilfred and his mates, they said that's who I should pursue. They told me I needed to find a way to get them together in the same place so they could all be taken at once."

"My god," said Gosha. "Where did they take them?"

"Herbert Road. After that, I don't know."

Johnny looked like he was about ready to punch Dudley, his fists clenched as Alfie stood between them.

"Thanks, Caspian. You were very helpful."

"Yeah, sure," he said as if they were old friends. "Anytime. See ya."

He strolled off toward the main road.

"Patastis," she said to negate the spell as he reached the corner.

Dudley stopped in his tracks and put his hands to his temples, but he recovered quickly and went on his way without a look back.

"We have to get Willy out," said Johnny.

"There was a phone box back that way," said Gosha pointing in the direction of the bar. "I'll call Adair and let him work his mojo."

"No," said Adair, his voice thin and distorted over the line. "If the police are involved, it's out of my hands."

The smell of urine and bleach in the call box stung her nostrils, even with the door propped open by Alfie so he and Johnny could listen in.

"But you saw what happened to Dougie Barber," said Gosha. "Whatever did that to him happened in police custody or after. At the very least we need to find out when they were released. What about the other three? Are they at all important to you?"

"They are all open accounts of significance," said Adair.

"Then get your people in Event Management on it."

Adair exhaled deeply at the other end of the line.

"It's not that simple, Mrs. Armitage. The police force has strong affiliations with the Sphere of Law. A research and analysis project directed toward them will create huge amounts of blowback. I'm not saying we can't make it happen, but it will take time and manpower. I'll get it started immediately, but it will take the time it will take. It can't be rushed. If the Lord Chief Justice gets wind of it, he'll shut it down."

"The Lord Chief Justice?" Gosha had understood none of that. "What does he have to do with it?"

"I don't have time to explain. I need to get the wheels turning. You've done great work tonight. The partners will be very pleased. Go home, Mrs. Armitage. There's nothing else you can do right now. Do not pursue any further leads until you get the go-ahead from me. Understood?"

"Yes," she said. "Yes, I understand."

"Good. I'll call you first thing in the morning. We'll be sure to have some movement by then."

She hung up.

"Well?" said Johnny.

"He won't do anything against the police."

"Fuck!" Johnny kicked the corner of the call box and winced.

She bowed her head, her eyes darting around unseeing as she thought.

"When I found Dougie Barber," she said, "he'd tried to slit his wrists."

"Oh no," said Alfie, stepping into the booth to wrap his arms around her, but she pushed him gently back.

"He didn't just try," she said. "He sliced deep into his forearms, but there was no blood anywhere. His body was dried up like a mummy. His skin was gray and his eyes were sunken into his skull."

Johnny turned pale.

"Just like Mick," he whispered.

"Just like Mick," Gosha nodded.

"Who?" asked Alfie.

"My best mate," said Johnny. "We had a band together."

"What happened to him?" said Alfie.

"He was killed for his Influence," she said. "Every ounce of it sucked out of him."

"We can't just leave it to these PR people of yours," said Johnny. "That could be happening to Willy as we speak."

"We're not leaving it to anyone," said Gosha, her mind made up. "We're going to Herbert Road."

19

HERBERT ROAD POLICE STATION WAS a large, gray brick and stone building with turrets and battlements, a spiritual cousin to the Tower of London, scaled down and modernized in the late eighteen-hundreds to intimidate the multifarious rowdies and ruffians of Cheyne Heath. Half-hearted concessions to the twentieth century littered the structure, signage, electric lights and a wheelchair ramp tacked on with little care for the building's history.

"It's eleven-thirty," said Gosha, checking her watch. "Will they be open?"

"They have a twenty-four-hour front counter," said Alfie. "There's always someone on the desk."

She caught a glimpse of her reflection in the hood of the Mini. Her outfit was respectable enough, but her inexpert drag wouldn't endear the police to her.

"I need a second," she said as she opened the car door and pulled her makeup kit from her handbag in the footwell.

She unzipped the pouch, laid out the contents on the hood and inspected her face in the mirror of her compact. The dark stippling Johnny had used to give her stubble was beginning to smudge. No matter, she thought. A quick application of her special face powder cleaned up her complexion. She needed to look sober and sensible, so she only applied the bare minimum of pigment to her eyes, and adjusted her slicked-back hair to a softer silhouette.

"What," she said to Johnny who watched her intently as she worked.

"You're very good at that," he said, tipping her chin back with his finger to inspect her work. "You must give me lessons sometime."

As she zipped up her pouch of goodies and tossed it on the dashboard, she looked at the others and pondered her approach. Her area of expertise was the domestic demimonde of Cheyne Heath. The Child Protective Services officer who came to her house the previous day was her first encounter with the authorities in years. She needed to find out what happened to Sir Wilfred in short order, and she didn't know how well Craft and the Metropolitan Police would mix.

"I think let me go in alone," she said.

"Are you sure?" said Alfie.

He knew she could take care of herself, had seen what she could do with Craft, and yet he still managed to be protective. Sometimes it could be irritating, especially when she was on the job.

"I might need to use Craft," she nodded. "It'll be easier if I don't have to worry about you two."

She kissed him on the cheek and crossed the street.

"I'll be right back," she said.

The lobby of the station was large and open, with posters and bulletin boards covering the walls and ranks of plastic chairs lined up across the floor. Harsh fluorescent lights, the whiff of chemical cleaners, and heavy, static Influence pressed in on her. On the far side of the lobby an overweight police officer in his shirtsleeves sat behind a closed window, a solid blue door to its right.

She walked up to the window and stood waiting for the policeman to acknowledge her, but he was buried in a book. She knocked on the window and made him jump.

"How can I help you?" he said, irritated, his voice muffled by the glass.

"A friend of mine was brought here last Tuesday. I wonder if you can help me find him?"

"You what?"

"A friend of mine," she raised her voice to be heard, "was arrested last Tuesday. I want to know what happened to him."

"What?" he said again, making no effort to slide up the window.

"Could you open up so I can talk to you?" she said, pantomiming lifting the window.

"Can't do that, Miss."

She did her best to stay calm and not throw one of her mother's spiteful hexes at him.

"My friend, Wilfred Stepney," she spoke loud and slow, articulating each word like a bad English tourist trying to be understood by a non-English speaker, "was arrested. In a raid. Last Tuesday night. He was taken here. I would like to see him."

"Can't help you, Miss. Detainees are processed here, but not housed."

"Where would they have taken him?"

"Can't tell you, Miss. You need to speak to the day shift."

"Is there anyone here I can speak to? Please, I'm worried about my friend. He has bad health issues. He needs to have his medicine."

She tried her best droopy-eyed expression to convince him. If the glass weren't separating them and she could touch him, she could have used her shiny new spell.

"Hang on," he said with a sigh, put his book down and pushed away from the counter. "Dinkins," he called out to another uniformed policeman in the office behind him. "What happened to the poufs the toff squad brought in last week?"

"I dunno," Dinkins shot back. "That lot do their own thing. You'd have to ask the guvnor."

"Cheers, mate," said the desk officer and ambled back to the window. "Come back tomorrow when everyone's in."

"What about your guvnor? Your colleague said—"

"Sorry, Miss. Can't help you. Come back tomorrow."

He picked his book up and started to read, making it clear the audience was over. Gosha swore under her breath. She needed to get in to talk to whoever was in charge.

She walked back to the front door and pushed it open as if to leave.

"Pezhvatek."

The lights dimmed around her and the colors of the waiting room, already washed out by the fluorescents, shifted toward gray as a feeling of warm and cozy seclusion enveloped her. She stepped back inside and went over to the door that led into the station. Pressing back against the wall to conceal herself from the officer, she put a hand on the door.

"Heckatisk."

The door shook with a heavy clunk, and the spell of concealment broke at her interaction with the world around her.

She ducked down to a crouch and pushed through the door.

"Pezhvatek," she said again as she cleared the door, and it clicked shut behind her.

The officer looked around, confused at not seeing anyone, and hit the door release a couple of times, making the lock clunk again. Satisfied that it was working properly and that no one had tried to sneak past him, he went back to his book.

A handful of desks manned by uniformed officers in their shirtsleeves with glassy eyes filling in paperwork were spread about the room. Only one officer was still in full uniform, lacking only his cap, at the coffee machine pouring himself a cup. One of the others nodded at him as he went past on his way to a wood and corrugated glass office at the far end of the room.

"Guv," said the officer in his shirtsleeves.

The officer in charge, thought Gosha as she dashed toward the office, taking care not to knock into anything as she ran.

She reached the door just as the inspector opened it and slipped in after him.

Standing with her back to the wall, she waited until he sat at his desk. She walked up behind him and put a hand on his shoulder, breaking the concealment spell.

He jumped at her touch and turned toward her, grabbing for her hand, but she cast her spell before he could do any more.

"Actalet," she said and Influence flowed between them in a brief spurt.

"Oh, it's you," he said with a laugh. "I didn't see you there. How are you? Do have a seat."

A witch's spell was a tool of cold precision, a scalpel that seamlessly linked intent and effect. These hybrid spells forged with the help of the dragon heads were grand gestures of will and hope she could never cobble together on her own. She had no idea how the spell worked to achieve its effect. Who knew what this man saw and felt when he looked at her? She smiled and did her best to reflect back at him whoever he thought she was.

"Thank you," she said, walking around the desk and taking the offered seat. "You arrested a friend of mine last Tuesday, Sir Wilfred Stepney. Where is he?"

"Last Tuesday." He frowned. "That was the task force. Not us, I'm afraid. They're very mysterious about what they get up to. Drives everyone around here bonkers."

"You've no idea where they would have taken him?"

He reached across his desk and picked up a clipboard filled with papers.

"One moment," he said, looking through the stack. "Oh yes, last Tuesday. That was an odd thing. Five homosexuals brought in for indecent behavior. We had them in the cells for all of an hour when they started to act mightily strange. Shrieking and speaking in tongues. Put the willies up Sergeant Hunt."

He put the clipboard down, crossed his hands on his lap with a smile and sat back in his chair, content to sit there until she asked him another question.

"What was wrong with them?" she asked, frustrated that she didn't think to build loquaciousness into the spell.

"Probably drugs. You know how that sort can be. We packed them off to the nut house."

"The nut house!"

"Yes, it was a bit odd. An order came in that morning that we should send anyone showing psychiatric distress to hospital."

He picked up his clipboard again and found the page he wanted.

"Banksville Psychiatric Hospital." He tossed it back on his desk. "Best place for a bunch of old shirt-lifters, if you ask me. Disgusting behavior. They should all have their balls cut off. Don't you think?"

Gosha was appalled. The casual ease the spell had given him coupled with his posh accent had lulled her into thinking well of him.

"No, I don't. Where's Banksville Hospital?" she demanded as she rose, ready to be rid of this awful man.

"Turncoat's Gate," he said getting up to see her to the door. "So lovely to see you. Do come again."

He watched her go from the door as she stalked back to the entrance, the officer at the window confused to see her storming out.

20

"WHATEVER AFFECTED Dougie Barber started after they got arrested," she said as she slipped behind the steering wheel and turned the key in the ignition.

"What happened?" asked Johnny from the back seat.

"They started acting erratic." She checked the rear-view mirror as she pulled away from the curb and headed toward Turncoat's Gate. "They were sent to a psychiatric hospital."

A finding spell led her to the hospital without interference. The buildings of Turncoat's Gate, a square at the southern edge of Cheyne Heath dangerously close to the border with Kensington, were all Victorian institutional monstrosities, multi-story buildings in a neo-medieval style with heavy doors and thick windows. She counted her blessings that the trail had, so far, stayed within her safe zone, and made a mental note to ask the dragon heads at the following full moon if they could come up with something that might protect her from George if she left the district.

Banksville Psychiatric Hospital took up the entire north side of the square, two vast wings spreading out from a central block with a neo-classical pedicle to crown it. Gosha found a parking space on the other side of the square.

"Want us to stay here?" asked Alfie.

"No, come with," she said, getting out of the car. "It's not the police."

There was a nip starting to build up in the air. She looked at the moon and wondered if she could re-tool her finding spells to give her the answers she needed, or perhaps she could come up with a different tack entirely. She had several hours to think of something before the moon set.

The main door was locked, but a sign pointed to a bell for after hours admission. The door buzzed open for them only moments after she pushed the button. Inside, the lobby of the hospital was much more welcoming than the police station. A large potted palm tree stood in one corner and generic art in soothing colors adorned the walls. A woman in a nurse's uniform sat behind the counter, an expectant smile on her face as she awaited their approach.

The Influence in the hospital flowed thick and slow in an orderly current through the room. Even in her limited experience as a witch, she'd felt a great variety to the quality of ambient Influence, from the clear organization of the auras of oath-bearers to the wild frenzy of football supporters emerging victorious from the local stadium. Something about the flow in here disturbed her in ways she couldn't quite articulate beyond a stale coppery taste in the back of her mouth.

"Hello," said the nurse, her navy and white uniform crisp and fresh, even at this ungodly hour of the night. "May I help you?"

"Yes," said Gosha. "Sorry to bother you at such a late hour. We just found out that some friends of ours were brought here last week. Can you tell us if they're still here?"

"Certainly," said the nurse, opening up a large three-ring binder organized with alphabetical tabs. "What are their names?"

"Wilfred Stepney was one."

She turned open the section marked 'S' and thumbed through a series of admittance forms.

"I have no record of a Mr. Stepney staying with us at the moment, but if he was already discharged, he wouldn't be in my book. Let me put in a call upstairs and see who's in the office."

She picked up her phone and pushed a button. Alfie's face lit up with an optimistic smile.

"It's reception," said the nurse. "I have visitors inquiring about a Wilfred Stepney. Yes, I'll tell them." She hung up. "Have a seat and someone from the office will be down to help you in a moment."

She gestured toward a wooden bench along one wall, but they had barely sat when the doors to an elevator to their left opened and out stepped a small man with close-cropped blond hair, a round face, and a scruff of beard.

"Edith," he said, walking over to the counter. "You needed me?"

"These people are looking for a Wilfred Stepney."

He spun on his heel to turn toward them and clapped his hands together with a jovial smile.

"Wilfred Stepney," he said as he approached the bench. "The painter? Are you friends?"

"Yeah," said Johnny, chiming in. "I work with him. I'm one of his models."

"Herbert Road Police Station told us he and four of his friends were brought here last week," said Gosha, standing to speak to him. "It would have been very late on Tuesday night."

The ambient Influence clung to his non-oath-bearer's aura, bolstering and inflating it to the size of an acolyte's. The effect could have been the result of whatever position of authority he might have at the hospital, but usually it poured off people of significance, like Johnny at her side. It didn't cling to them like that. Unless it was a sheath like Joel Adair's.

"Herbert Road?" he said. "Did they really? I'm afraid I can't help you. We haven't had such an illustrious patient in years, though I'm a great admirer of Sir Wilfred's work."

"And you are?" said Gosha, rising and offering him a hand.

"Doctor Gerhard Dropnick," he said taking her hand. Not a short man as much as he was built to a different scale, his handshake was wiry and firm. "I'm the chief of psychiatry here."

"Actalet," she whispered, expecting the spell to trigger twinned openings between the two of them, but the Influence of the spell flailed around him, unable to penetrate his sheath, and failed.

"I beg your pardon," he said. "I didn't catch that."

"Oh, nothing." She released his hand. "I'm just a little frustrated. He's been missing since last week, and I'm worried about him."

"I am so sorry, but I can't help you," said Dropnick with a shrug. He smiled and took a fountain pen from his pocket and fiddled with the cap, popping it on and off in an unconscious twitch. "The police so rarely bring us patients, I would have heard about it."

"Thank you for your time," she said.

"No problem at all." He clapped his hands together. "I wish you luck in your search. Good evening." He turned back to the counter. "Edith, may I use your phone?"

"Let's go," said Gosha and hurried out, the others behind her.

"That was weird," she said when they were on the pavement and heading back to the car. "I tried the confession spell, but it slid right off him." She touched the serpent ring on her finger and hung back. "I'll be right there. I need to try something."

As she looked up at the moon and began to speak the invocation that would open the Shadowlands to her so that she could forge a different spell that might help them, a black unmarked van careened around the corner and screeched to a halt in front of her. The back doors flung open and half a dozen men in suits and ties barreled out.

"Malgorjata Armitage," said the man in the lead as the others fanned out around the cars that separated them from her, blocking her off from Alfie and Johnny. "Please stop what you're doing and raise your hands in the air."

The other men reached into their jackets and took out guns which they aimed at her with locked arms.

"What's going on?" she asked, unable to process the sudden armed confrontation.

"RAISE YOUR HANDS IN THE AIR," shouted the man, pulling out his own weapon.

"Gosha!" Alfie ran toward her, but one of the men caught him with his shoulder, knocked him down and stood over him, training his gun on him. A second man moved toward Johnny, who cringed back against the Mini with his hands up.

She did as she was told, lifting her hands above her head.

"COUNTERMEASURES."

The man's shout echoed off the buildings surrounding the square.

A pair of suited men leaped from the back of the van and rushed toward her. One clamped a pair of barred iron manacles engraved with strange but familiar symbols about her wrists, the lock fastening with a crisp metallic click. The other took a black cloth bag and slid it over her head. Between them the two men lifted her off her feet and dragged her into the van.

"Alfie!" she cried. "Help!"

21

"WHERE ARE YOU TAKING ME?"

The van bounced along. She could hear the men surrounding her, could sense their auras, none of them oath-bearers, but they said nothing in return. She inhaled sharply when they crossed the border of Cheyne Heath and went beyond the protection of her wards. The weight of George's presence pressed into her temples. She could feel his awareness turning toward her.

"Boss," said one of the men. "System's showing a high-level incursion. Very big. Coming in very fast."

The pressure turned into pain, a vice threatening to squeeze her brains out of her ears.

"Jesus," said another voice to her left.

"Activate countermeasures," said their leader sitting in front of her on the other side of the van.

A scuffle ensued, men breathing hard and jostling her as they passed something across the van. The pressure crushing her abruptly vanished.

"Countermeasures holding," said yet another voice.

The boss chuckled.

"Is that someone trying to save you or to make you pay for your crimes? Either way, they're not getting to you."

The van stopped. She was dragged out, the cool expanse of night quickly replaced by the harsh echo of corridors, fluorescent light trickling through the weave of the hood. They pulled her down a stairwell, flight after flight, until a door slammed open and another door shut. Her captors pushed her into a chair, attached her manacles to a bar in the middle of a metal table and patted her down, taking her field kit and telling deck from the pockets of her jacket. Had they been women, they might have searched her body more thoroughly and found her lipstick in her bra. Thankfully, prudish awkwardness led them to avoid her chest.

The hood was yanked from her head. Harsh, bright light shone down on her, forcing her to scrunch her eyes shut. The door slammed again behind her, leaving her alone in a gray, featureless room with security cameras in every corner.

A tremendous racket of screeching noise assaulted her ears, as hard on her body as George's attempt to bring her down.

The racket suddenly stopped, replaced by a man's voice at the same brain-splitting volume.

"Are you working alone?" said the voice.

Silenced followed.

"Where are my friends? What have you done with Alfie and Johnny?"

The racket screeched at her again, rolling in wave after wave, jostling her brain. Deep bass notes resonated in her bowels.

"Are you working alone?" said the voice, breaking into the din.

"You saw my friends. What do you think I was doing?"

A pause of silence. Then noise.

"Who are the other witches in your coven?"

Her mother and the ladies had never once used the word 'coven' to describe themselves.

She said nothing.

More noise.

"What is your purpose?"

"I was just trying to find Sir Wilfred Stepney. He went missing—"

The screeching cacophony cut her off before she could finish.

"Who are the other witches in your coven?"

"There are no other witches," she screamed. "It's just me."

Noise and agony.

"What is your purpose?"

"I want to see a lawyer! You can't torture me like this—"

More noise.

"Who are your collaborators?"

She said nothing, tried to cover her head with her arms and blot out the noise.

"What is your purpose?"

The voice asked the same questions over and over again, and all she could do was weep.

The noise and questions finally stopped, after how much time she couldn't tell.

The lights turned off, blinding her with darkness. The door behind her burst open and a hood was pulled over her head once again. Rough hands unhooked her from the table and dragged her a short distance to another room.

"I want a lawyer," she said to the darkness. "This is illegal. You can't hold me here."

It was clear they could do whatever they liked with her, but something within her wouldn't allow her to submit meekly to whatever they had in store.

"You fucking bastards," she screeched. "This is illegal. I'm a British citizen. You can't do this to me."

They threw her into a hard-backed chair, removed her manacles and strapped her down. Someone tugged off her hood to reveal five men in black soldier's fatigues, balaclavas covering their faces. Two of the men held long metal shafts attached to the legs of the chair. They pushed the chair, rolling it on wheels until it hit a hard ledge and tipped, plunging her backwards, headfirst, into icy water.

With only enough time to take in half a breath, she struggled against the straps as cold water flooded into her nostrils, freezing her brain. They held her there until her lungs burned, her chest heaving as it tried to take in air, and she clamped every muscle in her body to prevent it.

When she thought she couldn't hold her breath any longer, when her thoughts turned fuzzy as her brain became starved of oxygen, they pulled her out. A rig of cables above her lifted the chair back onto its legs. She gulped air down and coughed up water.

"Who are your collaborators?" said the voice behind her, now unamplified. "What is your purpose?"

They gave her no time to answer before pushing her back into the water.

As she opened her mouth to take in the biggest breath she could, a spell came to her, jumping into her mind in Elsie's loving chirrup, a spell created to save an ancestor from just this kind of torture.

"Ochlandor," she breathed as the water flooded over her.

Such a stupid thing to do. The thought danced behind her eyes. *I wasted my breath.*

And then she found she could breathe.

A bubble of sweet highland air covered her nose and mouth, the smell of heather and loam and dew touching her crazed mind and calming her terror. Her body relaxed as she breathed in deep and realized her mistake. If they suspected she had saved herself, they would surely come up with some other torture she didn't have a spell for, so she writhed and struggled against the straps in her best performance of desperation. When they pulled her out, she pantomimed gasping and spluttering, though the bubble of air had kept the water free of her lungs.

"Who are your collaborators?" said the voice. "What is your purpose?"

"My name is Małgorzata Mierzejewska Armitage," she said, the highland air filling her with bravado. "I am a British citizen. I demand to see my lawyer."

They pushed her back into the water.

Defiance was probably not the best strategy, she thought as she writhed and yanked, but if she could keep this going for long enough, she might come up with a plan. She weakened her thrashing hoping to give the impression she was succumbing to their torture. Perhaps she could play dead and throw them off long enough to curse her way out of there.

When they pulled her up again, they threw the hood on her, unstrapped her and dragged her away. Worried they might have realized she had cast a spell, she steeled herself against what might come next, but they threw her into a tiny cell and slammed the heavy steel door shut. She heard bolts slide into place and pulled off her hood.

The cell was just wider than her arm span in both directions. High up on one wall, out of her reach, a grate opened to the night air, wire mesh across it. She peered out through a square of mesh cut into the door at eye level to see a balaclava-masked soldier with an oversized artist's paintbrush and a bucket of whitewash paint symbols on the floor outside the cell door.

"Oi," he said to another soldier when he saw her looking.

A metal cover slid across the grate leaving her soaked and shivering in darkness, a sliver of moonlight shining through the window in a pale square high up on the brick wall. She slumped back against the wall and hugged herself against the chill, a spell her mother had taught her to help with the laundry coming to mind.

"Osbeszta," she said.

The Influence flowed hesitantly from her lipstick, still well-lodged in her sports bra despite the abuse she'd suffered. At first she worried the symbols the soldier had painted had done something to stop her Craft, but the spell word flowered open within her and a flash of warmth spread across her body, drying her clothes in an instant and leaving them smelling fresh with a delicate scent of flowers, her chill gone.

She walked over to the cell door and pressed her ear at the grate, hoping to hear what was happening on the other side: muffled voices that grew louder and fell silent, the shrieking scrape of metal on stone, then nothing. She waited for a dozen heartbeats and a dozen more, but the room beyond remained quiet.

She considered her options. Her mother's unlocking spell could open the deadbolt on her front door. She saw no reason why it wouldn't work on the bolts that sealed the cell. If there was a guard outside, she could use the sleep spell on him, but she'd have to get close enough to touch him. So: unlocking spell, pull the door open, concealment spell, sleep spell. Rinse and repeat until she was out and safely away. She'd lost her field kit and telling deck, but they could be replaced.

"Hekatisk."

The complex spirals of the unlocking spell opened within her. Influence flowed through, but as it emerged, it dissipated like candle smoke in the wind. She tried it again, a second and third time, but the result was always the same.

She hugged herself and winced at a bruise on her elbow from all the dragging and struggling. Her wrists were sore where she had been shackled and bound.

"Rajequist."

The effervescent warmth of the healing spell spread through her, and the grazed and welted skin on her wrists began to clear.

Curious, she thought.

"Pezhvatek."

There was precious little light in the room to show color, but she felt the enclosed safety of the concealment spell envelop her. Personal spells still functioned, but whatever the soldier had painted on the floor was preventing her from affecting the world around her. She recalled where she had seen those symbols before: scrawled across the walls and floors of Emerson Margrave's prison for George where he planned to steal George's power.

Another mystery of High Influence, she thought, and remembered her serpent ring. Another thing the soldiers had overlooked.

The patch of moonlight was high up on the cell wall, beyond her reach no matter how high she lifted up on her tiptoes. Without direct contact of the light of the full moon, she wouldn't be able to summon the dragon heads.

She had no way out.

22

SHE WASN'T LEFT ALONE FOR long. The patch of moonlight drifted across the wall, marking the passage of time as it slid closer, brick by brick, until it was no more than an inch beyond her reach. The bolts to the cell thunked and the door clanged open. A soldier stepped through, three others at his back just beyond the doorway.

"Block the door," he shouted when he realized he couldn't see her, the spell of concealment still active.

His three associates pressed themselves forward creating a barrier with their bodies as he spread his arms, making it impossible for her to slip out.

"Get me a cannon," he shouted and the three at the door passed him what look like a large spotlight with handles, a giant cable trailing off between their feet.

He pointed the spotlight into the cell and flicked a switch. Light and Influence flooded from the open end of the cylinder, the light blinding her, the Influence blasting against her like a jet from a water cannon, pushing her back against the wall.

"Target acquired," he shouted and his associates pushed into the room around him and grabbed her, the spell of concealment breaking at their touch.

They pulled a black hood over her head, manacled her wrists and dragged her from the cell.

Up the stairwell they went, farther up than they had dragged her down. The flow of Influence increased around her, getting stronger the further they ascended. After ten flights of stairs beyond the ground floor, they dragged her from the stairwell to a room at the end of a long corridor and pushed her down into a chair.

"This is the witch?" said the clipped upper class voice of an elderly, aristocratic man.

Though she was blinded by the hood, her second sight was still strong. A single column of bright, powerful Influence shone from where the man's voice emanated. To her right stood three lesser columns close to what the flow of ambient Influence told her was the edge of the room. Where she guessed the wall to be was a shimmering, pulsing curtain of Influence. In front of her and to the left of the dominant column and of similar intensity, surely another aura of a saint, was one she recognized: diaphanous shifting layers like a series of veils caught in a summer breeze. Euphemia Graham, Saint of Mystery.

"Yes, Your Lordship," said a voice at her shoulder.

"Let's see her then," said the elderly man.

When the hood was yanked away, she found herself in a large office, the pulsing curtain of Influence anchored over floor-to-ceiling bookshelves filled with ancient, leather-bound tomes. The three lesser columns to her right were acolytes, two men and a woman, huddled over standing lecterns where they thumbed through ancient volumes taking notes. Their saint, behind a large carved wooden desk, leaned forward to peer at Gosha through wire-framed glasses, a long nose and high cheekbones beneath cold and piercing blue eyes. Euphemia Graham in a black tweed Chanel suit reclined on a leather couch to Gosha's left, long stockinged legs crossed demurely beneath her, a look of smug satisfaction on her face.

"She seems so ordinary," said the older saint.

"This is the heart of their perfidy," said Graham. "Tradition leaves one to expect they'd have some mark that gave an inkling of their inherent evil, but they look just like any other commoner."

"Do we need them?" said the elderly man, nodding toward the soldiers.

"I wouldn't be left alone in a room with one," said Graham, looking Gosha squarely in the eye.

"This is outrageous," said Gosha, allowing her indignation to flow. "How dare you—"

"The witch," said the elderly man raising two fingers in the air as if giving benediction, "will only speak when addressed directly."

A writhing, tangled knot of Influence burst out of the column of his aura and flew at her. She flinched as it hit, though she felt no impact, but when she tried to speak, her throat and tongue refused to obey.

"These were on her person, Your Lordship," said a guard emerging from behind her with a metal tray upon which sat her field kit and the pouch of cards. He placed the tray on the desk before the saint and walked back to his post.

The saint peered at the tray.

"What are they?" he asked.

"A witch's tools," said Graham. "Be careful. You know what they say about witches. They might be booby trapped."

This wasn't the first time Gosha had heard such a thing. She wished now she'd done something to her possessions to live up to the expectation.

"Officer," said the saint, pushing his chair away from the desk, and raised his two fingers. A thin membrane of Influence spread around him. Gosha noticed Euphemia Graham didn't bother to take the same precaution.

The guard who had brought him the tray walked over to the desk, opened the field kit and pouch and returned to his place. The saint pulled his chair back to the table, spread the cards and poked at the contents of the kit.

"Artistic postcards and a sewing kit?" he said with disbelief.

"Another example of the treachery and sedition of witches," said Graham, her tone suggesting disdain, though she rose to peer at the cards and field kit with the same curiosity as the elderly man. "They pervert the natural order by disguising the instruments of their Craft as common objects."

One of the two male acolytes stepped away from his lectern to hand the saint a piece of paper. The saint glanced at it and was immediately incensed, his cheeks flushing.

"No!" he said, the acolyte flinching and turning pale at the outburst. "No. This is not good enough. How many times must I tell you what I expect!" He crumpled up the paper, tossed it into a bin by his desk and waved at the guards behind Gosha. "Remove him. Tell Richardson to replace him."

The guard who had handed the saint the tray with Gosha's equipment took the offending acolyte by the arm, the acolyte following him meekly from the room.

"Give me the details," said the saint to Graham, steepling his fingers and leaning back in his chair. "From the beginning."

"She's a person of interest in the downfall of Emerson Margrave. She and her husband are suspected of conspiring together to cause his ritual of life extension to backfire and leave him in his current state."

Gosha's mother had masked the fact that Gosha had fought Margrave to stop the ritual that would have killed Miranda and scores of others. Euphemia Graham still didn't know the truth, that Margrave had helped George murder his father and steal the sainthood of Authority from him, but she knew enough to spin a tale that looked bad for Gosha.

"A terrible, terrible thing," said the male saint. "Poor Emerson. Such a delightful man. Richardson!"

The door behind her opened and a man's voice spoke.

"Your Lordship?"

"Bring me George Armitage straight away. Be sure to show him the proper respect, but make it clear this is a command."

"Yes, Your Lordship."

"After that," Graham continued, "she and her husband had a falling out. She succeeded through witchcraft to banish George Armitage from the entire borough of Cheyne Heath. He's been unable to step foot in it since then."

"She banished him?" said the saint, shocked. "How could she possibly have managed that?"

"My people have been working on the problem, but I've yet to discover the mechanism."

"Oh, no," said the saint. "No, no, no. This cannot be allowed to stand. This is very serious. She must be made to answer. Richardson! And you said she has committed offenses against you directly?"

"She and the saint of Shadow conspired to do irreparable harm to the populace of Cheyne Heath, and potentially the entire nation, in a repeat of the disaster at Tynecaster. Had I not intervened to stop them, there's no telling the damage that could have been done."

Gosha shook her head frantically and tried to stand, but the guards pushed her back down. Graham smiled at her, her eyes slitted with evil glee.

"And then she helped the saint escape with her necromancy."

"This rogue saint remains at large?" said the elderly saint with a shudder.

"My Lord Chief Justice," said Graham, nodding. "This woman is a clear danger to the safety of the realm."

Gosha slumped back in her seat. This man was the second-highest judge in the country.

"What have you to say to that, Mrs. Armitage?" The judge raised his fingers and Gosha found she could speak.

"Pauline Sutton came to me for help, your Lordship." Her words tumbled out in a mad rush. "Her acolytes were poisoning her, causing her to lose control of her powers. I stopped them before they could succeed. I was the one who prevented the disaster."

"She lies," said Graham. "Just like a witch."

"She was frightened of what Graham would do if she gained control of the Shadowlands, so I helped her disguise herself and escape."

The judge arched an eyebrow.

"So you admit to the accusations?"

"Pauline's acolytes had developed an elixir that corrupts people's auras so badly the Lords and Ladies consumed them. Graham wanted the elixir for herself."

Graham closed one hand into a fist and opened it again, causing a tangle of Influence to leap out at Gosha from within the folds of her aura, rendering Gosha mute once more.

"I most certainly did. It was a dangerous weapon. I didn't want it falling into the wrong hands."

There was a knock on the door behind Gosha.

"Bishop Worsley is here," said the judge's assistant.

"Thank you, Richardson," said the judge. "Send him in. And Armitage?"

"He'll be here shortly."

"I want to see him the moment he arrives."

"Yes, Your Lordship."

“Greetings, greetings,” said a voice behind her, the speaker striding into the room without invitation or challenge.

The speaker was an old man in full Anglican bishop’s robes, his tubby middle emphasized by the drape of his cassock, its deep magenta hue dark and rich against the wood and leather furnishings in the dim light of the room. His aura she recognized from the vision of saints she had been given by a curse on Emerson Margrave: a steady beatific glow about his body.

“Your Lordship,” he said as he approached the judge’s desk and gave a little bow.

“Your Excellency,” said the judge, indicating the sofa with a welcoming wave. “Thank you so much for joining us at such short notice.”

“It’s always a pleasure,” smiled the bishop, his round eyes wrinkling, his open face beaming with unctuousness as he sat on the sofa. “And Your Grace,” he said to Euphemia Graham. “It’s been far too long. Is this the creature?” He gestured at Gosha without bothering to look at her.

“It is, indeed,” said the judge, “and thank you for the timely warning.”

“Yes, how did you come to be aware of the incident?” said Graham. “The Metropolitan Police Force isn’t normally your stomping ground.”

“Ah, well,” said the bishop, adjusting the folds of his cassock and the ornate silver cross that hung from his neck. “It was the Herbert Road project. His Lordship and I have been working on a joint endeavor to strengthen the moral torpor of the general public.”

“Really?” said Graham, unimpressed. “I thought your philosophy was to let the plebs get on with it. Let them sink into the muck so that your lot can raise them up, that kind of thing.”

“You wound me, Ms. Graham,” said the bishop, clutching a hand to his breast and twisting his face into an excess of grief. “I have only ever had the best intentions toward the common man. And some things are so pressing I simply have to intervene. The sodomites have become far too comfortable of late, spreading their perversion among the youth. Your networks must have heard of this awful plague that's encroaching on our shores from America? Alexander and I have been working toward some very public prosecutions that will show the disgusting deviants their place."

"It's been most successful," said the judge. "We've been developing quite a list of offenders. If you're interested, I can read you in."

Graham shook her head. "Not my thing, although if any of them present a risk to national security, let me know. How did you end up with a witch?"

Bishop Worsley spread his hands in a self-satisfied shrug. "The deviant and degenerate revel in corruption of all stripes. Cast a line for a queer and who knows what you'll reel in. Thieves, seditionaries, spies, even witches."

Gosha couldn't believe what these horrific people were saying. Despite everything she'd witnessed these past four years since becoming a witch, some part of her had still clung to the notion that, even though she had become lost in the treacherous landscape of Craft and Influence, somewhere out there mundane law and order still meant something, but these three pillars of society sitting before her—a judge, a bishop, and a member of the security services—were a harsh lesson in how naïve she was. There was no due process or rule of law that would help her. She had to find a way out of there.

"And what," said Graham, arching an eyebrow at Gosha as she addressed the bishop, "is your opinion on what should be done about witches?"

"They are an inevitable fact of life," said Worsley with all the brightness of a university lecturer waxing enthusiastic on a pet topic. "In every ecological system there are vermin, parasites that spread disease and feed on the leavings of constructive participants. They can never be eradicated but, when an infestation occurs, it must be dealt with summarily, lest its filth contaminate the herd. The Convocation of Saints has a unique responsibility toward the nation's wellbeing, and we, as the saints of Faith, of Mystery, and of Law," He gestured toward himself, Graham, and the Lord Chief Justice, "must be custodians of that responsibility. We don't even know how witches come into being, do we, Euphemia?"

Graham set her face into an inscrutable expression that gave nothing away.

"It's a mystery I have yet to uncover," she said, "though I and my predecessors have never ceased searching for an answer."

Until Gosha had come to the rescue of Pauline Sutton, the saint of Mystery had always been the starting point of the Witch's Betrayal, the ritual that gave all witches their power. The witch would use the oath of fealty to the Sphere of Mystery to Craft her talisman, then confound the oath by burying an effigy of herself on holy ground, using the Influence of Faith to wipe the oath away. It had been that way since the dawn of the spheres in every realm of Influence the world over, until Gosha had infuriated Graham by refusing to hand over Pauline.

Interesting, thought Gosha. *She must have thought her involvement in the Betrayal a secret. Worsley clearly knows something.*

"The witch must be tried by the Convocation," said Worsley, "and we must ensure that the assembly reach the correct decision. Nothing short of full persecution will guarantee the nation's safety."

The judge grunted and snapped his fingers at the remaining pair of scribes to his left. One hustled over from his lectern with a sheet of paper which he handed to the judge before returning to his place.

"Upon conviction," he read, "the witch shall be taken from the court to the place of her execution where she will be given the chance to renounce her ways and publicly name and denounce her co-conspirators. If she so complies, her execution at the gallows shall be swift. If she refuses, she shall be hanged almost to the point of death, disemboweled, beheaded, and quartered."

He shuddered and tossed the paper on his desk. Gosha rattled at her shackles, the grip of the guards tightening to hold her down. She wanted to scream, but the spell had silenced her completely.

"So gruesome," said the judge with a frown. "Haven't we, as a society, moved beyond such displays?"

"She's shown herself to be a clear threat to the sovereignty of the Convocation," said Graham. "She's acted directly against both of us. We all know how sacrosanct you hold your police force."

"They are the backbone of our civilization," the judge nodded.

"And by denying me the saint of Shadow, she's done incalculable damage to every one of us with this prophecy of ruin hanging over our heads. Not to mention that she banished her husband, the saint of Authority, no less, from his home. She's a threat to us all."

There was a knock on the door behind her.

"Mr. George Armitage," said the unseen Richardson.

Gosha tensed as George's unmistakable aura, an ethereal suggestion of a suit of medieval armor, filled her second sight.

"Griffiths!" he blustered, striding into the room like he owned the place, sweeping past Gosha without seeing her. "What is the meaning of this completely unreasonable summons? I agreed to come to your interminable meetings, but usually you give me some warning. It's four in the damned morning!"

He looked older, thicker about the neck and waist, his taste in clothing shifted from bohemian cool to city finery. His tailored business suit encased him in an armor as ostentatious as his aura.

"Mr. Armitage," said Judge Griffiths, not bothering to rise to greet him, his expression steely. "As saints, we may be equals, but I am still the Lord Chief Justice of the realm. You will address me properly if you wish to be respected in return."

George frowned, unable to find a comeback. He hated not having the last word.

"Your Lordship," he said after a moment of seething.

"Better, Your Grace," said Griffiths. "I forgive your many offenses to decorum. I imagine the purview of your sphere makes it difficult to see yourself as anything other than independent, but the Spheres are a living ecosystem. None of us can exist without the others. You would do well to embrace your role in the Convocation of Saints. It will make your life much easier."

Gosha saw George's little finger twitch, a tell she knew intimately. He was furious, but knew enough not to show it. He looked around the room, taking in Euphemia Graham and Bishop Worsley.

"Your Grace, Your Excellency."

He nodded and turned to see Gosha for the first time. A jolt ran through his body like an electric shock as he realized who he was looking at.

"What's she doing here?" he said, his voice dripping with venom.

"Your wife is here to assist us in our inquiries," said Griffiths. "There are certain questions that have come to my attention upon which I seek clarification. Perhaps you could help clear things up for us."

A slight pinch around George's eyes and a stiffening of his lips. He was worried, probably wondering if Gosha had told them about how he murdered his father to assume the sainthood.

"Of course," he said. "What can I tell you?"

"You are acquainted with Emerson Margrave, Saint of Desire, are you not?" said Griffiths.

A grimace twitched up from George's lips to his eyes and was gone. His mind was racing, trying to think through the angles. Across the years of their marriage, Gosha had come to know him so well, and yet she'd never caught the relentless hunger for power that had driven them to this point.

"Yes," he said. "He was very kind to me when I first took the oath of fealty. How is the old man?"

It was possible George didn't know what had happened to Margrave after Gosha had rescued him from the attempt at merging their two spheres.

"Not well," said Griffiths. "He's still alive, but his mind is completely gone."

"That's terrible," said George. "What happened to him?"

Though concern softened his expression convincingly, Gosha could tell he already knew.

"That," said Griffiths, "is what I hoped you could tell me. Whatever befell him occurred in late September of nineteen-eighty. He was found wandering around Hastings in his current state. If I am to understand correctly, that would have been only a matter of days after the sudden death of your father and your ascension to his position. That does seem rather a coincidence."

"My father was grooming me to be his successor, but he was a difficult man." George's eyes flickered toward Gosha to see if she would call him a liar. "Emerson helped me understand what was ahead of me. When my father died, I was in London. It happened very suddenly. I wasn't ready for the transition effects after I took the oath. Margrave helped me through it, and then I had to run up to Liverpool to take care of my father's estate."

He was lying. Margrave gave George the means to murder his father, and when George came back, planned to consume the life force of her friend Miranda and a hundred other people to kill George and merge their two spheres. Gosha shook her head and struggled against the hands that held her down to grab the attention of the saints, but the guards held her fast. George's eyes narrowed as it dawned on him that she couldn't speak.

Worsley tutted.

"And you never once in four years thought to check in on your friend who had been so helpful to you?"

"I tried to contact him when I got back." George stared Gosha in the eye. "I even went down to his country estate, but the house was empty. I did look for him."

"It's entirely possible Margrave was up to his usual tricks," said Worsley. "We've had to reprimand the old roué before. He did like to get up to mischief with his followers. I'm sure you were devastated to lose two father-figures one after the other."

Worsley's face lit up with a broad, ingratiating smile of stellar wattage aimed at George.

"It was a great loss to me," said George.

"Euphemia?" said Griffiths.

She gave George and Gosha each a long, hard look before answering.

"We have no evidence to the contrary," she said. "And we do have a witch involved."

The word 'witch' was all George needed to understand the position Gosha was in and go for the kill.

"I never knew she was a witch until after I got back," he said, another lie. "She and her mother tried to manipulate me. They wanted me to kill my father for his money and his power. She bore my children so she could use them to keep me under her control. She's holding them hostage. I haven't seen them in years."

"Yes," said Griffiths. "Euphemia tells me she has found a way to banish you from the entire borough of Cheyne Heath."

George's face and neck flushed pink. Whether from fury or humiliation, she couldn't tell, but for all his self-control, he was unable to stop this reaction from the core of his being.

"She and her mother are a menace." He recovered quickly. "It's obvious they're the ones who did that to Margrave. He was a threat to their control over me. Is there nothing you can do about them?"

"Oh yes," said Griffiths. He slid the paper from his acolyte closer with his fingertips and glanced down at the list of horrors they intended to inflict upon her. "That's what we're here to determine. I think there's enough there for a trial, don't you?"

He turned to Worsley and Graham. Both nodded their agreement.

"Richardson!"

The door behind her opened.

"M'lud," came the assistant's voice from behind her.

"Summon the Convocation. Tell them it's for a trial. What time is it now?"

"Almost five, M'lud."

"Set it for ten o'clock this morning. Allow special dispensation for any who are outside London at the present time. That should still give us a quorum."

"Yes, M'lud."

"I want to appoint a Witchfinder General. Get me a list of candidates."

"Yes, M'lud."

"And send a unit to Mr. Armitage's residence in Cheyne Heath to arrest this woman's mother and return Mr. Armitage's children to him."

"Yes, M'lud."

Gosha had no voice, so she screamed with every other ounce of her being, struggling against the guards, desperate to get out of there and warn her mother. With so many oath-bearers in such a confined space, the flow of Influence in the room was slow and stifled, but it still reacted to the force of her emotion, whipping and swirling around her, rattling the books on the shelves and shaking the floor.

"Guards!" cried Griffiths.

A metal prod thrust into her back, a jolt of fire surged through her, and the world turned dark.

23

SHE CAME TO SPRAWLED ACROSS the cold stone floor of the cell, moonlight shining down on her face through the mesh-covered opening in the wall high above her. When she rolled over onto her side, her head screamed at her, her brain sloshing around inside her skull. Nausea flooded over her as she pushed herself up and steadied herself with one hand on the wall. She needed a spell to get out of here, and she needed it now, but as she raised a hand into the moonlight, the jasper ring dark against her glowing pale skin, a black smear appeared in the corner of her vision.

Widow's weeds, she thought. *Someone's going to die.*

She still knew so little about widow's weeds, a skill very few witches possessed. A response to the subtle Influence of death, the smear would progress around the very edges of her vision until, with its circle complete, tragedy struck. The speed with which it progressed along its arc told her something about when the death would happen, but little else. As premonitions went, it was frustratingly unhelpful.

But here she was in a building full of sorcerers. Perhaps they could help her figure it out.

She hammered on the cell door.

"Hey," she shouted. "Hey! I have to speak to the saints."

The slit in the door slid open with a clang to reveal a pair of eyes staring through the eye-holes of a balaclava.

"Quiet," he said, "Or I'll come in there."

"I have to speak to the saints. Someone's about to die."

The guard's eyes widened. He stumbled back toward a desk by the outer door, snatched up a walkie-talkie, and thumbed the talk button.

"Code 13," he said into the handset. "Code 13. The witch has issued a curse. Over."

Garbled words that Gosha couldn't understand came back through the walkie-talkie.

"No," she said. "That's not it. I had a premonition. Tell the saints." The stain at the edges of her vision had swept around half the circumference in the last few seconds. "Someone's about to die. Warn them."

Garbled and chatter squawked back from the speaker. A klaxon began to blare, and the lights beyond the cell clunked off to be replaced by deep red emergency light.

"Acknowledged. Over and out," said the guard as he darted back to the cell door and slammed the hatch over the slit.

Beyond the cell, she heard a series of metallic clangs as the guard slammed the outer door to the jail. Now that she had her voice back, she wanted to scream until her throat was raw, but succumbing to her frustration would only be a distraction. She stepped into the tiny square of moonlight and held the jasper ring.

"Lady Moon..."

She began to speak, but stopped, realizing how foolish it was to enter the half-world between reality and the Shadowlands to face the dragon heads without preparation, but all the offerings she'd brought with her were somewhere in the judge's chambers. She would have to think on the fly and hope for the best.

"Lady Moon, I stand beneath your light and beg admittance to your Shadowlands."

The grinding klaxons outside retreated to be replaced by the screech of shadow wraiths echoing through the cell as the jasper ring fell from her finger, its coils growing and growing, larger than should be possible in such a tiny enclosure. The dragon heads loomed above her, higher than the ceiling. Moonlight blazed through the high window like the fire of a sun. The nightmare dimensions of the half-world had never sickened her as much as here and now.

"Dear Małgorzata," said one of the dragon heads. "Twice in one night. Brother Aloysius, do you think people will talk?"

"I say let them," said Aloysius, its forked tongue slithering from between its fangs.

One giant head swept across the room toward the door, but, as it approached, a hazy ripple of purple light flashed out at it, and it flinched back.

"What is this horrendous place you've brought us to, my dear?" said Murgatroyd.

"I'm imprisoned. This is why I need your help. Can you help me forge a spell to get me out of here?"

Murgatroyd joined his brother at the shifting haze. They looked at each other and shook their heads.

"The Shadowlands are always open to you, oh illustrious and puissant witch," said Aloysius. "We can transport your soul from this place into the protection of the shifting dark, but your body will remain here."

"There's no way to get me through that door?"

Both heads tilted to one side as they regarded her.

"What door, kind Małgorzata?" said Murgatroyd. "Beyond is nothing but fire and oblivion."

They'd never been unable to come up with a solution to her requests before. Whatever the judge's men had done to neuter her spells was affecting the dragon heads as well. She took a deep breath to steady her nerves and cut through her disappointment.

"What about the widow's weeds?" she asked. She had to do something. Perhaps they could shed some light on the premonition.

"Widow's weeds?" said Aloysius. "What a delicious thought. So dramatic. To what could she refer, brother?"

"She is a creature of tragedy," said Murgatroyd. "An unheeded prophet. Look, brother, she has the sight of doom."

"Yes, that," said Gosha, cutting it off. Even though time in the half-world moved more slowly, these two could still waste far too much of it with their recursive swooning hyperbole. "It's called widow's weeds. It tells me someone's going to die, but not much else. Can you help me change it to make it more useful?"

The two heads pulled apart to hover over her on opposite sides so that she could only look at one of them at a time.

"Hold still, dear witch," said Aloysius as its forked tongue flickered around her. At the back of her neck she felt the shifting of air as its brother did the same.

"A delicate thread," said Murgatroyd. "It stretches out beyond the fire, a tenuous connection to the doomed."

"We can spin the thread thicker," said Aloysius. "Make it robust, an intimate bond between the witness and the damned."

"Yes," said Murgatroyd, its crest rippling in the moonlight. "It shall be a glorious making, a testament to wisdom and compassion. And what shall you pay us to be transformed into a banshee queen?"

She stood very still under their gaze, not daring to allow her thoughts wander, lest they pick them up and demand as payment whatever she inadvertently led them toward. She couldn't reuse the remaining two memories she'd presented earlier. They would reject them out of hand.

"We have decided," said Aloysius. "We want that."

It dipped its head to the level of her bra and the lipstick.

"For this service," said Murgatroyd, "we shall accept nothing else."

If she surrendered the talisman, she would be giving up witchcraft. That would certainly solve her problems with the saints upstairs.

"Then we have no deal," she said. "Aloysius and Murgatroyd, it was a pleasure as always. I regret summoning you needlessly from your station at the foot of your Lady's tower."

She spread her hands to begin the gestures that would return her to the waking world and the dragon heads to her ring finger. Endless bargains with Iron Jenny and the other merchants of Craft in Morel Market had taught her a thing or two about negotiating. Their mistress had charged them with helping her. Turning them down put them on the defensive. It wasn't a tactic she dared use often.

"Wait, wait, O eminent enchantress," said Aloysius, its scales flickering and pulsing down the length of its body, wending its way toward the head of its brother. "Surely there must be something else you could offer?"

In that moment, her thoughts slipped away from her to her mother and the boys, her worry at the thought of the judge's men taking them from the house weakening her mental control.

"That," Murgatroyd. "That is what we shall accept."

She looked at them, confused. She daren't speak without knowing exactly what the dragon heads meant.

"Your children," said Aloysius. "That which you value the most. We will accept your firstborn."

"My... No. Absolutely not. There must be something else."

"There is not," said Murgatroyd. "This is what we shall accept and nothing else."

"Then the negotiation's over," she said, spreading her hands to return her to the real world. "I won't give up my son."

"But, beauteous beldam," said Aloysius. "Never would we be so cold as to rip a child from its mother's breast. Not without giving her the chance to gamble for his return."

"Gamble?" she said, raising a suspicious eyebrow.

This was new.

"Why yes," said Murgatroyd. "A wager. We will open up your widow's weeds that you may see through the eyes of the doomed, and all you need do in return is enter a wager with us. We don't want your firstborn, do we brother?"

"Oh no," said Aloysius. "What would we do with a child? Such messy creatures with their emotions and their urges. And they grow! What would we do with all of that? We crave diversion, variety. It's the delicious uncertainty of the wager that we desire, not your child."

"What kind of wager?" she said, narrowing her eyes.

If her mother ever found out she had even considered this, there'd be hell to pay. And her mother's brand of hell Gosha would go to great lengths to avoid.

"We will set you a question," said Murgatroyd, "something to answer when next the moon be full. A simple question, one that should take nothing for a woman of such great perspicacity to answer."

"What question?"

"Tut-tut," said Aloysius. "When you agree, we shall give you your task. Just know it will be a simple thing."

The heads hovered above her, as still as if they had transformed back to jasper. Not even their forked tongues moved, a sign they wanted Edmund, and they wanted him badly. She should play it safe and let the matter drop, send the dragon heads back to their chamber at the foot of the tower at the heart of the Shadowlands, but she was trapped in this cell. The judge's men were after her mother and the boys, and someone close to her was about to die. Playing it safe could mean a horrific execution.

And the serpent heads were giving her an out. Whatever question they might give her, surely she and the other witches could come up with an answer.

"Yes," she said, her heart pumping a surge of blood and regret through her veins. "I accept your terms."

"Magnificent," said Murgatroyd. "Brother, let us spin a thread of such depth and richness as we never have before."

The heads began to dart and spin around themselves with terrifying speed in the tiny-yet-vast confines of the cell, their massive coils threading and weaving around themselves. The screech of shadow wraiths increased, doubling and tripling in density, setting Gosha's teeth on edge, rising in frenzy as if stirred up by the churning of the serpent coils.

The sound and movement stopped. One of the heads loomed above her.

"It is done. Return to us when the moon is once again full. Answer our question or surrender your firstborn son."

The head and its coils began to fade, the impossible dimensions of the half-world collapsing back into reality.

"What's the question?" she shouted to the empty cell.

"What are we?" said a whispering hiss in her ear.

24

IN THE DARK CELL, THE sliver of moonlight had begun its climb up the far wall on its slow journey to dawn. The klaxons outside the cell still blared loud enough to jangle her nerves.

Stupid, she thought. *Just the kind of cryptic twaddle you'd expect from a fairytale.*

In the darkness it was hard to tell how far the widow's weeds had progressed. She thrust her hand into the moonlight to give her a bright surface with which to see. The stain had smeared itself three-quarters of the way around its path and sped toward its completion.

"All right, you sniggering bastards," she said to the empty cell. "Show me what's costing me my son!"

The creeping film of black oil around her vision blotted out, blinding her momentarily. When it parted again, she could no longer see her hand or the dank cell, though the cold air still bit at her skin and the scrape of her shoes on the stone floor returned a familiar echo. Her eyes saw a train station. Paddington, it looked like. Whoever's eyes she was seeing through stood on the overpass to the tube station for the Metropolitan Line, looking down over the incoming trains as they disgorged the day's first commuters onto the platforms.

She looked over at a clock suspended above the stairs. Almost six in the morning. She, or rather the poor soul whose eyes she was looking through, walked down the steps to join the crowds as they made their way to the main concourse, the Circle Line, and the heart of London. A carriage door to her side slammed shut, drawing her attention. She barely recognized the reflection in the train window: Joseph Hobbs, one of Sir Wilfred's fellow abductees, though his face was haggard and his eyeballs rolled with madness in sunken eye sockets.

Others on the platform began to notice him, worried glances turning to horror as he reached a pair of long, withered arms in front of him and grabbed at the bustling commuters with gnarled fingers and nails he had worried to ragged talons. A young woman in a business suit tore her arm out of his grasp with a look of disgust and made to scurry away, but he snagged her by the hem of her raincoat and dragged her back, knocking her to the ground. He clambered on top of her, pinning her down as she opened her mouth to scream. Everyone around them scrambled to get away. He held her head back with one hand and thrust the fingers of his other deep into her mouth. Her eyes opened wide with horror as she struggled.

Someone behind pulled him off her, hauled him back and threw him down. A young man, blond and muscular in his shirtsleeves with a rugby-player's build, a leather satchel strung across his shoulder and his suit jacket over one arm, stepped on Joseph's chest, shouting at the young woman as she curled up into a ball on the polished stone platform, clutching at her face.

Joseph looked at his blood- and saliva-coated hand. In his palm was a large moth, its brown and gray wings fluttering, animating the markings on them, turning them into a grinning death mask. The moth took flight and launched itself at the rugby player, landing on his face as he shouted to the passers-by to get help. He stumbled back as he batted at the fluttering insect. Joseph grabbed at his foot and yanked him off balance, knocking him down. As the rugby player struggled to get up, Joseph crawled atop him as he had the young woman.

He bore down on the young man's chest with both hands. Shimmering Influence surged around him, seeping out of his pores to envelope them both. The young man's body tensed, every muscle gripping rigid. The Influence soured, twisting and turning with corruption, transforming into a cloud of quivering moth wings so dense they obscured the poor man's seizing body. The cloud exploded, the space where he had lain beneath Joseph Hobbs empty. Joseph waved his hands, and the wings scattered, spreading out across the platform and the chaos of screaming, fleeing commuters. Several moths landed and their victim's auras soured instantly, the innocent people stumbling and falling, vanishing into swarms of beating wings before their bodies could hit the platform.

Joseph looked down at himself and pulled back his sleeves. With the ragged fingernails of his right hand, he dug deep into his left forearm, scoring down the length of flesh from wrist to elbow, but instead of blood pouring from the wound, out crawled a moth that took to the air and fluttered around him. He cut open his other arm and a second moth emerged to join the first, attracting the clouds of beating ethereal wings to them until he stood within a shifting, thrashing swarm.

A few yards down the platform, a group of people pushed toward him through the commotion of bodies: men in dark suits surrounding a buxom woman with an hourglass figure dressed in a stylish navy business suit with vast shoulder pads, glittering with jewels about her neck, ears, and black-gloved wrists. Gosha recognized her immediately from the many pictures in the charlatan Denise Ogilvy's living room, and the lustrous vines and fronds of her aura: Portia Twill-Quimby, Saint of Abundance.

Twill-Quimby looked around at the scene, appalled, and raised a gloved hand. Her aura expanded, the vines growing fast and thick to enclose the expanding cloud of moths until they were surrounded by a dome of translucent, ethereal vegetation. Everyone and everything within, except for Joseph, fell abruptly to the floor. Bodies littered the platform leaving an open path between Joseph and Twill-Quimby.

Joseph approached her, slowly at first, but then speeding into a stumbling, interrupted run as the unconscious bodies beneath his feet slowed his progress. Twill-Quimby raised a hand and shouted for him to stop, a rush of Influence blasting out from her, but it had no effect. He kept on, bearing down on her. She called out a name and stepped back. One of her attendants, not an oath-bearer, took out a gun from his jacket and fired. Joseph's body jerked once, twice, and Gosha was plunged into darkness.

In her cell, she fell back against the wall, chest heaving as she caught her breath, trying to calm the shock of what she'd seen. When, at last, her heartbeat had calmed and her blood had ceased pounding in her temples, she slid down the wall and wedged herself in the corner beneath the shifting sliver of moonlight.

What could have done something so terrible to poor Dougie and Joseph? And what would have the power to transform reality so completely? In her experience, only a saint. Was this something cooked up by Bishop Worsley and Judge Griffiths? Or had Euphemia Graham's alchemist turned Vivien Drake's elixir into something infinitely more terrible?

The klaxons beyond the door of her cell stopped, and the bolts that sealed the door clunked back. She blinked in the bright light that flooded in as the door opened. A tall figure stood silhouetted in the opening.

“Mrs. Armitage,” said the figure. The voice was high, a deeper pitch constricted to a feminine register, the words a breathy whisper clear enough to carry to the cheap seats at the back of a theater auditorium. “I’m so sorry you’ve been put through all this. Let’s get you out of here.”

25

THE FIGURE STOOD BACK from the door, stepping out of silhouette so Gosha could see her in the light. Statuesque, she wore a long-sleeved, red sequin gown with a neckline slashed down to the navel. The split in her skirt revealed a long, tapered stem of a leg in matching sequinned heels. The woman gestured with her sparkling clutch purse for Gosha to step out of the cell, but Gosha was too awestruck by the woman's shimmering presence to move. Though the frock was a feat of sartorial engineering, sculpting the woman's body into an ideal shape of femininity rarely seen outside a museum, it was her aura that took Gosha's breath away.

Gosha's second sight normally interpreted the gossamer shapes and flows of a person's aura as a monochromatic wash of pale blue iridescence. This woman's aura was a shifting rainbow of color. A scintillating ball of energy swept around her in a slow orbit, the electric comet of the aura of

Strength, its radius large enough to envelop Gosha should she take even a single step forward.

"Please, Mrs. Armitage," said the woman, her voice soft and kind as she reached a gloved hand toward Gosha to beckon her out. "We don't have a lot of time. My name is Delilah Davina. You visited my hallow last night. I work very closely with Waterford, Wakefield, Winston, and Whorl. Mr. Adair has given me the bullet points of why you're here. It's important that we get you out so you can continue your investigation."

Not a woman, then, but a female impersonator, the most famous one in the country at that. And also a saint.

Gosha remained in the shadows, just beyond the column of light from the open door that cut through the darkness of the cell. She could push her way past La Davina, make herself vanish with spells and try to find her own way out, but she had no idea what other countermeasures these damned saints might have set against her. The whitewash symbols of the strange alphabet painted on the floor glowed bright against the dark stone. If she got out of this, she had to find out more about it.

"You can trust me, Mrs. Armitage."

La Davina's face was a mask of dense artifice—layers of foundation and blush contoured her features—but the worried expression beneath was genuine.

In for a penny, in for a pound, she thought, took a deep breath, and strode out of the cell.

"Judge Griffiths has sent men to arrest my mother and children," she said as she strode past La Davina, heading for the door the soldiers had dragged her in through. A dozen other cells lined the wall next to her own, each of them open. A single empty desk and chair stood by the entrance.

"The second we have you out," said La Davina as she fell in beside Gosha. "I'll send my people to your home to check on them."

She opened the outer security door to the stairwell—it was impossible to think of La Davina as a man—and let Gosha through.

"Stay close," she said, the glittering comet sweeping wide to include Gosha within its arc, "and keep your head down."

She led Gosha up five stories of sub-basement without challenge.

"Where is everybody?" Gosha asked as they reached the top of the stairwell.

"I pulled rank." The saint grinned at her as she pushed through the security door. "I have a knack for bluster and brio."

The door led them out to a medieval-style building with black and white checkered marble floors and carved wood everything else. To their left was a central courtyard open to the morning air, to their right, a row of stained glass windows. At the far end of the hall stood a gothic-arched doorway that led to the street. Facing out away from the security door to the basement cells in a protective half-circle stood half a dozen men and women, all in drag, with lesser versions of La Davina's aura sweeping around them in slow and steady orbits.

Mr. Granger—Bonita Fascinante, dressed in black capri pants with a deep blue crop top, neckerchief, and beret—wrapped her arms around Gosha.

"Oh, Gosha. It's so awful what they did to you!"

"Not now, Bonita," said La Davina, brushing her back to the circle with her sequinned purse. "We need to get her out."

Beyond La Davina's people stood a wall of flustered and irate guards in black army fatigues, all intent on getting through the circle to lay hands on Gosha.

"Bowie," said La Davina with low and level caution as she stepped away from the door. "Please lead us to the street."

Bowie Blades, in scuffed jeans and a biker's leather jacket, snapped his fingers and the other acolytes stepped into formation around them as they pushed forward. The guards stood aside only reluctantly, fixing them with angry glares as they passed. Behind them, a handful of guards rushed through the security door and down to the cells as the remainder followed close on the acolyte's heels.

"Please tell me His Lordship and the others remain unaware of our presence," muttered La Davina.

"A runner was sent upstairs shortly before you returned," said Bowie Blades. "If they haven't updated the intercom system, we have five minutes to get clear."

La Davina's eyes darted around at the expanse that lay between them and the door.

"Here's hoping His Lordship's refusal to concede to the Twentieth Century works to our advantage for once."

"Mistress," said the acolyte to her side, a male impersonator in his thirties with swept-up hair and rakish beard and smile. Che Guevara reborn as a new-wave sorcerer. He nodded toward the courtyard in the middle of the hall. Crossing at a brisk pace at the head of a phalanx of guards and civil servants, half of them his acolytes, marched the Lord Chief Justice and Saint of Law, Alexander Griffiths.

"Steady," said La Davina as Griffiths bore down on them, cutting them off with the street in sight through the pointed arch. "Stand firm."

"Madam Davina," said Griffiths. "What do you think you're doing? This woman is my prisoner."

Griffiths' acolytes spread out around them, though the guards, sidearms holstered at their hips, made Gosha infinitely more nervous. The acolytes couldn't kill, lest they risk tainting their connection to the source of Influence and be forcibly ripped from reality by their supernatural Lords and Ladies. A bullet remained a bullet. She didn't think she had any spells in her arsenal that could stop one.

La Davina's acolytes snapped to attention in formation around her, two fingers pointing to the heavens with one wrist clasped by the opposite hand, as if they were children playing cops and robbers in the park. Power built up around each of them, their individual comets expanding their orbits to join their saint's, until Gosha was surrounded by a single, powerful sweep of Influence. Gosha felt the prickle of static against her skin and wondered if these sorcerers could see Influence the way she did. She'd never been in a position to ask.

"Mrs. Armitage is an employee of Waterford, Wakefield, Winston, and Whorl," said La Davina, clasping her hands in front of her in a gesture that suggested diffidence, but was undermined in Gosha's second sight by the arcing Influence that flickered around them, "and is acting in her official capacity as a representative of Fate and Fortune."

"That woman, Your Grace," said Griffiths with a scowl, his distaste seeping through despite the honorific, "is a witch who has committed offences against members of the Convocation, myself included."

La Davina arched an eyebrow. "Good heavens, Your Lordship. What offences could a witch possibly commit against such an august figure of the realm as yourself."

"She has committed repeated acts of sedition and sabotage against members of the Convocation and their followers."

"Really," said La Davina with a mocking smile. "Mrs. Armitage is a mother of two and a photographer of some artistic renown. I find it hard to believe she has the time to spend committing acts of sedition."

"She's responsible for the downfall of Emerson Margrave and has proven herself a threat to the safety of the general public and the morals of the realm."

"The morals of the realm." One corner of La Davina's painted lips turned up in a sardonic curl. "Who's given you this information? Bishop Worsley? Euphemia Graham? You need better advisors, My Lord."

"She has committed offences against me personally. She is my prisoner. She is in my custody."

"And yet she stands among me and my acolytes, not your men at all."

Lord Griffiths' pale skin flushed pink with anger.

"You will surrender my prisoner this very instant!"

Hands shifted toward holsters and into gestures of power. The glittering comet sweeping around Gosha grew brighter in her second sight, becoming and incandescent star. La Davina raised her palm to the heavens, fireballs of ethereal lightning manifesting above her, their reflection gleaming in the eyes of the assembled, marking them as real.

The front doors only twenty short feet away parted and Portia Twill-Quimby burst in surrounded by her entourage.

"What a fucking mess," she announced to the hall, the profanity softened by her upper class tones, as she pulled off her elbow-length gloves one finger at a time, handed them to an attendant, and noticed the standoff before her. "Boys, boys," she said unfazed. "Put it back in your pants. We have more pressing concerns. I've just come from a serious balls-up at Paddington Station. All hands on deck for this one. Someone's meddling with powers they don't understand. If we don't get it in check, we'll all suffer."

Neither side backed down, Lord Griffiths and La Davina locked in a staring match, their followers hovering in anticipation for the first signal to act.

"KNOCK IT OFF!" shouted Twill-Quimby, tantacular vines of influence lashing out from her aura like some horrific creature from a dark nightmare, breaking the concentration of everyone assembled. The buildup of Influence began to subside. "I summon the Convocation to order under the emergency powers agreement of 1643."

Griffiths and La Davina turned to her in shock.

"Yes," Twill-Quimby nodded slowly as if trying to impress on a four-year-old the importance of what she was saying. "It is that serious."

She turned on her heel and stalked off toward the wide formal staircase that led up to the gallery. Griffiths gave whispered instructions to one of the guards and followed her.

"Bowie," said La Davina. "Take care of Mrs. Armitage. I must join them."

"The business in Paddington," said Gosha, placing a hand on La Davina's arm as she turned to go. "It's connected to the disappearance of Sir Wilfred. I think the judge and Bishop Worsley have something to do with it."

"Dammit." La Davina eyed the judge's remaining guards and acolytes. "I'm sorry, Mrs. Armitage. I don't think I can afford to let you go. Your insight might be valuable."

Gosha eyed the door. So close. She could conceal herself and try to slip out. Perhaps she could make it to the street before they pulled out that damned Influence cannon. She glanced at the brightening morning light shining into the courtyard. Hours must have passed since Griffiths had given the order to seize her mother and the boys. Agnieszka was no pushover. Gosha could only hope she'd whisked them away to safety.

"I promise you," said La Davina, "I won't let Griffiths barrel over you."

She beckoned to her followers without giving Gosha a chance to protest. They swept Gosha along toward the steps. There was nothing Gosha hated more than being trapped and forced to act against her will. That it was a kindly face who claimed to be on her side made it no easier to take.

26

THE OATH-BEARERS LED HER UP the staircase and around to where the gallery opened out into a waiting area before a large pair of carved double doors. A mass of people, acolytes and non-oath-bearers, mingled in clusters around the benches that lined the walls, the auras of the oath-bearers causing the ambient Influence to ripple and eddy like ocean currents through a rocky bay. Joel Adair spotted them from where he stood talking intently with a group of stylish young men and women all with the same not-aura about them of turning wheels. He detached himself and hurried over to greet them.

"Your Grace," he said to La Davina. "The partners have information that the incident at Paddington is connected to the disappearance of Sir Wilfred and to the prophecy."

"Yes, thank you, Mr. Adair." La Davina paid him only enough mind to not cause offense, her attention focused on the double doors. "Mrs.

Armitage has already informed me of that. If you'll excuse me, I must enter chambers."

The crowds parted as she strode to the doors unchallenged, two attendants in Tudor yeoman dress uniforms opening them for her as she approached. As a cluster of the judge's guards and acolytes came up behind them and surrounded them, another delegation swept up the stairs, with auras of shifting red and purple lightning licking off them like Tesla coils. The saint was a handsome man: ebon-skinned, close-cropped nappy hair, and a trimmed beard framing his face. He and his acolytes, women and men of varying ages and ethnicities dressed in multicultural bohemian finery, could all have graced the pages of a fashion magazine.

The saint broke off from his followers and headed toward the chamber as his acolytes pushed through the judge's guards to add to the ring of protection around Gosha, snaked lightning and sweeping comets interplaying dizzyingly in Gosha's second sight.

"Gosha." Bonita tucked her Gucci purse under one arm so she could clasp Gosha's hands. "Don't worry about the trial. Our faction in the Convocation is strong, and we're already in negotiations with the independent spheres. I'm confident we can secure the votes to overturn the formal charges before they go on record."

An electric bell trilled loudly, silencing the hubbub of the assembled. One of the attendants at the chamber doors rapped a ceremonial staff on the stone floor.

"The Convocation is now in session," he called out to the crowd. "The chamber is now sealed."

Everyone turned toward the door and waited quietly.

"Have a seat, my dear," said Bonita, gesturing to the nearest empty bench. "There's nothing we can do until they emerge."

A scuffle broke out between the judge's people and the press of acolytes surrounding her as they moved toward the bench, but it amounted to little more than posturing and shoving. She had seen the same kind of behavior between Edmund and his friends in the playground.

"She's just going to sit down," said Bowie Blades, staring down an imposing guard who backed away under his fierce gaze.

Adair joined Gosha and Bonita on the bench.

"This is why I didn't want you to follow up at the police station," he said, running a large hand across his buzzed scalp. "It's my fault. I should've been with you. The politics of the spheres can be very tricky. Lord Griffiths gets furious if anyone even looks at law enforcement askance."

"Griffiths is Saint of Law. Does that mean every police officer and barrister are part of his organization? There were no acolytes at Herbert Street Station."

"Not literally, they're not, but he considers them all under his protection."

If Gosha ever had a moment to herself again, she needed an oath-bearer to take pity on her and draw her an organizational chart of how this Convocation nonsense worked.

"Bishop Worsley told Griffiths about what happened, but if Griffiths is so possessive about his coppers, how wouldn't he have known himself?" Something about the chain of events wasn't sitting well with her. "The task force that arrested Sir Wilfred. Worsley said he and Griffiths were working on it together, but there were no oath-bearers of any sort at the station. How would he have known I was there? Was there some kind of detection system in place?"

She looked across the hall to the group marked as acolytes of Faith by the lesser radiant halo auras about them: two nuns in full wimple, a priest, two imams, and a woman dressed in flowing black weighed down by a surfeit of silver jewelry in the shape of five-pointed stars, Celtic knots, and zodiac symbols.

"It's possible," said Adair. "I only have a passing knowledge of the way a normal sphere works. We don't have saints and acolytes, only the partners."

"No," said Bonita. "The ancient codexes are more concerned with the inner workings needed for an oath-bearer to amass power, and the articles of the Convocation limit the development of technology to harness Influence. Any instruments built on the calls and keys would be very cumbersome, not an easy thing to conceal. Look."

She pointed at bundles of copper wire that lined the walls of the chamber fed by a giant trunk tucked away in a corner behind a wire cage.

"It's a dampening system to ensure equality among the saints while they're in there."

She put a hand on the seat of the bench.

"Do you feel that?"

Gosha did the same. A deep rumble at the limit of her perception vibrated through the bones in her hand.

"There's an enormous set of turbines in the basement powering it," said Bonita, taking a compact from her purse and patting down her nose with powder. "There have been precious few advances in the technology since the industrial revolution."

Across the hall, one of the nuns glanced furtively at Gosha. The woman wearing too much silver jewelry saw her and scowled, putting a hand on her arm in reprimand. The nun looked guilty and turned her back to Gosha.

"Excuse me," said a woman's voice from beyond the huddle of acolytes that surrounded Gosha. "Won't be a second. Mind your feet."

The huddle parted and a diminutive South Asian woman in overalls and a headscarf wielding a dust sweeper at the end of a broom handle made her way along the wall, cleaning under the benches.

"So sorry," she said. "Don't mind me. Nearly done."

The woman stooped next to Adair to get under their bench.

"Is this yours, sir?" she said as her sweeper knocked against his case.

"Here, let me get that," said Adair and stood with the case to let her past.

"Oh, my poor aching knees," said the woman.

Gosha looked down at the pink cotton scarf around the woman's head and realized she had no aura. Not the glaring effusion of a saint, nor the modest shaping of an acolyte. Not even the thin sheath of Influence bleeding off into the atmosphere of a normal person. No aura at all. This woman was a witch.

"And my back!" She looked up at Gosha, a twinkle in her eye. "This job will be the end of me, mark my words."

The face was different, younger, rounder, but Gosha would recognize the voice anywhere: Shreya.

"The job of a hard-working woman's never done," said Gosha.

Shreya was speaking to her in Witch's Cant, the coded language witches everywhere used to talk freely out in the open.

"You don't have to tell me about it." Shreya took a dust cloth from her overalls and began to wipe down the bench. "Luckily, all it takes is a uniform and a mop and people are only too happy to let a hard-working woman get on with it."

Gosha glanced around nervously. Sure enough, none of the people around them paid Shreya the slightest bit of attention, all their focus on the chamber doors.

"Only this morning," said Shreya, "I was talking to a dear friend of mine who was driven out of her house by rats. Rats, can you imagine that!"

Rats were code in Cant for any kind of authority figure that might have it in for a witch.

Bonita glanced over at them, but seeing nothing remarkable, she turned her attention back to the chamber doors.

"She got out of there mighty quick, I tell you. She wouldn't have thought twice about getting out her broom and scaring them off, but she had her boys to think of. So I put her up at my house."

Gosha breathed in a deep gulp of air, her hands suddenly shaking as she fought back tears of relief. Her mother and the boys were safe.

"You look a little peaky, dear," said Shreya. "You should splash some water on your face," she nodded toward a door on the far side of the hall bearing the universal symbol for the ladies' room, "and hum yourself a happy tune. That always makes me feel better."

Hum a happy tune? What could that mean?

"Personally," said Shreya when it was clear Gosha hadn't understood, "I like to look at the *stars*, but you'd have the *devil* of a time seeing them at this hour of the day."

Stars and the devil: the Devil's Star, a linking of witches' talismans to allow them to talk at a distance. Her mother and the ladies would be in contact with each other even now, able to hear every word Shreya was saying. Gosha needed to be alone so she could tune her lipstick to resonate with theirs.

"That does sound like a good idea," said Gosha as casually as she could. "Looks like rain."

Talk of the weather meant that Gosha was calling an end to the conversation.

"It certainly does," said Shreya. "There you go, my dear," she said to Adair, getting to her feet and tapping him on the shoulder. "All done."

He smiled at her and sat back next to Gosha as Shreya shuffled off unnoticed, continuing her charade of dusting every surface in the hall. Gosha watched her go, terrified that she'd be discovered, but her overalls and affected awkward gait never drew more than a glance.

"Joel," she said, putting a hand on Adair's arm. "I feel ridiculous, but I haven't peed since last night. I'm bursting."

It wasn't a lie. She'd swallowed a gallon of water during her dunking and, though there had been a drain in the cell, she hadn't had the time to take advantage of it.

"Oh heavens," he said, flustered, and stood again. "And you probably haven't eaten, have you? Here, come with me."

The huddle of acolytes parted to let them through, but a guard with a massive mustache stood in their way.

"Where do you think you're going?" he said.

"This woman needs to use the toilet," said Adair, indignant, and turned to Bonita. "Ms. Fascinante, can you help?"

Bonita rose and scowled at the guard. Though she barely came up to his shoulder, her fierce expression gave him pause.

"Shall we all go with her?" she said. "Would that make you feel better?"

An entourage of La Davina's acolytes and Griffiths' guards escorted Gosha into the ladies' loo. One of the guards made a great show of inspecting the four stalls for anyone who might be hiding as Bonita and Gosha looked on. Satisfied no accomplices were there to help Gosha escape, he crossed his arms and stood in the middle of the room.

"Really?" said Bonita. "Leave the woman to pee in peace. She can't get out of here. We can wait outside."

She glared at him until he huffed out.

"Take your time," said Bonita to Gosha with a smile as she followed him. "They're usually in chambers a while."

27

THE MOMENT THE DOOR CLOSED, leaving her alone, her bladder decided it could hold on no longer. She scrambled to get to the stall in time for the longest pee of her life. When she was done, she splashed water on her face as Shreya had suggested and patted herself dry with a paper towel as she looked toward the door and waited. After a handful of breaths no one had come to get her, so she fished into her bra, took out her lipstick talisman and rubbed at the sore spot where the plastic had been digging into her ribs since dinnertime the night before.

It didn't take her long to tune the lipstick to the frequency to which the ladies had set their own talismans.

—did they do to her? Elsie's worried twitter siddenly filled Gosha's ears. *Did she look hurt? Did she look pale?*

—She looked fine, snapped Shreya. *I can't talk. People are starting to get suspicious.*

"I'm here," said Gosha. "I'm on the line."

Her ears exploded with five concerned voices asking her how she was.

"I can't hear you if you all speak at once," said Gosha, and the din subsided.

"Mamusha, are you there? Do you have the boys?"

—*They're perfectly fine,* said her mother. *We just finished breakfast when I saw the soldiers traipsing through my azaleas. They ruined my heirloom courgettes. It took some finesse, but I got the boys out without the* shchury *seeing us.*

Agnieszka used the Polish word for 'rats.'

"Were the boys frightened?" She'd gone to such great lengths to keep any hint of the supernatural from bleeding into their lives.

Agnieszka grunted her distaste.

—*Of course not! What kind of a novice do you think I am? We walked out of the house like we do when we go to the park and they were none the wiser. We had to leg it when we got to Manor Road, but I told them I was late to meet Shreya.*

"How are they now?"

—*Edmund's being difficult, as usual, but I took him to the newsagent and told him he could get as many of those awful bash-bang papers he loves.* Gosha smiled at Agnieszka's use of her disapproving name for Edmund's favorite superhero comics. *Timothy's reading quietly as he always does, the little angel. The boys are fine. What did you do to get into so much trouble?*

Relief turned to irritation. Her mother always knew how to push her buttons.

"I cast a spell on a police officer."

—*So what?* said Agnieszka.

"So the saint of Law sent his people to arrest me. They're putting me on trial."

Five mouths inhaled sharply with shock.

—*But why?* came Eleanor's deceptively youthful voice. *We've all cast spells on policemen and no one's said boo about it.*

"Apparently the saint of Law gets funny when his people become ensorceled."

—*Nonsense,* said Mei. *I had my fingers all over Notting Hill Police Station when I was a young one. Had a thing for girls in blue and no compunction about using a love potion to get what I wanted. Never once got even a sniff of trouble. Someone must be putting ideas in the lord high mucky-muck's head.*

"Well, the saint of Faith said he found out about it first."

—*Oh no, said Eleanor. Bishop Worsley? Oh dear. He's a nasty piece of work. I've come across him over the centuries.*

—*Centuries?* cried Mei. *Just how old are you?*

—*Not as old as he! He's a devious one. Very political, very ambitious, very greedy. If he has the Lord Chief Justice's ear, he must be the one who put him up to it. He can be very convincing.*

"But how would he have found out?"

—*Someone must have told him,* said Elsie. *What kind of spell did you cast?*

"It was one of my new ones. It makes people trust you enough to tell you their secrets."

Oohs and aahs filled Gosha's ears, along with a skeptical harrumph which could only have come from her mother.

—*Enough chatter, ladies,* said Agnieszka. *How are we going to get her out of there? We all know what comes at the end of a witch trial.*

Gosha thought about the vision of Joseph Hobbs and the chaos he caused. That kind of transformation would require a lot of power.

"This case I'm working on—"

—*Case?* said her mother. *What, you think you're a detective now? Is the house going to be overrun with hoodlums and women of ill-repute?*

"This case I'm working on," Gosha barreled on, talking over her mother, "has High Influence written all over it. I keep seeing moths and moth wings. Does that mean anything to anyone?"

The witches all said no.

"Listen, this is an absolute mess," said Gosha. "I need your help. Five men were arrested by the police because of Bishop Worsley and the judge. They were being transported to a psychiatric hospital but they never got there. Now two of them have turned up dead. Just a couple of hours ago, one of them walked into Paddington Station and started turning people into swarms of moths."

—*Not possible,* said Eleanor. *Influence can do many things, but it can't create a complete metamorphosis like that. A person always remains a person underneath.*

"No," said Gosha. "These people were gone. Completely gone. And you remember that terrible business with Tracey Dobbs and Terry Kirby's son? I found in two of the men's houses artifacts they created that do the same thing: corrupt a person's aura until they're rendered to the Lords and Ladies. I'm worried there's more out there. Can some of you go and look for them?"

With all the commotion of La Davina getting her out of her cell, she'd forgotten about the deal she'd made with the dragon heads.

"And Pauline Sutton. I need to speak to Pauline Sutton. Can one of you try and get word to her."

—*We don't have enough people to do all that, dear,* said Elsie. *We're going to need everyone if we're going to get you out of there.*

"More people will die, Elsie. Not only Sir Wilfred and the rest, if Paddington repeats itself. We have to find the other artifacts and Sir Wilfred."

—*Where would we even look?* said Eleanor.

"Someone needs to go to Paddington and see if the artifact's there. I can give you the other men's names and you can try their homes or workplaces."

—*No!* said Agnieszka. *Absolutely not. I will not allow it. These monsters will hold their trial and at the end of it, my daughter will be dead. Everything else can wait. We get her free, then we take care of the rest.*

"Mamusha," said Gosha, "we can't leave people to die."

—And I will not allow these wicked saints to kill you. Think of your children. Do you want them to grow up without their mother? Think of yourself for once in your life.

Gosha was used to her mother accusing her of being selfish. This unsuspecting about-face surprised Gosha into acquiescing. The saints were discussing the incident in Paddington right now. Perhaps they could come up with a solution.

"Okay," she said. "After you get me out, will you all help me?"

—Of course, dear, said Elsie. *We witches stick together.*

—We'll need paraphernalia on the spot, said Mei. *What does everyone have on them.*

—I have buttons, said Eleanor, *silk thread and a length of yarn.*

—I have dress pins, a silver spoon and a comb, said Mei.

—I have buttons, too, said Elsie. *And twine, copper wire, and scones.*

"Scones?" asked Gosha. All the other items the women had listed were special ingredients, prepared with Craft to be the foundation of the charms and recipes that were a witch's stock-in-trade, but she had never heard of a scone being used. "What are they for?"

—Oh, I just brought them along in case anyone needed a snack. They're lovely. Lemon and poppyseed. My mother's favorite recipe, bless her dear, departed soul.

Gosha's mouth watered and her stomach rumbled. She hadn't eaten since dinner and it was now well past breakfast.

—We'll have to find a way to get the supplies to you, said Elsie. *What do you have on you, dear?*

Gosha's heart sank.

"My field kit and telling deck are still in the Lord Chief Justice's office."

Elsie exploded in a wave of Scottish that was cleary swearing. Agnieszka cackled with glee.

—We will not just leave them there, said Elsie once she'd run out of steam and caught her breath, the faintest hint of Scottish brogue coloring

her voice. *A telling deck is too powerful a tool to lose. It would be too easy for the wretched saints to use it to uncover all our secrets, even an unfinished one like yours. Don't you worry, my dear. We'll sort it out. Let's get planning, ladies.*

Gosha took a deep breath.

"I should get back out there," she said. "I won't be able to talk."

She paused with her hand on the doorknob.

"Please get word to Pauline Sutton. It's important."

—I can send Margie out to beat the bushes, said Elsie. *She's a resourceful girl. She'll find her.*

—Just remember, said Eleanor. *We're with you. We can hear everything you say.*

28

GOSHA EMERGED FROM THE LADIES' loo to a wall of scowls. Five grumpy soldiers, Bonita Fascinante, and two more of La Davina's glammed-up followers hovered around the door.

—Ideas please, ladies, said Agnieszka in Gosha's ears. *How do we deliver my daughter from her poor decisions?*

Her heart pounding, Gosha looked around at the guards, but they gave no sign they could hear.

—You lot figure it out, said Mei, *while I sort out how to get her the materials. I think I saw a cat down in the rubbish bins.*

"Better?" said Bonita, ruddy lightning crackling around her sweeping comet.

"Much. Thank you," said Gosha.

"Happy, Sergeant Perkins?"

Bonita turned to the guard with the large mustache.

"Wait here," he said as he brushed past her to search the loo.

"What do you expect to find, Sergeant?" Bonita taunted. "Better check her bog roll for hidden messages."

She curled her lip at Gosha in a sly smile.

—*What about the time Elsie's son was in trouble with the Hell's Angels?* suggested Eleanor in Gosha's ears.

Gosha did her best not to look guilty.

—*Explosive diarrhea?* said Elsie. *I don't think so. The Ministry of Defense will be on us like mold on a supermarket loaf accusing us of chemical warfare!*

Sergeant Perkins came back from the ladies' loo satisfied that Gosha hadn't got up to any funny business.

"You can go back to your bench."

"Thank you so much," said Bonita, her voice dripping with acid.

As she and her entourage walked back to where Adair sat at the other end of the hall, Gosha's eyes fell on the thick cable of wire lining the chamber. She dropped her head and fiddled with her collar to cover her mouth.

"They have some kind of Influence dampening system in their meeting room," she whispered. "It might throw things off. It's powered by turbines in the basement."

—*I can take care of that,* said Eleanor.

"What was that?" said Bonita.

"Oh, just complaining to myself," said Gosha, trying to appear nonchalant. "My stomach's growling. Haven't eaten since yesterday."

"I'm sorry you have to go through all this," said Bonita. "It's a travesty. I think what you do is beautiful."

Not what she expected from an acolyte, Gosha thought with surprise as she sat back down next to Adair, who had moved to the far end of the bench so he could talk on his briefcase phone. He looked up at Gosha with a serious expression as he talked and glanced down the hall behind her. She turned to look and saw Shreya's dusty blue overalls. Resting her elbows on her knees, she leaned forward and ran her fingers through her hair, the

Brylcreem she'd used to style it the night before heavy and greasy in her hands.

"Shreya, they might be onto you," she whispered.

—*Oh bugger,* said Shreya. In the distance, she stuffed her dust cloth in her pocket and slipped away around a corner. *Don't worry. I'll stay close.*

—*I've located the telling deck,* said Elsie. *Fifth floor. I'm heading up there now.*

—*Bastard!* cried Mei, loud enough in Gosha's ears to make her jump. *It bit me. Honestly, if we did have familiars, I would never choose a cat. Willful, malicious creatures. What are we getting to Gosha?*

—*I gave my buttons to Eleanor,* said Elsie.

—*Buttons it is,* said Mei. *They'll be the most useful, whatever we decide. What did we decide?*

—*Someone create a big distraction outside,* said Agnieszka. *Then we use the buttons to create doppelgangers to confuse them and she slips away. Just like we did before.*

—*Except it didn't work before, did it?* said Mei. *That hideous oath-bearer had her trapped.*

Gosha thought back to the basement below the Comet Club and the dark cell she and Alfie had woken up in after the ladies' last attempt at freeing her from a difficult situation. Her life was punctuated with enforced stays in dark and dank places.

—*It worked perfectly well when I freed my husband from the Communists. And now we all have experience,* Agnieszka snapped back, *we won't make the same mistakes. If anyone has any other suggestion, I'm all ears.*

—*I've got my hands full steering this bloody cat.*

—*We'll go with Agnieszka's plan until we come up with something better,* said Eleanor.

—*Can't talk,* said Elsie. *There's soldiers everywhere.*

—*I'm heading in, too,* said Eleanor. *I'll check in when I can.*

Adair slid back next to her on the bench.

"I was just on with our statistical modeling department. Their prognostication for the outcome is very strong. There are thirteen spheres represented in there, including our proxy with La Davina. There are two main voting blocks in the Convocation: us, Strength, Liberation," he nodded toward the glamourous scruffs, "and Devotion. That's them over there."

A cluster of men and women stood apart from the others in the middle of the hall. Gosha blinked and squinted, their auras making her eyes water. Each acolyte appeared doubled or tripled, ghost images of themselves superimposed over each like some sophisticated music video effect.

"What about the other side?" she asked, looking away when she could no longer tolerate the disorientation.

—*I made it down to the basement,* said Eleanor. *It's a labyrinth down here.*

"Law, Faith, Mystery, Abundance," said Adair, "and now I have to assume Authority. Your husband has never attended the Convocation before, but Authority and Abundance are usually paired."

She counted off the spheres on her fingers.

"Wait, that's four of ours to their five. How is that good?"

"The other four spheres in attendance—Creation, Introspection, Surrender, and Inspiration—are independent. They'll vote according to the merits of the proposal. Our statistical modeling is confident all four will vote with us."

"That's good," she said, not believing it.

"Yes, it's very good. There's every chance his Lordship's accusation will be struck down. When it is, La Davina will table a proposal to recognize you officially. It would be very good for you, Mrs. Armitage, for you and all witches. It would be a great shame if anything happened to jeopardize it."

His eyes flickered meaningfully to where he'd seen Shreya before she slipped away. What had his statistical modeling department told him? She relaxed her face as best she could, a feat not helped by the sight of a sleek, calico tail weaving toward her between the legs of the benches.

—Nearly there, said Mei. *This damn cat steers worse than my old Citroën Deux Chevaux.*

Gosha watched the tip of the tail bob and weave between the bench and the wall as the cat stalked up underneath her.

—Got it, said Mei. *They're right underneath you. Alright you manky bastard. Let's get you out of there without tipping anyone off.*

"It would be a great shame," said Gosha, molding her face into a frown of worry and trying desperately not to seem like she knew to what he was referring. "What do you think could happen?"

"Mrs. Armitage," Adair said pointedly, raising an eyebrow.

Several yards behind him a black and brown streak launched itself across the hall and down the stairs.

"I want a positive outcome to all this as much as you do, Mr. Adair," she said, leaning down to redo the laces on her boots. "My mother and children have been threatened."

She slipped a hand further beneath the bench and felt a small velvet pouch. The electric bell rang, long and shrill, and all eyes turned toward the door of the chamber, allowing her to slip the pouch into her pocket unseen.

The attendant at the door rapped his staff on the ground three times and called out.

"The Convocation has paused its session. The chamber is now unsealed."

The saints emerged and went to their respective huddles of followers. Bonita and Bowie rushed to La Davina's side as she approached Gosha. Behind them, a queer couple made their way toward the acolytes of Devotion, hands clasped and held high as if about to perform a formal court dance. He was in his twenties, she in her eighties. Unlike the other acolytes, these two had no aura of shifting mirages. Instead, the blue radiance of Influence flooded from their eyes. They stood in silence among their acolytes as they all joined hands in a circle to form a tableau that would have seemed sweet had it not been so creepy.

—*So many soldiers!* whispered Elsie. *And acolytes everywhere. It's like a minefield up here. I'm outside the office. Should have your things in a jiffy, Gosha dear.*

The Lord Chief Justice, Bishop Worsley, Euphemia Graham, and Portia Twill-Quimby stood in a group around George, who glared at Gosha across the hall with an evil smile.

"Worsley is clearly at the center of this mess," said La Davina. "Every time someone tried to suggest action, he had a counter-argument and Griffiths acquiesced. I don't know how Worsley got his claws so deeply embedded in that man's arse. Twill-Quimby eventually shouted him down. The Convocation has voted to send a party to Paddington to investigate and clear up the aftermath. Bowie, I want you to represent us."

"Yes, Mistress," he said with a bow.

"Griffiths' steward is coordinating."

A skeletal man in a suit ripped from the costume department of a nineteen-fifties period drama with the single column aura of Law detached himself from the group surrounding George and his new friends. Other acolytes, including one of Worsley's nuns, joined the acolyte as he strode to the top of the steps and waited until his group of investigators had fully formed.

La Davina turned to Adair. "I pushed to allow one of your people to join. Do you have someone you can send? I'd rather you stay close."

"Yes," said Adair. "Let me call the office."

"Send them directly to Paddington."

Adair stepped away and snapped open his briefcase to retrieve his phone.

—*I have your things!* said a breathless Elsie. *Now I just need to get them to you. Mei, do you still have the cat?*

—*The little bastard's long gone,* said Mei.

—*Never mind. I'll figure it out.*

"Bowie, please inform Mr. Richardson that the representative of Fate and Fortune will join you at the scene."

"Yes, Mistress."

He bowed again and turned to join the odd, mismatched group by the steps like pieces from a dozen different board games.

"Mrs. Armitage," said La Davina. "What exactly can you tell me about what happened to Sir Wilfred?"

"Worsley and Griffiths have a task force set up to entrap and prosecute gay men," said Gosha. "They used an informant to target Sir Wilfred and four of his friends. Joseph Hobbs, the man who did all that at Paddington, was one of them. They were arrested and taken to Herbert Street Police Station, but they started to act strangely and were shipped off to Banksville Psychiatric Hospital. They never arrived. Adair and I found artifacts at the homes of Sir Wilfred and Dougie Barber giving off the same kind of dangerous Influence emanating from Joseph Hobbs. And we found Dougie Barber's body at his home. There's no question his cause of death was supernatural."

—*Matka boska!* said Agnieszka, listening in across the link of the Devil's Star.

"Someone's on their way," said Adair, rejoining the group with the cumbersome telephone in one hand as Gosha finished her account. "Who were the other men in the group?"

"Richard Howell and Andrew Mills."

"Two famous painters," said Adair, "a famous sculptor, a renowned graphic designer, and the illustrator of the biggest-selling children's book of the past decade. That's a lot of raw Influence to have locked in a room together. The kind of Influence someone could take advantage of."

"I've heard it said that Bishop Worsley is centuries old," said Gosha, well aware from her experience with Emerson Margrave that Influence could be sucked from the living to extend the life of a saint. "Could he be using them to keep himself alive?"

"That's just a quirk of his sphere." La Davina frowned. "Jed Norton over there," she nodded toward an anemic young man with the saintly aura of a single spear of brightly glowing Influence lancing up from his feet to blossom into a shower of fireworks sparkling from his head, "is a hundred and six. The Lovers," she pointed to the strange hand-holding couple with glowing eyes, "have been around in one form or another since the fourteenth century."

Gosha channeled her mother's innate skepticism for all things and harrumphed, drawing a curious expression from Adair.

"The trial is next on the agenda," said La Davina. "I've tried already to dismiss Griffiths' charges, but Worsley wouldn't allow it. It might get tense in there, but I promise I won't allow them to run roughshod over you."

Gosha wondered if La Davina knew exactly what lay in store for her if she lost the trial. She wanted to like this glamorous creature, but she was far too casual for Gosha's taste when the outcome could be her entrails spread out across the street for all to see. The moment an opening presented itself, she would have to make a run for it.

"I must confer with the others," said La Davina. "The Convocation will summon you shortly."

The Lovers with their hands entwined and the saint of Liberation with his aura of snaked lightning were already deep in discussion as La Davina joined them. The bell trilled, calling the Convocation back to the chamber. Bishop Worsley split off from his group as they made their way inside to confer with his acolytes. He tried to seem nonchalant as he spoke, but the tension in his body was clear. He placed a hand on the shoulder of the woman with too much jewelry and a dark twist appeared in the beatific glow of his aura. The twist fluttered and grew, transforming itself into a single moth that detached itself and flew into the woman's copious curls. The woman bowed, turned, and strode at a rapid clip toward the stairs.

Gosha grabbed Adair by the sleeve and pulled him close.

"I don't have time to explain," she hissed into his ear. "Just pretend I'm talking to you. Ladies, there's a woman dressed in black with long hair and tacky jewelry about to leave the building. She has one of the moths on her. Someone has to follow her!"

She waited for a response, staring into Adair's widened eyes.

"Hello? Can anyone hear me?"

—*I'm here,* said Mei. *I see her.*

—*Don't you leave, Mei,* said Agnieszka. *Don't you leave my daughter.*

"Hush, Mamusha, this is important. Go after her, Mei. She's our only lead to the missing men. Who knows how many people could die if we don't find them?"

—*Okay, okay,* snapped Mei. *Sorry Agnieszka. Your girl's in perfectly good hands.*

Agnieszka grunted in disgust.

"Who are you speaking to?" asked Adair.

"I told you before. You have your people," said Gosha. "I have mine."

"Should I send my lot to assist?"

"No."

Mei would never trust a stranger with a peculiar aura who suddenly showed up offering help.

Sergeant Perkins marched toward her, a soldier at each shoulder.

"They want you in there, witch," he sneered. "Come with me."

His two subordinates fell into step behind her. The eyes of every acolyte assembled in the hall followed her as the soldiers marched her to what she fully expected to be a sham of a trial.

—*I found the engine,* said Eleanor. *Lords and Ladies, it's va—*

The doors of the chamber clicked shut behind Gosha, her access to the Devil's Star severed.

29

A DOZEN PAIRS OF EYES bore into her as Sergeant Perkins led her across the chamber to a small dais behind a circular rail. Once he had her in position, he stepped back to the carved wooden walls behind her. The chamber stretched up to the heavens, the upper walls lined with stained glass windows depicting scenes of men and women kneeling before exalted figures that glistened with color in the morning light. Gosha counted thirty leather-upholstered chairs arranged around a raised circle to either side of her. Across the circle, lounging in an ornate throne—a king before his court—sat Lord Griffiths, a gavel and block resting on one arm of his throne. He traced the circular head of the gavel with his fingertips, his aura a thin column of light jutting up toward the roof, as he surveyed the other saints. Only a dozen or so of the remaining seats were filled. La Davina and her faction sat to Gosha's left, George and his new cronies to her right. The unaligned saints sat spread out across the remaining chairs.

Outside, the combined presence of so many saintly auras had pressed against Gosha's temples, the ambient Influence whipped into blustery staccato currents. Within the chamber, the saints' auras were still grand and ostentatious in her second sight, but now it seemed as if they existed under glass, torpid and withdrawn. The air of the chamber was thick with Influence that clung to her like treacle, tingling against her skin with a dull electric smoldering.

Perkins and his two subordinates were stationed behind her, and two more guards flanked the chamber doors. A half-dozen others were spread out, standing at attention around the chamber walls, disappearing in their stillness against the dark wood. All were unarmed, even Perkins having somehow lost his sidearm on the way in.

La Davina rose as soon as Gosha reached the dais, her red-sequined dress an arresting splash of color against the drab browns and grays of the hall, matched only by the bright magenta robes of Bishop Worsley. Gosha had no idea what the pantomime ahead of her would entail, but she had to keep it going long enough for Eleanor to kill the dampening field so the others could get her out.

"My Lord," said La Davina, addressing Griffiths.

"The chamber recognizes Delilah Davina of Strength," said the judge, an edge of irritation turning his consonants brittle.

"This is ridiculous." Though the dampening field restricted her aura, it glowed with a shimmering rainbow. Its comet, small and tight, spun around her in an urgent sweep. "We haven't had a witch trial in the realm for centuries."

"Do you have a motion, Ms. Davina?" He spoke her name with ironic weight.

"I do. My Lord, I move that the Convocation strike all rules, regulations, and conventions from the codes of governance regarding the treatment of witches."

"My Lord," said the saint of Liberation, rising from his seat next to La Davina. La Davina's skirt shifted in a phantom breeze.

Griffiths rolled his eyes.

"The chamber recognizes Colin Dancy of Liberation."

"I second the motion," said Dancy.

He and La Davina retook their seats.

"It is moved and seconded," said Griffiths without raising his head from the cradle of his hand, "to strike all rules, regulations, and conventions from the code of governance regarding the treatment of witches. Is there debate?"

La Davina rose again to speak.

"Witch trials are a mark of ignorant behavior, fear-mongering, and oppression of women. They have no place in modern society or the affairs of this august institution."

Euphemia Graham stood.

"My Lord."

"The chamber recognizes Euphemia Graham of Mystery," said Griffiths, his affectation of boredom deepening to exasperation.

Graham frowned, put out by his rudeness, but soldiered on.

"The occult sisterhood of witches are an unregulated power within the realm that requires oversight and restriction. The codes of governance laid down for us by our founders grant us little guidance for the administration of that power. The rules and regulations surrounding witch trials are the only authority the codes give us over potentially dangerous misuses of Influence such as the one we face this very day. To strike from the codes our one recourse would render us impotent in the face of a potential threat to the security of the realm."

"Why is the saint of Mystery," said La Davina, leaping to her feet to speak before someone else could, "suddenly so against the notion of witches when we all know she and her predecessors have benefited from their presence in the realm since before the founding of the Convocation?"

"How I conduct the administration of my sphere is no business of yours." Graham turned to face Griffiths as she spoke, refusing to address

La Davina directly, "according to the very codes you seek to savage. I have a responsibility to a higher authority than even the Convocation."

La Davina snorted with derision.

"The Crown has invested confidence in me in my role as advisor on national security," she scowled, "and through me, the Convocation itself. If we cannot—"

"Her Majesty, the Queen, knows nothing of the Convocation," interrupted La Davina, "and the Ministry of Defense scratches its head every time you issue a report, wondering why on earth they have to listen to you."

"If we cannot govern ourselves," Euphemia barreled on, "as individuals blessed with the privilege of fealty to the Lords and Ladies and the benefits we derive from them, then what use is the Convocation to any of us? Tampering with the codes will be the first step toward anarchy. As much as you and yours may thrive on such lawlessness, the rest of us value the order the Convocation demands of us."

"My Lord," said Portia Twill-Quimby, rising and smoothing out the wrinkles on her skirt with her gloved and adorned hands.

"The chamber recognizes Portia Twill-Quimby of Abundance." Griffiths cast an appreciative glance at her.

"This is a tiresome debate we've had over and over again." She smiled as she spoke, filling the room with her easy and confident presence. "If it's not about witches, it's about alchemists. If it's not about alchemists, it's about necromancers. We all know the outcome. There are more pressing problems than this knocking at our door."

"Absolutely, Ms. Twill-Quimby," said Griffiths and rapped the gavel on its block. "Is the chamber ready for the question?"

"My Lord," said La Davina.

Griffiths rapped the gavel again, overriding her.

"The question," said Griffiths, "is on the adoption of the motion to strike all rules, regulations, and conventions from the codes of governance regarding the treatment of witches."

"Strength carries the proxy for Fate and Fortune," said La Davina.

"Yes, yes," said Griffiths. "We all know that. You don't have to keep reminding us. All those in favor?"

La Davina, Dancy, the Lovers, the saint of Introspection with his Roman candle aura, and a man with scraggly hair down to his shoulders in a worn and ill-fitting tweed jacket, a manic cast to his eye and an aura that pulsed around him like a neon sign outside a Soho strip club, all said "aye."

"All those against?"

The remainder of the saints voted no.

"The nos have it, seven to six," said Griffiths and rapped his gavel. "The motion is lost."

"My Lord," said La Davina, leaping to her feet once again.

"Ms. Davina," said Griffiths rolling his eyes. "Could perhaps another of your little cabal do the interrupting? Even you must be tiring of the sound of your own voice by now."

Twill-Quimby might have confidence on her side, but La Davina knew how to command a stage. Her words echoed to the rafters. "My Lord, I move that the Convocation repeal the punishments for a conviction of witchcraft outlined in the rules, regulations, and conventions of the codes of governance."

"On what grounds?"

"On the grounds that they are cruel and inhumane, and directly contradict the articles of the European Convention on Human Rights."

Colin Dancy stood.

"I second the motion."

"It is moved and seconded," said Griffiths with a look of exasperation to Bishop Worsley, who shrugged and shook his head with a condescending smile, "to repeal the punishments for a conviction of witchcraft outlined in the rules, regulations, and conventions of the codes of governance. Is there debate?"

Worsley rose to claim the floor before La Davina could speak.

"My Lord," he said.

"The chamber recognizes Bishop Worsley of Faith."

"My Lord." Worsley smiled ingratiatingly as he addressed the judge. "We are not subject to the temporal laws of the realm, and for good reason. We deal in forces that would destroy common men and women. Has not each of us suffered abominably from the crushing power of Influence at the taking of our oaths?"

Graham, Quill-Twimby, and the four unaligned saints chimed in with a round of "hear! hear!"

"Do we not struggle every waking hour with the constant demands of our Lords and Ladies chattering in our ears?"

The chorus of agreement continued, the saints rapping the arms of their seats with their knuckles to add to the cacophony.

"Witches exist outside our control." Worsley turned to acknowledge his supporters as he spoke. "They have, through dark pacts with forces we cannot know, access to all the benefits and privileges of Influence with none of the accountability. They are the greatest threat those of us who seek betterment through devotion to our Lords and Ladies have ever faced. They prey on the innocent and unprotected. They are con artists and schemers—worse than the Romanichal Travelers who plague our lands—but, unlike filthy gypsies, they carry the added bite of necromantic corruption that, left unchecked, could bring us all to ruin—"

La Davina leaped to her feet to interrupt.

"Hanging, disembowelment, beheading, and quartering. I put to the Convocation that these are not the actions of civilized people. These are the actions of despots and tyrants. These are the atrocities of demagogues and oppressors. We are the privileged few who have seen the truth of the world. We are above petty vindictiveness and bloodthirsty brutality."

"But the witches are not," said Worsley. "They're not like us. They have no moral code. They aren't answerable to any higher power. They exist in the darkness and multiply like cockroaches. The punishment is there to send a message, to make it clear that we who are the keepers of virtue in the realm will not tolerate their destructive villainy."

Griffiths rapped his gavel. "The question before the chamber is on the adoption—"

"My Lord!" said La Davina, outraged that Worsley be allowed the last word.

"The question," Griffiths hammered away at his block, undeterred, "before the chamber is on the adoption of the motion to repeal the punishments for a conviction of witchcraft outlined in the rules, regulations, and conventions of the codes of governance. All those in favor?"

La Davina and her faction chimed in with their "ayes." None of the unaligned saints joined in.

"All those against?"

Every one of the unaligned saints voted with Worsley's block.

"The motion is lost." He rose from his throne, all his bored languor gone, and pointed a long, bony finger at Gosha. "As Saint of Law I accuse the woman, Malgorjata Armitage, of the crime of witchcraft. Who will stand with me in my accusation?"

His mispronunciation of her name grated in Gosha's ears.

"As Saint of Mystery," said Graham, rising to point at Gosha, "I accuse Malgorjata Armitage of the crime of witchcraft."

Worsley rose and pointed. "As Saint of Faith, I accuse Malgorjata Armitage of the crime of witchcraft."

Gosha did her best to not roll her eyes, the drama of the moment careening past camp to crash head-on with amateur dramatics of the most indulgent kind.

George, who up to now had watched the proceedings in silence, rose to join in.

"As Saint of Authority, I accuse Małgorzata Mierzejewska Armitage," the correct pronunciation of her full name from his lips cut into her, bleeding from her a hot and angry brew of hurt and anger, "of the crime of witchcraft."

"Bailiffs," said Griffiths, as he and Gosha's accusers sat, "bring forth the first witness."

From a small door at the back of the room emerged the police officer Gosha had bespelled to find out what had happened to Sir Wilfred and his friends. A black-fatigued soldier led him to a spot on the floor beside Griffiths' elevated throne, his head coming up to the judge's elbow.

"Please identify yourself for the chamber," said Griffiths

The police officer frowned and looked around at the chamber, bewildered by the assembly.

"Inspector Evan Whitaker," he said, looking up at the judge, "of the Metropolitan Police Force."

"And you are the supervising officer in charge of the night shift at Herbert Street Police Station, are you not?"

"Yes, m'lud."

"Do you recognized this woman?"

He looked at Gosha.

"I do, m'lud."

"Did this woman present herself to you last night in your office at Herbert Street?"

"She did, m'lud, at approximately twenty-three-thirty hours."

"And did she question you about the whereabouts of the homosexual, Sir Wilfred Stepney, who had been arrested for public indecency under the Sexual Offenses act?"

"Yes, m'lud."

"And you answered those questions?"

He looked at her again and furrowed his brow. "I did, m'lud."

"Are you accustomed to volunteering information to unidentified women who approach you in the middle of the night."

Whitaker flushed.

"No, m'lud."

"Explain, please, to the chamber why you answered her questions?"

Whitaker's eyes flickered around the room, his mouth open but silent as he tried to come up with an answer.

"I thought I knew her," he said after a long moment.

"You thought you knew her?"

"Yes, m'lud. I can't explain it. I mistook her for someone I've known for a long time. I thought I could trust her."

"And so you volunteered sensitive information to her. Are you in the habit of discussing the business of the Metropolitan Police Force with your personal acquaintances?"

"Absolutely not, m'lud," he said, upset by the accusation.

"Then why would you do so with this woman?"

"I... I don't know, m'lud. I felt like I would have done anything for her if she'd asked me." His chest dropped and his shoulders rolled forward, a perfect statue of dejection and dismay.

"Thank you, Inspector. You may go."

Whitaker slunk away, the bailiff leading him out the way he came.

"I put to the chamber that the witch enchanted an upstanding representative of the law to get what she wanted in a brazen display of disregard for even the most fundamental pillars of our society. What else might she do to undermine order and propriety should she be allowed to continue with her actions unchecked?"

"My Lord," said La Davina, rising yet again. "Mrs. Armitage was working in an official capacity as an agent of Waterford, Wakefield, Winston, and Whorl. She is in the middle of an extremely important investigation with relevance to every one of us in this chamber: the incessant portents of doom we've all been experiencing for the past few years, no matter how much members of this chamber wish to deny it."

"Have a care, Strength," said Griffiths, with a sharply raised eyebrow. "It sounds like you're suggesting a sphere of the realm has acted directly against one of its peers. Continue with that line of argument and we open up an entirely different array of contingencies and powers. Is that what you want?"

Gosha had no idea what Griffiths was talking about, but the threat was apparent in his bearing. La Davina had no retort, quailing under the force of Griffiths' stare.

"I thought not," Griffiths sneered as La Davina sat. "Bring in the second witness!"

The bailiffs escorted in a face it took Gosha several seconds to remember: Hugo Morrison, round and sweaty chief alchemist to Euphemia Graham.

"Please identify yourself to the chamber," said Griffiths as Morrison took his place at the foot of the judge's throne.

"Hugo Morrison, My Lord," said the small, round man, removing a handkerchief from the sleeve of his jacket to dab at his sweaty brow. "John Dee Chair of the Royal College of Alchemists."

"Do you recognize this woman?" Griffiths pointed his long, bony index finger at Gosha.

"I do, your Lordship," said Morrison, without looking at her. "Three years ago, in the summer of nineteen-eighty-one, she smuggled into the hallow of my saint, the Queen of Secrets," Graham squirmed in her seat under the outraged stares of the assembled drawn by the mention of her title, making Gosha realize it must be an affectation of which the others didn't approve, "a singularly dangerous elixir which, left unneutralized, would certainly have killed everyone it came in contact with."

"And what was her intent in secreting such a concoction into the presence of the saint of Mystery?"

"Truthfully, I couldn't say, your Lordship, but the formula itself could have no other purpose than to cause death of a most horrible nature. It created in every living, Influence-exuding creature it came in touch with a corruption so deep, the very ground of reality rejected them."

This caused a stir among the saints, even the four that were supposed to be on Gosha's side.

There was no clock in the chamber, but as she stood in her dock watching the proceedings, the light pouring through the stained glass windows had begun to shift. Time moved on, and Gosha had no idea how many more witnesses Griffiths had to trot out.

Best get on with mucking things up, she thought. *Can't throw the cat among the pigeons if the pigeons have throttled the cat.*

"That formula," she said, loud so that the sound of her voice bounced back at her from the chamber walls, "was the work of Vivien Drake, an acolyte of Shadow, who intended to plunge the entirety of Cheyne Heath into the Shadowlands."

"THE WITCH," shouted Griffiths, veins bulging in his forehead, "WILL SPEAK ONLY WHEN ADDRESSED DIRECTLY."

He flicked his wrist in the same gesture of benediction he had used in his office to silence her. His aura brightened and flexed around his fingers. A tendril snaked out at her, but traveled only a matter of inches before being drawn back into the rigid column of Influence from whence it came. The dampening field in action.

"Pezhvatek," she whispered under her breath, with no expectation that the spell of concealment would work, but she wanted to see how the dampening field affected her. She only had an inkling of how the sorcery of oath-bearers compared to a witch's spell, but perhaps they were different enough to allow her some wiggle room.

The spell created within her its familiar opening. Her lipstick, tucked away in her sports bra, grew warm against her ribs as it struggled to channel Influence through the opening. A trickle of viscous flow pushed through to be shaped into the spell, but went no further, becoming a living sheath around her that shifted and thrust against the dampening effect, ready to spring once the restriction dropped.

No one around her seemed to notice.

"I brought the elixir to the Queen of Secrets," she said, bolstering her courage in the face of the aggressive glares of the saints by digging at Euphemia with her self-styled nickname, "in the hope that she might help stop Vivien Drake, but instead, she took the formula for herself and sealed off the entire borough of Cheyne Heath, leaving us all to die. She was more interested in capturing the saint of Shadow than anyone's safety."

The spell of concealment continued to swirl around her without fading. Perhaps she could cast a sequence of spells that would launch into effect the moment Eleanor was able to kill the dampening field, or when they dragged her out of here to kill her. She had no illusions this was where the trial was going to end. La Davina and her faction had no leverage over Worsley and the judge.

"My Lord," said Euphemia, leaping to her feet, "This is nothing short of calumny. We all know what happened at the fall of Tynecaster." This drew a sharp look from Twill-Quimby. The disaster that had wiped out an entire city almost a thousand years ago had come as a result of a petty squabble between their two predecessors. "I was simply trying to contain a tragedy that could have consumed the entire city."

"By leaving everyone in Cheyne Heath to die?" said Gosha.

"The witch will not speak!" said Griffiths. "Perkins, silence her."

Sergeant Perkins stepped up on the dais to restrain her, grabbing her by the arms, but she had learned enough self-defense from Alfie to twist out of his grasp. A well-placed kick to the shins unbalanced him and knocked him back off the dais.

"Don't you touch me," she hissed at him, playing the part Griffiths and the others seemed to want her to play: the vicious, treacherous witch.

Perkins gestured to his two subordinates and the three of them mounted the dais. She could leap over the railing and lead them on a merry chase about the chamber, prolonging the trial as much as possible for the ladies' plan to kick in, or she could play on events she knew were inevitable. She had no idea what stood between Eleanor and success, but she knew for certain they'd be dragging her out of here in short order. She let the guards grab her, two holding her by the arms, Perkins coming up behind and gripping her in a loose choke hold with one hand across her mouth. The smell of cigarette tobacco on his fingers flooded into her nostrils as his hot breath blew against the nape of her neck. It was the perfect cover for her to cast spells unnoticed.

"Thank you, Sergeant," said Griffiths.

The spell of concealment straining to get free was useless now. The three soldiers would be drawn into the concealment with her, and whatever spell she cast next would shatter it, anyway. Her first step had to be getting free of them.

"Puthut," she said.

The sound of her voice was muffled by Perkins' hand, but it didn't matter. The spell created its opening within her and the sluggish, tarry Influence flowed through to create a propulsive expanding shell between her and the spell of concealment. That would push them away. Then she'd need to make sure none of them came back at her. The sleep spell might work, but it was so easy to break. She'd have to use the spell of her mother's that she hated the most, the one that froze her in place. Of all the horrendous things her mother had done to her as a child in her attempts to curb Gosha, this was the worst.

"Vezhramak."

She repeated the word, one for each of the guards in the room, and clenched fists of power darted around inside her dampening shell like angry snakes in search of prey.

The buildup of unexpressed spells amped up her nerves, leaving her breathless and nauseous, but she needed to hold it together. There were more spells she had to cast.

"And what of the elixir?" asked Griffiths. "Did you dispose of it?"

"Of course, your Lordship," said Euphemia. "It took a lot of work, but Morrison was able to eradicate it safely."

"Yes, My Lord," Morrison chimed in. "The underlying oppositional qualia were extremely complex to—"

"Yes, thank you, Morrison," said Euphemia. "We don't need to bore the chamber with technicalities. Suffice it to say, the elixir was destroyed. There is nothing left of it, is there?"

Morrison's balding pate furrowed for a moment with confusion at what she asked him before the penny dropped.

"Yes, your Grace," he said with an over-enthusiastic nod. "The elixir was destroyed."

Morrison was a terrible liar, Graham clearly still had the elixir, but no one challenged him.

"This would seem like very important information," said Griffiths, "that should be shared with the rest of the Convocation."

"I would be happy to," said Graham and sat.

"Thank you Mr. Morrison," said Griffiths. "You may go. Bring in the final witness!"

Gosha would need as much confusion as possible to cover her escape. Her mother's spell to plunge the ordered division of the spheres into chaos would certainly do the job, but it would affect her as much as anyone else, and she'd have to leave a lengthy time before the disruption it caused calmed itself enough for her to safely cast the spell again. Best to save it as a last resort.

"Alutroyd," she mumbled instead, casting the spell of intimidation that opened a window into the Shadowlands

When the next witness was brought in, she froze.

Pushed in on a wheelchair, dressed in wrinkled cotton pajamas, a thick woolen robe and slippers, and swaddled in a blanket, was Emerson Margrave. The old man looked much the worse for wear, his head lolling against the high back of the wheelchair, his eyes unfocused and drool seeping from the corner of his mouth. He was alive, but barely, his attendant nurse in an old-fashioned white-starched uniform with a navy blue hat and cape following him closely with a watchful eye.

His arrival caused a stir in the chamber.

"Behold," said Griffiths, "what remains of Emerson Margrave. Margrave was a charming man, a personal friend to many of us here. He was often chastised by this chamber for his many indiscretions, but he was generous and passionate, committed to the betterment of humanity. She did this to him."

Emerson Margrave was a manipulator and a murderer, she thought. Though she was shocked to see what her handiwork had done to another human being, she didn't regret what she'd done.

"Any individual or group," said Griffiths, "that has the power to do this to one of us must not be allowed to remain at large. Not only must we convict this hag for her crimes, but we must send the strongest possible message to her kind that evil of this magnitude will not be tolerated! Furthermore, I have begun the search for a witch-hunter general to spearhead a vigorous program of prosecution."

Several of the saints, La Davina and Dancy included, glanced between Margrave and Gosha with appalled expressions. George watched Griffiths' tirade with open glee, while Bishop Worsley sat back with his hands crossed contentedly over his paunch, a satisfied smile plastered across his face. As powerful as the Lord Chief Justice might be, he wasn't the one pulling the strings here.

A saint could tear her spells to shreds without a second thought. That meant she couldn't use her mother's curse, or anything else offensive against them, but Agnieszka's all-purpose hex acted on the environment of the victim, causing often-ridiculous mishaps to vex them.

"Vekshatep," she muttered behind Sergeant Perkins' hand, once for each of the saints, including those who claimed to be on her side. She couldn't trust that whatever secret machinations they were wrapped up in wouldn't leave her on the sharp end of a butcher's knife.

The pressure of the accumulated spells ravaged her body. Random tremors eddied through her. The guards took her wobbling as an attempt at escape and tightened their grip, allowing her to relax into them. She used the respite for a moment of reflection, allowing the layers of spells fighting to be free to insulate her from the farce being performed around her. Was there more she could do to prepare? Could she manage any more spells, or would one more be enough to incapacitate her?

To her surprise, she found what she wanted more than anything was the cold, heavy certainty of her switchblade. She'd left it in the house, on a high shelf in her studio, away from the boys' curious hands.

"Tatlet," she said, casting the spell that would call it to her. She had forged the spell because of the many times she had fumbled and dropped the knife when she was first learning to use it. She'd never tried to summon it from so far away.

"Pezhvatek."

She cast the concealing spell once more, the last spell she thought she could handle. Hopefully the torrent of spells beating at her as they tried to get free would be sufficient to get her out of there.

"I call a vote," said Griffiths. "Convict this woman of witchcraft!"

—did it! came Eleanor's voice across the link of the Devil's Star. *I finally stopped the bloody thing! Let's get her out of there!*

30

THE SPELLS RIPPED AWAY FROM Gosha like a virus her body was trying to shed with one massive convulsion after another. Had the guards not been there to restrain her, she would have tumbled off the dais and fallen to the floor in a spasming heap.

She couldn't tell if the spells took longer than usual to reach their marks, or if the disorientation from their explosive release had slowed her sense of time to the point that seconds passed like minutes. The world around her dimmed, colors turning from bright to gray, the commotion in the chamber muffling as the spell of concealment took hold. Taken into the spell with her, Sergeant Perkins and his subordinates loosened their grip in surprise as they realized something was amiss, allowing the knockback spell to rip them away from her without dislocating both her shoulders and breaking her neck. She offered a prayer of thanks to anything that might be watching over her that her miscalculation hadn't ended her escape attempt before it began.

The three guards slammed against the wall behind her and fell to the floor, their attempts to get up stilled by the paralysis spells that froze them and all the other guards in place. The concealment spell broke, returning the world around her to brightness, only for it to darken once more as the intimidation spell hit.

"Guards," shouted Griffiths. "Seize the witch!"

The stained glass windows above her darkened as the barrier between the real world and the Shadowlands became porous. Wolves howled and shadow wraiths screeched in the distance, setting Gosha's nerves on edge.

With the first howl, Griffiths and all the other saints flinched in instinctive terror. The collapse of the dampening field had allowed their auras to leap once again to life, but the seep of the Shadowlands into the chamber transformed them, making them stronger and wilder, smooth sweeps and flows becoming jagged edges that writhed aggressively against their owners. The saints, to a man, leaped from their seats and scattered about the room, each trying to get as far away from the others as possible.

"Stand your ground," shouted Griffiths. "The witch seeks to divide us. This is all her doing. Guards!"

He finally realized that all the guards around the chamber were paralyzed, locked in place with their backs against the chamber walls, their eyes, the only part of them that could move, darting frantically from side to side. He raised a hand to cast some kind of release on them just as her mother's hex landed on him.

The canopy above his throne came loose and collapsed, leaving him covered in a tent of green velvet. The Influence he cast whipped around the room, breaking the paralysis spell and forcing the guards to stumble as if the ground lurched beneath them. The other saints found themselves tripping, suddenly entangled in their clothing, or forced to duck to avoid falling segments of wood paneling that had inexplicable come loose, or tottering on twisted ankles from breaking heels. It all had a flavor of absurd humiliation that Gosha recognized well, the hallmark of her mother's sense of humor.

The spell to summon her switchblade was next in the sequence, but she had no way of knowing if it met its mark. The chamber dimmed around her again as the second concealment spell did its work. She stepped back off the dais, beginning to recover from the shock of the rapid release of so many spells, and darted to the edge of the chamber, as far away as she could get from where she had been standing. Three guards descended upon his platform to pull Griffiths free while another three rushed to the remaining saints to help them out of their entanglements and to corral them away from where Gosha had stood before vanishing.

"Fan out!" shouted Perkins, and the remaining half-dozen men spread out across the chamber, arms held wide in an attempt to block her path, six grown men playing a game of hide-and-seek that would surely end in her gruesome death if they caught her.

As they forced her into a corner as far away as she could possibly be from the chamber doors, the pouch of buttons Mei had sent her began to vibrate. With four loud pops, the buttons exploded and the concealment spell broke as four identical versions of herself appeared around her.

"Get to the doors," one version of her turned to whisper. "I'm outside waiting for you."

The doppelganger winked as she and the others stepped out to act as a shield. If Gosha hadn't already experienced so much strangeness in the past twenty-four hours, the sight of four different versions of herself might have reduced her to a gibbering pile of nerves. Instead, in a mixture of narcissism and curiosity, she watched, fascinated by the four very different bearings of the doppelgangers before her, each one clearly a different woman, and none of them herself.

The one who had spoken to her planted her feet wide and, with one hand on her hip, she stretched out the other arm and thrust her palm forward as if to declare: 'you shall not pass.'

Could that be Elsie?

The doppelganger to her left arranged her body as if she were a ballet dancer preparing to perform a grand feat of athletic grace.

Eleanor or Shreya? she wondered until she saw the soft and serene stance of the third version of herself that had to have been Shreya.

The final doppelganger she knew, instantly, as her mother, the stooped posture with fists clenched and chin jutting forward as familiar to her as Edmund's severe correctness and Timothy's loving softness.

Behind the approaching melee of Goshas and guards, Griffiths and the rest of the saints were being ushered toward the chamber doors by the remaining guards, a perfect opportunity for her to slip out.

"Pezhvatek," she said to conceal herself again, and immediately regretted it as the room wobbled around her and her stomach lurched, her nervous system still enervated by the explosion of spells. Though the disorientation forced her back against the wall, the room turned gray and muted around her, the spell unbroken by her contact with the wall.

Just as well, she thought, her legs shaky beneath her.

One of the half-dozen guards confronting the doppelgangers lunged forward to grab Elsie's outstretched arm, but she muttered something and he dropped to the floor with a look of confusion as if his body suddenly weighed a thousand pounds.

"Cannons!" shouted Perkins. "Get me cannons!"

A guard pulled open the chamber doors and rushed out, followed by three of his compatriots and the cluster of saints, the door slamming shut before Gosha could edge past the guard Elsie had driven to the ground. The remaining guards joined the wall of bodies blocking her way, forcing her back to her corner, as one of the guards attempted to drag his fallen comrade to one side. He couldn't even lift an arm, the man's body was so heavy.

The remaining guards closed in on the doppelgangers, two on each except for Elsie, the second guard giving up on moving his comrade and stepping over the body to bear down on her. Their tactics appeared to be assault and subdue, each of the men lunging at the witches to either knock them off balance or grapple them down to the ground.

Eleanor moved with fluid grace, stepping out of range of her first attacker and parrying his blows with ease, angling the trajectory of his attacks to place him between her and his second to act as a shield. Pirouetting into him while somehow avoiding his blows, she locked him in a firm embrace and planted a kiss on his lips. His eyes rolled back into his head and he collapsed to the floor, unconscious, dropping down around her as if he were a slip she had let fall seductively from her shoulders. She stepped across his body and blew a kiss to his second, who also collapsed into oblivion.

Elsie tried to outmaneuver her remaining attacker, but he grabbed her and pulled her to him, spinning her around to get her in a half-nelson, but she thrust her head back hard, smashing it into his nose and forcing him to loosen his grip enough that she could spin around and tap him lightly on the forehead between his eyes. He froze with both hands halfway to his bruised and bleeding face.

Shreya's first attacker took a swing at her, but she calmly raised a hand as if answering to her name called across a crowded room. The guard's arm swung wide. Instead of striking her, his fist connected hard against his second's jaw, the momentum throwing him forward and knocking both of them to the ground.

Agnieszka went on the offensive, thrusting forward to grab her assailant by the throat and claw him with her fingernails as the chamber doors burst open and three guards rushed in, each carrying one of the spotlights that had forced her back in her cell, a fourth guard manning the thick cables that trailed behind them, keeping them untangled. The guards turned on the lights simultaneously and three torrents of Influence swept across the room, burning away the doppelgangers. One of the torrents caught her and broke the concealment spell as it pinned her to the wall. Perkins and his remaining subordinate tried to get to her, but the blast forced them back.

"Stand down!" he shouted, and the force cut out, leaving her clutching the wood paneling, panting.

—*What in mother's name was that!* said Shreya through the link of the Devil's Star.

—*What do we do now?* squealed Eleanor.

—*The buttons,* said Elsie. *I gave her eight of them.*

—*I'm trying them,* said Agnieszka, *but they don't respond. Whatever that was knocked the Craft out of them.*

The link filled with a cacophony of chatter as the ladies talked over each other trying to come up with a new plan to help. Gosha push it to the back of her mind. She needed to focus.

Perkins took the lead, edging toward her past the bodies of incapacitated guards strewn across the floor, the three cannoneers spreading out behind them trying to get a direct shot at her. She dropped into her best fighting stance—fists up and elbows in to protect herself—and wished she had Alfie by her side.

"Give it up, witch," Perkins sneered. "Put your hands behind your head and get on your knees or I'll have these beauties," he cocked his head toward the nearest cannon, "put you in your place."

Above him, a pane of stained glass shattered as a small, heavy object flew through it toward her. She raised a hand and snatched it out of the air.

Her switchblade.

She snapped the blade open and grinned. Now she was in business.

"Aw, you think you're hard do you, witch?" sneered Perkins, dropping into his own fighting crouch. "I'm going to enjoy this."

"Puthut!"

She thrust a hand out at him, throwing her pushback spell at him with all her might, and he flew back, knocking into the cannoneer behind him and sending them both tumbling. The cannon clattered on the ground.

"Pezhvatek."

The room dimmed as the concealment spell wrapped around her and she rolled into a somersault through a gap between the dock and the platform that supported the saint's chairs as the two remaining cannoneers turned on their weapons to blast at the spot where she had just been standing. She ran across the center of the hall and hid behind the covered remains of Griffiths' throne.

"Sweep the chamber!" shouted Perkins as he scrambled to his feet. The cannon beams arced out across the open space.

She ducked down and curled herself up into a ball against a torrent that never came, the mound of fallen canopy massive enough to break up the remaining twin torrents of Influence, though it rattled and groaned under the onslaught until the beams swept past. If they figured out she was there, it wouldn't hold as a shield for long.

The doors were open, but blocked by the two sentries and the man feeding cable to the cannons. There was no way she could slip past them, even concealed, and the cannoneers would surely take her down before she got to them. She needed to take them out if she was to have any chance of escape.

Realizing she might be hiding somewhere around the edges of the room, the cannoneers changed their search pattern to scour every corner. She peeked out from behind her barrier for as long as she dared, got a fix on the nearest cannon and ducked back down, edging around the throne as its beam angled toward her.

She stood, aimed the switchblade at the center of the cannon's lens and spoke the spell that would turn the knife into a projectile weapon of perfect accuracy.

"Pakkat."

The blade hurled from her hand, smashing into the cannon and shattering the glass. The torrent of Influence abruptly stopped, the cannon arcing violently with jagged lightning that shocked the cannoneer and knocked him unconscious.

The room grew brighter, the concealment spell breaking and leaving her vulnerable as the torrent from the one remaining cannon arced toward her.

"Pezhvatek."

She dropped into a sideways roll as the gray muting wrapped around her, hiding her from the guards.

She scrambled to her hands and knees to scuttle across the floor and nearly fell flat on her face as nausea gripped her and her brain twisted inside her skull. Only the lip of the seating platform saved her from the beam. She rolled in tight next to it, stretched out across the floor.

"Rajequist."

The healing spell fizzed through her and perked her up better than a shot of espresso.

"Pezhvatek," she said and hid herself again, rolling out from her bolt hole and scuttling to wedge herself into a corner the beam had just swept past.

The healing spell may be a refreshing tonic, she thought as the concealing spell jolted through her, but she was still casting too many spells. Push it too far and she would find herself passed out on the floor at the mercy of Griffiths' men. She hoped one or two more would be okay.

She locked onto the remaining cannon and pointed her open hand at it.

"Tatlet."

The concealment spell broke, taking with it any calm the healing spell had brought her as the knife handle flew into her grip.

"Pakkat."

The knife hurled itself at the remaining cannon which shattered and sparked, taking out its operator.

"Pezhvatek," she said and took two steps to the left, narrowly missing Perkins as he lunged at where she had just stood in a rugby tackle that would have been devastating had it connected.

She took a deep breath to steady her nausea and staggered to the door. *Just one more spell.*

The pushback spell could knock down the guards covering the door and allow her to get out of the chamber where Elsie, she hoped, could take over the heavy lifting.

She ran toward the doors, stopping far enough away that the projected cone of the spell would catch the two sentries and the guard manning the cables.

"Puthut."

The three men were yanked off their feet and thrust out of the chamber into the hall, the two doors ripping off their hinges and blasting out with them.

The floor lurched hard to the right as her brain protested, sloshing around inside her skull. She didn't dare cast the spell of concealment again lest she faceplant before she even reached the threshold. Hopping over the tangle of cables, she darted for the opening and freedom, only to be knocked off her feet, hurled against a wall and winded by the unstoppable blast of a cannon. The first cannon, she thought, realizing she had assumed that its operator had gone down for the count.

The beam blasted into her, pressing against her chest, making it hard to breathe. When it finally stopped, she had barely enough breath to summon the switchblade to her.

"Tatlet," she whispered, and it leaped into her hand, though she hadn't the strength to do more than clutch it.

"Got you," sneered Perkins as he stooped over her, grabbed her by the collar and pulled her to her feet.

She wrapped her hands around his wrists. There was one last spell she could cast, though she had no idea if it would do what she needed.

"Actalet," she said. "Help me."

The spell ripped through her and, for a moment, she lost consciousness. When she came to a fraction of a second later, Perkins held her still, the sneer wiped from his face, replaced by confusion as he looked around him as if waking from a dream. He released his grip on her collar, slipping a hand around her wrist.

"Stay behind me," he said, pulling her with him toward the ravaged open doorway.

"Sarge?" said the one remaining cannoneer, the only other guard left standing, as he stepped between them and the door. "Sarge, move away from the witch."

Perkins let go of Gosha's hand and rushed the guard, yanking the cannon from his grasp and smashing it on the floor.

"Sarge?" said the guard, still not getting what was going on, though it all became clear when Perkins punched him squarely on the jaw.

Gosha tottered back as the men fought, picking her way over cables and unconscious bodies to edge around them toward the door. She stuck her head through the opening, saw no one except the three guards she had blown out of the chamber, and stepped through.

A woman came out of nowhere. Tall with long legs in high heels and a skirt slit up the side, she smiled broadly at Gosha and beckoned her forward.

"Quickly," said the woman. "We don't have a lot of time."

Gosha hesitated, but at this point she was quite prepared to consider anyone not attempting to kill her on sight to be a friend.

"Give me your hand," said the woman as she took Gosha gently by the elbow and led her toward the stairs.

"Elsie, is that you."

"Of course, dear." The woman smiled and winked. "I told you I'd be outside waiting for you."

She stopped them at the top of the stairs and wrapped a length of copper wire around Gosha's wrist, twisting off the ends.

"There. Now no one will recognize you."

Elsie waved a hand in front of her face and her long, straight hair suddenly became wildly disheveled, her white shirt ripped and smudged.

A dozen guards in their black uniforms, pistols at the ready, rounded a corner and rushed up the stairs toward them.

"Okay," whispered Elsie. "We need to sell this if we're going to make it outside."

She shrieked in terror and clutched at Gosha, cowering from the guns.

"Oh my god," she said, gesticulating up at the gallery. "It's terrible. She would have killed us. You have to help them!"

Most of the guards rushed past them up to the chamber, but two remained behind to see them down the stairs.

"I thought I was going to die," said Elsie, clutching hold of one of the guards as if her life depended on it. "She threatened to turn us into frogs."

"You're safe now," said the guard, peeling her off him. "Wait outside until you get the all-clear."

Their escorts turned and ran back up to join the rest of their squad.

"Not bad, eh?" said Elsie with a grin. "You know I trod the boards a little bit in my youth!"

They stepped out of the main doors to the street unchallenged.

—*Are you out?* said Agnieszka across the Devil's Star.

"Can't talk now," said Elsie through clenched teeth as they crossed the road.

Some forty or fifty men and women stood on the other side of the street huddled together in clusters, staring up at the building. Twenty yards away, the saints stood arguing among themselves, George apart from then, scanning the crowd.

—*We're waiting for you at the end of the street,* said Shreya.

"Let's walk very slowly in that direction," said Elsie under her breath, leading them past the circle of saints. "We're both a little shaky. It's all been a bit much, but we're holding it together. We're just walking off our nerves and getting a breath of fresh air."

George stared hard at them as they walked past him, but he didn't recognize them. They wobbled slowly down the street unchallenged and turned a corner to find Shreya's Volkswagen van idling in wait just out of sight. Gosha realized she had barely taken a breath since they set foot outside the building.

31

SHE STUMBLED AS SHE STEPPED up into the van, her legs watery beneath her, but Eleanor slid forward with open arms to catch her.

"I'm so happy you're safe," she said, hugging Gosha tight. A hint of floral perfume wafted off her skin.

"Come on, girls," said Elsie, standing in the street, still wearing her statuesque glamor. "Spit-spot. The hounds are at our heels."

"We were so worried," said Eleanor as she helped Gosha onto the green and white vinyl bench. Elsie slid in behind her and pulled the doors shut.

"Everyone in?" asked Shreya, looking back from the driver's seat.

—*You've got her?* said Agnieszka across the link.

"She's safe and sound," said Shreya, looking back. "Strap in, please."

—*Lady be praised,* said Agnieszka.

Shreya floored the gas pedal, pushing Gosha back into her seat as the van accelerated with more kick than it would have had fresh off the assembly line.

Gosha began to shiver, a ripple of goosebumps across her skin deepening into spasms that wracked her body.

"Oh, dearest," said Eleanor.

She muttered something that sounded vaguely Italian and a wash of heat warmed Gosha's bones, but it did little to lift her spirits, the relief she felt at being free and among loved ones quickly crushed by the weight of knowing she'd barely escaped. She had struggled against great and mysterious forces before. In the past, her ignorance had given her license to be bold and reckless, had pushed her from one trial to the next as she discovered the extent of her newly awakened potential. Now she'd been at this business of Craft long enough to know her limitations. She had just pushed herself as far as she knew how and it had barely been sufficient, a hideous death averted only because of the intercession of her friends.

Shreya raced them through the crowded streets of London, throwing spells left and right to clear their path.

"Wait," said Gosha, pulling herself up on the bench in front of her to look out the windows. "Where are we going?"

—Your fancy man and fairy doll have proven not to be completely useless, said Agnieszka. *They've found a car big enough for all of us. I daren't go back home in case the rats are still swarming, so I sent them for provisions.*

"Provisions?"

—I traded with Iron Jenny for the name of a witch in Bristol who will shelter us until we can find a boat. I think we should go to Spain or Portugal. I hear it's lovely there. Lots of witches and only a handful of oath-bearers. And good wine. Sounds like heaven to me.

"For god's sake, Mamusha. Why is your first response to trouble always running away? Shreya, stop the van."

—Ignore her, Shreya! The little idiot will have you up to your nethers in vermin before you can twitch your elbows.

Shreya turned onto the embankment to the Thames, slowed her breakneck pace, and pulled to a stop on the curb.

"She has a point, dear," said Elsie as her glamor of a disheveled office-worker shimmered and dissipated, revealing her familiar plump and indefatigable cheerful face. "They put you on trial, and I saw the state you left them in. They're going to be out for blood. It's hard enough being a witch without every saint in the realm screaming for your head."

"I remember the last spate of trials," said Eleanor. "I watched too many of my sisters fall. If the saints have regained the taste of witch blood, we'll all suffer. Think about your little dears. Do you want them to grow up in fear for their mother's life? Or worse, do you want them to grow up without you?"

—Yes, said Agnieszka. If you won't listen to me, listen to her. She's seen it all a hundred times over. I can hear your foolish mind ticking away with plans that will only bring you misery.

Her mother was right. For a moment she'd toyed with the idea of being free of George completely, of starting again somewhere warm, just her and the boys. With Agnieszka, of course. And Alfie and Johnny. And Elsie and Mei and Eleanor and Shreya. But before she knew it, her thoughts had returned to Dougie Barber and Joseph Hobbs, to the scene on the platform at Paddington and the poor, unsuspecting commuters ripped to nothing on their way to work. The Convocation had sent people to investigate, but could she trust them to get the job done? If she ran away now without the certainty that whatever strange force working through the men to create such artifacts of destruction had been stopped, she'd never be able to rest.

Five men had been kidnapped. Adair and his firm had two of the artifacts, hopefully properly neutralized. Did Hobbs have his on him when he went to the station? There could be two more out there unaccounted for. And where were Sir Wilfred and the other men?

"Mei, are you there?" said Gosha. "What's going on?"

—*See,* said Agnieszka. *You see! I was right. You're going to get yourself killed.*

"Mei." Gosha did her best to ignore her mother. "Do you have the acolyte?"

—*Shit,* said Mei. *I'm so sorry. She drove off in a fancy car. I couldn't follow her. I tossed a finding charm at her, but I lost it once she got to Cheyne Heath. If I can get to a kitchen, I'm sure I can find her again.*

Gosha looked at the others watching her silently, waiting for her decision.

"We need to go to Paddington," she said.

Across the link, her mother bellowed with exasperation.

—*Idiot girl! If you won't leave, I'll take the children. I won't see them harmed.*

"I'll leave, Mamusha, but Sir Wilfred's kidnapping has turned into a complete bugger's muddle and I don't trust that lot back there to get the job done—"

The van and the ladies twisted sharply around her and, although the padded bench was a firm support beneath her, she felt herself falling.

"Gosha!" screeched Eleanor. "Elsie, help!"

Gosha's body shook violently, her head knocking against the back of the bench, her limbs sliding on the slick vinyl covering.

—*What's going on?* Agnieszka shouted. *What's happening?*

Blood rushed in Gosha's ears, a gush of white noise that blotted out even the echoes of her mother shouting in her head. The world grew blurry, Shreya's pink and mango van reduced to shifting blobs of color obscured by darker shapes as the witches clustered over her. The spasms increased in violence until she thought her arms and legs would break. Her ribs froze so she couldn't breathe. The rushing in her ears grew and grew, blood pressing into her skull as if it might explode.

And then there was quiet, her body suddenly light and cool as if her fall had finally been broken by a cloud. The misty blur of the van resolved itself so she could see again. She found herself looking down from a great height on a huddle of women, fussing over a figure she didn't recognize.

Is she hurt? she thought, wondering if there was anything she could do as the women made frantic signs with their hands over the figure, muttering to themselves as they placed insignificant objects on her body: buttons and lengths of thread, a playing card and a square of cloth.

A siren blared somewhere behind her and she found herself standing on a street, by a river. Police cars and ambulances rushed past in the fading light of dusk. Smoke filled the air, blowing into her eyes and leaving a bitter taste on her lips. Stunned and dust-covered people drifted past her in groups of two and three, many of them with ripped and tattered clothes, many of them bloody and bruised. She turned toward the direction from whence they came. Thick black clouds billowed up from the end of the embankment where it met the bridge. The road was familiar to her, though something was different. Something was different that shouldn't be, something gone from where it had always been. She set off against the stream of people and vehicles to investigate.

Where the bridge met the street, a barricade had formed: low, interlocking metal fences bolstered by vehicles and uniformed officers who ignored her as she approached and stood at the barrier to see the source of the smoke. A field of rubble stretched out before her. Hills and cliffs of shattered limestone masonry covered the ground. The fractured remains of a tower jutted up from the debris like a broken tooth. At its foot lay the warped and shattered remains of a giant clock face.

She stood amid the chaotic throng, trying to remember what had stood there before, until a keening voice crested in her awareness, a sound she knew well.

That baby's hungry, she thought. *Someone needs to see to the poor little thing.*

It took her a moment in the commotion to locate the direction of the cry which showed no sign of stopping. She wove through the crowd, back the way she came along the embankment, past buildings made of stone and wood until the cry led her to an alley and a cellar door open in the dirt.

As she stood at the top of the steps and peered into the darkness, some vague memory niggled at her consciousness as if to warn her against tunnels that spread into the dark, but the baby's cries grew more and more desperate. She had no choice but to go down.

The cellar was crude, with stone walls, a dirt floor, and a low wood-beamed ceiling. At the center grew a ten-foot ring of toadstools. Thick and dark glistening caps overlapped, turning the ring into a low wall. The dark matter within the ring rustled and shifted, the baby's cries coming from somewhere beneath.

Hello, little one, she said, though no sound came out of her mouth. *Everything's going to be fine. Where's your mother? Did she leave you here?*

Twin pinpricks of red light blinked open beneath the mound of dead leaves and branches within the circle and the crying stopped. She froze under their gaze, her breath coming in short gasps as fear overtook her. Whatever was beneath writhed and thrashed, kicking up a mound of leaves and twigs. As the stench of rot assaulted her, she tried to turn and run, but her legs refused to obey. A figure rose up out of the mulch, towering over her as it spread massive insect wings that filled the cellar, giant mottled sails emblazoned with terrifying amorphous shapes that suggested the denizens of nightmare.

The creature reached out a pair of leathery limbs and wrapped her in its claws, lifting her off her feet. Its head and body obscured by darkness, a lavender tongue snaked toward her, lapping at her face and neck, tasting for something it didn't find. Disappointed, it dropped her into the mulch.

She fell and fell, into the rot and darkness, falling and falling as if she might never come to ground.

She awoke to a hard slap across her face.

"She's awake," screeched Eleanor. "Thank the Lady, she's awake!"

The other witches moved back so Gosha could sit up, though her muscles protested.

"What happened?" she croaked, her throat dry.

"You're spellshocked, my dear," said Elsie from the back bench. "Too many spells in too short a time. We thought we'd lost you."

Her head had begun to clear, and her joints loosened, the passing of her seizure leaving her with little more than a crick in her neck. But something was different. Her second sight was gone. She had no sense of Influence around her. The world was nothing more than metal, vinyl, earth, and air. Placing a hand on her chest, she realized her lipstick was no longer digging into her ribs.

"Where's my talisman?"

"I have it here," said Eleanor, presenting it to Gosha, but Elsie snatched it away.

"No, no. You mustn't. Not for a few hours yet. It could be dangerous. We nearly lost you."

"I need to speak to my mother."

She held out her hand and Elsie grimaced as she gave her the lipstick.

—*Is she awake?* shouted Agnieszka through the Devil's Star as the flow of Influence brushed against Gosha's skin with the hardness of shards of glass. *What's going on? Someone tell me what's going on?*

"I'm fine, Mamusha," she said.

—*If I were there, Goga, I would smack you so hard.*

"Yes, I'm sure you would." To her surprise, Gosha found this comforting. "I'm fine. Really, I'm fine."

—*She has no sense in her. Shreya, bring her here immediately. She can't be trusted on her own.*

"Hush, Mamusha. Can you hear that?" she asked the others.

The crying child, desperate with hunger, still rang in her ears. What had she experienced while she was having her seizure? It wasn't a trip to the Shadowlands, she knew that for certain.

"Excuse me," she said, brushing Eleanor to one side so she could slip out of the van.

On the street, she spun around to get her bearings and saw Big Ben and the Houses of Parliament at the end of the road.

The prophecy, she thought. *I was inside it.*

In the vision, the monster's cry had come from her right, but the buildings across the road had been different. She could see no side street where the cellar and the toadstool ring had been, and turning her head from side to side gave her no sense of what direction the keening came from, making her wonder how much of what she'd seen she could trust.

A long smudge of darkness towered above the buildings, stretching up into the sky. It had an inky substance, writhing and flickering in the afternoon air like a candle flame or a banner of black fabric.

"Do you see that?" she called to the ladies, who joined her on the pavement of Victoria Embankment.

The three witches followed her outstretched arm to see where she was pointing.

"No," said Shreya. "What do you see?"

The flickering smudge had the same quality as her widow's weeds, though now it had leaped from the periphery of her vision out into the world, no doubt thanks to the manipulation of the dragon heads.

I have to find Pauline Sutton, she thought, a pang of worry for Edmund cutting through her concentration.

—*What is it?* screeched Agnieszka. *What does she see? I curse you witches for your uselessness. I would never treat you like this. A pox on each of your heads!*

Big Ben was at Gosha's back, so that meant she was facing northeast. The smudge was to her left, so that meant Paddington. She spun around to face Cheyne Heath. Two columns of smudge snaked up into the sky close together near the border between Cheyne Heath and Kensington where the offices of Wakefield, Waterman, Winston, and Whorl would be. Those must represent the two artifacts Adair had taken. Three more columns of smudge snaked up into the sky further west, deeper into Cheyne Heath. She counted them out on her fingers. Five columns for each of the artifacts, including the two unaccounted for, and a sixth column. What could that be?

"My widow's weeds have changed," she said.

"Changed?" said Shreya.

—That's impossible, said Agnieszka. *Małgorzata, what have you done?*

"What are they showing you?" asked Eleanor.

"I see them there, there, and there, rising up over the skyline."

She pointed out each of the columns.

"That one's Paddington," said Elsie.

"Yes. It's the closest. I need to go there next."

—You cannot be serious, Małgorzata. You are entering the lion's den. Didn't you say the saints sent their men to deal with it? Why are you concerning yourself with this? Let them handle it.

"Mamusha, they don't know what they're facing."

—And you do? What makes you think you're so special?

Gosha thought back to her vision of the terrifying moth-creature in the cellar and shuddered.

"I've agreed to flee with you when all this is finished, Mamusha, but my knees ache and my neck is gripped like a rock," she said, using the traditional opening that indicated she was switching to Witches' Cant. "This may not be my house, but I've been given the keys to the door and there's an unholy stench in the cellar. Who else but a hard-working woman is going to get down on her hands and knees and scrub out the rot? There's rain coming and I need to get on before it drives out the rats."

She glanced up at Big Ben as she awaited her mother's objection, but none came.

"Well," said Elsie. "You can't go alone. Cast one wrong spell and you'll be no good to anyone. You'll be fit for the asylum."

Asylum, thought Gosha, and a knot of irritation she'd been worrying at in the back of her mind since the night before unraveled. *The doctor at the hospital. What was his name? Dropnick, with his strange not-aura like Adair's. He was the one who turned the saints onto her.*

She turned to the columns of smudge above Cheyne Heath. The sixth one she couldn't account for hung over Turncoat's Gate and Banksville Psychiatric Hospital.

There, she thought. *That's where I'll find Sir Wilfred.*

—Um, ladies? said Mei. *Do you think you could come pick me up?*

32

THEY PICKED MEI UP FROM Grosvenor Square where they found her pacing around under the Roosevelt Memorial.

"Good god, what happened to you?" Mei exclaimed upon laying eyes on Gosha in the back of the van being warmed by another of Eleanor's spells. "You look like you were dragged backwards through a privet hedge and dunked in a pond of frogs."

"Oh, leave her alone, dear," said Elsie, closing the door behind her as Shreya screeched away from the curb and shot an evil eye at the security guards around the American embassy who watched the psychedelic-colored van tear past with a worrisome professional interest. "She's spellshocked."

"Spellshocked?" said Mei, slipping into the bench next to Elsie. "Nicely done, girl."

She slipped her fingers into the waistband of her frumpy denim skirt and took out her talisman, a porcelain thimble, and placed it on the seat next to her.

"How cross do you think Agnieszka is?" she said, her connection to the Devil's Star broken now that her talisman was no longer in contact with her bare skin.

Gosha tucked her lipstick into her trouser pocket and Agnieszka's chorus of disapproving tsk-tsks and judgmental grunts cut off.

"She's just grumpy she's not here to lecture us all in person," said Gosha. "She'll be fine."

"Eyes front," said Shreya. "We're nearly there."

She slowed the van as she turned onto Praed Street and approached the entrance to Paddington Station. The driveway to the platforms was blocked off by police stanchions and uniformed officers.

"Station's closed, ma'am," said a young constable as she slowed to a halt.

"What's happened?" she asked.

"Suspicious package. Sorry, ma'am, you can't stop here."

"Thank you, constable," she said as she drove off.

They circled round the perimeter of the station. Every possible entrance was blocked off. Shreya drove them a few streets away and found a parking spot.

"How do we do this?" Shreya turned off the ignition and swiveled in her seat toward the others.

All the witches turned to look at Gosha, making her want to crawl under Elsie's hand-knitted shawl and hide at the sudden attention. She looked up at the column of smudge still staining the sky above Paddington.

"The widow's weeds are still hanging there. I suppose the artifact must be there as well. We should go in and see what the acolytes have done with it. Joel Adair seemed to think his people could manage them."

"Who's that, dear?" asked Elsie.

"He works for Wakefield, Waterman, Winston, and Whorl."

This drew blank faces from the others.

"The Sphere of Fate and Fortune."

Four pairs of eyes grew wide, and four jaws hung open.

"What?" said Gosha.

"My Auntie Isla was asked by them for help once," said Elsie.

"What happened?"

"No idea. She would never tell us. She went off for two weeks without warning and came back with a tan, a taste for cumin, and a collection of the most exquisite bejeweled slippers. From then on, every time she saw an aubergine she'd burst out laughing."

"Yes," said Shreya. "Yes, my grandmother came across one of their minions shortly after she had taken her Betrayal in Agra. Same thing. She disappeared, came back, and was never the same. Couldn't stand India anymore. That's why we ended up coming here."

"Do you all have stories like that?" asked Gosha.

Mei nodded. "My three great aunts were all whisked away by one of them right before the Autumn Harvest Uprising in the twenties. Eleanor, have you ever had dealings with them?"

Eleanor's face flushed bright red.

"Who, me?" she said, entirely unconvincingly, and shook her head vigorously. "No, never. I think I would remember something like that."

Mei narrowed her eyes to slits and opened her mouth to speak, but thought better of it.

"Best pick up your talisman, my dear," said Elsie, who pointed to her ear and mouthed the words "she's getting upset."

—*What's happening?* said Agnieszka in Gosha's head as Gosha slipped her hand into her pocket and pulled out her lipstick. *What am I missing?*

"We're just making a plan," said Gosha. "I think I trust Adair, but that Bishop Worsley must be up to his elbows in this."

"You're right not to trust him," said Eleanor.

"And how do you know that, Eleanor," said Mei. "Did you know him a thousand years ago when you were a nun?"

"Hush, *beta,*" said Shreya, putting a gentle hand on Mei's arm. "Not now."

"If it looks like Adair can get his hands safely on the artifact," said Gosha, "without interference from anyone else, I'll be happy. We can head off to find the remaining two artifacts and get them to him somehow for safe-keeping. If it looks like anyone else is going to get their fingers on them, we need to steal them away."

"How are we going to do that?" said Eleanor.

Gosha looked out the window as a police car drove past, its lights and sirens flickering and blaring.

"I have no idea. I'll have to come up with something."

"Alachrotha," said Elsie, one hand on Gosha's shoulder, the word in her own secret language she used to cast the spell of concealment, and the bright colors of Shreya's van muted. "Let's go."

She entwined her arm around Gosha's and led them toward the entrance to the station as Eleanor, Shreya, and Mei winked out around them. Shreya and Mei were to act as lookouts, each finding a vantage point to give them the lay of the land, while Eleanor and Elsie accompanied Gosha to cast any spells that might be needed.

The vast cathedral that was Paddington Station, normally bustling with travelers and echoing with announcements, was eerie and silent, huddles of policemen and policewomen spread out across the expanse, radiating strategically away from the broad strip of concourse between platforms eight and nine where Gosha had witnessed Joseph Hobbs and his victims die. Gosha slowed as they entered, awed by the great vaulted roof, and jumped when a nearby walkie-talkie squawked through the silence.

Ambient Influence in a place like this would normally be strong and fluid, streaming with current that mirrored the path of the many people passing through, or vibrant with potential during off-peak hours. Now, thin and trembling, it twitched around Gosha even in Elsie's cocoon of protection, leaving her with an acrid taste in her mouth and an unnamed anxiety that tweaked at her chest.

"Lords and Ladies," said Elsie. "What happened in here?"

The scene of the catastrophe had been enclosed in a large tent constructed of metal joists and white plastic tarpaulin. Though the police presence in the station numbered in the hundreds, the space was so vast Elsie and Gosha made their way with ease through the clusters of policemen to the tarpaulin tent where they were forced to stop. No opening presented itself for them to enter through. The single flap on the side of the tent facing the main concourse remained resolutely closed.

—*I'm in position,* said Shreya.

—*Me, too,* Mei chimed in.

—*I approach the tomb,* said Eleanor.

Elsie shot Gosha a worried glance. Eleanor was slipping into her gibberish, a side effect of her advanced age.

"Eleanor, dear," said Elsie, "take one of those pastilles I gave you. They'll do you a power of good."

Elsie had a panoply of herbal concoctions she used to help Eleanor keep her wits together. Without them, she'd quickly become useless to anyone and, in this environment, a danger to herself.

"How on earth do we get in?" asked Gosha.

—*What about a brisk wind,* said Mei and, before anyone could respond, a strong breeze whipped up around Gosha's ankles, growing in strength until it rattled the metal posts of the tent on the polished stone floor. The wind caught and lifted the flap, but not enough that they could slip through.

"Mei, stop it," said Elsie. "You're not helping."

The flap burst open and a dozen people, the task force the Convocation of Saints had sent to take care of the mess, streamed out in a panicked dash, backing away a hundred yards to what they felt was safety.

Mei tittered across the link.

They stood there and watched until Bowie Blades thrust his hands on his hips and stormed back toward the tent.

"Pathetic," he called back to the others as he pulled the flap to one side and ducked in.

The flap fell into place before Gosha and Elsie could get to it, and the sudden, sheepish return of the remaining acolytes forced them to step back from the tent.

—*Someone's coming,* said Mei.

"Where are you both?" asked Gosha.

—*I see him,* said Shreya. *Big man carrying a suitcase and holding something up to his face. I'm at the top of the steps heading to the tube station.*

—*Look up,* said Mei.

High above them, arms wrapped around one of the massive iron girders that supported the roof, stood Mei. She smiled down and waved.

—*Can you see me?*

"For the Lady's sake, be careful," said Elsie.

—*The bird flies so high,* said Eleanor with a giggle. *Never shall it return to earth.*

Elsie kneaded her temples with her free hand.

"Eleanor, dear, perhaps head back to the van and have a nice rest, yes?"

—*I go, I go, faster than an arrow from a tartar's bow.*

—*Shakespeare,* said Shreya. *That's a new one.*

—*Probably an old boyfriend of hers,* said Mei.

Gosha watched the figure approach, a small dot marching across the concourse toward them, growing larger and larger with each step: Joel Adair with his portable phone glued to his ear. A police officer stepped out from his huddle and intercepted him before he reached the platform.

The officer barred his way until he got a squawked message on the walkie-talkie attached to his lapel to let Adair through.

"I know him," said Gosha. "He's the one who hired me."

—*Maybe he can get you in,* said Mei.

"How do we talk to him?"

—*Let me think,* said Shreya.

Adair slowed and frowned as he approached the tent, listening intently to his mobile telephone. He stopped at the flap and looked around, cocking his head to one side as if to listen.

"Are you sure?" he said into the phone and squinted at a point in mid-air three feet to Gosha's left.

"I think he might know we're here," said Gosha. "This happened once before. An acolyte was able to sense my presence while I was concealed."

Adair pulled the flap to one side and launched into a very poor pantomime of having a serious conversation on his phone. He tucked the briefcase under his arm to free up one hand so he could make a slow and surreptitious beckoning wave.

"Come on," said Gosha, pulling Elsie with her through the flap.

"Eleanor, dear," said Elsie. "Did you go back to the van? Don't come in with us."

—*Marbles,* said Eleanor. *A dangerous game, and one I've never cared for.*

"Bugger," said Elsie.

"Will she be all right?"

Elsie shrugged.

"She'll just have to be, won't she."

33

THOUGH THE TENTED ENCLOSURE WAS large, the throng within—each acolyte with their own overpowering aura—made the space feel cramped.

"Lords and Ladies," said Elsie in an awed whisper, even though the concealment spell enclosing them meant no one other than Gosha could hear her. "I've never seen so many acolytes in one place."

She tittered, her bright, staccato laugh colored with anxious tension. Her laughter turned to convulsion and she wretched as if to vomit, placing a hand to her lips to prevent anything from coming out of her mouth.

"Are you okay?" asked Gosha, the pressure of the combined auras pounding against her skull.

Elsie swallowed and nodded.

"Too many auras."

Had anything come out of her mouth and fallen to the floor, the concealment spell would have broken. She slipped from a pocket of her dress a pair of boiled sweets wrapped in twists of wax paper and handed one to Gosha.

"Take this." She unwrapped her own sweet and popped it into her mouth. "It'll help the spellshock."

Gosha did the same and grimaced as a sour and bitter taste spread across her tongue, making her salivary glands spasm and her mouth water. The pressure in her temples eased just a fraction. A tension behind her eyes she hadn't known was there released, bringing tears.

Gosha counted twelve acolyte, as well as Adair and another woman with his same non-aura of concentric, spinning wheels. At the center of the enclosure lay the corpse of Joseph Hobbs, twisted and dessicated into a mummified statue, one arm pulled across its chest in protection, the other outstretched as if to hold its killer at bay, its mouth frozen open in a scream of protest. An oval perimeter had been taped off around the corpse. Along the perimeter, stationed at the corpse's head and feet, and level with his hips, were four low columns that captured the ambient Influence and spun it into a domed shell around the body. Each was made of a hodgepodge of high-tech boxes with winking lights and exposed cogs and gears that could have just as easily been works of art as strange technologies able to manipulate the stuff of sorcery. Within the dome, wings fluttered, a tiny storm of ethereal moths in a cloud over the body.

"Do you see that?" asked Gosha.

Elsie's eyes widened as she took it in and nodded. "I've never seen anything like it."

"It's what killed Terry Kirby's boy. It's coming from something on the body. Adair and I," she nodded toward Adair in whispered consultation with Bowie Blades, "found two more objects like it. And there's another pair of them somewhere in Cheyne Heath."

—*What is it?* asked Shreya.

"Some kind of projection," said Elsie, "like an acolyte's aura, but there's nothing to give it life. Do you know what's powering it?"

"Remember the elixir I took from Vivien Drake? Euphemia Graham's alchemist said something about the effect coming from competing qualities. Does that make any sense?"

—Sounds like High Influence malarkey to me, said Mei. *They've no idea what they're messing with half the time. Bunch of blaggers and con artists. They stumble across something and lie to make it seem like they meant it.*

Adair's associate, a severe-looking white woman in her forties with close-cropped, bright orange hair and giant earrings to match her enormous shoulder pads, stood a foot back from the perimeter with one eye placed to the viewfinder of what appeared to be an elaborate, high-tech video camera, a grid of green and red lights winking on and off on its side, with a microphone embedded in a giant parabolic dish aimed at the dome. She had her own briefcase phone, the case resting on the floor beside her as she held the receiver to her ear and conferred in whispers with someone on the other end.

Adair's associate wasn't the only acolyte inspecting the body. The acolyte of Devotion, a thin man in his early twenties dressed in chic black, his overlaid aura of phantom figures confusing Gosha's second sight, stood at the edge of the perimeter, hands waving and clapping in slow choreography like a multi-limbed Hindu deity playing an elaborate game of patty cake with itself. To his side, an acolyte of Mystery dressed in sensible corduroys and sweater appropriate for a hike across the moors, her aura of shifting veils rustling in a non-existent breeze, surveyed the corpse with an elaborate brass sextant. At the corpse's feet, Bishop Worsley's nun stood glowering in her black robes and white wimple, her hands thrust into the folds of her robes, elbows sticking out to spread the fabric into a pair of bat wings at rest that reminded Gosha of the creature she had seen in the toadstool ring in her vision. A shiver rippled across her skin. The remainder of the acolytes stood with their backs against the tarp, as far away from the body as possible.

Adair pulled back from his conference with Bowie Blades, returned his phone to his ear and looked around the enclosed space. Seeing nothing, he went to his associate.

"Granville, a word?"

He led her to an empty corner of the tent.

"Please give me an update," he said, a little too loudly for the enclosed space. Granville looked at him oddly. "Spare no details, please."

He waved his phone at her and put it to his ear. She did the same with her own. She glanced around frantically as she listened. Gosha rolled her eyes. Subterfuge was neither of their strong suit.

"Of course, Adair," said Granville, also a little too loudly. Bowie Blades looked over with a curious raised eyebrow, but no one else bothered with them, all attention consumed by the corpse. "We arrived to find the police had cordoned off the area in a satisfactory manner. Perkins pulled strings with the Metropolitan Police to allow us to take over the investigation. The body has been successfully isolated by the barriers loaned to us from the Convocation's applications and technology committee, as you see. A vote was taken to empower ourselves, Mystery, Devotion, and Faith to conduct a thorough analysis of the situation."

Both Adair and Granville briefly turned their attention to whoever was speaking to them on their phones.

"It's been a complete clusterfuck," said Granville, leaning in and lowering her voice. "Everyone's claiming it's their turf. Liberation and Surrender nearly came to blows."

"And what results have you come up with so far?" said Adair, frowning and shaking his head sharply to warn her off the topic of politics.

"They're very impressive, aren't they?" said Elsie, riveted by the amateur dramatics.

"Post-mortem emanations are nil," said Granville.

"Unusual," said Adair in a normal tone. He checked his watch. "The incident was only eight hours ago. He was a famous sculptor. He should be giving off trace emanations until at least a week after his obituary's published in the Times. The equipment must be off. Have you recalibrated it?"

"Six times," said Granville. "And this is the second unit I had brought in. The only thing I've been able to detect is an unusual burr in his tertiary field characteristics."

"Tertiary field?" said Adair, rubbing his free hand across his scalp. "What made you think to look there?"

"Something Sister Mary Constance said. I heard her muttering a prayer for the deceased's 'evanescent body.' The girls in research told me it's what that lot call the tertiary field." She leaned in again. "I don't trust her. She keeps pushing to drop containment and physically examine the body, but Bowie Blades keeps shouting her down."

"What are they talking about?" said Elsie. "Can't they see what's happening to that poor man's aura?"

"I don't think they have second sight the way we do," said Gosha.

"Why would she be bothered with his tertiary field?" said Adair. "There's nothing there but the deep unconscious. Can you run a close analysis?"

Granville shook her head. "I don't have those functions enabled. Whoever looks at a person's tertiary field?"

"I'll get the functions cleared for you." He lifted his phone to his lips. "Cherry, put me through to Event Management."

Gosha watched Granville return to her equipment. Something was off about Sister Mary Constance. All the other acolytes looked appropriately worried by the mummified corpse of Joseph Hobbs, while she looked almost gleeful, her green eyes glittering in the glare of the floodlights positioned around the interior of the tent.

"Adair and his people have a way of isolating these artifacts and making them safe," said Gosha. "We need to ensure whatever Joseph Hobbs has on him gets into their hands. Is there any way we can communicate with him?"

—I know a spell to project whispers, said Shreya, *but it requires an unobstructed line of sight.*

"What if one of us acted as a medium?" asked Elsie.

—How would you do that without being seen? asked Mei.

"We can use the link," said Elsie, removing her talisman, a simple hairbrush with stiff bristles and a wooden handle, from the waistband of her skirt where she had it tucked against her bare skin.

She began to sing in a high, reedy voice a song about a woman standing on a bridge lamenting her lost love. Her voice trailed off after the first verse, just as the young woman in the song prepared to throw herself into the river. Gosha's sight clouded and her vision doubled, a faint overlay of the tent from Elsie's perspective mixing in.

—Oof, that's unpleasant, said Mei. *You could have warned me. I nearly fell off my bloody perch.*

Next to Gosha, Elsie stood quietly with wide, unseeing eyes.

—Excellent, said Shreya. *Point her in the direction of this fellow you want to talk to.*

"Elsie," said Gosha. "Are you okay?"

—She won't be able to speak to you while she's channeling, said Shreya. *Point her at your man and tell me what you want to say to him. I need to see his ears.*

Taking care not to break contact and lose the effects of her spell of concealment, Gosha shuffled Elsie around so she could see Adair, the double-exposure shifting as she turned.

"Tell him I'm standing next to him."

—Just talk to him as if he could hear you. It'll be simpler, said Shreya.

"Mr. Adair, it's Gosha Armitage. I'm standing next to you."

Adair flinched, startled, his eyes bulging.

"Joel," said Bowie Blades, coming over to put a hand on his shoulder. "What's the matter?"

"Oh, nothing," he stammered and pressed his receiver against his chest. "Just the partners demanding an update."

He turned away from Blades and covered his mouth to obscure his words as he put the phone back to his ear. Blades returned to watching over the strange gesticulations of the acolyte of Devotion.

"I'm so glad you're okay," said Adair.

"This lot doesn't know about the other objects, do they?" said Gosha.

"No, and we'd like to keep it that way. If Griffiths finds out, he'll demand we hand them over."

"Do you have a plan to secure the artifact?"

"Event Management are standing by with their equipment, but I don't know how to get them in here. If I try to make a play for it, there'll be a fight. If I don't, this lot will stand around bickering forever."

"There are two more artifacts. Send your people to Andrew Mills and Richard Howell's work places."

"Do you know what they should look for?"

"Your guess is as good as mine. Some piece of artwork."

She glanced over at the swarm of fluttering wings hovering over the pelvis of Hobbs' corpse.

"This one must be small. It's in his trouser pocket. Have your people look for the anomaly your partner spotted."

"In his tertiary field?"

"Yes, is that something you can search for?"

It would be so much easier if Gosha or one of the other ladies could do the search, but there wasn't time. The remaining artifacts needed to be secured, and fast, before anyone else was harmed.

"Yes," said Adair. "Let me talk to Event Management."

"Ladies, we need to figure out how to get the artifact away from these acolytes and to Adair's people. Any suggestions?"

—An explosion outside to draw their attention, said Agnieszka.

"Mamusha, you're not helping."

—You can't touch the thing, or it will kill you, yes? said Shreya.

"That's right. It has to be contained in some way."

—If you can wrap it in a piece of cloth or something, said Mei, *I have a spell that will seal the bundle. Nothing will get in or out, not Influence or anything. My aunties used it when we fled China. They had to pack up my grandmother's entire kitchen and keep it from the revolution. Mao's saints would have loved to get their hands on my nai nai's precious goods.*

"Adair, if you can arrange for us to be alone with the body, we can steal the artifact."

"How on earth am I going to do that?"

"I don't know," snapped Gosha, her impatience at how absurdly complex this had all become bubbling to the surface. Why did she have to come up with everything? "This is important to your partners, isn't it? Get them to do something, and quick."

A fluttering in the corner of her eye caught her attention, and she turned back to Joseph Hobbs' corpse. The beating cloud of Influence had surged into a greater frenzy, spreading out across its containment, wings thrusting themselves against the confines of the barrier the acolytes had erected.

"Something's happening," said Gosha. "It looks like the artifact woke up."

Sister Mary Constance noticed it, too, her eyes brightening as she looked to the other acolytes to see their reaction. Her aura shifted, the radiant glow that emanated from her body spreading and dividing into two lobes that shook with slow momentum, a massive pair of beating wings. The change vanished, the wings merging back to the usual beatific glow of her aura as she stepped through the barrier.

"No!" shouted Gosha, reaching to stop her, not realizing she had let go of Elsie.

If she'd broken the spell quietly, it might have taken the assembled acolytes minutes before they noticed her, so focused were they all on the body. As it was, she couldn't have made herself more conspicuous if she'd set off a firecracker in the enclosed space. The acolytes all turned toward her. Only the acolyte of Mystery standing on the far side of the barrier witnessed the sight of the nun lunging for the corpse's trouser pockets. To Gosha's second sight, the noxious aura of beating wings swarmed about her, devouring her own as she pulled from Hobbs' pocket a perfect ball of polished black stone that fit snugly into her palm.

"Sister Mary Constance," exclaimed the acolyte of Mystery, who dropped her sextant and stepped toward the nun, pulling up short at the edge of the barrier.

The acolyte of Mystery's outburst and the sight of the nun in her black robes stooped over the corpse like some ghoulish revenant divided the attention of the group, paralyzing them with one unexpected occurrence too many to process. Bowie Blades recovered first, stepping between Gosha and the rest.

"You shouldn't be here," he hissed.

Bowie's decision had been a good one. Once the others saw she was dealing with the intruder, they turned their attention on Sister Mary Constance, who pulled herself up, face beaming with triumph, and held the stone before her.

"For the glory of the Lord," she said, but her joy quickly turned as the beating wings that consumed her aura darkened, becoming effervescent twists of corruption that spread around her body, an effect Gosha had seen before. The nun's death would be quick to follow.

"What's she doing?" said Perkins. "Sister Mary Constance, put that thing down!" He turned to the acolyte of Abundance at his side, a middle-aged woman in a coordinated dusty blue-gray business suit, the thick vines of her aura coiled around her limbs. "Do you sense that? Her emanations are disrupted."

The nun's skin began to darken, to become wrinkled and cracked like the body at her feet as her entire aura became a cloud of tiny fluttering wings that spread out to fill the barrier around Joseph Hobbs' body. She spoke again, but the words came out garbled, her voice cracking.

"Stupid woman," said the acolyte of Abundance. "What would have possessed her to do that? Is she safe in there?"

"The barrier will contain her," said the acolyte of Mystery at the nun's side, the swarm cloud beating at the invisible wall that separated them.

As if to spite the young woman, the nun reached through the barrier, grabbed her by the throat and pulled her close, knocking down the nearest protective column. The barrier failed. The bubble that contained the noxious aura burst and the swarm expanded into the tent, though none of the others noticed the buzzing around them. The acolyte of Mystery clutched at the nun's hand at her throat, pulling at her fingers to free herself, but to no avail. Before anyone could move to help, the swarming wings entangled themselves in the graceful veils of the acolyte of Mystery's aura, consuming them. The acolyte was quick to die, her body drying up and crumbling in the nun's grip.

The nun turned on the acolyte of Devotion, seizing him by the arm and pulling him into her embrace.

"Jarvis!" cried Bowie as he leaped forward to stop her.

The radiant glow of the nun's aura was gone, but in its place coalesced a phantom form, part human, part twisted creature, as if she were both herself and this other thing, this other thing that Gosha recognized from the dark cellar in her vision of the Houses of Parliament's destruction. Jarvis, the acolyte of Devotion, resisted with all his limbs, both real and ethereal, but his aura was quickly consumed, his body reduced to a husk.

Bowie screamed with outrage and thrust out a hand. Lighting lashed out from his circling comet, striking the corrupted nun, real-world light refracting around her from the intensity of the blast, but Sister Mary Constance and her monstrous aura opened their arms as if to embrace it. Perkins and the acolyte of Abundance at his side launched their own attacks, Perkins' aura splintering into spinning scythes as it burst from his fingers, the vines of the acolyte of Abundance swiping out in thick whips. The power surged at Sister Mary Constance and all it did was feed her, her aura of beating wings growing thicker, the monster growing more defined, with limbs half human, half insectoid.

"Stop," said Gosha, putting a hand on Bowie's arm. "You're making it stronger."

He dropped his arm, and the lightning vanished.

"Can you make them stop?" Gosha pointed at Perkins and his companion.

"Perkins," cried Bowie to get his attention, but he and the acolyte of Abundance were too absorbed by the surge of power flowing through them.

Bowie swept his hands in front of him as if clearing crumbs off a tablecloth, and a wavefront of ruddy Influence rolled off him, knocking Perkins and the acolyte of Abundance off their feet and throwing them into the tarpaulin. The entire tent shuddered on its frame.

Sister Mary Constance stepped over the body and knocked over Granville's tripod to get to her. Granville stumbled, and the nun was on her, digging her fingers into the woman's neck. Granville lasted only a fraction of a second, her faux-aura of concentric circles ripped from her. Her small and simple aura was quickly sucked away.

"It's eating your auras," Gosha shouted so all the acolytes could hear. "Get away from it! Get out of here!"

Bowie didn't need a second hint. Grabbing hold of the back of Adair and the acolyte of Liberation's jackets, he dragged them out through the flap. Elsie stood unmoving, her gaze still distant as she continued to channel what she was seeing across the link of the Devil's Star.

"Elsie," shouted Gosha as she shook the diminutive witch, snapping her out of the trance. "Go! Go now!"

She spun her around and pushed her toward the flap. Glancing back, Gosha saw Perkins and the acolyte of Abundance get to their feet as the auras of the remaining acolytes, of Introspection and Surrender, spontaneously exploded into beating wings without the nun being anywhere near them. Perkins and his compatriot watched in horror as the two men turned into mummified corpses before their eyes.

They turned and fled through the flap leaving Gosha alone with Sister Mary Constance and the creature that rode her.

—*I'm coming down,* shouted Mei.

A loud thud reverberated across the roof of the tent as a large object struck it from above, bringing down its aluminum frame. The ungiving sheet pressed down on Gosha for only a second before tenting up around the flow of wing-tainted Influence that emanated from the nun.

—*Get out of there so I can seal it in,* said Mei, her voice doubling up in Gosha's ears, at once clear through the link and muffled by the tarp.

Sister Mary Constance leaped at Gosha, flowing through what little space there was between them without her feet touching the ground. She landed on Gosha's chest, knocking her down, and wrapped one hand around Gosha's throat while she pressed her face down with the other. Tiny wings fluttered around Gosha, her exposed skin tingling.

The nun released her and turned toward the edge of the tarp.

Just like in my vision, thought Gosha. *No aura to feed on and it loses interest.*

She rolled over to get her feet beneath her and launched herself at Sister Mary Constance, bringing her down before the nun could reach the flap. The nun elbowed Gosha in the face and twisted, throwing Gosha off her back. Before Gosha could pull herself up, Sister Mary Constance dropped down on her and wrapped her dessicated, bony fingers around Gosha's throat, cutting off her windpipe. The ghostly face of the monster looked down at her, superimposed over the nun's rapidly deteriorating features.

At her healthiest, the nun would have been a fraction of Gosha's weight. Now, with the creature ravaging her body, she was little more than a bundle of twigs. Gosha swatted her away effortlessly with a maneuver Alfie had shown her for situations just like this. The nun rolled across the floor, but was up on her feet in a flash.

—*Gosha,* screamed Mei. *I can't do anything while you're in there. The rats are moving in.*

—*I'll handle them,* said Elsie.

A low rumble spread across the platform under Gosha's feet. Shouts of surprise came from beyond the tent.

Sister Mary Constance roared with frustration as Gosha placed herself between the nun and the flapping opening of the mangled tarp. She jumped and flew through the air at Gosha, her feet inches from the ground.

"Puthut," said Gosha without thinking to cast her push spell, and immediately regretted it. Her eyes crossed, and the world spun around her, throwing her to the floor, the force of the spell dissipating among the beating wings of Sister Mary Constance's aura.

By now, the nun's face suspended above Gosha resembled a monster from one of Edmund's comics, her eyes large above brittle cheekbones and sunken cheeks. Her gums had receded back to the bone, turning her teeth into sharp blades, her tongue a long, writhing spike in the fetid cavity of her mouth. More interested in breaking free to search for auras to consume, Sister Mary Constance made to leapfrog over Gosha's supine body, but Gosha grabbed her and pulled her down, scrabbling for the flap herself. It didn't take much to get ahead of the nun, her body growing more and more frail with each passing second. A good kick to the head pushed her far enough away that Gosha could crawl out of the flap and hold it shut to prevent the nun from getting out.

"Cast the spell," she shouted to Mei, Shreya at Mei's side.

"You wrap," Mei said to Shreya. "I'll seal."

Shreya tapped the index finger of her right hand on the webbing between forefinger and thumb of her left three times as she muttered something that sounded vaguely Hindi. The edges of the flap yanked out of Gosha's hands and fused together. The lower border of the tarp curled under, wrapping itself into a long tube like an enormous rolled cigarette with Sister Mary Constance trapped inside, flailing against the plastic. Mei clapped her palms together softly as she sang a quiet chant and Sister Mary Constance ceased her struggling.

"There," said Mei. "Safe as trees."

34

GOSHA HUNCHED OVER TO CATCH her breath, her eyes widening at the sight of the chaos on the platform. Elsie stood a few feet away with one shoe tucked under her arm and picked odds and ends out of her palm: bits of fluff and string, buttons and copper pennies. She tossed them in the air and muttered spells that caused the stuff to disintegrate and launch their stored-up Influence at the wall of acolytes and police officers rushing toward them. Great gusts of wind whipped all manner of rubbish and grit into spinning dust devils that created a wall of confusion that none of them could push through.

"Dears," shouted Elsie, half-turning her head back to Gosha, Mei, and Shreya. "I'm running out of materials."

"Stop, Elsie," said Gosha. "It's done. Mei wrapped the creature up."

The dust devils blew themselves apart into nothing and all the trash tumbled to the ground as Elsie dropped her shoe.

"Thank the Lady," said Elsie and slipped the shoe back on.

"Did you get the others?" Gosha said to Adair as the surviving acolytes approached, a squad of police officers edging their way cautiously up the platform toward them.

"My people are on their way," he said, looking down at the long roll of tarpaulin.

"Others," said Perkins, his eyebrows hitched up high at the news. "This is outrageous. You knew of more of these things and you kept it to yourself? This goes against every article of the Convocation."

Adair was unimpressed by Perkins' bluster. "The Convocation's proved many times over it can't be trusted to do a good job in situations like these."

"But what about us," said Bowie, the acolyte of Liberation at his side in her wrap skirt and hooped earrings, both looking just as put out as Perkins. "We have agreements for the free exchange of information between us."

"I'm so sorry. The partners wanted it kept secret."

Adair seemed genuine in his contrition.

"This is why none of us fully trust you," said Bowie. "You think having no saint and having direct access to your Lords and Ladies puts you above the rest of us, when, in fact, it means you're vulnerable to their every capricious whim."

"I assure you," said Adair, palms up to placate them. "It's nothing like that."

"I'm with Adair," said Gosha. "What happened in there makes it clear Lord Griffiths and Bishop Worsley were involved in some way. None of this would have happened if their task force hadn't arrested Sir Wilfred, Joseph Hobbs, and the others

Perkins gave her a long look.

"Officers," he called out to the ring of policemen that had reached them. "These women are terrorists. Arrest them."

The officers, finally given something to do, perked up at the order and pushed passed the acolytes toward the witches. Mei grabbed Shreya and Gosha by the hand.

"Get Elsie," she said, and muttered something that might have been Mandarin as Gosha wrapped her fingers around Elsie's palm.

The echoes of the station muted, all the colors shifting toward gray as the concealment spell enveloped them all.

"Run," said Mei, pulling them toward the wide staircase that lead up to the tube station.

"Seal the area!" shouted Perkins. "I want them found."

Mei's instinct to cut and run under the cover of Craft had been good, but running four abreast up the stairs holding hands would have been a disaster had it not been for the concealment spell and the slow-moving policemen wrestling with the unlikely sight of four ordinary-looking women being hailed as terrorists and then suddenly disappearing. Gosha was the fittest of them by far and Mei, surprisingly, the least. Without the other three holding her back Gosha would have been out of the station and onto the street without a second look behind her. To their great fortune, the tube station was empty, the whole area already cordoned off by the police, so no one saw them as they broke the concealment spell to clamber over the turnstiles and make their way through the empty tube platforms to the street exit.

They came out on the far side of the station, halfway to Royal Oak and a ten-minute walk from Shreya's van, having concealed themselves individually, Elsie once again taking Gosha with her in her shell of seclusion. Agnieszka began to badger them for updates, asking questions to fill in the blanks that she hadn't been able to glean from what she heard across the Devil's Star.

The police were everywhere: roadblocks at every intersection and helicopters buzzing in the sky above them. As they turned onto Praed Street, a caravan of three black, unmarked vans with large, circular wire antennae on the roof approached. A static charge pressed against Gosha's skin as the vans drove past, her stomach turning and every inch of skin on her body spasming. Elsie stopped in her tracks, feeling it too.

"Oh, I don't like that," she said. "I don't like that at all."

—*There's more coming,* said Shreya. *No time to dally, ladies.*

Sure enough, just as the trio of vans turned a corner and disappeared from sight, another group turned onto their street.

"Can they tell where we are?" said Gosha as they started off once more at a good clip.

—*Who knows,* said Shreya, *but that antenna was doing bad things to my gunas. Let's not risk it, shall we?*

It quickly became obvious the police could tell where the witches were as three of the helicopters hovering over Paddington broke formation and headed in their direction.

—*Bugger,* said Mei. *Run!*

They made it the two blocks to Shreya's Volkswagen without passing another black van, but as they piled in, breaking their concealment spells, the helicopters repositioned themselves directly above them. A procession of five vans turned onto the street, heading their way.

"Mei," said Shreya from the driver's seat. "Will the spell you used on that creature work on the van?"

"Oh yes," she said, as bright and carefree as if she had been asked if she knew how to make a pot of tea. "Nothing in, nothing out. No light, no air, no Influence, nothing."

"But will we be able to get out again."

"Of course," said Mei. She frowned, opened her mouth as if to speak and closed it again.

"Mei," Shreya chided, one eye on the approaching vans.

"Well, probably. A few of nai nai's crates we couldn't get open and had to bury in the garden."

"How many crates exactly?" said Shreya, the black vans with their looming antennae only five car lengths away.

"Four."

"Out of how many?"

"Eight."

"Mother preserve us," said Shreya.

"Just do it," said Gosha. "A fifty-fifty chance is better than what we'll have without it."

Mei kissed the porcelain thimble on the tip of her index finger and muttered a word. The windows turned black, plunging the interior of the Volkswagen into darkness.

"Mei!" shouted Shreya.

"I said nothing in or out," she protested.

Shreya turned on the interior light, a single weak glow from the roof revealing four unhappy faces.

"Best not speak much," said Mei. "We don't know how long before we run out of air."

"How will we know when it's safe?" said Gosha.

Mei shrugged.

They sat in silence for what seemed like an eternity, the only marker that time was passing the increasing heat in the cramped space, the air growing heavier with each breath. Gosha's mind replayed the events of the last twenty-four hours over and over again in a loop, every poor decision she had made, all of which had led them here, churning in her gut. Not only had she ruined her own life, she had ruined everyone else's as well.

"I can't breathe," gasped Elsie.

"We can't leave trying to get out until the last minute," said Shreya. "If Mei can't break the spell and we're already half-dead, we're buggered. Go on. Try it."

Mei muttered a word and nothing happened. She tried another, and a third.

"There's only a tiny bit of Influence left in here," said Mei. "I used most of it to seal us up in the first place."

"So you can't get us out," snapped Gosha.

"I can. I just need the right word."

Gosha began to feel woozy. Elsie next to her looked ashen, her face drenched in sweat.

"I know, I know!" said Mei and muttered again.

Light flooded into the van. With her last ounce of strength, Gosha pushed the door open and staggered out into the fresh air, the others close on her heels. The street was empty, the vans and helicopters gone. The spell had worked.

"Oh my goodness gracious," said Elsie in a sudden panic. "Where's Eleanor? We've forgotten Eleanor!"

"I'm right here," said a voice behind them and they all jumped.

"What a lovely nap," said Eleanor with a yawn as she sat up on the back seat of the van. "I feel like myself again. What's been going on?"

35

GOSHA LOOKED UP AT THE evening sky. A golden glow to the west faded into dusk, the evening star bright against a backdrop of deepening blue. The plumes of churning, flickering widow's weeds towering above Cheyne Heath winked out one by one, leaving only the one above Banksville Hospital. It called to her, pulling at her, demanding her attention like a screaming child.

"Come," said Elsie, placing a gentle hand on her shoulder as they piled back into the van. "We need to move."

Yes, they did need to move, all of them.

"They've seen you now," said Gosha. "They know who you are. Not you, Eleanor. You're safe, but how long until they find out who the rest of you are?"

"Hearts are blue," said Eleanor from the back seat as Shreya pulled away from the curb. "Only the king in his bunker can push the saplings to the surface."

Elsie shuffled closer to her on the luminous pink vinyl and passed her a boiled sweet.

"Take this, dear."

Eleanor undid the wrapper, popped the sweet into her mouth and intertwined her arm with Elsie's as she laid her head on her shoulder. Elsie patted Eleanor's knee absently and kissed her hair as she gazed off into the middle distance, her eyes unfocused.

They all sat like that, in tense silence, alone with themselves as Shreya drove them away.

"Where are we going?" said Shreya after ten long minutes weaving through traffic to avoid police roadblocks, making her way west.

"I think you should all go with my mother and the boys," said Gosha. "Flee to Bristol and out of the country."

None of them protested.

"I'll stay. I have to." Behind her eyes, smoke poured out of the crater where the Houses of Parliament should have been. "That thing on the platform is connected to the omen. I saw what's going to happen. Hundreds of people will die. It's like Joel Adair said. If Lord Griffiths and Bishop Worsley are in on it, we can't trust the Convocation to do the right thing. Whatever's going on in is centered at Banksville Hospital. I need to go there."

Across the link, Agnieszka grunted her disgust.

—Just like your father.

"If I can stop what's happening, perhaps I can broker a deal with the Convocation so that you can all come back. I could hand myself over to George. He'd love that."

Shreya slowed when she reached Bayswater, and turned onto a side street off Notting Hill Gate.

"If we're going to my house, we should part ways here," she said as she pulled into a parking spot.

"I'm so sorry," said Gosha, her eyes welling up with tears as she hunched over, a long, protracted sob wringing her out. "I've ruined everything for you."

Elsie and Mei were suddenly at her side wrapping her in their arms and hugging her tight.

"Oh, no, no, no," cooed Elsie. "This wasn't you. You didn't do this."

"She's right," said Mei. "This was all happening anyway. Think how much worse it would have been if you hadn't been there. I've seen firsthand what happens when history rolls over and smothers everyone in its bedclothes. Some things you can't stop. You just have to do your best to help save as many people from suffering as possible."

"The Inquisition comes for us all, eventually," said Shreya from the driving seat. "It's part of what it means to be a witch."

"Gosha," said Eleanor, moving to kneel on the front bench and lean over so she could take Gosha's hands into her own. "Jackfruit."

She said it as if Gosha would know exactly what she meant.

"And columbine. And tenterhooks."

Gosha wiped her eyes and smiled.

"You should probably take her with you," she said.

"Yes," said Elsie. "I think that would be best."

"Five spells and five spells only." Elsie's voice echoed in Gosha's ears as she watched the hospital from around the corner. "Even five could be too many. And certainly nothing big, or you'll find yourself flat on your back again, and I won't be there to help you."

Gosha removed her telling deck from its pouch and took out the three aces Elsie had told her would help calm the spellshock: buttons, needles, and brushes. As she fanned them out and looked at them, her nerves settled, and the nausea that had been nipping away at the edge of her consciousness grew a little less insistent. She slipped them into the breast pocket of her jacket in case she needed them in a hurry.

Elsie had given her permission to use the deck to cast spells, though it was an awkward process made worse by her lack of practice and the fact that her deck was missing an entire suit of cards. The aces were the only minor cards she understood anyway, so she separated out the major arcana and the remaining Ace of Cups, put the rest back in their pouch, and tucked them away in her inside pocket. The contents of her field kit were useless, denatured somewhere along the way. The usable telling cards she put in one of her front pockets, her switchblade in the other, its weight giving her comfort.

The Devil's Star was still active, though the ladies didn't say much as they made preparations to flee to Bristol.

She wished Alfie were here.

As the streetlights turned on, Banksville Psychiatric Hospital sprung from the twilight gloom like a ghoul leaping from a cupboard to shock its victim into cardiac arrest. Stark shadows thrown by the pale sodium light turned eaves into darkened brows hiding the sightless eyes of its barred windows. The faux portcullis above the main doors became teeth over a giant maw.

In the half hour she'd spent watching from her vantage point and contemplating her next move, no one had come in or out of the front of the building. Lights inside had turned on and off, windows on the upper of the three stories staying mostly lit, only one or two windows on the second and ground floors showing evidence of habitation. Priorities jostled for dominance in her mind. She had no idea what she was walking into and needed to sort that out quick. She needed to find Sir Wilfred and the other two men and get them out, possibly to Adair and his people who could take care of them. How to manage that was a problem for later. If she could have used spells with her usual abandon, she would have cast a finding for a way in, an unlocking to get her in there, and a hiding so she could explore, unseen. Elsie's admonition to only cast five spells made her realize how dependent she'd become on them.

She did her best to approximate the spell commands she wanted using the cards from her telling deck. Elsie had shown her how to project a tiny amount of Influence through the cards she chose to test the combination's effects, a process that quickly became instinctive for Gosha, as easy as checking her watch to tell the time, but the entire procedure was fiddly and took time. She had to hold the cards so she could see them as she cast the spell, and would need to keep them available in case she felt the effects of the spell falter. Finding combinations took time. She made herself groupings for hiding, finding, and unlocking, and a few others, and put them in her trouser pockets, wishing she had her photographer's utility vest with her, with its multiple compartments.

Time to go, she thought, and pulled out the cards she'd chosen for her finding spell: the Known, the Unknown, and the Ace of Needles. For a finding spell it was clumsy and inelegant, like pulling out the contents of every drawer in the house to find a single pair of socks, but she lacked the time and the skill to do better. Squatting, she placed the Known card on the pavement and turned it to match the orientation of the hospital. The Unknown and the Ace of Needles she held in front of her as she touched the lump under her clothes at her breastbone where her lipstick pressed against her skin. She'd been wearing the same clothes for more than a day now, and the fabric felt stale against her skin.

She imagined herself opening a door and stepping into an empty hospital corridor as she gently nudged Influence toward the cards. She felt a twinge of nausea flutter deep inside her, but it was as if the spell was happening around her, not channeling through her in the way evoked by a spell word, and the nausea dissolved. At first nothing happened, but after a minute, a short, sharp gust of wind came from Gosha's right and blew the card over onto its face.

A door on the west side of the building, she thought, interpreting the effects of the finding.

The combination for her concealing spell was a touch more elegant: the Ace of Needles, the Unknown, and the Unseen. The coolness of the evening air dissipated as the spell took hold, the colors around her changing little as so much had been leached out of them already by the street lights. She found the door, an innocuous-looking security door with a small wired glass window. Above it, a boxy security camera pointed down to cover the entrance.

Dammit, she thought. The second she cast her unlocking spell, she'd be seen.

She pulled out her cards and shuffled through them for a series of images that might disable the camera and nearly dropped the concealment spell by accident, the cloud of Influence around her beginning to dissipate as she lost concentration, drawn in by the pictures on the cards. An image of a broken wine glass, its contents spilled over the table, caught her eye.

Good enough.

She took the Ace of Needles from the trio forming the concealment spell and held it up with the image of the broken glass beneath the camera so she could see both at the same time, and willed Influence through them at the device. The glass over the opening of the protective box that covered the camera shattered. The wires feeding into it sparked and smoked.

The combination for her unlocking spell was a picture of a large iron key, a majestic wooden door she'd come across at the Tate in Trafalgar Square, and a shot of Timothy emerging from a crawlspace under the basement stairs. The lock clunked heavily, and the doorknob turned in her hand.

Of course, there was another camera covering the inside of the door. She swore copiously under her breath, something filthy she'd once heard one of Alfie's bouncer friends say, as she fumbled through her cards to put back together her camera-breaking trio.

The camera shattered and sparked as she recomposed the set of cards that would hide her. When the concealment spell had enveloped her once again, she skimmed down the corridor and pressed herself into a corner in case her luck had been bad and someone had been looking at the security cameras before she'd broken them, but after five minutes nobody came. She listened as she bided her time, wondering how the others were faring, but the Devil's Star was silent.

She pushed herself out of the corner, the unnaturally turgid flow of Influence lumbering through the corridors suffocating her, and peered down the hall. Institutional walls and doors stretched out around her: linoleum floors and whitewashed walls glowing under the fluorescent lights, doors labeled only with numbers etched on the walls in black vinyl Helvetica digits in a generic labyrinth devoid of personality. Around a corner and three steps beyond and she had already lost her sense of direction.

A custodian in dingy whites shuffled down the corridor toward her pushing a wheeled cart covered in stacks of files, his back rounded and head drooping in late shift apathy. He looked like he might be going somewhere important, albeit slowly, thought Gosha, and decided to follow him until she was able to get a better sense of the layout. He led her around an endless succession of corners, numbers on the doors growing larger, then smaller, shifting from three-digit codes to number and letter combinations and back again. The source of his sagging apathy became apparent. The atmosphere in the building was dense and oppressive, the ennui of the decor inducing soporific submission. She wondered if it was an intentional choice, a way of calming the frayed nervous systems of the patients, and if the treacle-slow torpor of the ambient Influence was merely a side effect.

Just as she felt her spirits sag and thought she might never see color again, the custodian turned a corner and led her to a suite of offices. A nurse's station with a low counter stood in front of a large records room and a handful of other offices. Two nurses sat at the station, one reading a pulpy novel, the other thumbing through a dog-eared copy of Vogue. Neither bothered to look up as the custodian squeaked past them to deliver his load to the records room.

Security cameras pointed everywhere. If she could find the security office, the camera feeds would give her a great sense of where everything was and where she might find Sir Wilfred and the others. When a cursory glance around the nurse's station yielded nothing concrete she could use, she retraced her steps, following the cameras, until she found what she hoped was a blind spot in their coverage.

Shuffling through her cards, she selected the finding combo and took the Ace of Needles from her concealing trio. The spell that cloaked her broke and the ascetic walls grew brighter as she concentrated on the finding combo, pictured a wall of security monitors, and gently pushed Influence toward the cards. Thick and inert, the ambient Influence refused to cooperate. She pushed harder, bearing down on it with her will. It moved sluggishly, but move it did, and the finding spell released into the atmosphere. The strip of fluorescents in the corridor to her right flickered in sequence away from her in an invitation to follow.

She released her control, and a wave of pressure built up inside her skull, forcing her back against the wall as stars sparkled before her eyes. It faded quickly, leaving a dull ache. Elsie obviously hadn't accounted for the bizarre atmosphere in here when she gave Gosha carte blanche to cast spells with her deck. Gosha reassembled her hiding sequence. The spell affected her and her alone, and hadn't required so much force, but now that her spellshock had been triggered, even the thought of casting it caused the ache in the base of her skull to throb. It was late, and there were so few people around. Gosha decided to risk proceeding without cover.

The flickering fluorescents led her on a twisting trail. By the time they came to a halt, in a part of the building clearly marked for maintenance by the blue-gray color of the walls, Gosha had lost all sense of direction. The building couldn't possibly be as large as her passage through the labyrinth of corridors suggested. She wondered if her disorientation were a result of the spellshock, the peculiar Influence, or a combination of both.

If there was a guard inside, she'd need to cast her hiding spell. If not, and the door was locked, she'd need an unlocking spell. Either way, there would have to be Craft involved. She prepared her hiding cards, knocked sharply on the door and took a step back, cards held before her.

"Come in," a man's voice called from behind the door.

She knocked again.

"Door's open," he said.

She knocked a third time.

"For fuck's sake, Jeffries," said the man.

The doorknob turned and Gosha cast her hiding spell before the door opened. A security guard dressed in a matching gray shirt and trousers with a truncheon hanging from a large leather belt stuck his head through the doorway.

"Jeffries?" he called, stepping out into the corridor. "Did you check the side door?"

Gosha slipped into the room and slid out of the way as he closed the door behind him.

"Idiot bastard," said the security guard and sat at a desk before a dozen television monitors bolted into the wall, each monitor cycling through the feeds of three or four cameras. The cycles of the screens were out of sync with each other by a few seconds, creating the visual equivalent of a deafening cacophony to Gosha's spellshock-addled eyes.

The guard crossed an ankle on one knee and unfolded a copy of the Sun.

The screens mostly covered common areas of the facility. Gosha recognized the entryway and the receptionist's desk, shown from three different angles. Two feeds, presumably from the cameras she'd disabled, were black. The right-hand column of screens showed the insides of patients' cells, grim and austere boxes with little more than a bed and side table in them. The patients either lay catatonic on their beds or stood listless, staring into the middle distance.

With so many screens showing so many images, Gosha couldn't take them all in at once, and was forced instead to spend long minutes watching each screen until it cycled through all its feeds. The office was unventilated, the atmosphere stifling from the combination of lack of air, their two bodies and all the electronic equipment generating heat, and the dense Influence that threatened to congeal around her and encase her in amber. Her mind wandered, and the second it did she felt her hold on the concealing spell falter. The guard looked up from his topless glamor models and glanced around as she lifted her three spell cards so she could see them.

"Shit," she swore as the Ace of Needles slipped from her fingers and fell face down on the floor.

"Strewth!" said the guard, dropping his paper and looming over her as she crouched to retrieve the card. "You shouldn't be out of your room."

He reached down to grab her.

"Falethta," she said without thinking, reaching out to touch his arm.

His eyes rolled back, his lids drooping, and he sank to the floor, asleep. Gosha's brain twisted in her skull and the room lurched around her, forcing her down next to him. She lay there, panting, as the floor took its time to right itself, several score breaths passing before she could clamber to her feet and turn the lock on the door. She sank into the guard's chair.

On one of the screens appeared a figure she recognized. Bishop Worsley stepped out of an office into a corridor accompanied by his black-clad acolyte with too much jewelry and the little doctor who had called the Bishop to warn him she had been asking questions. What was his name? The Bishop looked pleased as he talked to the doctor who bobbed obsequiously and gestured for the Bishop to follow. They walked out of frame and Gosha looked frantically from monitor to monitor until she found them again chatting amiably as they wandered down the corridor.

She followed them across screen after screen until the doctor led them through a security door and up a flight of stairs.

“No, no, no,” she moaned, looking frantically from monitor to monitor, but they didn’t re-emerge on any of the other screens.

“Dammit.”

She smashed her fist down on the table, spilling the sleeping guard’s coffee.

As the dark liquid spread across the newsprint of his paper, the black stain of widow’s weeds blotted out her vision. She felt herself falling.

36

SHE LOOKED DOWN AT A wrinkled and calloused hand wielding a thin paintbrush with the delicacy of a surgeon. The brush traced a line of brownish purple across a tiny painting of a ghostly figure standing before a poster on a brick wall. Rendered in amazing detail for something so small, Gosha could see every smudge and tear, every bubble where the paper pulled away from the wall. The brush drew strange symbols on the poster, the same arcane alphabet she'd seen used by saints and acolytes, in a dense script. Gosha couldn't read the words, but the meaning was somehow clear: it was a summons. The cold and queasy weight of dread gurgled in the pit of her stomach.

Bright light shone down from above over the large table at which the person whose eyes she was looking through was working. She reached out to put the brush down and select another, the vision giving her the illusion of agency, though as much as she wanted to raise her head and look around, she wasn't in control here. Softening her gaze, she opened herself to the periphery of her perception. Two others sat around the worktable, each laboring over their own tiny image. To her left sat Andrew Mills, his furrowed brow chasing his receding hairline across his scalp, the tip of his tongue poking out between his lips as he drew careful strokes with a gold-nibbed ink pen. To her right, Richard Howell made angry marks with pastel sticks on his miniature. Around them on the table were spread boxes, trays and jars of every kind of art supply. Had the men's faces not been so deeply marked by the intensity of their concentration, she might have thought herself observing an art class or therapy session.

Scattered around the table were the results of the men's work: chips of card covered with images. Gosha recognized immediately what they were doing. They were creating a telling deck, although the images were all strange and unsettling. She had seen the decks her mother and the ladies had fashioned. Even though each was as distinctive and individualistic as the women themselves, the images on the cards all had similarities. Even Gosha's incomplete deck, cobbled together from a thousand different sources, followed the same rules. Any card from any telling deck would be recognizable for what it was. These cards were downright peculiar, depicting disturbing scenes, moments of savage beauty captured and frozen by ink and pigment. Many cards from a witch's telling deck depicted the shadow and darkness of life, but all were balanced out by images of wonder and joy. Every image Gosha could see from the corners of her eyes depicted a world of anger, violence, and dread.

It took a moment for Gosha's second sight to resolve in this new perspective, but as her awareness of Influence seeped through the link the dragon heads had forged for her out of her widow's weeds, the emerging cloud of beating wings that covered the table filled her with horror. The seething mass hovered in clumps over the cards and art supplies and flickered out over Andrew and Richard, feeding off the thick waves of Influence that flowed off them, growing larger, brighter, taking on more distinctly the shape of moths.

"And here," came a voice from the darkness that surrounded the table, "is the workroom where our talented artists toil at their magnificent creations."

The doctor—Dropnick, that was his name—Worsley, and his lackey stepped into the reflected glow of the table, the radiance of the saint and his acolyte bright in the phantom overlay of Gosha's second sight. The flurry of wings rippled at their arrival, a few drifting tentatively toward the auras of Faith, only to be burned away by the intensity of their radiance. The turgid Influence of the hospital clung to Dropnick him like a gelatinous shell, the moths apparently uninterested.

"I sense so much power coming from them," said the woman. A hint of an accent reflected her strong Mediterranean nose and kohl-lined eyes. A silver pentacle suspended around her neck by a chain glittered in the glow of the overhead light.

"Sister Bernadette is one of my most perceptive acolytes," said Worsley, his maroon robes standing out against the blackness around him. "Do explain again how you achieve such a pronounced effect."

"I have developed through my researches," Dropnick smiled and bobbed with enthusiasm as he spoke, "a system of purification and conditioning that opens up the deepest channels of connection to the essential spiritual nature of man. The three fields, as your John Grey puts it in that volume you gave me. I must thank you for that, by the way. I had arrived at similar conclusions through my own research. It was illuminating to hear it from one as knowledgeable as he."

"John Grey?" said Sister Bernadette. "But he was declared anathema and his writings a dangerous heresy. How did you come to possess such a thing, Your Excellency?"

"The ways of our Lord, the Prince of Faith, are uncanny and unfathomable," said Worsley, dismissing her with an indulgent and patronizing smile. "When He asks we must not question Him, we must simply do. Herr Dropnick, please continue."

"Yes, with the channels open, the most fundamental manifestation of the psychospiritual force you call Influence is able to gush forth with great vigor. The channels available to these gentlemen were already considerable given their creative prowess and long careers, but my technique can do the same for anyone."

"But how are you able to get them to craft these amazing artifacts?" Worsley eyed the cards on the table with naked lust.

"It requires intense grooming. These gentlemen, as you know, were prepared under my personal supervision for many, many months."

"Mm," said Worsley. "I delivered five to you, but here you have only three."

"Yes, unfortunately the process is still undergoing refinement, which is why your patronage has been so greatly appreciated. I could not have done it without you, Your Excellency."

Sister Bernadette walked around the table and inspected each man individually, the cloud of beating wings shifting and adjusting around her aura to avoid its radiance. Sir Wilfred, whose eyes Gosha must be seeing through, didn't turn or flinch when Sister Bernadette brought her face close and waved a hand in front of him.

"These men are catatonic," she said, returning to Worsley's side. "Excellency, this is an atrocity. You can't treat people like this."

"A moment, Sister Bernadette." Worsley raised a finger to silence her and turned back to Dropnick. "And the special artifact you promised me, where is it?"

"I have it here, Your Excellency."

Dropnick took from his pocket a leather envelope which he unfolded to reveal an elegant silver cross of minimalist modern design, about four inches in length, attached to a delicate silver chain. He dangled it before him to show Worsley. The turgid Influence in the room slowly drifted toward it to be absorbed and transmuted into what Gosha could only describe as an aura, the kind of emanation only a living person should have.

"And it works?" said Worsley with an eager smile, hands reaching to grab it.

"As far as I can tell, though I've only been able to perform the most rudimentary tests."

"Where did you get the idea for such an instrument?" Worsley took the cross and held it with all the care you might hold a child.

"From a woman I found in, of all places, a bookshop near Morel Market. She had a gift for creating interesting artifacts able to manipulate the psychospiritual force. I've been meaning to ask you about her, in fact. She styled herself a witch. Would this be real, or merely the fancy of a deluded hysteric?"

A bookshop near Morel Market. A witch with the knowledge to Craft objects that manipulated Influence. Gosha was certain he was talking about Auntie Rosamund, the witch who had saved her from going mad at the hands of Emerson Margrave. For years, Gosha had attempted to track her down and thank her, but no other witch Gosha had asked had been able to help, and no finding spell had been able to locate her.

"Oh, quite real, I assure you," said Worsley with a rueful sigh. "They give us no end of problems."

"The woman who came here yesterday in search of Sir Wilfred, I believe she was one of these women. I would very much like the opportunity to work on another of them. They have a very different understanding of the psychospiritual force than your John Grey. I learned much from my patient. Perhaps this other woman could be surrendered into my care?"

"I'm afraid not, Herr Dropnick. That one has made herself a particular nuisance. She's far too dangerous. The Convocation will require dealing with her directly, although, given the current state of affairs, I'm sure many other witches will be available for you to study in the coming months. What happened to your patient?"

"The process I have developed is not always kind. The more potent the connection to the psychospiritual force, the more consuming the effects, though with every procedure I refine it further. These gentlemen, for example, will remain functioning and useful for many days more, though eventually the intensified flow of emanations through their three fields will render them incapacitated."

The bishop raised an eyebrow at the word 'render.' Gosha wondered if this had been the fate of poor Auntie Rosamund.

"How can you associate with this monster!" Sister Bernadette's sudden outburst drew the attention of the three men away from their work. Sir Wilfred turned his head, allowing Gosha to see better.

"Sister Bernadette!" snapped Worsley, his sudden, frothing anger shutting her up. "Do not presume to understand the intent and motivation of your betters! You are merely an acolyte. You have no comprehension of what it means to be sanctified by our Lord. I will thank you to hold your tongue."

Sister Bernadette's mouth dropped open as if she might respond, but the rebuke sank in and she closed it again.

"I do apologize for the ignorance of my underling," said Worsley, all trace of his fury gone.

Dropnick shook his head with a smile and spread his hands as if to brush the outburst away.

"Your Excellency, I would very much like to see the instrument in action," he said. "Would you put it on?"

"A moment, Herr Dropnick."

With surprising dexterity for such an old man, Worsley reached out and tapped Sister Bernadette on the brow with a fingertip. Before she could react, her expression grew slack and her eyes unfocused.

"It's best we do this without interference. Sister Bernadette is one of my inner circle. It wouldn't do for word of this to spread."

"Of course, Your Excellency. I understand completely."

"How does it work, exactly?" asked the bishop as he slipped on the cross and arranged it next to the gaudy one he already wore.

He inhaled sharply and his eyes lit up.

"I feel it already."

"That is simply from the freely available psychospiritual force—"

"Influence, Herr Dropnick. I do wish you would call it by its traditional name."

"Influence, yes."

Dropnick took from a pocket of his jacket a square object, five inches to a side, with a large lens embedded in its center surrounded by the kind of electronic sliders you might find on a high-end stereo. Holding the square up before him so he could look through the lens, he adjusted the sliders with his thumbs.

"Yes," he said, "as I suspected. The free Influence in the air is, sadly, insufficient for the effect you desire. I experimented rigorously with different intensities, but it turns out not to be a question of amount. The ambient supply is simply too unrefined. Only the purified fields of oath-bearers—is that the correct term?—can provide the kind of sustenance you require. May I have the instrument?"

The bishop removed the cross and returned it to Dropnick, a sad reluctance in his face, a hesitancy in his hands.

"Not to worry, Your Excellency. I will give it back to you momentarily. I must simply calibrate it."

Dropnick rested the lens on the table. To Gosha's second sight, the glass was clouded with a swirl of Influence. From another pocket he took a small metal box made of wood and brass with a hinged lid and placed the cross in a customized recess embedded in a sheet of brass within. He closed the lid and adjusted concentric-ringed dials on its surface. He picked up the lens and held it before him to peer at the bishop and Sister Bernadette, made an adjustment on the dials of the box and checked the lens once more. Satisfied, he replaced the lens on the worktable and removed the cross, handing it back to Worsley, who put it on. The ambient Influence no longer flowed into it. Instead, a tiny stream of Sister Bernadette's radiant aura leached away from her to be drawn into it.

"Oh," said the bishop, eyes wide with delight. "Oh, yes. I see what you mean. Much better."

"I have it calibrated to draw only the tiniest amounts, and only from the fields of your own acolytes, but it will be sufficient to sustain you indefinitely. This is what you wanted, yes?"

"You're able to increase the draw further?"

"Oh yes, but any more would negatively impact those you would be drawing from."

"Show me how it works," said Worsley, gesturing to the box in Dropnick's hand.

"Are you sure, Your Excellency? If the draw of the instrument exceeds the output of a subject's fields, it will consume them whole. The oath would effectively be broken. They would be nothing more than human and with severely compromised mental faculties at that."

"But they would still be alive?"

"Yes, but in name only. There would be nothing left of the person they once were."

"Herr Dropnick, to sustain myself all these centuries I've been forced to consume entirely one of my followers in every normal human lifespan. It's a complex and laborious process of decades to prepare the chosen one for the sacrifice. I am required to keep the intended close at all times, and when it's done, I must literally consume them and incorporate them into my own being. It's the only way to get around the limitation to not take a life all we who serve the Lords and Ladies must observe. Sister Bernadette is my current chosen. Her help has been invaluable, but these are difficult times for my sphere and I've been forced to enlist her in acts that would create great problems for me among the Convocation should they become known, my association with you included. I was going to have to cull her soon, anyway, but it's a messy process. Lots of blood and other fluids. It sounds like this would be a much cleaner way to go about it. And I thought you might appreciate studying the unrestrained effects of your creation."

Dropnick's face lit up with excitement, as if Worsley had offered him the opportunity to observe him bake a cake, not destroy another human being.

"Oh, yes." Dropnick reached for the cross as if grabbing for a box of jelly babies. "Let me show you how it works."

Worsley returned the cross and Dropnick replaced it in its box.

"This dial calibrates its sensitivity to the emanations of a particular sphere, and this the intensity of the draw."

The bishop turned the dial all the way to maximum and winked at Dropnick with an impish smile.

"Let's try it, shall we?" He removed the cross and put it on again. "Do I need to do anything to get it started?"

"No, no. Exposure will be sufficient." Dropnick picked up his lens to watch.

Sister Bernadette's aura was sucked away from her in a matter of seconds, like smoke drawn out of a crowded bar by the sudden opening of a window. Her hair grew brittle and gray as her skin aged, the fullness of her cheeks draining into sunken grooves. Whatever Worsley had done to paralyze her had already robbed her face of the ability to express itself, but a light went out of her eyes. When the process was finished, she was left a ravaged husk, a faded reflection of a human being.

37

GOSHA WANTED TO SCREAM, WANTED to leap from her chair and rip the cross from Worsley's neck, wanted to smash Dropnick's devices against the linoleum floor, but the eyes she looked through were not her own. The fingers that continued to paint despite the horror going nearby belonged to Sir Wilfred, and she had no control over them. Worse, the force of her revulsion pulled her back from her connection, the room retreating from her down a tunnel of black smudging.

Back in the security station, she commanded herself to breathe deeply and shed the charge exploding through her limbs, and regained enough composure to concentrate: Sir Wilfred's hands, the table, Andrew Mills and Richard Howell at work across from him, Bishop Worsley and Dropnick, and poor, doomed Sister Bernadette. The widow's weeds blotted across her vision and she found herself in the room again.

"Magnificent," exclaimed Worsley, stretching his arms in the air as if waking from a deep and renewing sleep. His aura blazed in Gosha's second sight with such power that, had it been real light, she would have been blinded. "In a thousand years, it's never been this easy."

"May I suggest," said Dropnick as he reached for the box, "that we reset the instrument immediately? We don't know what would happen if you accidentally absorbed more psychospiritual force before your current charge has dissipated."

"Oh yes," said Worsley, heeding the warning and handing him the cross. "A very good point. Thank you for being so thoughtful."

Dropnick replaced the cross in the box and fiddled with the dials.

"I will reduce the draw to its bare minimum. I suggest you keep it at that until you begin to feel the effects of depletion. If even that's too much, you may always keep the instrument in the box. It will insulate it fully. When you do increase the draw, I recommend keeping it as low as possible. Small quantities over an extended period will serve you better in the long run than infrequent binges."

Dropnick might have been explaining a treatment plan to a patient rather than telling Worsley how to suck the life force from the men and women who had placed in him their trust.

"Excellent advice, Doctor." Worsley took back the box and put the cross on once more, tucking the box into a pocket beneath his surplice. "Might you take Sister Bernadette into your care? Perhaps she could help you with your research."

Dropnick hovered next to him, his body language clear he wanted Worsley gone now that their transaction was over.

"Yes, of course, Your Excellency. It would be my pleasure. We can make her quite comfortable."

Dropnick barely succeeded in masking his impatience as he attempted to usher Worsley toward the door.

"It's wonderful to finally see the results of our combined efforts, Herr Dropnick." Worsley turned to inspect the work on the table rather than take the hint. "At first I had reservations about our association. You asked for a great deal when you first approached me, and your claims were preposterous." He ambled over to watch the studious efforts of Andrew Mills and his ink pen. Dropnick started to follow, hands out ready to pull the bishop back, but he stopped himself. "The secret of the fundamental nature of Influence and the Spheres is an undertaking every saint and acolyte has struggled with since the founding of the realm five thousand years ago, and you're not even an oath-bearer. Had all this failed, the personal cost to me would have been staggering."

"Your Excellency, are you not satisfied with the instrument I produced for you?" The professional confidence with which Dropnick had dominated the room had dissipated to be replaced by the manner of someone suddenly worried for his future prospects.

"Oh, most decidedly so." Worsley's perfect white teeth glowed in the work light with a smile that didn't reach his eyes. "When we discussed how your research might benefit me, I never expected results as powerful as this. It makes me question the true nature of what you're trying to accomplish here."

"I explained my interests in great detail, Your Excellency—"

"I remember. While treating a patient you uncovered what you thought, at first, was an elaborate delusion about psychic forces and spiritual struggle. I tracked down the monograph you wrote at the time. I'm convinced your patient must have been an oath-bearer, by the way, probably an acolyte of Surrender. The funny business they get up to often leaves them deranged."

He wiggled his fingers in a dismissive gesture and leaned in to get a better look at the card Mills was working on, a hunched, agonized figure sifting through a field of rubble.

"You read that?" Dropnick's brow furrowed with worry.

"It was quite hard to find. Published by a small press bought out by a mysterious benefactor who promptly closed the business and destroyed all the stock. Well, not all." He smiled again, and Gosha felt a distant chill run down her spine. "It's a wonderful read. You are a most gifted writer. Your patient gave you a very detailed portrait of the Spheres and what it means to give your oath to the Lords and Ladies. It's quite a leap, however to get from that to this. Technologies that manipulate Influence are a carefully guarded secret of the Convocation of Saints. Their development is heavily regulated and generally frowned upon. We all fear an escalating arms race. If the Lord Chief Justice ever found out what you were up to, he'd have his stormtroopers in here immediately."

"Your Excellency," said Dropnick in alarm.

"I, of course, would never betray your confidence, Herr Doctor." Worsely spoke without looking up from the table. "I think what you're getting up to is remarkable. I thank my Lord, the Prince of Faith, that you chose to approach me and not one of the other saints. I'm a firm believer in the patronage of the brilliant. It's something I have encouraged among the spiritual institutions of the realm since Roman times. How did you come across the idea of using physical materials to manipulate Influence? Such things are hard even for an oath-bearer. Was it the witch?"

He looked up from Andrew Mills' work and waited for an answer.

"Ah, no. Not the witch," stammered Dropnick, clearly unsure in what direction Worsley was leading him.

"Another of your patients, then?" Worsley raised his eyebrows in a pleasant inquiry, his expression belying the trap Dropnick, from the defensive posture of chin high and chest out, could tell he was building around him.

"Yes, a different patient. I can't reveal more, I'm afraid. Doctor-patient privilege."

Worsley put a hand on Mills' shoulder. A cloud of ethereal wings fluttered up at him and were burned away by the intensity of his aura.

"Yes, I do understand the relationship between Doctor and patient. It's very similar to that of a man of the cloth and his flock."

The shambled remains that were once Sister Bernadette shifted, her robes rustling. Worsley's pointed way of speaking reminded Gosha of conversations in Witches' Cant, where subtext was the entire purpose

"I see you have these gentlemen working on another project. It seems quite elaborate."

He waved a hand across the table to encompass the cards spread across it and stirred the cloud of wings.

"It's a form of art therapy," said Dropnick, refusing to cede ground in the face of Worsley's implied threat that lingered heavily in the air.

"It's a peculiar form of art therapy that causes so much chaos."

"I beg your pardon?" said Dropnick, confused at the turn in Worsley's oration.

"You haven't been honest with me. What exactly happened with the other two gentlemen I procured for you?"

"I told you. They were not strong enough to benefit from the procedure as it currently exists."

"Douglas Barnes was found dead in his home yesterday morning, a victim of an apparent suicide," said Worsley, staring Dropnick in the eye, "though his body was disfigured in a way that suggests mummification. Joseph Hobbs was killed this morning after causing untold mayhem at Paddington Station during the commuter rush, having created an artifact that caused the deaths of six acolytes. Either you're intentionally getting up to something quite dangerous here, or you've unleashed forces you are incapable of controlling. Which is it, Doctor Dropnick?"

"He created something? What was it?" Dropnick's defensive posture expanded into curiosity.

"It's unclear. Apparently the object had to be isolated permanently. What happened to the men?"

Dropnick fell silent and held himself as perfectly still as a living person could.

"Doctor." Worsley smiled amicably and returned to Dropnick's side. "I'm not here to accuse you of wrongdoing. I'm not here to turn you over to Griffiths and the rest. I'm here to help you, and I can't do that if I don't know what you're up to. Tell me what you're really working on and I will do my utmost to further your cause. We've established a wonderful relationship from which both of us can continue to benefit if we can just get the current situation under control."

"Under control? Is there more?"

"Well." Worsley pursed his lips and nodded his head from side to side to undermine the seriousness of what he was saying. "We're having a problem with witches, but not to worry. It's just the sort of problem the Lord Chief Justice loves getting stuck into, and we can blame the whole mess on them. You see? If we work together, we can achieve so much."

Dropnick gave Worsley a long look before speaking.

"I've had to push the process to its limits for this."

He picked up one of the cards and, for a moment, lost himself in its illustration.

"It's an idea I got from the witch. She possessed an elaborate deck of cards used for divination that described the complex interactions of the psychospiritual force. I wish to create my own version, but one that will detail the inner function of what you call a Sphere in a sort of map. It would be the ultimate tool for my research. I misjudged the intensity of the process I used on my subjects. By means I have yet to understand, Barnes and Hobbs escaped their confinement. My current theory is that the process gave them the ability to manipulate the new surge of force flowing through them. It would explain this artifact you say Hobbs created. I would very much like to see it."

Dropnick had lost Worsley's attention at the mention of the Spheres. He stood over the table and turned the cards toward him.

"A map of the Spheres," he whispered. "I'm afraid it will be difficult to give you access to the artifact," he said, coming back to himself and the conversation. "My people tell me the witches did something to make it unreachable, but perhaps I can arrange for it to disappear from the vaults of the Convocation and be brought to you. It may take some time. Herr Dropnick, would this map of the Spheres show one how to control the flow of Influence? To prevent it from drifting?"

Dropnick gave him an odd, assessing look.

"Drifting? I suppose so."

"My Lord, the Prince of Faith, has made it clear to me that there's another who seeks his favor. He's playing this usurper off against me. I'm not worried. It's happened before, and I've learned how to defend my position, but the Lords and Ladies are fickle and capricious. Would this map of the Spheres help me curtail him?"

"Would this deck of cards help you control the anthropomorphic representation of the psychic drive that gives you your power?"

Worsley's smile was genuine this time, the veils of caution and manipulation gone.

"Yes. You understand me perfectly."

Dropnick nodded slowly.

"Yes. I do believe it would."

"Excellent." Worsley clapped his hands with delight. "Carry on, Herr Doctor. I look forward to seeing the results of your fine work. I must head back to the Convocation and ensure that your efforts remain hidden."

He swept away, his robes fanning out behind him as he passed Sister Bernadette on his way out the door without a second glance. Dropnick leaned on the table, watching the men work. Wings fluttered toward him and settled on the dense cloak of Influence that encased him.

No sooner had the bishop left than someone else came in, a young man in an orderly's uniform, the white cloth catching the light and glowing in the corner of Gosha's perception.

"How did it go, Doctor?"

"Quite well, quite well," said Dropnick. "Up to a point. There have been complications, not least of which an unwanted level interest from our patron, the bishop. We must abandon the hospital immediately and evacuate to the backup location. Start moving out everything important. I want it all gone by the time these gentlemen finish."

"Yes, Doctor. And what about this one?" he asked, seeing the remains of Sister Bernadette.

"Leave her. She's harmless. She can die with the rest of them when we gas the building."

38

A JOLT WRENCHED HER EYEBALLS in their sockets, tearing her away from the sight of Dropnick leaning over the table and surveying the work of Sir Wilfred and his friends as if he were a general pondering a map of his field of battle, his forces spread out before him in wood and plastic figurines arranged across the paper. A black ring of widow's weeds smudged around her field of vision as if reality had ripped, the darkness growing, blinding her completely before parting to leave her back in the security guard's station, the wall of television screens in front of her. She barely noticed the commotion of nurses and orderlies rushing from screen to screen, packing up files.

"What the fuck did you do to Dibble?" said a man behind her as he placed a hand on her shoulder, pulled her back away from the table and spun her to face him. Lanky and thin, his uniform was crumpled and he stank of BO.

"Puthut," she said without thinking, and immediately regretted it.

As his body was thrust back to knock against the wall behind him, her brain twisted in her skull and a nausea gripped her that was so intense her muscles locked up in spasm. Two spells she'd cast. Elsie had given her leave to cast five, but it felt like even a third might kill her.

Her spasm relaxed, her entire body losing all tone in an instant, causing her to melt out of the chair and tumble to the ground, knocking into the first guard and breaking the delicate sleep spell. He took one look at Gosha and his coworker sprawled on the floor opposite each other and scrambled to his feet to help his partner up. Gosha rolled onto her stomach and attempted to gather her limbs beneath her, but the room span wildly about her and she pressed her head against the cold and hard linoleum in a vain attempt to make it stop.

"Stop faffing around," said Dibble as he pulled his friend up by the arm.

"She pushed me," said Jeffries. "Knocked me clear across the room."

"Oh, I believe it! Useless, you are. Call the nurse's station. Tell them one of the nutters went walkies."

He stooped over Gosha as Jeffries dialed the phone.

"They keep 'em so drugged up, I don't know how she got down here. Look," he said as he hooked his arms around her and pulled her to her feet. "She's a bloody sack of potatoes."

Gosha remembered feeling this bad after a night out carousing with George in the early days, when love and infatuation had transformed his arrogance and vanity in her eyes to strength and confidence. Three bottles of champagne, a fifth of whiskey, and a dodgy curry had forced their way out of her in a humbling few hours spent crouched over the toilet. This was worse, an assault on her nervous system and not her gastrointestinal tract. She wasn't sure she could have held herself up without the guard's help.

"They're not answering," said Jeffries.

"What the fuck's going on?" Dibble looked up at the commotion on the screen.

The door opened behind them.

"Must we always be so unclear in our commendations?" said a familiar cheerful voice. "Butter and jam is hardly fit for a queen."

The two men's eyes rolled back in their heads and they crumpled to the ground. Gosha felt herself falling, only to be caught by a pair of strong arms in a silk blouse.

"Bless you, my child," said Eleanor, her face beaming as she drew a circle on Gosha's brow with her fingertip. "In the name of the mother, the begonia, and the boiling kettle."

All Gosha's nausea and disorientation melted away, the ground firm beneath her feet and gravity a reliable constant once more.

"What are you doing here?" she said as she hugged Eleanor tight.

"A bastard child should be loved as much as the first born of wedlock." Eleanor pulled away from the embrace and stooped over the recumbent guards to adjust their crumpled shirts and straighten their ties.

"Oh, Eleanor. You should be back with Elsie getting ready to drive to Bristol. I don't know how to take care of you."

"Oh, don't be silly. Rain. It's as simple as rain."

She snapped her fingers six or seven times and laughed like an actor from a nineteen-thirties movie. Plump and delicate snowflakes drifted down from the ceiling to land on Gosha's nose and lashes. Gosha sighed. Despite the situation, the blanket of whiteness softened something inside her.

"Well, you're here now. Perhaps you can help. See all this running around?" She pointed up at the screens. "They're evacuating. When they've gone, they're going to kill everyone that's left. We have to stop them. Can you cast a finding to lead us to Sir Wilfred? He's upstairs somewhere."

"Hmm," said Eleanor. "I like popcorn best."

The tips of her fingers sparked and glowed.

"That would be a no, then," Gosha sighed.

The settled snowflakes were beginning to melt. Gosha picked her dampening telling deck from where she left it on the desk and brushed it off on her jacket. The three cards for her finding spell were on the top. It took her seconds to cast. The encouragement she felt at the process becoming that much easier was instantaneously chased away by a hard tweak of nausea turning over between her ears. Still not nearly as bad as casting with a spell word, but worse than it had been.

"Darling," said Eleanor, grasping Gosha's shoulders with concern and pulling her close to stare deep into her eyes. "You've never looked so much like an elephant."

She isn't entirely delirious, thought Gosha. *She's reacting to some things, but not consistently, and everything she says is gibberish.*

The overhead fluorescents flickered in response to the spell.

"Come on," she said, taking Eleanor's hand and leading her out into the corridor to follow the path of flickering lights. "Perhaps we can find a quiet place to put you while I sort this all out."

She should have, perhaps, specified to the cards that she was looking for an unobstructed path to whatever dark corner Doctor Dropnick was holding Sir Wilfred and his friends in. She would have been happy to meander for a bit, even in the stifling dullness of the Influence that crawled through the corridors of the hospital. Instead the finding spell delivered her to five orderlies, all young and strong, carrying boxes of files and equipment.

"Crap," said the nearest, spotting Gosha over a stack of boxes. "Livestock. Benny, take care of them, will you?"

"Why am I always the one that has to clean up the shit?" said Benny from the back of the group as he put down his boxes.

"'Cos you're the dumb one," said the leader. "Stan, help him out. Find a room you can lock 'em up in, doesn't have to be a cell. It won't matter in a few hours."

What kind of travesty of a mental health facility is this fucking place? thought Gosha.

The remaining three disappeared around a corner with their loads leaving Benny and Stan to deal with Gosha.

"Come on, luv," said Benny, reaching out to grab her by the arm, but Gosha twisted away from him. His brow furrowed in confusion.

He must not be used to livestock being quick on their feet, thought Gosha.

He lunged for her again, but she stepped back and would have cleared his reach had Eleanor not been directly behind her to get in her way.

"Lawks!" crowed Eleanor as Gosha stumbled into her and Benny wrapped a large hand around her arm.

He twisted her arm and wrenched her shoulder up before she could wriggle away and turned her so her back was to him to march her off to whatever prison would hold her until they released the gas that would kill everyone left in the building.

Big mistake, she thought as she stamped down hard on his ankle and thrust her head back and bashed into his nose.

He squealed and staggered, trying to nurse both wounds at once. She spun to face him and used the momentum to power a solid punch to his temple with the full force of her back. His head bounced off the wall and he slumped to the floor, dazed.

"Benny!" said Stan, rounding on her rather than help his fallen friend. "You fucking cow."

Gosha slipped her switchblade out of her pocket and thumbed the release. The blade snapped open with satisfying force, but before she could even raise it in threat, Eleanor stepped between her and Stan.

"Hello, young man," she said, as breezy and carefree as if she'd been introduced to him at a garden party. "How would you feel about a lovely game of whist?"

He reached out to sweep her aside, but she laid a hand on his arm and he screamed a loud, blood-curdling wail of abject horror, fell to the floor and curled himself up in a ball.

"What did you do to him?" said Gosha as she took Eleanor by the hand and led her away at a run toward the flicker of the finding spell in the ceiling lights ahead of them.

"He's just a silly billy," she twittered.

From behind them came the commotion of Benny and Stan's friends rushing back to see what the ruckus was.

"Wait, wait," said Eleanor, digging in her heels and pulling back her arm from Gosha's grasp. "I forgot my linens."

She turned back to the approaching orderlies and raised her hands as if to pray, but instead began to clap them together in a quiet, brisk rhythm as she muttered to herself. The rumble of distant thunder quavered through the walls and the fluorescents dimmed as a thick fog seeped up from the floor, encasing them in impenetrable white. Stan's pathetic wails distorted and diffused, appearing to come from everywhere and nowhere all at once.

"There we are," said Eleanor turning back to Gosha. Had she been a foot further away, she would have been nothing more than a shadow. "Now the little rabbits will have carrots for their tea."

Gosha buried her head in her hands and swore.

"Thank you, Eleanor," she said, pushing down her irritation. The woman was likely a thousand years old. Without the brew that kept her lucid, she couldn't help herself. "But now how are we going to follow the finding spell?"

Eleanor cupped her cheek.

"Sweetheart," she said. "Never fear. The darkness will always find you."

Gosha took a deep breath, the smell of damp twigs and churned earth filling her nostrils. She would have to re-cast the finding spell and hope that it would work through this pea-souper. She took out her working deck. The cards were hard to see in the gloom. Perhaps she could do a better job this time. To the Known, the Unknown, and the Ace of Needles she added Unity, to keep them from running into anyone else, and Liberation, an image from a photo shoot she'd done for an alternative fashion magazine: a man and woman dressed in flowing op-art stripes, leggings, and sparkly tutus chained to a tower of mannequins dressed in restrictive suits and formal dresses, pulling them down with their chains, the best representation she could find for Sir Wilfred and his friends toiling away in the basement creating artifacts of horror against their will.

She held the cards up before her, concentrated, and willed Influence through them to launch the spell. The thick and slow-moving Influence surrounding her resisted, and she pushed harder, her temples throbbing with the effort, the acrid taste of bile rising up in her throat. Once the Influence met the cards, it shifted. Like straw spun into gold, the leaden and unresponsive force became light and dynamic. The spell tumbled away from them, swirling through the fog, leading them toward their destination.

39

THE REFINEMENTS SHE ADDED TO the finding spell made all the difference. The shifting tunnel through the dense clouds of fog led them safely past blinded orderlies stumbling around with boxes, and huddles of nurses and doctors rethinking their planned evacuation to account for the inexplicable fog. This Dropnick wasn't yet another oath-bearer acting in solitude away from the prying eyes of the Convocation. He had an entire organization of people working for him. Gosha marveled at what might motivate all these people to willingly cause so much harm to others in this mockery of a place of healing. Was it money? Was it devotion to the doctor? Did they think themselves doing noble work in the name of science?

The tunnel in the fog led them to the foot of a stairwell. Gosha stopped and took Eleanor's hands in her own.

"Stay here, Eleanor," she said, touching their foreheads together. The tunnel the spell had created was still thick with mist and Gosha needed to be sure Eleanor saw how serious she was. "It's going to be dangerous up there. I love you dearly, but when you're like this you're only going to get in the way. Promise me you'll stay put?"

"Porcupines," said Eleanor. "Possibly priapic, but perpetually prosaic."

"I don't know what that means. Please stay here. Please."

She backed away smiling toward the stairs gesturing for Eleanor to stay. Eleanor seemed to get the message, waiting patiently, but when Gosha turned to go up, Eleanor ran to catch up and hugged Gosha's arm.

"I do so love the museum," she whispered in Gosha's ear.

Gosha sighed.

The tunnel through the fog led them up three flights of stairs to what must have been the top floor of the building, pausing them twice on the way so frantic staff could scuttle from one floor to the next without bumping into them. It led them safely out of the stairwell and down a corridor to a pair of swinging doors with frosted glass in the windows, and then it collapsed, encasing them in fog.

Gosha put an ear to the door, careful not to disturb it, and heard muffled voices coming from the other side. In her vision she'd seen Dropnick in there and one other orderly, but Sir Wilfred's point of view under the bright light over the worktable had left the far reaches of the room in darkness. She had no idea how many people were in there.

She couldn't risk being incapacitated, even for a second, so casting spells of any kind was out. Thinking back over the time she'd spent in the boxing ring with Alfie over the past three years, she offered a prayer of thanks for all the hard work he'd made her do. Dropnick was the man in charge. His lackeys wouldn't gas the building without his order, and if she held him hostage, she could use him as a bargaining tool with the Convocation. He'd be concrete evidence that Bishop Worsley was behind the disaster at Paddington. Turning Dropnick over to them would surely convince the Convocation that witches were a valuable asset and not a threat. If not, she might be able to negotiate freedom for the ladies in exchange for turning herself in.

Okay, she thought. *Slip in, get the lay of the land, disable whoever's in there, take Dropnick and get Sir Wilfred and the others out of there. Without Craft. Sure, no problem. All in a night's work.*

"Eleanor," she whispered. "I'm going in. Please be as quiet as you—"

She turned back to find herself alone in the fog.

"Eleanor?" she hissed, waving her arms through the murk in search of her, but Eleanor was gone.

She sighed and tried to put her worry for the other witch out of her mind along with all the other things she didn't have time to worry about. If she thought about anything beyond what lay on the other side of the doors, she'd never move forward.

She pushed the door to open it a crack, just enough to feel the strength of the springs tethering the doors and find out how creaky they were. Four spells that might have helped popped into her head, along with three different combinations of cards she might have used to get into the room, none of which she dared cast for fear of blacking out. But she was in luck. Though the springs were surprisingly strong, they were mercifully quiet.

She ducked down and slipped through the smallest gap she could make between the doors. The room beyond was medium-sized, with space enough for several tables and their accompanying chairs, most of which were folded and stacked racks against the wall to her left. One round table stood in the middle of the room, Sir Wilfred, Andrew Mills, and Richard Howell seated around it, still working away on their tiny masterpieces. To her right, with eyes that saw nothing and an expression devoid of emotion, stood the remains of Sister Bernadette, as if caught in a pause between one thought and the next, though the next would never come. Three orderlies, all heavier than she, stood around the room, two with their backs to her, the third facing sideways, though he was fully absorbed by the work of the three men and didn't see her, as were Dropnick and another man dressed in street clothes who manned a device like a stubby telescope mounted on a tripod with wires and what looked liked precious stones embedded along its length. The wheeled racks housing the stowed chairs and tables hadn't been pushed flush against the wall, leaving Gosha room to slip behind them and work her way unseen toward the nearest of the orderlies.

The fluttering wings of corruption were everywhere now, an ethereal plague feeding on the eyes, mouths, and hands of the unsuspecting watchers, nibbling at their auras and growing brighter in the phantom superimposition of her second sight. It took only a moment for the wings to find their way to her. She did her best not to flinch, nor to swat them away as they swarmed around her, but with no aura for them to feed off, they passed her by, uninterested.

"How are we doing, Mr. Devereux?" asked Dropnick standing at the table with hands on hips as he surveyed his captive's work.

"Nearly there, Doctor," said the man at the scope without lifting his head. "Power levels are increasing substantially, but the waveform still lacks cohesion."

"Perhaps if I arrange the cards," Dropnick said, thinking out loud rather than asking for permission. "My research has shown that relative position can make a significant difference."

He took from his pocket a pair of latex surgical gloves and snapped them on. It had no effect on the fluttering swarm that continued to nibble at his fingers as he gathered up the cards the men had finished working on and patted them together so he could shuffle through them with ease and select the ones he wanted.

"Let's try a circle first," he said, laying out cards face up on the table.

The fluttering wings reacted with the fourth card he placed on the table in the root position of a simple cross layout. She wondered if he understood the significance of the spread he'd chosen, knowledge he must have stolen from poor Auntie Rosamund. The wings swarmed into the center of the room as if sucked there by a vacuum, more and more of them pulled in with each additional card he lay down until his spread numbered a dozen cards.

"It's making a difference," said Devereux from behind his device. "The power levels spiked."

"And the waveform?"

"A little clearer, but still not well defined."

"Hmm." Dropnick rubbed his chin as he pondered. "Perhaps a different order."

He rearranged the cards, trading pairs around the circle and looking to Devereux for confirmation.

"There," said the technician. "It's coming together."

The wings that had been fluttering about within the invisible boundary of the circle of cards in random jostling began to swirl as if someone had stirred them. Whatever effect Dropnick was looking for, Gosha needed to stop it now.

The first two orderlies still had their back to her, but number three would see her the moment she broke cover. Sir Wilfred, Dropnick, and poor Sister Bernadette stood in his way and would hopefully slow him down while she dealt with orderlies one and two. If she could take out all three of them, there'd be nothing to stop her from taking Dropnick hostage. It was a mad plan, but she knew she was fast and strong. She might succeed.

Might.

Taking out her switchblade, she hefted its weight in her hands. She could stab Orderly Number One in the back, but she'd only ever wielded it as a threat, to slice and jab, or used it as a tool. The idea of drawing blood was too much for her. She closed her fingers around the dense heaviness of the haft, the blade stowed securely inside it. It would work just as well as a weight to harden her punches.

Without the space to limber up her stiff and tired body, she took a deep breath and willed her muscles to soften in readiness for the exertions to come, and duck-walked at a crouch from behind the chairs and tables to come up behind Number One. She called up the memory of how to launch herself at him the way Alfie had shown her, allowing muscle memory to prime her. She stood, placed her feet and threw a punch at the back of Number One's head, hoping she'd judged it right and would only knock the man and not kill him.

Her fist made contact with the crack of bone against bone. Gosha's hand throbbed sharply from the impact of the blow as Number One went down.

"Oi!" shouted Number Three, seeing his associate crumple, and stepped out from behind the table toward her.

She didn't wait to see how the room would react, plowing ahead and reaching Number Two as Number Three pushed past the uncooperative form of Sister Bernadette. Number Two turned to see what was going on, the commotion only now beginning to register for Dropnick and Devereux, so engrossed were they by the swirling cloud of corrupted Influence spinning within the ring of cards.

She threw a punch at Number Two, but the man was quick and sturdy. A meaty arm blocked her blow and knocked the switchblade from her hand. Alfie had taught her a lot about the sweet science of boxing, but he'd also taught her how to fight dirty. She spun with the momentum from Number Two's block and lashed out with a donkey-kick to his right knee. As he folded over with a grunt of pain, she brought her own knee up sharply and struck him between the eyes. He went down heavy.

By now, Number Three had made it past Dropnick, drawing the full attention of the doctor and his technician. He grabbed Gosha from behind and tried to slip an arm up under hers to immobilize her in a half-nelson, but she stamped down hard on his foot, wrapped her leg around his and threw him off balance, rolling him across the floor to crash against the worktable. The table scraped across the floor, the jolt breaking

Dropnick's careful arrangement of cards. The invisible container around the wings broke and they scattered chaotically about the room.

"Blasted woman!" shouted Dropnick, arms above his head in outrage. "Look what you've done!"

Gosha retrieved her switchblade and thumbed it open, the blade deploying with a satisfying click.

"Idiots!" shouted Dropnick, eyes wide at the sight of the blade, and stepped back, away from her. "Stop her this instant."

Number Three sprung up off the floor and stepped between her, Dropnick, and the table. The blade was purely for intimidation's sake, but she couldn't let him know that. She lunged out at him, slashing the air in front of her in a cheap imitation of a Musketeer, but he pulled back beyond her reach. As they lunged and feinted at each other, behind Number Three Dropnick hurriedly rearranged the cards.

"The waveform's collapsing," said Devereux, his eye back against the scope.

To Dropnick's right, Eleanor appeared out of thin air standing next to Sister Bernadette, distracting Gosha and allowing Number Three to slip under her guard. He knocked the blade from her hand and barreled forward, slamming his forearm into her throat and driving her back against the wall, the force of it knocking the wind out of her.

"You poor dear," said Eleanor to Sister Bernadette. "What have they done to you?"

"Rick," shouted Number Three, "Jake. Fucking help me out."

Out of the corner of her eye she could see that Number One wasn't moving, but Number Two pushed himself up off the floor and limped toward her. Dropnick finished rearranging the cards and the fluttering wings were drawn back to swirl in their containment. Gosha tried kneeing Number Three in the gut, but she didn't have good leverage.

"I'm so sorry about this," said Eleanor, and whispered in Sister Bernadette's ear.

The woman's vacant eyes lit up with purpose. She hurled herself across the room, a screeching cloud of flowing black, and launched herself at the unsuspecting orderly, wrapping herself around him, clawing at his eyes and digging her fingers into his cheeks. He released his grip on Gosha as he struggled to fend off Sister Bernadette's feral attack.

"And you've been very clever and very naughty," said Eleanor to Dropnick as he watched the commotion with fascinated horror.

She placed a hand on the table. With a concussive crack that reverberated about the room, the table shattered into splinters of plastic and metal. Art supplies and cards tumbled to the floor, the fluttering wings bursting from their containment once more. Sir Wilfred and the other two men sat back in their chairs, hands still, and stared into space, entranced.

"My God!" shouted Dropnick as he backed away from her, knocking into Devereux and the scope.

Orderly Number Two—Rick or Jake, she didn't know which—loomed over her as she reached for the switchblade, a giant bruise darkening across his face. She came up underneath his reach with an uppercut to his solar plexus, knocking the wind out of him. A one-two punch to the head and he crumpled to the floor, unconscious.

Beyond the tangle of struggling limbs that were Sister Bernadette and Number Three, Eleanor stepped between the three seated men into the remains of the table and grimaced at the mess spread across the floor and the clouds of fluttering wings.

"What are these monstrosities?" With a gesture, she made the cards float up from where they'd fallen. "You're playing with forces you don't remotely understand," she said to Dropnick. "You're about to create a very dangerous mess."

Dropnick pulled from his pocket a metal and leather cylinder about the width of a large flashlight covered with circular dials and sliders wrapped around its circumference. He turned the controls to a particular combination and pressed a large button on the end. The ambient Influence immediately changed from torpid sludge to thick, writhing tentacles that lashed around like angry snakes coiling around Gosha's limbs, battering at her with physical impact and wrenching her to and fro. She'd had gentler experiences in the mosh pit at punk gigs at the Marquee Club. The fluttering wings frayed and shredded to nothing by the turbulence.

"These women," said Dropnick to his technician, watching intently as Gosha and Eleanor were flailed about, "are susceptible to the psychospiritual force like the activated patients. After Mr. Barber and Mr. Hobbs escaped their confinement, I developed this device to ensure it didn't happen again."

He turned knobs and rings, and clicked the button once more. The tentacles merged into a labyrinth of moving walls that pressed into Gosha, sandwiching her between them.

"Oh, dear boy, no," said Eleanor, and waved a hand as if saying a reluctant goodbye across the platform of a crowded station.

A slow and implacable wavefront of Influence moved away from her toward Dropnick and Devereux, pushing them against the wall. Dropnick changed his settings once more and clicked the button. The Influence transmuted, thick walls becoming an angry mist of static that buzzed and burrowed into Gosha's bones and brain, immobilizing her body and making it impossible to string together coherent thought.

Eleanor was affected, too, her body rigid as a look of shock crossed her face. The suspended cards dropped. On the floor, Sister Bernadette continued to struggle with Number Three, but he soon put a stop to it with a swift kick to her temple.

Dropnick moaned as he stepped into the pool of bright overhead light. "This is a disaster! Devereux, quick. Tell me what's going on?"

Devereux reset the scope, turned a few dials and put his eye to the viewfinder.

"The waveform's completely collapsed," was his verdict.

Dropnick's fair cheeks flushed.

"Blasted women! Bishop Worsley was right about witches. So much trouble!"

He stooped to retrieve the fallen cards as Number Three helped up his fallen comrades. Both Rick and Jake, whichever was which, looked very much the worse for wear.

"Keep an eye on them," said Dropnick. "I don't want them creating any more mess. Devereux, help me out here."

Dropnick fiddled with his device, found a new setting, and pressed the button. The aggressive buzzing haze smoothed out into static thickness. Gosha felt as if she'd been encased in amber, her body as rigid as before, but now, at least, she could think clearly.

The technician got out from behind his device and followed Dropnick to the back wall to retrieve another table and set it up between the three catatonic men, but Eleanor stood paralyzed in the way. Number Three moved to help, hooking his arms underneath Eleanor's armpits and dragging her, stiff as a board, out of the pool of light so Dropnick and Devereux could set up the table.

Satisfied, Dropnick reset the cards in their circle, the fluttering wings beginning to reform within their confines.

"We have confluence," said Devereux, at his post behind the scope.

Dropnick stood back to look at his arrangement.

"I think I have it, now," he said and shifted the positions of four of the cards.

A slow change worked its way through the fluttering wings, the random chaos of their beating organizing itself into waves.

"The waveform's stabilizing," said Devereux.

The fluttering waves slowed until the wings all beat in unison.

"Excellent." Dropnick beamed. He turned to Number Three. "Hold off on the final evacuation. We're so close to finishing. I don't want to waste the subjects we already have prepared for the next phase."

"What do you want done with the women?" asked Number Three.

"That one's useless," said Dropnick, nodding toward the fallen lump of limbs, black fabric, and silver jewelry that were the remains of Sister Bernadette. "But I want these two for further study. Wait a moment."

He went to the edge of the room and picked up an old-fashioned leather medical bag that he placed on the table and clicked open, revealing a series of small drawers and other containers. He opened one of the drawers and took out what looked to Gosha like a crown made of copper wire with small copper washers welded about the circumference. Handling it with great care, he carried it to Eleanor and placed it on her head. She began to scream, a loud and high-pitched shriek that curdled Gosha's blood. When she ran out of breath, Eleanor screamed again.

"Puthut," said Gosha, directing the pushback spell out around her without thinking about the effect it might have on her, but the Influence in the room resisted, held rigid by Dropnick's device.

With all her might, with every ounce of emotion she had in her, she grabbed at the Influence of the spell with her will, accepting no other possible outcome, and pushed it through the opening within her the spell word had created. Force swept outward from her, blowing back all the men, Sir Wilfred and his friends included, even the body of Sister Bernadette, but leaving Gosha and Eleanor, still screaming her throat raw, untouched. The cars on the table remained where they were, the beating wings within the circle fluttering in ominous unison.

Gosha's brain did a somersault inside her skull, the only thing stopping her fall the rigid Influence that held her. She didn't know how much more she had in her before spellshock took her. There was only one more spell she could think of casting. Hopefully, in the aftermath, Eleanor could summon enough control of herself to pick Gosha up off the floor.

How did Elsie's rhyme go, she thought, her mind refusing to focus.

A spell to bind, a spell to break, the words rolled through her battered brain.

A spell to find, a spell to take,

And one more spell to use but once, when all is lost and darkness comes.

"Gorogoltha," she said.

40

SPEAKING THE WORD WASN'T ENOUGH. Once again, she fought with every ounce of will she had to force Influence through the terrifying shape the chaos spell created within her, but when it was through everything changed. Influence flowed wildly hither and thither. The beating wings vanished in the flow. Sir Wilfred and his friends awoke from their trance, blinked and looked around, confused to find themselves together in this strange room.

Eleanor stopped screaming.

Without the Influence to hold her up, Gosha tumbled to the floor. Her head struck the ground, but she didn't feel the pain for, although her body was at rest, splayed out across the cold and hard institutional linoleum, she continued to fall. Her vision grew cloudy and a chill spread through her limbs. She felt tired, more so than she ever had before, too tired to even draw breath. Too tired to think.

She might have fallen for seconds or for years, she lost all sense of time, but eventually she found stillness, the cool resistance of dewy grass at her back. Above her domed a twilight sky, to her right the amber and gold of evening, to her left, the deep blue of night right before the last trace of sun drained from the sky.

"There you are," said a woman's voice. "I've been waiting for you."

Gosha tried to press herself up, but she was too tired and rolled over onto her side instead. The woman was old, her skin waxy and brittle, her voice dry and cracked. A bush of wild salt and pepper hair hung down her back, tamed by a bronze ring shaped into Celtic knots. Her robes were coarse, a deep indigo the color of night. She sat on a low stone worn smooth by weather, and around her wrist was a thin bronze shackle, its chain looping across the grass. She was a severe and fearful sight to behold sitting over Gosha, her knotted fingers stroking the grass, but something familiar about her meant Gosha wasn't afraid.

"Eleanor," she said. "Is that you?"

"It's me," said the old woman, a smile creasing her lined face. Her eyes, though rheumy and clouded with age, looked down upon her with the same humor and light as the Eleanor she knew. "You can get up. The exhaustion is nothing more than an illusion. You're not here in body, only in mind."

Gosha pushed herself up and the heaviness in her bones melted away. "Where are we?"

"Between."

Gosha looked around. They sat on the peak of a large hill looking out over a broad and flat landscape. To her right and far below them, almost at the edge of the horizon where the light of day still lingered in the sky, stood a shining city. To her left, behind Eleanor at the edge of darkness, a vast storm cloud lingered over the land, flickers of lightning shining purple through the billowing condensation.

"Over there," Eleanor pointed to the city, her chain clinking as she moved her hand, "is the real world. And there," she pointed to the storm, "is the other place, where the Lords and Ladies live."

"Is this the Shadowlands?" asked Gosha, her mind latching onto the only other experience like this in her comprehension.

"Oh no. You see that dark streak of land at the edge of the storm?"

A shadow fell across the wild moorland that rolled away from the hill toward the rumbling clouds.

"That's the Shadowlands. Over that way is Faerie." She pointed a long, gnarled finger in the direction of a patch of land shrouded in gently shifting blue-green fire. "And there is Hell, or one of them, at least."

Angry spires of rock jutted out of the ground beyond the blue-green glow, their surfaces glistening with the reflected lightning from the storm.

"Hell?" said Gosha, alarmed.

"Yes, but not the way you're thinking. The only people in there are those who want to be. Nobody goes there after death, or anything like that. No one goes anywhere after death. That's why I'm here."

Gosha looked at Eleanor again, taking in her frail limbs and stooped back. Is this what a thousand years looked like on a woman's body?

Eleanor laughed.

"A thousand years?" she said, responding to Gosha's thought. "I assure you, I'm not a year older than eight hundred and twenty. I was like you." She patted Gosha's hand, rough skin scratching against her. "Spellshocked, though it's not the affliction everyone makes it out to be. This is the problem with witches, you see. We're obsessed with control because we have so little of it. Once the other place," she pointed toward the storm, "was tamed and we could make talismans, we abandoned the old ways. Making use of the Between is too demanding. Much easier to issue a command and have your talisman do the hard work for you."

Eleanor raised her unchained arm to show Gosha. A slender vine with sprouted leaves wrapped itself around it from wrist to elbow.

"Look at yours," she said with amazement. "Very striking. You always have such a creative eye."

Gosha realized she could no longer feel the hardness of her lipstick poking into her ribs. Instead of her clothes, she wore an indigo robe to match Eleanor's. A spiral of deep oxblood pigment wound about her forearm like a tattoo.

"They come at a price, though," said Eleanor as she ran her fingers across her transformed twig in a gentle caress. "We give up too much when we turn our backs on the Between. We have an advantage oath-bearers will never have, even with all their sorcery and the gadgets they've created to force Influence to bend to their will. The Between is our birthright. Craft and Influence are in our blood."

She leaned over to face Gosha and picked a stalk of grass as she talked, chewing absently on its end.

"I know you've heard the adage that the first oath-bearer was a woman and the second was a witch, but there were witches long before the Keystone and the Lords and Ladies. If you head that way, you can see it for yourself. Just walk a few thousand years in that direction," she pointed down the hill, "and you'll come across some fearsome old witches. The future's back the other way, but don't concern yourself with it. Too confusing, too many possibilities."

"So this is how you've stayed alive for so long?"

"Yes, but I don't recommend it. The big makings require you to bind part of yourself here." She raised her arm and shook her chain. "You've seen what it does to me. If I were a stronger woman, I would have met my end when it came to me."

She picked herself up with more agility than a frail body that age should have, and stood, beckoning Gosha to join her. Gosha brushed her hands against her robe out of habit, but her hands were clean of grass and her back was dry.

Eleanor clasped Gosha's hands.

"Don't be afraid of the Between. Embrace it. Learn to use it. Spellshock is only one way in. There are much gentler paths. See that?"

Eleanor led them down the hill in the direction of the shining city, her chain stretching out endlessly after them, where a huge and complex circular labyrinth had been carved out of the turf into the chalk beneath. At its center sat a ghostly figure, a woman in a rough-woven skirt and prim bonnet who stared into space without seeing them.

"This was Crafted by a very skillful witch a thousand years before I was born. What you see sitting there is the part of her she left behind when she died. Walk her labyrinth and you can go anywhere in the world. You can even come here to the Between in body as well as mind. It has its dangers, though. Stray from the path and you might get lost, or worse. It helps to have a beacon to follow, like an invitation."

She picked up a small fragment of chalk from the edge of the labyrinth and was about to hand it to Gosha when she stopped and pulled it back.

"There are a few rules you should know about, safety precautions. Only ever accept a gift from another witch in the Between. There are other creatures abroad in these parts who will take accepting what they offer as an agreement of terms, and you never know what you've signed up for. Anything given by a witch you can consider safe."

She handed Gosha the chalk.

"This will only exist in the Between, but you will always have it with you. It will open the labyrinth. When we get back, I can show you how to use your telling deck to harness it."

At the mention of her telling deck, the peace Gosha had felt upon awakening in this place burned away.

"We're not safe," she said. "Back in the real world, we're not safe."

"Yes, you're right. Time works differently here, but we shouldn't dawdle. Come."

Eleanor led them further across the plain, toward the shining city, until they arrived at a stretch of sod that had turned brown within a large ring of malignant-looking toadstools, their surfaces glistening with moisture.

"Look at this," said Eleanor. "I've been watching it grow for days."

"I've seen it before." Every detail of the low cellar from her vision flooded back into her memory. "When I was spellshocked the first time. I had a vision."

"Mm," Eleanor nodded. "You didn't fully enter the Between, only grazed its surface. The membrane would have shown you something. Past, future, or something hidden from you. Which was it?"

"The future, I think. I saw the Houses of Parliament blown to rubble. And this thing," she pointed to the ring of fungus, "underground. Something hideous emerged from the center, the same creature that caused all that trouble in Paddington."

Eleanor shuddered. "In all my many years, I've never seen anything like that."

The dead matter in the center of the ring pulsed and grew into a small mound about the size of a soccer ball.

"It's starting," said Gosha. "Can we do anything to stop it?"

Eleanor stuck out her arm. The talisman wrapped around it grew, the wood spreading, twisting and reshaping itself until it became an axe heavy in her hand.

"You can do this, too," she said. "Simply picture what you want your talisman to be."

The first image to pop into her head was the blade her cursed lug wrench had become in the Shadowlands. The pigment on her arm reacted quickly, before she realized it was happening. Before she knew it, the sword was in her palm, dark fire licking off it, the curse whispering its yearning in her ears. Forged in a moment of desperation, the weapon had been a mistake she'd come to regret. She shook her head and thought of one of the swords on the covers of Edmund's fantasy novels, something righteous and filled with light. The weapon in her palm shifted and grew into a glistening steel two-handed sword, its silvery blade tinted oxblood.

"Chop up the ring," said Eleanor. "Get rid of the toadstools. We'll make our way around the circle from different sides."

She began to hack at the ring. With the first blow, a metallic shriek came from the mound at the center of the circle, and light flickered out beneath the dead sod that spread to the toadstools in a network of veins, making their scales ripple and flash. Gosha swung at a large, bulbous toadstool head, its dense stalk resisting when she tried to pull back the blade, slowing her down. She put more into it from then on, hacking at the ring with every ounce of strength she could muster. As she and Eleanor made their way around the circle, mushroom caps flying, the metallic screech grew stronger, the flickering light grew more frantic, but the mound ceased to expand.

"I thought you said exhaustion was an illusion," panted Gosha as she joined Eleanor on the far side of the ring.

"The exhaustion of your physical body is an illusion." Eleanor's eyes flashed with glee at the exertion. "Effort is effort, no matter where you are. Step back."

She beckoned Gosha away. Satisfied that Gosha had retreated far enough, she turned back to the ring and raised a fist in the air. With a massive crack, a bolt of lightning lanced down from the clear twilight sky and struck the mound, which burst into flames. The screeching and flashing subsided.

"How did you do that?" said Gosha, her face lit up with marvel.

"It's like when you make a button or magnetize a needle. You do it with imagery. The Between is highly responsive, even more than Influence, but you have to be very careful, very clear and robust about what you want. You have to hold in your mind all the ramifications of what it might entail, or the effect will be weak. Or worse, something other than you intended. This is why witches abandoned the Between as soon as the first witch came up with the Betrayal. Working it requires a lot of skill and talent, and not every witch has that. A talisman and a spoken spell are much more reliable, but we lost so much by binding ourselves to the Spheres and their way of doing things."

Gosha thought about the Craft of her mother compared to that of the other ladies. She was effective more because of her tenacity and sheer bloody-mindedness than her subtlety and skill.

Without warning, the earth beneath them shook with such force that she and Eleanor were knocked into the grass on their backsides. A few feet away from them, just beyond the still-smoking remains of the toadstool ring, a giant slab of stone thrust up out of the dirt, a runic symbol roughly hewn into its surface.

"What's going on?" asked Gosha as she helped Eleanor back to her feet. "Did you do that?"

"Not me." Eleanor walked around the circle toward it, taking care not to step on the charred earth, and placed a hand on the stone's surface. It towered over her at twice her height. "I've never seen this symbol before, have you?"

The earth shook again and a second stone thrust up across the remains of the toadstool ring, a different symbol on its face. Gosha ran over to it and checked both sides.

"The rune's only facing in."

Eleanor checked her own. "Here, too."

A third and fourth stone thrust up out of the ground halfway between the first two.

"I know this sequence," said Gosha, stepping back as a fifth and sixth stone emerged. "This is the way the doctor arranged his cards to contain the corrupted Influence."

Eleanor joined her as half a dozen more stones rumbled up from the ground.

"The Between is a reflection of the real world. Perhaps this is him trying again."

"Trying what? To create that monster?"

Between the standing stones, five spears of black crystalline rock thrust up out of the ground, jagged and malformed teeth compared to the clean surfaces and orderly planes of the standing stones. Fingers of crystal snaked out of the stalagmites and dug into the stones in an irregular lattice of spiked fronds that spread like a cage around and across the circle to join in the middle.

"Destroy it," said Eleanor stepping back and raising a fist. "Bring the whole thing down. Leave nothing standing."

Lightning showered down from the sky in a deafening cascade. The lattice and stones shook with each bolt that stock the circle, but remained standing.

"Fire," shouted Eleanor above the din. "We need fire as well!"

Here in the Between, Gosha still had her second sight, but what it showed her and allowed her to feel was very different from the tempestuous flow of Influence. The substance of the Between was like a glistening sheen that made all the colors in this twilight place brighter and deeper. She looked at her hands and thought of flames as she willed the substance at the ring as if she were pushing Influence, but her robes ignited and began to burn. She dropped to the damp grass and put them out as Eleanor's lightning fell.

"Don't push," shouted Eleanor. "You have to ask nicely. You have to coax the Between."

Sloppy, Gosha thought, chiding herself for making such a crude mistake.

Eleanor said the Between responded to imagery, the kind she used to create all the special ingredients in the locked cupboard in the kitchen. This was something Gosha was good at, better even than her mother and the other ladies thanks to her training as a photographer. She needed to be clear, precise, and meticulously detailed.

In the center of the ring, the mound began to grow. The dead vegetable matter thickened and piled up on itself into a massive, unburning pile that reminded her of autumns on Cheyne Heath after the parks department had been through and raked. The smell of smoldering leaves filtered through her memory. A bonfire was a good image, but fallen leaves were damp and took time to ignite. She needed something stronger.

Guy Fawkes. Last November, she'd taken the boys to the heath to watch the burning of the Guy and the fireworks display after. Now, that had been a bonfire! Bundles of kindling had been stacked high, the sticks and logs arranged to amplify the flames into a raging furnace. By the end of the night, the fifteen-foot pile had been razed to the ground, nothing remaining but ash and char.

She pictured the ring of stones, the stalagmites, and the horror forming within burning with the same intensity, every molecule ravaged by flame until nothing was left. She pictured a flat and smoldering plain where the ring had stood.

Please make this happen, she thought, and released the plea to providence as if wishing on a star.

The earth was the first to ignite, the mulch smoking and bursting into flame, the sod beneath it following suit. Then the stones and stalagmites began to glow, red to orange to white, until the entire ring burned with heat so fierce it pushed Gosha back.

The fire began to spread, leaking out across the grass.

"Stay with it!" shouted Eleanor above the roar and rumble of flames and lightning, her long hair breaking free of its ring and sticking out from her head. "Guide it! Shape it, or we'll all burn!"

Gosha cast her mind back to that chilly November night and the crowd that had gathered around the bonfire, turned toward it with awe and delight in their faces. She imagined all that focus pressing in on the flames, containing the baking heat. The flames before her shrunk back to the perimeter of the stone circle.

Deep within the maelstrom, the mound continued to grow despite the onslaught, its amorphous mass gaining shape, as if the creature were molding itself into being out of nothing. Limbs like fractured branches thrust out of the mass, giant caps of fungus emerging from its back and flickering like wings. Its body elongated and a head, little more than three bulbous roots, sprouted from the top of the fibrous, hairy barrel of its torso. The flames danced around it, jumping from the mulch to its twisted leg stumps, up its back and around its wing-growths, but they burned weakly, flames spilling like liquid across the creature's surface without taking hold.

She pictured the Guy on the bonfire on the heath, a dummy made of canvas stuffed with newsprint and dressed in an old thrift store suit, a pointed hat made of black construction paper and a store-bought mask with its eyeless grin, upturned mustache and pencil-thin beard. Such a gruesome tradition to burn in effigy a three-hundred-year-old revolutionary, yet it was so beloved by children and adults alike. She pictured the flames, the figure crumbling in on itself, and asked the Between to make it happen to the creature.

"Good!" shouted Eleanor, arms raised to the sky to summon down lightning in great, deafening cracks. "Good girl. Keep it going."

The flames that had danced across the creature's long, spindly limbs, its hairy barrel torso and chitinous wings took root, growing stronger and brighter. The monster opened its maw, a jagged rent in the malformed domes of its head, and screamed the same metallic screech that had reverberated off the toadstool ring, the jarring grate echoing off the slope of the hill at Gosha's back.

The dark, crystalline stalagmites came to life once more, branching veins growing inward from each stalk toward the creature, following the path of flames and climbing up its body, encasing it in a protective shell that caught the flickering arc light of Eleanor's onslaught. Flames and electric charge flowed across the crystal armor.

Gosha watched, appalled at the turmoil. Eight stones around the circle like the cards Sir Wilfred and the others had created under Dropnick's eye. Each man had made an artifact on their own without Dropnick's knowledge that spouted corruption powerful enough to create this hideous creature. And there were five ragged stalagmites disrupting the orderly ring of standing stones and protecting the creature. Twelve cards and twelve standing stones. Five artifacts and five stalagmites. The penny dropped. She kicked herself for not seeing it sooner.

"The black crystals," she shouted to Eleanor. "Focus on the crystals!"

It was too late. Protected from the witches' attack by the crystal armor, the creature was free to grow until it towered above the stones. Eleanor's lightning and Gosha's flames ripped at the stalagmites, but they sloughed off the attack in rivulets of fire and spark. The creature stumbled on twisted legs toward one of the standing stones and beat at it with its limbs. The stone crumbled, shot through with crystal veins that made it brittle and weak, and broke in great chunks. The creature staggered from the circle.

"The labyrinth," shouted Eleanor. "Don't let it get to it or it'll burst through into the real world!"

Gosha and Eleanor broke into a run, but Gosha was closer and put herself between the creature and the white chalk labyrinth glowing with the reflected light of the golden city. She summoned the sword from her talisman as the creature staggered toward her, but the long blade was heavy and cumbersome and she had no idea how to use it. She summoned again, desperately reaching for the feeling of some weapon that might be familiar. Oxblood pigment flowed from her right forearm across her body and spun itself into the form of her switchblade in her right hand, blade deployed and glistening in the twilight, and the cast-iron skillet from her kitchen in the other.

The creature's fungal wings fluttered behind it as it swept a limb to knock her aside, but she blocked it with the skillet, spun the blade in her hand to reverse her grip on the hilt so the tip pointed back, edge out, and spun her body to slash at the creature's arm. The blade cut through the crystal and black fluid oozed from the rent. The creature opened its maw and screeched.

Remembering a nature documentary on the BBC she saw once about wolves hobbling their prey by severing their hamstrings, she rolled between the creature's feet and sliced up at the backs of its legs. She dropped the skillet and held the hilt of her blade with both hands to stab at the creature's back, but its wings beat and knocked her down. It turned to loom over her, jagged teeth dripping ichor on her face, but as it reached down with spiked claws to rip at her, the surrounding air began to glow. Shimmering veils of northern lights folded and unfolded around it, growing brighter and brighter until Gosha was forced to cover her eyes. When the glow subsided, the creature was gone.

"What did you do?" said Eleanor as she reached Gosha and helped her up off the grass with thin and wiry arms that were surprisingly strong for one so ancient.

"It wasn't me."

She looked down at the earth where the creature had stood. The turf was burned away, the ground beneath it fused to slag. Behind it, the stalagmites had grown to encase the standing stones in a thicket of crystal thorns, the ruins of the broken stone now the root of a new growth, a crystal spire that stretched up into the sky.

"I think we should get back," said Eleanor, looking up at the spire, her ancient face creased with worry.

41

THEY RAN BACK UP THE hill. Eleanor gathered up her chain as they went.

"All you have to do is touch the stone," she said as they reached the top, "and you'll wake up in your body. But wait a moment."

She approached the rock and laid the chain across it. A jagged stone appeared in her free hand and she struck the chain hard.

"There," she said when she'd broken one of the links after several blows. She unthreaded it, popped it in her mouth and swallowed. "I'll be a little more use to you when we get back."

She pinched the two severed ends of the chain together and rubbed them between finger and thumb. The links began to glow, and the ends fused.

"Do you have the piece of chalk from the labyrinth?"

Gosha pulled the tiny chip from the pocket of her robe and held it up.

"Excellent," said Eleanor. "Now swallow it."

"Swallow it?"

"Yes, that's how you bring its power back to the real world. Here." She stooped and dug her fingers into the grass and pulled up a handful of turf and soil. "These, too. That way you won't need psychedelic drugs or spellshock to commune with the Between. It's fine," she said at Gosha's hesitation.

She nodded down the hill to the darkened strip of land at the border of the storm cloud.

"None of this is material." She smiled, lifting Gosha's hands to her mouth to get her to eat. "It's all metaphor."

Gosha awoke with a strong taste of chalk and grass in her mouth, the floor cold and hard against her back, above her a single overhead ceiling sconce was covered in a thick wire cage, its light dim and stark. Somewhere in the distance, a man screamed the wail of desperation of someone who knew they were about to die.

"Eleanor," she said, pushing herself up off the floor.

They were in one of the many patient cells Gosha had seen in the security cameras. Eleanor sat up on the bed. She looked older, her features a little more defined by deepening lines around her eyes and lips. Far from the withered crone Gosha had met in the Between, it was the face of a woman in her late thirties and not the jarringly youthful twenty-five-year-old Gosha was familiar with. Taking the link from her chain had cost her.

Another scream rang out, muffled by the thick security door to the cell.

"What's happening out there?" said Eleanor as she went to press her ear against the door.

Gosha joined her and placed a hand on the lock.

"Heckatisk," she said, and immediately regretted it.

As the door unlocked with a click, the room lurched sideways and she lost her balance, falling into Eleanor's arms.

"Careful," said Eleanor, leaning Gosha against the wall. "The spellshock takes a long while to work its way through you. *Aricantas.*"

Gosha's nausea faded, and the room ceased cavorting around her.

"That should keep you on your feet, but no more regular Craft. When your pee loses its green tinge, you'll know you can use it again, but that won't be for at least a week. Until then, you'll have to use the Between."

She put her hand on the lock.

"Petitin," she said, and the lock clicked shut. "Try it now."

Another scream came from outside, a woman.

"There's no time, Eleanor." Gosha frowned. "Open the door."

Eleanor held Gosha by the shoulders and pressed her firmly against the wall to stare her squarely in the eye.

"Listen to me," she said, the stern set of her face creating wrinkles between her eyebrows. "You're fearless. I've seen you rush into situations without a care for yourself that would make any other witch balk. You've done tremendous good in the world and made your mother proud, but you've pushed yourself to the edge. Most of my power is caught up in the enchantment that keeps me alive. All I can do is parlor tricks, only the most rudimentary spells. The link I consumed will help me stay coherent, but if I overdo it, I'll be batty as a seamstress without any pins, and no use to anybody. You're going to have to do the heavy lifting. Be thoughtful. Consider the consequences before you act. You can't push through this like you always do. Spellshock will have you stuck in the Between and it will take an entire coven to get you back. I've given you a gift. Learn to use it."

Had anyone else talked to her like that, Gosha would have bristled. She would have nodded and made nice until she could get away and get on with it, but coming from Eleanor, who had always been so quiet and good natured, with never a harsh word for anyone, the words hit home.

"Okay," she said. "Okay, how do I do it?"

"Take out your talisman."

Gosha fished it out of her bra and held it in her palm.

"You must never use emotional force the way you do when casting unseeded spells," said Eleanor, cupping Gosha's hand in her own. "You cannot compel the Between to carry out your whim, the way oath-bearers try to bring creation to heel with belligerence and willpower. The Between must be evoked and courted. You must be clear in what you ask of it and trust that it will come to do your bidding in the way that it sees fit. Push and it will push back. Demand and it will comply to the letter of your request and not the spirit, or worse, it will do the opposite. Be clear, be trustful, and be patient."

"Sounds exactly like dealing with my mother."

A wry smile spread across Eleanor's face.

"Your mother has always been a force to be reckoned with."

"You said I have to evoke the Between. How do I do that?"

"You've eaten its soil. You carry it with you. In another age it would have required meditation, poetry, and consciousness-altering drugs to reach it, even after consuming its substance. But you have an advantage not available to witches before the creation of the Keystone that bound and tamed Influence. You have your talisman."

She closed Gosha's fingers around the black and gold tube of lipstick. Another scream echoed through the halls, drawing Gosha's attention.

"Focus," said Eleanor. "There's nothing you could have done that would have helped that poor soul. Get this quickly and you'll be able to help the next."

Gosha nodded. "Yes, I'm sorry."

"Use your second sight."

Gosha softened her gaze to sense the thick and turgid Influence that clung to her skin like a humid night in the tropics.

"What do I look for?"

"Think back on when we were in the Between. What struck you most about the landscape?"

Gosha thought a moment, recalling the twilight sky that shifted from gold to the deepest purple as day transitioned to night across the canopy of the heavens. Under that sky, all the colors were a little brighter, a little richer, suffused with the warm glow of fond memories of late summer evenings. The stillness of the air and the quiet that blanketed the landscape touched something inside her that calmed her fears and made her yearn to go back.

"The light," she said. "It was breathtaking."

"Good." Eleanor took a step back to allow Gosha to observe the featureless room and the flat, unforgiving fluorescent light that filled it. "Look for that light. It's there under the surface, so close it will burst through if only you give it a chance."

"How could I even..." Gosha began to protest at the feat of imagination it would require to picture it in this relentlessly dreary place designed to numb the soul into submission, but before she could finish the thought, the room began to glow. It came slowly at first, a hesitant sheen across the blank white walls, but it quickly grew stronger, a filter of warmth and humanity against the absolute negation of the cell.

"That's it," said Eleanor with a smile. "You have it. Now ask for the door to open. Remember, it's the same way of thinking as when you're preparing ingredients for a recipe or Crafting a card for your telling deck. Tell me when you're ready."

Another scream broke Gosha's concentration. Frustration, impatience, and outrage wove themselves into a spike that stabbed at her gut, dimming the glow of the Between, but she calmed herself. She pictured all the people out there on the other side of the door who needed her help. She pictured herself, trapped in the cell, stewing at her imprisonment. She pictured the door opening and herself and Eleanor charging through it.

"I'm ready."

"This is the hardest part of all. Release it. Send it into your talisman. Let go of any scrap of worry that your wish won't be granted. Trust in the Between."

"How can I do that? That's impossible."

"You must," Eleanor shrugged, "or we'll be two crippled witches without a spell book between us."

She released the image into the talisman and felt the turgid Influence shift around her, no more than the lightest puff of power flowing through the lipstick, but all her rage and anxiety still bubbled within.

"Let it go," said Eleanor.

The glow of twilight, rich in color, flickered about her, and she remembered the moment of quiet and stillness when she had first awoken on the hill, by the stone.

The door clicked open.

Eleanor clapped her hands.

"Well done!"

42

THE LIGHTS OUTSIDE FLICKERED AND buzzed. The cell they'd been confined in was at the end of a long corridor. Identical doors lined the walls at regular intervals, all locked when she tried their handles. Gosha peered through the mesh-covered slit in the door across from theirs. A young woman huddled in a corner with her knees pulled up to her chest, her face buried in the tent she'd made of her nightgown around her legs.

"We have to get these people out."

Gosha reached for the door handle, but Eleanor pulled her arm back.

"With that thing out here, don't you think they'll be safer in their cells? If we get rid of it, we can come back and set everyone free."

"You're right." Gosha took a deep breath and nodded. It tore at her to leave these people locked away, but what good would it do if freeing them now would lead them to the creature?

She patted down her jacket. She still had her telling deck on her, but her switchblade was gone.

"We have everything we need," said Eleanor at the look on Gosha's face.

Gosha tucked her lipstick back in her bra. If she got out of this, she needed to devise some kind of pocket that would hold it against her skin without it digging into her.

"Hold the Between with you as you go," Eleanor whispered as Gosha peered around the corner. "That way it will be there for you when you need it."

The twilight glow had already begun to fade. Gosha cleared her mind and allowed it to flood back, but to stay like that was going to require energy and attention she wasn't sure she had.

The corridor was long, stretching off into the gloom of the malfunctioning overhead lights. At the end was a pair of double doors like the ones leading to the room where Sir Wilfred and the others had been held. For a moment her heart leaped thinking she might find them so easily, but then she remembered they'd been on the top floor, and the stairs up were right behind her. One of the doors had fallen to hang from a single hinge like a broken limb dangling useless from the joint.

She rounded the corner, resisting the urge to crouch. They were fully exposed. No amount of shrinking would prevent Dropnick's men or the creature from seeing them, but it felt reckless to stand tall and stride down the corridor. As she passed the broken door, the sight beyond made her stop in horror.

"Oh, my Lady," said Eleanor from behind her as Gosha entered.

The room was another open space like the one upstairs, with collapsed and stacked tables and chairs around the walls. At the center, three tables had been pushed together to create one large surface around which sat a dozen people, three to a side, wearing hospital gowns, robes and cheap slippers. All twelve appeared dead, some half-fallen out of their chairs, some slumped on the table, each of them withered and mummified, expressions of pain and fear etched on their faces. Each had around their neck a copper picture frame containing one of the cards Sir Wilfred and the others had created. Copper wires attached the frames to crown contraptions similar to the one Dropnick had placed on Eleanor that caused her such agony. A copper cable led from the back of each crown to a device placed at the center of the table: a hefty octahedral crystal mounted on a brass base, the crystal cracked and the base half-melted. Her heart condensed into a cold lump that burned in her chest. She had seen a device like this before at Emerson Margrave's country estate four years ago.

"This thing is designed to suck the Influence out of people," she said as she reached across the table to grab it.

She turned it over to examine the base. The switches and dials underneath were identical to the device she'd seen before and were of the same construction and workmanship as all the other gadgets Dropnick was using in the hospital. And hadn't Margrave made some comment about getting his device from a doctor? It had to have been Dropnick.

"I would never have thought to use it without the tip from our mysterious friend."

The words of Vivien Drake, acolyte of Shadow and co-conspirator with Roy Merton to seize the sainthood of Shadow from Pauline Sutton and kill everyone in Cheyne Heath in the process, sprung into her mind with a force of realization that staggered her. This man, Dropnick, had been the architect of all the misery in her life since she'd become a witch.

"Gosha," said Eleanor from the other side of the table where she had righted one of the slumped victims. "This one's alive."

Gosha ran to her side as Eleanor cast her healing spell and the woman's eyelids flickered. Her dark skin was gaunt and ashy, but as she opened her eyes, Gosha realized she knew her.

"This is Rosamund, the witch who helped me when the spirit of Johnny's friend was threatening to drive me mad. She gave me the wode sump."

“That explains why she’s still alive,” said Eleanor, looking around at the other corpses. “These people were all attacked by the creature. It consumed their auras. A witch doesn’t have an aura, so it passed her by.”

“Auntie Rosamund?” Gosha squatted next to her. “Do you remember me? My name’s Gosha. You were very kind to me once.”

Rosamund looked back and forth between her and Eleanor, frowned and shook her head as she rubbed her temples. She placed a hand on Gosha’s cheek as her lips worked, but no words came out.

Gosha looked up at Eleanor. “Can you do anything else to help her?”

Eleanor shook her head. “The healing I cast is still working on her, but it’ll take time.”

“Rich tea, shortbread, ginger snap,” croaked Rosamund.

“What’s that?” Gosha squeezed her hand.

“Jaffa cake, digestive biscuit, jammy dodger.”

Rosamund was gaining strength, her eyes clearing.

“Chocolate bourbon, custard cream, hobnob.”

“I don’t understand what she’s saying.”

“Her mind’s been addled by whatever happened here.”

Frustrated, Gosha stood and stepped back to look around the circle at the bodies.

“Can you move, dear?” asked Eleanor with a hand under Rosamund’s arm.

Rosamund nodded.

“Garibaldi, fig newton, chocolate finger,” she said as Eleanor helped her up.

Around the table the glow of the Between darkened to a purple hue that deepened to black around the device where Gosha had left it at one edge of the table. Twelve sacrificial victims, twelve cards and twelve standing stones, five artifacts and five stalagmites.

“This is where he summoned the creature away from the Between,” she said, half to herself. “He thought he could contain it with the cards, maybe even trap it in the crystal, but the artifacts Sir Wilfred and the others made interfered. It broke free."

"Wensleydale," said Rosamund, on her feet with Eleanor's help.

"I think I'm beginning to understand her," said the ancient witch, the flickering gloom around them granting her an illusion of the decade of youth she'd sacrificed to be coherent. "She's agreeing with you."

Rosamund nodded.

"Colby, Manchego."

"They took her talisman, but her second sight is still strong," translated Eleanor.

"Halloumi, Camembert, Roquefort."

"The little doctor had big plans."

"Emmental, Taleggio, Pecorino."

"He thinks he understands, but he has a lot to learn."

"Burrata, Stilton, Mimolette."

"The moment the summoning went wrong, he and his men fled." Eleanor put an arm around Rosamund. "Are you okay to come with us?"

"Caciocavallo." Rosamund nodded vigorously. "Fontina, Morbier, Tilsit."

"She says she needs to find her talisman. She can feel it's still in the building."

"Could I find it for her?" asked Gosha.

"Sweetheart," said Eleanor as she helped Rosamund shuffle toward the doors, "you can do anything you set your mind to, and doubly so now you have the Between."

"Benedict, deviled, egg drop soup," said Rosamund, staring at the other witches with awe.

"Yes, dear," said Eleanor. "We've had quite an evening."

"How do I find it?" asked Gosha.

"Well, you know how to cast a finding, and you know how to summon an object to you. Do you know what her talisman is?"

Gosha cast her mind back to that day in the bookshop when she and Johnny were searching for some clue as to who had killed Mick Trash, Johnny's friend, before George came home from murdering his father and upended her life.

"It's a clear plastic ruler, like one you'd have in your pencil case at school."

"Well, there you are. What do the Christians say? Ask and ye shall receive."

Gosha pictured Auntie Rosamund in her workshop in the basement of the bookstore, waving her plastic ruler over Gosha as Gosha did her best not to throw up. She took in Rosamund as she was now, diminished and addled, missing an essential part of herself, and wished her to be whole. Sending the wish into her talisman, she took a deep breath and allowed herself a moment to bask in the loveliness of the twilight glow.

The ruler appeared in her hand.

Rosamund gave out a little cry of joy, took the talisman and held it to her chest, clasping it with both hands.

"Huevos Rancheros," she grinned.

"She says 'thank you.'"

"I think I got that one," said Gosha.

They moved cautiously, Eleanor and Rosamund several paces behind Gosha. The corridor spanned the entire length of the building, stretching off into the flickering gloom ahead. Cell doors on either side had been ripped clear off their hinges, their inhabitants lying dead and mummified within. Halfway down, they passed a nurse's station where a handful of dessicated men and women lay lifeless, spread out across the counters and collapsed in corners.

From a room to her left came the sound of a struggle, the scrapes and thuds of furniture being hurled around with abandon. She edged forward to peer in, but one look at the commotion inside and Gosha grabbed the other witches and pulled them with her behind the cover of the nurse's station counter. Three orderlies struggled, two carrying large batons with metal prongs on the end attempting to corral the third. The third was the source of horror that had sent Gosha scurrying for cover. The young man was withered, in an advanced state of mummification, but around him the aura of the creature was strong, clearer and more vivid than Gosha had seen it before, its fungal wings spreading behind it, the darkened glow of the Between shrouding it in purple ink.

Peering over the counter Gosha watched as the two orderlies jabbed at the creature over a barrier of pushed-together beds, their batons flashing with sparks that confused it and forced it back, though only for a moment. The creature—it rode the poor, half-dead man like a horse, animating the fading body—threw its head back in a silent roar and leaped over the beds with inhuman strength, and crashed into one of the orderlies. The mummified body fell dead across its new host as the creature jumped bodies. The creature absorbed the young man's aura into its own and grew a little brighter, a little more defined in Gosha's second sight. If it consumed enough people, she wondered, would it become real?

The new host screamed as his life force was drained from him, thrashing about desperately as if he could shake off the unseen thing that was killing him. His partner swore and backed out of the room, slamming the door shut and fumbling to get his keys in the lock. When he succeeded in locking the door, he turned and fled.

"We need a plan, and quick," whispered Gosha, ducking back down and slumping against the counter between the corpse of a male orderly hanging limp on one side and the crumpled form of a nurse on the other. "That thing was in the Between and now it's here. Dropnick's cards created it and would have contained it if the artifacts hadn't interfered." She pulled her telling deck out of her pocket. "Could we trap it with my cards?"

The orderly's screams grew weaker behind the locked door.

“I could devise a sequence of cards for you,” whispered Eleanor as she peered over the counter, clutching the twig that was her talisman so tightly her hand had turned white. “But how would you empower them? We can’t kill twelve more people.”

“What if we take it back to the Between? Won’t the cards be more powerful there?”

“Yes, but you’d need a great making. You would have to leave some part of you behind. And you’d always have to be vigilant. How would you even get the monster there?”

“Through that labyrinth you showed me. You said it can take you bodily into the Between.”

“The path is extremely complex. The slightest misstep and you have to go back to the beginning. You couldn’t just lure it there with a carrot on a stick. How would you subdue it? I can’t go with you, or the Between will addle me and I’ll be useless again. I’d waste a decade of life for nothing”

Gosha stopped a moment to immerse herself in the calming twilight glow so she could think. The orderly’s screams stopped. An idea began to form in her mind. Like all her ideas, it was dangerous and reckless. Eleanor had admonished her to think about the consequences before she acted, but all Gosha could imagine was what would happen if she didn’t.

“It feeds on auras,” she said.

“But you don’t have one.” Eleanor said with a scolding firmness that told Gosha they were thinking along the same lines.

“Adair and the other acolytes of Fortune have manufactured auras that wrap around them.”

“No,” said Eleanor, understanding where Gosha’s train of thought was leading. “Absolutely not.”

“Could we make one for me, to draw it to me? Then you could guide me through the labyrinth before it consumes it. You said it yourself, I have no aura. It won’t consume me. In the Between there’ll be no one else with an aura it could feed on.”

Eleanor stared at her, livid. The creature began to hammer at the door.

"Give me your deck," she said, thrusting out a hand. "Your mother will kill me. I'll do this for you, but you'll lose the cards you use to contain it. You'll have to leave them behind in the Between. You'll never be able to replace them. If you do, it could break the bindings and we'll all be back here again."

She began to rifle through the cards. The entire wall shook with the force of the creature's attempt to get out.

"Go and do something about that," Eleanor snapped. "I need time to work."

43

THE DOOR SHOOK, STRAINING ON its hinges as the creature within worked furiously to get out. If Gosha could have used spell words, she could have sealed it in by binding the door to the wall around it, a strategy that had served her well in the past. Instead, she pictured a welder sealing an iron hatch shut, a rising tide being held back by a concrete seawall, and a wild animal growling within a cage. She sent her wish into the talisman and the Between took it. A web of fine, glowing threads appeared around the frame of the door.

"Here," said Eleanor, scurrying out from behind the counter to hand her two stacks of cards. "This one is for your aura, this one is to trap the creature."

Behind her, Rosamund stuck her head up from the shelter of the counter.

"Bisto gravy," she squeaked and ducked her head down once again.

"She says to be careful. Good luck."

The stack of cards to create an artificial aura was thick, twice the size of the other.

"How do I make this work?"

"No idea." Eleanor shrugged and kissed Gosha on the cheek before disappearing back behind the counter.

Gosha pocketed the smaller stack and thumbed through the cards, a mixture of major and minor arcana. She tried to string together meaning out of the disparate images, but taken as a whole, all they gave her was a complicated jumble with no through line to inspire her.

How do you ask for something you don't understand? she thought and ran her fingers through her lank and heavy hair to massage her scalp as if she might somehow rub an idea into her head.

She flinched as the entire wall shook with a blow from the creature on the other side.

Fanning out the cards, she held them in front of her at arm's length, the twilight glow of the Between shifting through the photographic emulsion and giving the images an illusion of life. The card on top was that of Mystery inverted, a portrait of a veiled woman sitting on a rocking chair and stroking a large, long-haired cat, a still from the last fashion editorial she had shot before she became a witch, the same card Elsie had given her to hand to Euphemia Graham when she took her Betrayal. For a terrifying and miserable half hour, before her mother had helped her complete the ritual, she'd suffered under the burden of bearing an oath to Euphemia Graham. Influence had raged around her, beating her into the ground, threatening to crush the breath from her lungs.

But I was an oath-bearer, if only for a moment, she thought. *I had the kind of aura the creature would love to feast on.*

She summoned the memory in as much detail as she could, down to the uncomfortable outfit her mother had forced her to wear and the smell of freshly cut grass and morning dew. She sent her wish into the talisman and blanked her mind, basking in the calm of the twilight glow.

At first, she thought she'd failed, but the turgid Influence around her began to shift and swirl, began to brush against her skin and rustle through her hair, whipping up into a frenzy that she feared would dash her against the wall, it beat against her with such force.

It's now or never, she thought.

She pictured a giant fist crashing through the wall, dust, plaster, and splinters of wood bursting everywhere, sent it into the talisman and tried again to blank her mind, a feat that grew harder and harder the more urgent her need became. She had to figure out a better way to handle this. Casting spells this way took too much time.

The entire wall wobbled, plaster cracking in long gashes that snaked away from the door, which ripped from its frame with a concussive crack to be thrown back into the cell. In the ragged opening stood the dessicated corpse of the orderly, animated by the towering ghostly image of the creature, maw open and jaws gnashing, twisted insect-limbs snapping in her direction as giant wings spread out from its back. A long tongue lashed out toward her, tasting her newly-fashioned aura. The corpse fell, shattering into dust as it hit the floor. The creature leaped at her.

As it draped itself around her and began to consume her simulated heath of Influence, she screamed. Even though the aura had been hers for only a handful of seconds, she felt as if she were being eaten alive, as if her fingers and toes were being ripped from her, her limbs ground into meat inch by inch back to the joints.

"Eleanor!" she shouted, unsure of how long she would last. "How do I get to the labyrinth?"

"Two steps forward," Eleanor shouted back.

"What?"

"Follow my directions exactly! Two steps forward."

She did as she was told.

"Turn to the right, then one step. To the left, then three steps. To the right and four..."

The pattern was complex and erratic. She shuffled through the corridor like a game piece being moved on an invisible board, somehow never running into walls, always moving, getting further and further away from the sound of Eleanor's voice, the creature burrowing into her skin, into her organs and veins until she thought she'd collapse, but she kept on moving, one foot in front of the other, turning this way and that until the corridor spun around her and she thought she might fall, until the hard linoleum floor became soft as grass, until the sterile, antiseptic air became sweet and cool, a gentle breeze brushing across her face, and she found herself once again in the Between.

This time the Between was different. Entering in mind only through the violent disorientation of spellshock, she had arrived and found peace, the calm of refuge in a place that was both unfamiliar and to which she knew she belonged. Now, having passed through the membrane that separated reality from this strange half-place in body as well as mind, the Between was an untamed landscape where menace loomed over the horizon, the colossal storm clouds of the other place visible from where she stood at the edge of the labyrinth on the plain below the grassy hill.

A metallic screech cut through the air from behind her and a massive blow struck her back, knocking her down, the cards that had given her the simulated aura spilling across the grass. She rolled over on her back to find the creature towering above her, once again a physical, material threat. Its head thrashed about, bulbous, segmented eyes rolling around in confusion, and settled on Gosha. It spread its wings, the moist, oozing scales blotting out the sky, fluttered them and leaped at her, covering the scant few feet between them in the space of a heartbeat.

She rolled out of its way and, without thought of what images to use or giving up the wish and trusting the Between, reached out to call weapons to her hands. Blade and skillet appeared: the knife in her right hand heavy and ornate with Celtic knots, the blade sharp-pointed and serrated along its edge; the handle of the iron skillet in her other elongated in her grip, the pan small and dense like the head of a mace.

Before she could swing up to her feet, the creature struck out, backhanding her with an unnaturally segmented limb, but she blocked the blow with her skillet mace. The limb crunched and wept black ichor.

As it pulled its arm back to nurse the wound, Gosha spun to her hands and knees, pushed herself into a squat and launched herself at the creature, stabbing and ripping up into its undefended lower torso with the blade. The blade sank into fur and flesh, leaving behind a ragged slice in its abdomen. A black, oily ooze seeped out, and it screeched its metallic cry, the wail of an infant distorted through layers of electric guitar, and struck out with its other arm, lifting her off it and throwing her a dozen yards away. She landed hard, her joints aching at the impact, the wind knocked out of her.

They had emerged from the labyrinth close to the circle of standing stones and crystal growths. Fearing what would happen if she succeeded in trapping the creature so close to either, she staggered to her feet, gasping for air, and ran for the open plain with the grassy hill at her back. She pumped her legs harder than she had ever before, her lungs bursting in her chest, but behind her the pounding of the creature loping toward her grew closer and closer until it hit her from behind and knocked her down. Rearing up over her, it slammed down with both its arms.

She screamed a shout of defiance as she raised her arms to protect herself and clenched her eyes shut in anticipation of the blow, but instead of the impact came a wooden crunch above her. She opened her eyes to find herself encased in a shell of interwoven roots grown up out of the ground protecting her from the creature's onslaught. The Between had interpreted her cry and her gesture of self-protection as a wish and had given her the letter of what she had wanted, but the complete lack of thought for the ramifications had left her trapped in place. The shell shuddered with blow after blow from above, creaking and splintering a bit more each time. It wouldn't be long before the creature burst through.

Even though the shell blocked out the sky, she could still see, the twilight glow radiating from every surface around her. She pulled from her pocket the second stack of cards Eleanor had prepared for her, certain her only hope was to get the cage built and the creature trapped. The top card was the Known, a photograph she'd taken of an elderly gentleman reading at the local library, shelves of books spreading out behind him.

The Known, she thought, realizing she had no idea in what order to arrange the cards. *How ironic.*

Dropnick had said that sequence was important when he was experimenting with his own circle. He had twelve cards, but Eleanor had only given her eight, enough for the four cardinal points on a compass and the half-steps between. But did she cast the cards clockwise or widdershins? Widdershins would suit the contrary nature of all witches, but Dropnick had arranged his cards by switching pairs. She didn't have the luxury to keep fiddling until she got it right.

She held up the Known, ready to cast it the moment her protective shell broke, with no idea where the second card should go. She needed to keep the card in sight to cast the spell which meant she only had one free hand for a weapon.

The shell didn't break so much as shatter into splinters, but Gosha was ready. She spun up into a squat and launched herself up at the creature, driving the tip of the blade deep into its chest and twisting until it staggered back, screeching with outrage, clutching at the knife trying to pull it free. She recognized that screech: Edmund when he was six, overtired and overagitated, jacked up on ice cream cones playing on the beach.

She held up the card, pictured the creature contained within a circle of stones and wished.

The card vanished in a glowing swirl. From the earth in front of her emerged not a monolithic standing stone, but a giant statue of the elderly man at his table in the library turned to face the creature. Distracted from its agony by the rumble, it saw the statue and screeched with fear, flinching back until she made the mistake of peering around the carved granite to see what it was doing. At the sight of her, it roared and bounded the dozen paces toward her. She ducked to hide behind the statue, and it flinched back again, staring up at the carved rock with its segmented eyes, howling.

Enormous, terrifying, and not very bright, she thought. *A dreadful combination, but one I can turn to my advantage.*

As it paced and bayed on the other side of the statue, she looked at the next card: the Witch, a candid shot of her mother Gosha had snapped in the kitchen when Agnieszka was absorbed in the details of a recipe she was making. The card after that was Chaos, a photo of a cloud of ink swirling in a glass of water. The fourth was Creation, her supplier at the photographic studio adjusting a towering enlarger, the fifth Law, the sixth Balance, the seventh Will, the eighth Purity.

Chaos and Creation, Law and Balance, Will and Purity, she thought. *Definitely matched pairs.*

Great. That meant she had to get to the other side of the creature to cast the second card. She took a deep breath and pressed her back against the statue. The glowing city in the distance Eleanor had said represented the real world shone out even brighter than the golden strip of sun across the far horizon behind it.

The creature screeched behind her, snapping her out of the fugue her exhausted mind had fallen into for the briefest of instants. She'd won enough games of tag with Edmund and Timothy for a strategy to form in her mind.

She pulled herself up and broke right, emerging from cover long enough for the creature to leap for her, then feinted left to the other side of the statue, keeping it between them for as long as possible as she edged her way around to the other side of it, and broke into a sprint, her feet pounding into the earth to propel her across the grass. The creature screeched with fury as it bounded after her. She stopped, turned, raised the next card and wished. The card was snatched from her hand and from the earth burst up a statue of her mother grinding herbs in a mortar and pestle. The creature dug its feet into the grass and scrambled back.

If the first two cards were north and south, the next two would be east and west. She bounced on the balls of her feet, edging from side to side, ready to dash should the creature lunge for her, but nothing happened. The statue between them blocked her view.

"Oi, wanker!" she shouted. "Come and get me!"

It took the bait and broke right to barrel around the statue toward her, but she dashed left to the halfway point between the two statues and cast the next card. The shape that ripped up out of the ground was an amorphous cloud, eerily like the gigantic storm that loomed on the other side of the hill.

She didn't stop to admire the statue, instead taking advantage of the creature's hesitation at this new appearance, and dashed the long way round for the far side of the compass cross she was building to the statue of the old man reading. She skidded to a stop behind it as the creature turned to track her. Giving herself no more time than it took to gulp in one deep breath, she ran for the fourth position and cast the card. A giant photographic enlarger emerged from the earth, reimagined as some kind of arcane astrological device, its scope pointing up at the sky.

The creature's pacing grew frenzied, the four statues staring down at it causing it distress. It tore up the grass with its ragged claws, churning the ground within the cross to peaty mud as it lashed around trying to reach her and avoid the statues at the same time. The other side of the cross was suddenly very far away, despite the protection of the statues. One wrong move and it would have her. She reordered the cards so she could cast them in a loop, run widdershins around the circle, of course: Law, Will, Balance, Purity.

Law was an Art Nouveau statue of Lady Justice complete with blindfold, sword, and scales, Will a giant sphere, and Balance a child's see-saw. By the time she'd cast Balance, lungs bursting with exertion, the creature realized what was happening and leaped for the one remaining opening. It flapped its wings, though they weren't yet strong enough to lift it more than a few feet as it hurled toward the opening, forcing Gosha to cut across the circle and block the gap with her body. The creature grabbed her by the shoulder. Its sticky, jagged fingers wrapped around her torso and lifted her off her feet toward its snapping jaws.

The hilt of her knife stuck out of the creature's chest close enough that she could reach out and curl her fingers around it. She yanked, and the creature wailed with agony, its metallic screech drilling into her skull, but the knife was buried deep in its hairy torso and wouldn't budge. As it grabbed her with its other hand and began to squeeze, she kicked her feet up and pushed at its body. The blade came free, leaving a gash that oozed black ichor. It released her and she fell heavily to the ground on her feet, her thighbones jamming up painfully into her hips with the impact.

She rolled out of the way and cast the final card, Purity. A single column of stone lanced up out of the ground between them. She collapsed back, breath heaving, as the creature threw itself at the column to get at her, but a force she couldn't see repelled it. It slunk back to the scooped-out center of the circle and paced, clutching at its wound with one hand, head thrown back to howl at the indifferent sky.

She took her time on her back, the cool and springy grass supporting her, with one eye on the creature as it stalked about its new cage, testing its limits.

The soft earth grew hard and rough beneath her. She sat up and found herself surrounded by veins of the black crystal from the manifestations of Sir Wilfred and his friends' artifacts that snaked across the ground toward the circle of statues.

"No, no, no," she moaned as she rolled onto her hands and knees to survey the advance.

She hacked at the nearest vein with the knife. It cracked and withered, but fifty more slow-moving seams creeped toward the circle.

She rose to her full height and, remembering the figure of aged Eleanor summoning lightning, raised an arm to the heavens.

"Stop!" she screamed at the sky, frustration surging up within her.

Instead of lightning striking down from above, the ground beneath her feet rumbled and cracked, matching the fury that made her heart pound and sent hot blood throbbing through her temples. The earth dried and split, a rough and uneven fissure that spread across the advancing crystal, breaking its path. Waves of heat rolled off the fissure as the earth and rock within it began to melt into a river of lava that slowly flowed toward the remains of Dropnick's summoning circle, consuming the crystal and standing stones.

The more she allowed her fury to rise, the further the lava rolled, as if her mounting anger were its source. Part of her mind cowered, shocked at what she wrought, but most of her surrendered to the abandon, glad, after so much angst, to be able to release all the pent-up wrath that had been simmering inside her at the way she'd been treated by the Convocation of Saints and the mysterious Doctor Dropnick.

She roared with triumph until her throat grew raw, her cry mingling with the creature's wail, until the entire plain from where she stood to the other circle was engulfed and the last of stalagmites had shattered and melted. When it was all over, all trace of the circle devoured by the lava, she turned back to the creature, slapped her palm into the crook of her elbow and thrust up her fist at it in the universal sign for 'up yours.'

The feeling of triumph began to recede. She looked around her, the shining city an impossible distance away.

"Fuck," she said out loud to no one. "How do I get back?"

44

SHE STARTED UP THE HILL to the stone that she and Eleanor had used to return to the real world. Eleanor's chain was still there, looped around the stone, the manacle at the end mclasped around the woody stem of a small shrub heavy with pink blossoms. Nothing happened when she touched the stone.

Down below, the chalk lines of the labyrinth glowed in the twilight beyond the darkening scar the now-cooling lava cut across the ground.

Perhaps I can figure out how to use it to get back, she thought, and scurried down the hill.

Standing with her feet at the opening of the labyrinth she tried to remember the directions Eleanor had given her, thinking she might somehow reverse them for the return journey, but the pattern had been so complex, Gosha couldn't even summon up the first step. She ran her gaze along the path through a few turns and realized this wasn't the same kind of maze Timothy loved solving with his chewed up pencil in the Sunday paper. The lines before her traced a single, serpentine path within the circumference of the labyrinth. Perhaps all she had to do was follow it.

"There's no place like home," she whispered as she took the first step—

—And found herself in the hospital corridor, the thick, dense Influence clinging to her skin.

"Gosha!" whispered Eleanor, her face popping up from behind the counter. She ran around to wrap Gosha in a bear hug. "You made it back safe."

"How long was I gone?" Gosha inhaled the scent of jasmine wafting off Eleanor's hair.

"Five minutes at the most."

Eleanor released her from the hug, but kept a grip on one hand, as if Gosha might vanish into the Between again.

"Shetland, Rambouillet, Dorper." Rosamund's head bobbed behind her.

"What happened?" asked Eleanor.

"It worked. I trapped it."

Eleanor's gaze unfocused, staring through Gosha as if she weren't there. It only lasted a moment.

"Damson jam was always my favorite apparition," she said. When she registered the look of confusion on Gosha's face, she squeezed her eyes shut and kneaded her temples.

"Targhi, Ile-de-France, Boreray." Rosamund gently stroked her hair.

"Sorry, sorry. I shouldn't have done that. I can keep it together. I promise I can. Yes, it's there. I saw it. Did it do all that damage?"

Gosha shook her head. "That was me," she said.

"Oh Gosha, dear." Eleanor hugged her again. "You might turn out to be the best of us."

A commotion echoed down the corridor toward them. Rosamund grabbed them by the hand and pulled them back to hide behind the counter.

"Kerry Hill, Awassi," she hissed.

Five sets of footsteps clomped down the corridor and stopped at the shattered doorway.

"Des," said a man's voice. "Oh, crap."

"What happened?" said a woman. "Des!"

"Fuck this," said a second male voice. "We've got about five minutes before the doc brings the place crashing down."

"We can't leave them," said the woman.

"They're dead, Cathy," said the first voice. "Come on. If we don't hurry, we'll be jelly like the rest of them."

The footsteps scuttled on down the corridor.

"Jelly?" said Gosha as she rose up out of hiding. "What does that mean?"

The lights went out and emergency spots turned on with a loud clunk.

"We have to get everyone out." She walked out into the corridor and looked left and right, unable to decide which way to go. "We don't know how many other patients there could be in here."

"Unlock all the doors," said Eleanor.

"That'll take forever."

"If you do it one at a time, yes, but you're not thinking properly. Frame it the right way and you can open all the doors at the same time. A building like this is a closed system, an entity in and of itself. All the doors are part of it. Wish for every door to open and let the Between do the rest."

Gosha closed her eyes and imagined herself flying through the corridors, doors opening as she passed.

"No, no," said Eleanor. "Not like that. You have to see the building as a place where the doors are always open, have always been open, will always be open."

Gosha was well familiar with this kind of thinking. She'd twisted her mind into countless impossible shapes to Craft buttons, swatches of fabric, or roasted acorns, but she was getting tired. It was becoming harder and harder to hold subtle thoughts together.

As she took a deep breath and cleared her mind to prepare, her skin began to tingle, the Influence effervescing like a tablet of bicarbonate of soda dropped into a glass of water.

"Fry's Angel Delight?" said Rosamund.

The atmosphere exploded, ambient Influence buzzing with static a thousand times worse than when Dropnick had activated his wand device. The static penetrated her brain, digging into her synapses, taking her to the edge of unconsciousness and leaving her there stranded, unable to move or even collapse to the floor, unable to rub two brain cells together to generate a coherent thought. Eleanor and Rosamund stood rigid, every muscle in their bodies gripped tight, their faces twisted into inhuman expressions of agony.

The static penetrated deeper and deeper, obliterating memory, obliterating all sense of self. As Gosha faded into agony, her last thoughts terrified for what might happen to Edmund and Timothy and her mother without her, indignation flared up within her. Fury at the injustice of what this man Dropnick had perpetrated against innocent people, outrage at the determination with which the Convocation had persecuted her, all of it coagulated into a burning rod within her that refused to be extinguished.

The Between listened.

Pale fire ignited on her skin, a shifting purple-green phosphorescence that burned away the static and allowed her to think, making her whole again.

Eleanor and Rosamund remained trapped, unaffected by the fire. She gathered them up in her arms and hugged them close, expanding her outrage to include the prejudice the Convocation had about all witches, extraordinary women who had done nothing wrong other than to embrace their own power and dare to use it to help others.

The pale fire flickered and spread, wrapping the others in its fingers. Gosha felt their muscles relax, the deadly seizure abating.

"Gaussian integers!" exclaimed Rosamund as Gosha released them, the pale fire clinging to their bodies.

"How is he doing this?" said Gosha.

"The Convocation used enormous turbines in the basement to create their dampening field," said Eleanor, rubbing her jaw to release tension in her muscles. "He must have a giant version of that beastly wand of his."

"Let's go," said Gosha, turning at a run toward the staircase.

Oh, great, she thought. *Another hole in the ground.*

A deep hum thrummed through the stone floor of the basement, the vibrations rattling Gosha's teeth as she stepped out of the stairwell into a low, dank space that was filled by a giant framework of brass and steel containing an elaborate clockwork mechanism. Deep within, three large metal drums shook violently, the vibrations reverberating in the confined space. Directly in front of them stood a console, a small wooden lectern with gauges, dials and switches embedded in the surface. A strip of red lights flashed on and off down one side.

"How do we turn it off?" asked Eleanor.

"A finding spell, maybe," said Gosha. The dials and switches were identical to the ones on the device Margrave had used to harvest the Influence from his followers. A finding spell had worked back then, showing her the sequence needed to turn the device on and off. She patted down her pockets. "I don't have anything to use as a medium to tell us which switches he used."

Rosamund pulled from the pocket of her robe three blue pills and handed them to Gosha with a grin.

"Royal jelly," she said, a beam of self-satisfaction spreading across her face.

As Gosha took the pills and ground them to powder with her heel, Rosamund lost interest and wandered away from them to examine the machine. Gosha scooped up what she could of the powder and held it in her palm.

She pictured Dropnick pulling switches and turning dials on the console, pictured all the patients in the hospital frozen in death spasms, pictured them suddenly free—

"Gosha, stop," said Eleanor, placing a hand on her arm and pulling her away from the console.

The pale fire around her and Eleanor had faded to nothing. Static began to buzz against her skin and grab at her synapses.

"You left too much of yourself behind to keep the creature contained. You can only do one thing at a time. Let me try."

Gosha tipped her hand to pass the powder to Eleanor and focused once again on the purple flames. The crippling effects of the device began to fade as Rosamund tugged urgently at Gosha's sleeve.

"Chutney, chutney, chutney!"

"Better go with her," said Eleanor as she stepped up to the console and surveyed the apparatus. "I can take care of this."

Rosamund dragged Gosha around the corner. In an alcove built into the side of the machine lay two women and a man strapped into gurneys with brass and copper crowns attached to their heads that were linked to the machine by wires. Their skin was pale and dry, their cheeks sunken below staring, unseeing eyes.

"Eleanor!" Gosha shouted. "Don't bother. Come quick."

"Chutney," said Rosamund as she stooped over the woman to peer in her eyes and shook her head. "Tomato, ginger, mango."

"Lady save us," said Eleanor as she came around the corner and saw the tableau.

"I bet they're powering the machine," said Gosha. "Let's get those things off them."

They each went to one of the invalids to free them, but as they removed the crowns from their heads, each of them began to shake violently. Their eyes rolled back in their sockets and saliva frothed from their mouths. Within seconds, they were dead. A loud creaking shook the machine, and the drums fell silent.

"Dammit!" shouted Gosha, appalled at herself that she wasn't able to do anything to help them.

They stood in silence over the bodies.

"Mitochondria," said Rosamund in a small voice.

"Yes," said Eleanor. "You're right. The machine's stopped. We must hurry and get everyone out of harm's way in case that horrid little man has anything else up his sleeve."

"Remember," said Eleanor as they stood in the middle of the hospital lobby, "without the Between, the freeform casting of spells requires deep concentration. It requires emotional heft. None of that will work with the Between. Only lightness, clarity, and absolute, sustained conviction will get you what you want." She waved her arms in the air and performed a little pirouette to punctuate her meaning. "All this is even more important when you try something large scale."

"Okay," Gosha nodded, rolling her neck and cracking her knuckles as if she were about to step into the ring for a boxing match.

"In your mind it must be as if this hospital is a place where the doors are never closed and never have been closed. Patients are free to come and go as they want. Got it?"

Rosamund crossed her arms and frowned, unconvinced.

"Romanesque, Gothic, Muscovite," she said, shaking her head.

"I have it."

Gosha cocked her head and found the stillness inside her that allowed the twilight glow of the Between to seep through the cracks in reality and pictured the hospital in the way Eleanor had asked. She pictured the twilight glow in every nook and cranny of every cell and treatment room, every office and workstation. With the ambient Influence freed of its turgid stasis by the dismantling of the machine downstairs, it returned to its usual gentle flow, making it easier to imagine this place a center of healing and renewal rather than the prison Dropnick and his followers had made it. She pictured calm and happy people wandering from room to room in pleasant conversation, or sitting and reading quietly. In her mind it became a spa she would happily check herself into. She sent the wish into the talisman.

With all the force of a puff of air, the spell was whisked away from her. A solid click echoed through the ground floor and all the doors she could see swung open.

"Now what?"

Eleanor shrugged. "I suppose we wait."

The electric clock on the wall above the reception desk clicked to mark the passage of a minute and then another. No one came.

"They can't all be dead," said Gosha. "Rosamund, how many patients are there in the building?"

"Baroque, Palladian, Pombaline," she said.

Gosha looked to Eleanor for translation.

"At least thirty or forty people. They're probably too addled to think for themselves, like those poor men painting the cards. Perhaps you should summon them. You've got the hang of it now."

Gosha let out a breath, closed her eyes and imagined herself speaking into a microphone welcoming a crowd of people as they filed into the lobby in steady streams down the stairs and from the back of the building. In the spell's puff of release, she realized she missed the intense feeling of timeless bliss that enveloped her whenever she spoke a spell. This way of doing Craft was so ephemeral. She could see how witches gravitated to the Betrayal and abandoned the old ways.

It took less than a minute for the first patients to come shuffling in from the corridor behind the reception desk, all looking pale and weak. Soon the lobby was packed.

"What are we going to do with them?" asked Eleanor.

"Let's get them all outside first," said Gosha. "Then we can find a public phone box and call for ambulances. We can be away and back to the others before anyone arrives."

Eleanor held open the front door as Gosha began to usher the crowd through two or three at a time. Rosamund stood by the door nodding as they passed, a Queen receiving her people.

Sir Wilfred, Andrew Mills, and Richard Howell were last, Sister Bernadette in tow.

"Sir Wilfred," said Gosha, clasping him by the shoulders. "It's Gosha Armitage. Do you remember me?"

He regarded her amiably, his eyes clear and bright, his mouth open as if to say something, but no words came. His eyes crinkled with distress.

"It's okay." She pulled him into a hug, something she would never have dared at the club. "Don't worry about a thing. We'll get you taken care of."

"How, though?" said Eleanor.

"I have Joel Adair's number memorized. I'll tell him to come and get them. Then we can bugger off. Come on."

She took Sir Wilfred and Andrew Mills by the arm.

"Take the other two, would you," she said to Eleanor as she led them across the now-empty lobby. "Maybe Adair can do something for Sister Bernadette as well."

As she stepped out the front door into the cool night, arm-in-arm with the two men, a wall of glaring lights cut through the night and blinded her.

"Gosha Armitage." An amplified voice echoed across the square. "The building is surrounded. Surrender immediately and no one will get hurt."

45

GOSHA PULLED THE TWO MEN back inside with her and slammed the door shut.

"Fucking hell."

She ducked down below the pebbled glass windows embedded in the doors.

"Ballista, cannon, trebuchet," hissed Rosamund as she ran to peer through a window.

"Soldiers?" said a confused Eleanor.

"Barzhed."

Gosha spoke the binding spell to seal the door without thinking and the room twisted sharply to the left. She staggered back into Sister Bernadette.

"Gosha, be careful!" Eleanor rushed to her side to steady her.

"I'm okay." Gosha pushed her away and joined Rosamund at the window.

The glare of lights caught on the grimy glass, but she was able to make out the scene outside. The patients were being ushered away by the Convocation's soldiers in their black uniforms and riot helmets. Helmets poked up from behind parked cars staring down the barrels of rifles pointed at the hospital door.

Gosha's heart pounded in her chest.

"If we use the labyrinth, can it deposit us back in reality somewhere else?"

Eleanor came up behind her. "Yes. It can take us anywhere you want."

"Let's do it, then—"

"Mrs. Armitage." Gosha recognized the voice: Perkins, Griffiths' steward. "Your co-conspirators have already been apprehended. Your children are being returned to their father. There's nowhere for you to go, any of you. We know who you are, who you all are. Dame Graham has shared with us her files on all the witches in the realm. The nation's security services have turned their attention upon you. All witches will be in custody of the Convocation within the next twenty-four hours."

"Lady preserve us," whispered Eleanor.

At first Gosha couldn't breathe. Only forty-eight hours ago she was at home in her kitchen worrying about putting food on the table. Now every witch in Britain faced execution because of her. Her mind raced back in time, as if she could somehow undo all the decisions that had led her here. But, as she forced herself to become calm with long, deep breaths, she found that same column of fury deep within her that even Dropnick's terrible machine couldn't extinguish.

"I've had enough of this shit," she said, more to herself than either of the others. "I have all this power, we have all this power, but we can't do a damn thing with it to help ourselves."

"This is what I meant about surrendering power to the saints," said Eleanor. "We have so much potential, but we've always been content to put our heads down and work in seclusion at the edges of the world, unwilling to stick our necks out for anything that would jeopardize our precious independence, even though we bargained it away centuries ago."

Gosha paced the length of the lobby and back, thoughts rushing through her brain so quickly she could barely track them.

"We have to warn them," she said, a plan forming in her mind. "We have to tell everyone what's coming."

"How, though?" said Eleanor.

She took her lipstick from her bra and held it in her hand.

"The Devil's Star, but on a large scale like all the doors."

"Scarab, weevil, ladybird, firefly," said Rosamund, nodding her head vigorously.

"Global thinking," said Eleanor. "Yes, it could work. One giant network of all the talismans in the realm vibrating as one."

Gosha's anger turned to excitement as the plan began to deepen in the back of her mind.

"It won't be enough," she said.

"Witches are resourceful," said Eleanor. "If we warn them quickly, I'm sure many of them can go into hiding."

"What then?" said Gosha, shaking her head. "How many witches are there in Britain?"

"Across the entire British Isles? Five hundred? A thousand?"

"How will a thousand witches hide from the authorities? Can we all just show up on the beaches of Dunkirk and expect to be taken in? We have to take a stand. We have to lay this nonsense to rest or none of us will ever know peace."

The idea seemed preposterous as the words came out of her mouth, but now that she had given them voice...

"Can you bring them here through the labyrinth?"

"What, all of them?"

"A thousand witches flooding Turncoat's Gate will send a message the Convocation can't possibly ignore."

"I can't," said Eleanor, shaking her head, her face creased with worry. "To open the labyrinth for so many people is more than I can manage. Too much of myself is tied up in the Between. And even if I could, I can't force them here. They'd have to come of their own volition."

"You and the others have only ever spoken of the saints with contempt." Gosha began to pace again, the movement helping her think. "Is that just you, or do all witches feel that way? And what about the portents? Every witch on Morel Road has been muttering dour warnings about them for the past three years. Something terrible is brewing for us all. If it's not Dropnick and that thing he called into being, then it's something coming from one of the saints. I've been a witch long enough to know nothing good comes from the meddling of oath-bearers."

"I can show you how to open the labyrinth," said Eleanor, her head bowed in thought. The light shining through the window caught on her tight black bob, turning it white. "But you won't be able to do it and open the Devil's Star to everyone, or the creature will surely escape."

Her gaze unfocussed as she looked into the Between. She sighed.

"I'll do it," she whispered.

"You'll show me how?"

"No. You cast the Devil's Star, I'll open the labyrinth."

"I thought you said—"

"It will cost me, but I've been on the sidelines for far too long."

"Greengrocer, laundromat, chemist's, library." Rosamund placed a caring hand on Eleanor's shoulder.

"I'll get a little older and a lot battier. I'll be fine."

The heat fueling Gosha's piss and vinegar cooled at the thought of Eleanor sacrificing herself.

"Mrs. Armitage." Perkins' electronically amplified voice rang out across the square. "You have five minutes to obey. After that, I cannot guarantee your safety."

At that, the heat within Gosha burned brighter than ever.

"Okay." She realized her hands had clenched into fists. She shook them out. "Let's go."

Gosha closed her eyes and recalled the relief she'd felt in the ladies' room at the Convocation hall when the Devil's Star came to life and she could hear her mother, Elsie, and all the others. She recalled the feeling of not being alone, of hope that with the support of her sisters she might find a way out of the mad predicament she'd found herself in. She thought about the other witches she knew: Millicent Harkness working away at the hairdresser's on Bolton Street; Iron Jenny at her stall in Morel Market, and all the other specialist vendors dotted around Morel Road in their secret shops and stalls that only other witches could see. And Rosamund, who had been so badly abused by Dropnick. Holding all those attachments in her mind, she imagined all the other witches across the country with their talismans watching over their communities and working unseen. She imagined her own little circle and how it might connect to everyone else in a giant web of community, hidden away from those who would judge and condemn them as they had for centuries, the traditions of Craft flowing across the web for generations.

Letting the thought go, she felt it whipped away from her and into the lipstick. Now came the hard part, trusting that the Between would interpret her wish properly and make it happen.

"How's it going?" she asked Eleanor.

Eleanor ignored the question, absorbed in concentration as she walked a complicated pattern across the lobby floor muttering to herself.

"Beret, fez, kepi, bowler?" asked Rosamund, but without Eleanor to translate, Gosha had no idea what she meant.

When the whispers began, Gosha knew the spell had worked. At first all she could hear was one half of a conversation between a witch and her daughter, explaining the properties of garden plants, but it was quickly followed by layers upon layers of interactions: bargains being struck, recipes given to kitchen visitors, cackles of laughter and whimpers of fear, gossip exchanged in Witches' Cant and normal speak, even the sound of lovemaking.

Gosha took a deep breath to steady her shaking hands.

"Four minutes," came Perkins' voice from outside.

"Sisters," she said, and the cacophony of witches across the Devil's Star was immediately silent. "My name is Gosha Armitage. I am a witch of Cheyne Heath in London. We're all in danger. Euphemia Graham, the Queen of Secrets, has betrayed us and given our names to the Convocation of Saints. They're coming for us, all of us. I offer you a choice: drop everything, abandon your homes, your loved ones, and your communities and flee. Flee because there'll be no hiding. They mean to wipe us out, down to the last woman. Or join me. Step out from the shadows, face this injustice with me and take a stand against the Convocation. We've all worked too hard and done too much to care for and protect our communities to be extinguished by a group of men and women whose only concern is the pursuit of power and immortality. Our very existence is a threat to their power. Let's make good on that threat and stand up to those who would persecute us. You've all seen that a great disaster is coming, something that could spell ruin for everyone: witch, oath-bearer, and common man alike. Can we trust the saints to protect our parents and children and cousins once they've wiped us out? Can we afford to surrender our lives to an organization that hates us for no other reason than that we refuse to submit? Join me. Join me and resist."

She looked over at Eleanor, who finally stopped pacing. Around her, the twilight glow traced the circular path of a labyrinth that spread out across the lobby, through the walls and into the square outside. Eleanor nodded her readiness.

"I've opened the labyrinth to you all, a lost pathway forged by a great and forgotten sister. Follow the beacon and it will lead you to me. Please join me. Without you I can't stop the Convocation from killing us all. Without you I can't stop the nightmare that's coming. Sisters, I beg you, stand with me for all our sakes."

"Three minutes," said Perkins.

Gosha held her breath.

The twilight glow of the Between grew brighter. Ghost images appeared walking the path of the labyrinth and became solid, depositing Iron Jenny, Millicent Hargreaves, and several other of the stallholder witches with Gosha in the hospital lobby.

"Of course it would be you," said Millicent, the twilight glow fading. She was her usual ultra-fashionable self, with her asymmetrical pomegranate-red haircut, turquoise bustier, and fuschia tutu skirt. "Never happy unless you're looking for trouble, aren't you."

She looked around the lobby.

"I always knew this pace was no good. One of my clients started seeing a shrink here and was never the same again. Ended up mad as a hatter. There was nothing I could do for her."

"Rosie!" said Iron Jenny, looking radiant as ever in Gosha's special home-brewed makeup. She hugged Rosamund. "Look at you. Aren't you the worse for wear."

"Ooh," said one of the stallholders, a sturdy woman in her early sixties dressed in the standard market uniform of unfashionable jeans, a sensible top and jacket, from the window. "Marsh mist. Haven't seen that since I was a girl in East Anglia. This should be fun."

Gosha ran to join her as the glare of the floodlights dimmed and a thick, gray mist rolled into the square.

"Two min—" Perkins' megaphone cut out with a squawk.

Shouts rang out across the square, most of them male, and then there was silence.

"Job well done, if you ask me," said the stallholder with a grin.

"Heidi," said Iron Jenny to the stallholder. "Get that window open won't you? She's done a right number on this door."

Heidi placed a hand on the window frame and whispered a spell. The window shook once and the layers of hardened paint sealing it shut cracked so she could slide it open with ease. She climbed up on the bench beneath it and straddled the opening, one leg in and one leg out.

"Looks like that lot will need a little help getting through," she said, nodding toward Sir Wilfred and the others.

"What happened to her?" said Millicent as she led Sister Bernadette to the window.

"Long story," said Gosha as she helped the frail woman through the window.

"I've no doubt." Millicent raised a sardonic eyebrow as she inspected the ragged remains of Gosha's over-styled attempt at a man's haircut. "Interesting. You should come by the salon and let me take care of that for you."

Outside, the mist was a real pea-souper. Gosha was unable to see much more than four feet ahead of her. She helped Eleanor down from the window to the pavement. She had aged by a good thirty years, her hair now salt and pepper, her back just a little stooped.

"Stay close," said Gosha as Eleanor stepped out into the street.

A cluster of familiar figures loomed out of the mist: Alfie, Johnny, Agnieszka, the boys, and the rest of the ladies.

"Mummy, mummy." Edmund and Timothy ran at her. She crouched and wrapped them up in her arms.

"We were so worried," said Timothy. "The police came and took us away. They kept saying you'd done terrible things."

"I didn't believe them," said Edmund. "They weren't even real police. Their uniforms were all wrong."

"Don't worry," said Agnieszka. "I'll see to it they'll wake up in their beds in the morning and think it was all a dream."

"Nothing they said was true, darling," said Gosha between kisses. "Everything's going to be fine."

"Is it?" said Agnieszka with a scowl and looked out at the mist.

"We'll see if a group of hard-working women can rout the rats," said Gosha, not bothering to give the verbal sign she was shifting to Witches' Cant. Her mother knew what she was saying. "Can you look after them a while longer?"

She handed the boys back to her mother and kissed Alfie full on the lips.

"Are you okay?" he asked when she finally pulled back.

"It's not finished yet. Johnny," she said as she hugged him. "We found Sir Wilfred. He's in bad shape. Can you talk to him? See if you can bring him round?"

Sir Wilfred was only a couple of yards away from him, but Johnny would never have known in the dense fog had Gosha not pointed him in the right direction.

Another figure, a stranger, strode from the mist, a handsome woman with long, reddish-brown hair tied up in a loose ponytail, wearing a hand-knit gansey sweater, a long tweed skirt with leggings underneath, and sturdy hiking boots on her feet.

"Which one of you hard-working women is the Armitage witch?" she said in a thick Scottish accent.

"That's me," said Gosha.

The woman reached out with a steel grip and shook Gosha's hand with three no-nonsense pumps.

"Grace Kinnaird from the Outer Hebrides. That was some trick you pulled. Wasnae any witch not gonna come after that. Those hoity-toity bastards have gone to ground in the park, but the lasses have them surrounded. Want us to knock some heads, or do you want to talk sense into the dickheads yourself?"

"Mamusha, Alfie, will you stay here with the boys?" she asked, turning back as she followed Grace Kinnaird into the mist, passing a pair of men in Convocation uniforms lying unconscious, spreadeagled on the tarmac.

"Don't worry about them," said Grace with a chuckle. "They'll wake up in a few hours with the worst hangover of their lives."

As they went deeper, other figures began to emerge. Women of all ages, all ethnicities, and all walks of life stood silently, patiently looking toward the park.

"Out the way, ladies," said Grace, pushing her way through the throng. "Armitage witch coming through."

Bodies stood shoulder to shoulder as far as Gosha could see in every direction, which, she admitted to herself, wasn't very far at all. She thought she counted two or three hundred as they wove their way through the park.

The crowd spread out when they got to the center. A dome of clear air, free of the mist, thrust up among the ring of women. Within were the saints she'd seen in the Convocation hall and several acolytes eyeing the crowd nervously. In the middle, Joel Adair chattered on his enormous mobile telephone.

No George, she thought with a sigh of relief that the wards around Cheyne Heath had held against him. At least she had that going for her.

"Mrs. Armitage," said the Lord Chief Justice with a sneer when he saw her emerge from the mists. "I suppose you think you're very clever with your amateur theatrics. This changes nothing. It's only a matter of time before reinforcements come. We will have you all in custody by sunrise."

"Feckin eejit," Grace Kinnaird muttered under her breath before Gosha could respond. She looked behind her and shouted. "Mina, Dolores, drop the smoke screen!"

A wind blew up out of nowhere. The mist was gone in seconds, revealing a sight that filled Gosha's heart with awe. Not two hundred or four hundred, not even five hundred or a thousand witches filled the square. The press of bodies was so great in number that it spilled out along the side streets in all directions under the bright moon. Eleanor had miscalculated terribly. Easily five thousand women or more stood, watching and waiting. Griffiths and the other saints—even Adair and Delilah Davina, her supposed allies—blanched at the sight.

"How about now, ye poxy wanker?" said Grace Kinnaird. "Sorry, love," she grinned at Gosha. "Carry on."

A witch standing behind Grace raised a small cut-glass figurine of a cat that glittered in the moonlight and hummed a note that spread from witch to witch, from the circle all the way back out to the square and down the side streets, each witch raising their talisman into the air to re-join the Devil's Star, a gesture that, multiplied by several thousand, became a fearsome salute of defiance.

—Can someone tell us what's going on? said a voice across the link. *We can't see a damn thing in the back!*

A chorus of whispers flooded the link as witches in the front of the circle narrated the events before them.

"Lord Griffiths," said Gosha, ignoring the whispers. "We've done nothing wrong. All we've done is try to help."

"You are terrorists, anarchists, and seditionaries. You unleashed unholy hell on the populace of London. We will not capitulate!"

"Your Lordship." Gosha did her best to sound as reasonable as possible, but it was a struggle. "I'm a mother of two. I make a living on homemade artisanal cosmetics, fertility charms, and cures for nicotine addiction. All these women are the same. We're not terrorists. We're your mothers, your sisters, your daughters. This hatred you have for us is based on centuries-old prejudice fostered by the Church who didn't like it when parishioners paid more attention to their midwives than their priests."

"What about that horror you unleashed today on Paddington Station?" Griffiths sneered. "A dozen good men and women are dead because of you."

"Witches are an abomination," said Bishop Worsley, elbowing his way past Perkins and another of Griffiths' acolytes to get to the edge of their protective bubble. "They are vectors of sin and an offense to God!

Those poor, tragic souls who died at her hand are all the proof we need of their immorality."

"Is that so?" An evil smile spread across Gosha's face. She'd had just about enough of this shit for one lifetime. "You know a lot about sin and immorality, don't you, Your Excellency." She turned and shouted back at the crowd. "Can someone bring me Sister Bernadette and Sir Wilfred?"

Worsley turned green about the gills as the circle of women separated to reveal them, both oblivious to their surroundings, led gently forward by Millicent and Johnny.

"He's the one you should be turning your disgust on." Gosha pointed an accusing finger at the bishop. "He conspired with a man named Dropnick to kidnap Sir Wilfred Stepney and four of his friends to force them to create artifacts of power, but they didn't know what they were messing with. Under their sway, the men also created the objects of corruption that caused the tragedy at Paddington. I and my friends were only there to help, and we wouldn't have been there at all had it not been the request from Waterford, Wakefield, Winston, and Whorl."

"Preposterous," said Worsley, studiously not looking at Sister Bernadette. "Where's the proof?"

"The proof? Back there." She cocked a thumb behind her at the hospital. "Dropnick was experimenting on innocents, altering them to control their Influence. He killed a dozen people completing a ritual to contain the entity that did all that damage at Paddington. Who knows how many more bodies you'll find in there?"

"Your Lordship," said Worsley, leaning in as if to speak in confidence, though his voice remained loud and clear so everyone could hear the weasel's performance. "This Dropnick character sounds like an unspeakable threat to every one of us. She is clearly in league with him. Don't let this show of intimidation cloud your vision."

"Apparently," she cut in, "Bishop Worsley has lived so long because he feeds on his followers." She immediately regretted her words. Griffiths' face hardened at the outrageousness of her claim, spurred on by the pantomime of bemused horror Worsley put on beside him, but she pushed on. "I have the proof right here."

She went to Sister Bernadette and led her to the edge of the protective bubble.

"He had Dropnick create a device to make it easier for him to consume the Influence of his followers in small amounts so he doesn't have to explain why one of his closest followers mysteriously disappears in every generation."

This touched a nerve in Griffiths and Euphemia Graham, both of whom turned on the bishop an appraising eye.

"He used the device to consume Sister Bernadette's essence and leave her a mindless husk."

"Gracious! What a story this woman is telling," Worsley blustered. "And where is this fantastical device?"

He placed a hand over the cross Dropnick had made for him and slid it behind the collar of his robes.

"There," she said, pointing at the cross, but Worsley waved his original crucifix in front of him.

"What, this thing? This is a gift from a cherished parishioner. It's nothing more than gold leaf and paste."

"No," said Gosha. "The other one. It's working as we speak, siphoning off Influence from his acolytes."

His three acolytes standing with him in the circle regarded Sister Bernadette with horror.

"Perkins," said Griffiths, calling his steward over. "Your viewer, please."

Perkins took from his pocket a sheet of glass in a silver picture frame which he handed to the judge. Griffiths held it up to peer through at Worsley and his acolytes.

"The device is under his robes," he said, pointing to it. "Get it."

Perkins strode over to the bishop and, ignoring Worsley's protests, patted him down, found the cross, and took it from him.

"You have no authority to do this!" squealed the bishop. "You have no right. A saint is sovereign to his Sphere."

"And yet, he is also accountable to the Convocation," said Griffiths, examining the cross with his viewer. "Restrain him," he said to Perkins, who signaled to two other black-uniformed acolytes of Law. The men seized the bishop by the arms and pulled him away from the edge of the bubble.

"Your Lordship," said Adair, pushing to the front. "The partners can provide you with a detailed dossier to support Mrs. Armitage's claims. We have evidence stretching back several centuries of Bishop Worsley's activities."

"You have been surveilling the saint of another Sphere?" said Griffiths, incredulous at the news. "This is an outrageous violation of the principles we have all agreed upon."

"Oh, come on, Griffiths," said La Davina, her red sequins shimmering in the moonlight. "You and Graham are as bad as they are. Every one of us has spies keeping tabs on the others. Don't be a hypocrite."

Griffiths looked like he was about to say something in response, but the rejoinder died on his lips as he allowed his gaze to travel across the wall of witches staring him down.

"This persecution of witches has to end," said Gosha, reclaiming the floor before the saints got caught up in their petty politics. "We won't sit passively in our kitchens and wait for you to drag us to our deaths, when all we've done is care for our families and communities."

"Is that a threat, Mrs. Armitage?" said Griffiths.

"It's a statement of fact, Your Lordship. We're an army of women with secrets and powers you couldn't even imagine."

A murmur of approval spread across the Devil's Star, bolstering Gosha's train of thought.

"Witches were here long before there were ever saints and acolytes, and witches will be here long after you're all dead, no matter what you do to try to wipe us out."

—*Here, here,* said a chorus of voices.

—*Sod the bastards.*

—*Go for the throat, lass.*

"It's time you accepted that we do not recognize your power, that we will never kowtow to you."

Beside her, Grace Kinnaird covered her mouth and muttered into her lapel.

—*A flashy display wouldn't go amiss right about now, ladies.* Her voice came in clearly across the link.

Clouds rolled suddenly across the sky, accompanied by a deep and threatening peal of thunder that rumbled in Gosha's gut. Sparks of static electricity flickered through the crowd from center to edge and back again, and a giant unkindness of cawing ravens flew across the moon.

—*Good, good,* muttered Grace. *Don't overdo it.*

The static subsided, and the clouds rolled away as suddenly as they had come.

"Do you want this army turned against you?" said Gosha. "How effective do you think MI-5 and the SAS would be against us? Wouldn't it be more prudent to come to favorable terms with a power such as ours with this portent of doom that's hanging over us all?"

—*Have we all been seeing signs? I thought it was just me,* said a voice Gosha didn't recognize.

—*Hush, Mabel. You're not the only one who can read tea leaves.*

Even Euphemia Graham looked unnerved at the thought of a battle with the witches.

I bet she really regrets accepting our oaths now, thought Gosha.

"My Lord Chief Justice, Speaker for the Convocation," said La Davina, her voiced raised as if in the council chamber. "We have present a quorum of saints. I, Delilah Davina, Saint of Strength, formally request to address the chamber."

"The chamber recognizes Delilah Davina of Strength," said Griffiths, raising a wary eyebrow.

"My Lord, I move that the Convocation strike all rules, regulations, and conventions from the codes of governance regarding the treatment of witches."

"My Lord," said Colin Dancy, the saint of Liberation at her side, his skin glistening in the moonlight. "I second the motion."

Griffiths surveyed the crowd.

"It is moved and seconded, to strike all rules, regulations, and conventions from the code of governance regarding the treatment of witches. Is there any debate?"

"Witches are anathema to the Convocation and to God," shouted Worsley from where he was being held in the middle of the bubble. "Thou shalt not suffer a witch to live."

Grunts of disgust reverberated across the link.

"His Excellency Bishop Worsley, Saint of Faith, is under investigation for crimes against the Convocation," said Griffiths. "Until such time as the council can be satisfied the accusations are without merit, the Saint of Faith is stripped of all voting rights. Is the chamber ready for the question?"

No one spoke.

—*This is great,* said another voice unknown to Gosha. *Just like Crown Court on the telly.*

"The question," said Griffiths, "is on the adoption of the motion to strike all rules, regulations and conventions from the codes of governance regarding the treatment of witches."

"Strength carries the proxy for Fate and Fortune," said La Davina.

Griffiths rolled his eyes and shook his head. "All those in favor?"

All except for Euphemia Graham said "aye." She glared at Gosha with the predatory eyes of a lizard.

"All those against?"

"No," she said and cocked her head at Gosha in challenge.

—*Ooh, I always hated that stuck-up cow.*

"The ayes have it," said Griffiths, "eleven to one. The motion is carried. All rules, regulations and conventions from the codes of governance regarding the treatment of witches are struck forthwith." He turned to Gosha. "There, are you satisfied? Can we all go back to our business now?"

He waved his hand as if he could dismiss five thousand witches with a gesture.

—Ugh, bloody toffs. Think they own the place.

—Is that it? Did we win?

—How do we get home? I left my purse with my rail pass on the kitchen table.

Grace stepped up, turning her back on the Convocation to face Gosha and whisper.

"Seems good, yeah? Satisfied?"

"I think so," said Gosha. "There's a couple of things I need to take care of, but that's the worst of it."

Grace crossed all four fingers of both hands.

"Ye can get us all back home can't you?" The echo of her voice across the Devil's Star was muted by the gesture.

Gosha looked over at Eleanor, a little faded, a little stooped and a lot older, and hoped she would still be coherent enough to show Gosha how to open the labyrinth.

"Yes. It may take a few minutes."

"Mm. Best not keep us up too late. I don't imagine the fine folks of Cheyne Heath will appreciate the presence of every witch in England, Ireland, and Wales on their doorstep when they open the door to pick up their milk."

She uncrossed her fingers.

"Make way, ladies, for the fine men and women of the Convocation." Her voice echoed across the link once more.

Griffiths spearheaded the exodus of saints and acolytes, shooing witches aside with the full expectation that he would be obeyed.

"Your husband," said Euphemia Graham as she passed with a tart gleam in her eye, "had an unfortunate accident crossing Wegman Street. Suddenly lost control of all his faculties. Had to drag himself back across the road on his hands and knees in front of everyone. Very embarrassing. I don't imagine he'll take well to that. You'd do well to watch your back."

She eyed Kinnaird up and down with a distasteful curl of the lip and sniffed.

"How's the pig shit?" she said as she walked away through the corridor opened up by the parting crowd.

"Never liked that woman," said Kinnaird.

Gosha pulled Joel Adair aside as he passed.

"Can you do anything for these poor people? There's hundreds of them."

She led him over to Sir Wilfred and Sister Bernadette. Sir Wilfred watched the departure of the saints with a bemused smile. Sister Bernadette remained as blank as ever.

"Grace," she called across the clearing. "Where are the rest of the patients?"

"We've got them penned in on the corner."

"Let me call Event Management," he said, clicking open his briefcase to take out the handset of his phone. "Can you take me to them?" he asked Kinnaird, who led him away.

With the saints and acolytes gone, the tone of the assembled witches loosened. Conversations began, soft chatter overlapping across the Devil's Star. Gosha went over to Eleanor.

"We should get everyone home."

"Pastel colors never look good on—" Eleanor shook her head. "No, no. I still have a little sense left in me. I'm going to need sleep. Lots of sleep. Do you think you'd watch over me? It could be a month or two."

"Of course. You can stay in my room. I'll put a cot in the studio and move down there. Can you show me how to open the labyrinth?"

"It will be my pleasure. We can do it right here. There's plenty of room."

She hugged Gosha's arm and walked with her to the center of the clearing, two old friends taking a stroll in the moonlight.

"Are you ready?"

Gosha relaxed and allowed the twilight glow of the Between to seep through the cracks in reality.

"Good, you'll need to drive. Follow me exactly, step for step."

The vast crowd of witches watched as Gosha followed Eleanor in a complicated pattern across the grass. The labyrinth appeared, its complicated weaving spreading out across the square and into the streets beyond. One by one, the witches shimmered and vanished, returned to where they'd come as easily as they'd been brought there. When they were done, all that was left were Gosha, the ladies, her children, Alfie, and Johnny.

What a family we've become.

"I think I've given all I've got for now," said Eleanor, patting Gosha's hand. Her eyes glazed over and crinkled with confusion. "Bitter fruit. Not my favorite flavor, but I'm sure I can make a delicious pie. Just needs enough sugar."

"Elsie," said Gosha, leading Eleanor toward the opposite side of the park where everyone was waiting. "Can you look after her?"

Elsie scuttled over and pressed Eleanor into her ample bosom.

"Oh, Eleanor, darling! You brave, brave soul!"

"She's going to stay at our house until she feels better."

"Wonderful idea. We'll make you comfortable," Elsie cooed at Eleanor. "I'll get in all your favorite treats."

Gosha let Elsie lead Eleanor away and closed her eyes for a moment to enjoy the night, cool and quiet once more now that the five thousand bodies cramming the square had disappeared.

An eerie screech echoed across the buildings and a wolf howled in the distance.

She opened her eyes. Above her, the moon had grown into a giant disk that filled the sky, its light so bright she had to shield her eyes. As she raised her arm, she realized the jasper serpent ring was gone.

"Dear Mrs. Armitage," said a camp, plummy voice behind her. "Did you think we'd forgotten about you? Time to pay up, my dear."

She turned. Two enormous dragon heads hovered above her.

46

SHE FOUND HERSELF STARING into two vast caverns lined with sharp and gleaming white teeth, and a pair of long, thin tongues darting from side to side, sipping at the air.

A high-pitched shriek of fear behind her tugged at her maternal instinct. Behind her, all on his own, stood Edmund, face pale and eyes wide with fear, Agnieszka and all the others gone. She ran to him and wrapped her arms around him, putting herself between him and the dragon heads.

"It's okay sweetie," she cooed. "They won't hurt you."

If she could have, she would have swept him up in her arms but he was far too big for her to carry. She clasped his hand tightly and pulled him behind her as she turned to face the serpent heads.

"We had an agreement. I have a month until I need to pay you."

The heads slid back and forth, scaled coils rolling over each other as they crossed their paths.

"Such an analytical mind, don't you think, brother Aloysius?" Murgatroyd shook its head, sending a rippling wave of scales down the length of its body.

"Oh yes, brother Murgatroyd, and yet she did not tend to the letter of our agreement."

"Oh no, so foolish of her to act in haste," said Aloysius. "So foolish of her to presume she understood, when she only heard what she wished to hear, and not the words that were actually said. The agreement was that you would come to us upon the next night that the moon's countenance is turned toward the earth, and its power is at its greatest strength."

"Yes, the full moon was last night. I have four more weeks before your payment is due."

"Surely a witch would know the moon's power is at its greatest strength for a full three days before and after the Lady Moon is at the apex of her journey?" said Murgatroyd.

"Surely," said Aloysius, "a witch would understand the rules which govern the Craft she has devoted her life to perfect?"

"Our Lady Moon is as powerful this night as she was the last, as she was the night before," said Murgatroyd. "This is the time we agreed upon, whether you understood the commitment you were making or not."

Her mind was cloudy with weariness. Her body tried to produce adrenaline, but couldn't, its supply exhausted after twenty-four hours of running for her life. She gripped Edmund's hand harder in the hope that she might squeeze from it some solution that would get him home safe from the Shadowlands and these treacherous creatures.

"There must be something else I can offer you, something else that would satisfy you?"

Aloysius shook its head and curled back a lip to expose an even greater length of glistening sword-fangs.

"The agreement has been made. Our services were given. Now we want what is ours."

Four enormous eyes blinked as the heads edged around her to peer at Edmund, who wrapped his arms around her waist and whimpered.

"What are they talking about?"

"Nothing sweetie. They're just silly old things."

Both dragon heads rumbled deep in their gullets, a sound that made her sweat and dried her throat all at once.

"We will be generous," said Murgatroyd, pulling back and rising up on the tree-trunk of its body. "We will give you three guesses. Fail to answer correctly and we will take what is ours."

"Answer the question," said Aloysius as it slithered around them, trapping them in a loop of giant coil. "What are we?"

Gosha had hoped to reach Pauline Sutton, Saint of Shadow and the mistress of these creatures, to find out the answer, and though the dread of this moment had been a tiny knot in the pit of her stomach, she hadn't given the question a moment's thought. They were dragons, they were a ring on her finger, they were guardians at the foot of the shining white tower at the center of the Shadowlands. Clearly the question was a trick, but she had always been useless at riddles, unable to even solve the silly ones that fell out of Christmas crackers the boys loved so much.

Nothing. Nothing came to mind, not even the vaguest notion.

She turned and crouched so that she could wrap Edmund in her arms again.

"I love you sweetheart. I love you so much," she murmured into his ear as she clenched her eyes tight trying to concentrate.

Out beyond the edge of the square, a shadow wraith screeched, its unnerving cry making Edmund whimper again.

Their bodies might still be in Turncoat's Gate, outside the psychiatric hospital, but their minds had been transported by the dragon heads to the Shadowlands. But the Shadowlands were themselves nestled within the Between, at the border of the other place where the Lords and Ladies dwelt. She was, essentially, in the Between, and in the Between she had power.

She let out a deep breath to calm herself and find the twilight glow. As stillness descended, something deep inside her unlocked, and she found it. It was faint in this dark and twisted reflection of reality, but there it was, a soft diffusion in the flush of Edmund's cheek, in the reflection of burning moonlight in the surface of the pond at the center of the park, even in the evil glitter in the dragon heads' eyes.

She pictured what she wanted—a doorway out of this place that would take them to safety, back to the house on Canterbury Gardens, where she could tuck Edmund in and tell him the happy ending to this story—and sent the wish into her talisman nestled against her breast.

A dozen feet ahead of her, the glow intensified in one tiny mote of light that pulsed like a golden firefly floating above the grass. The speck of golden sunlight elongated, a split in the unreal stuff that made up this awful place. It grew and grew until the split became a tear through which Gosha could see the grassy hill with the stone on top where she had awoken to find the aged Eleanor, the stone they had touched that had brought them back to the real world.

"Edmund, run!"

She grabbed him by the hand and ran as fast as she could, dragging him behind her.

"Treachery!" shouted Murgatroyd.

"Deceit!" shouted Aloysius, his voice growing closer even as they ran.

Edmund lagged behind her. She practically dragged him along as they passed through the tear from darkness into twilight.

"See the top of the hill," she panted as her feet pounded into the soft turf. "Do you see it?"

"Yes," he screamed.

"At the top is a large stone sticking up out of the ground. Touch it and you'll be safe."

She yanked him forward and pushed him ahead of her.

"Don't look back," she shouted. "I'm right behind you."

She stopped and watched his little legs carry him off into the distance and up the hill. Without a moment to catch her breath, she spun to face the dragon heads. Above her loomed the enormous storm cloud of the Lords and Ladies of Influence. The dragons had reached the tear, but it was too small for them to pass. They threw themselves at it, biting with their sharp teeth and powerful jaws, worrying it open.

She put her hand to her chest, realizing the pressure of the lipstick against her skin was gone and the great swirl of oxblood pigment spread across her arm. She pictured what she wanted, and in her hands appeared two blades, two large knives with sharp points and vicious serrated edges. For a moment she felt powerful, invincible, but then the dragon heads burst through the tear and slithered across the grass to tower above her, and the feeling of power drained away. She wasn't one of the heroes in the boys' storybooks who tilted fearlessly at ogres and dragons.

She wasn't one of those heroes, but she was a witch.

She flipped the blades into a reverse grip, stabbed them into the turf and sliced, willing the ground to quake and cleave. The Between obeyed. An immense split ripped out from where her knives stuck out of the earth. The ground shook, and the split became a ravine, the baking heat of molten lava rushing up at her from the bottom. The serpent heads reared back, hissing and gnashing their teeth, unable to pass.

She didn't need to slay the dragon. She just had to get her child home and safe.

The fissure was wide and deep, but it didn't spread far. The serpent heads realized this and darted left to race around it, but it had bought her time. She turned and ran.

Though Edmund was strong and athletic, he was still only ten. She caught up with him halfway up the hill as the dragon heads reached the base.

"Keep going," she shouted, pushing her before him as the dragon heads gained on them.

At the top they were almost upon them. She grabbed Edmund's hand and, with a might that she would never have in the real world, swung him at the stone. His fingertips grazed the rough, pocked surface and everything stopped.

The world froze between one heartbeat and the next, twin pairs of enormous jaws swooping down upon her to bite off her head, Edmund suspended in mid-air, one hand holding hers, the other touching the stone. The twilight glow deepened, her whole world turning incandescent with purple, gold, and orange hues. The inner quiet she'd been struggling to find to cast her spells descended upon her and seeped into her cells. All the anguish and drama of the past twenty-four hours fell away in a receding tide, and Gosha understood what Eleanor had told her. The Between was in her blood.

Reflected in the black slits of the dragon's eyes, she saw as clearly as if peering through a window a young girl's bedroom. The room was small, a bedroom in a council flat, one she recognized as Becklow Towers, where Pauline Sutton had grown up. On the bed sat a small, frightened girl with full red lips and violet eyes, Pauline aged no more than seven. She slid from the bed and ran to the door, pushing it shut. She grabbed a long fabric tube stuffed with something heavy like sand or wheat and wedged it into the crack under the door. The door shook with the force of someone hammering on it from the other side. It pushed open, but the tube was wedged firmly in place and stopped the door from opening more than a crack. The young Pauline hid behind the bed and cried.

Gosha looked closer at the fabric tube: brown satin decorated with pink and green argyle diamonds down its back. At each end was a wedged-shaped head with animal toy eyes and red snake tongues sewn in.

"You were the draft excluder Pauline Sutton put under the door to protect herself when she was a child! You've always been her protector, even before she became Saint of Shadow."

Time rolled forward again and Edmund vanished.

"You cheated!" said the dragon head on the left. She'd lost track of which was which.

"How? How have I cheated? The agreement was to answer the question, wasn't it? I answered."

"You guessed!" said the one on the right.

"You had help!" said the other.

"You deceived us! You never intended to be fair!" they said together.

"I did nothing of the sort! You took advantage of me in a moment of desperation. You sought to extort from me the life of my son. I'd say you're the deceivers."

The serpent heads snarled and gnashed their teeth, swaying back and forth on their shared tree-trunk of a body.

"Our arrangement is over," said the one on the left.

"No more shall we come to your aid," said the other.

"No more shall we debase ourselves with your petty concerns," said the first.

"Our association is hereby broken!"

"No, it's not," said Gosha, her fear diminishing in the face of the irritation she always felt around these ridiculous creatures. "Your saint instructed you personally to help me. Will you defy her?"

Both serpent heads hissed, their tongues darting about behind their sharp teeth, making Gosha quickly regret her cockiness.

"We serve the will of our lady in the tower," said the one on the left, "but we do so under protest. Be very careful the next time you summon us. You have made of us an enemy, no matter the bond of our word."

They turned and slithered back down the hill and across the plain toward the dark shadow beneath the storm cloud. Her hand shook with spent fear as she touched the stone—

—and found herself in the park in Turncoat's Gate. Edmund stood between Alfie and her mother, Alfie's hand resting affectionately on his shoulder, his mouth agape and the deep grooves of a frown chiseled into his face. From the look of everyone else, they'd been gone for no more than a second. No one seemed to have noticed that their minds had been elsewhere.

Over the past four years she'd done her best to keep all trace of the supernatural out of the boys' lives. As far as they knew, their father had left them for another woman, a lie she hated, but how could she tell them that their father was a sorcerer who had murdered their grandfather in his pursuit of power? It broke her heart a thousand times over to see the hurt she and George had caused them, but she'd been determined that they grow up normal children in a normal world where Craft and Influence were the sorts of things that only existed in stories.

"Hey, kiddo," she said, ruffling his hair as if nothing had happened. If there was one thing she was good at, it was denial. "Ready to go home?"

He gave her a long, serious look, too serious for someone so young, and glanced up at the moon.

"Good. Me, too," she said. "I'm exhausted. It must be well after midnight. You've never been up this late before, have you?"

She kissed him on the cheek. The twilight calm began to fade, and she felt her hands tremor with delayed shock, but she held herself together.

"Yeah," he said, long and drawn out as if trying to process something he wanted to say, but instead of an awkward question Gosha would have given anything to avoid, "Can I have a bowl of Weetabix when we get home?" popped out of his mouth.

"Anything you want, Eddie Bear."

"My name is Edmund," he said as they walked out of the square toward the main road. "I'm too old for that name."

"Of course you are, sweetie. I'm sorry."

She let out a sigh of relief, but as they turned the corner, he glanced back at the square and up at the moon. She was going to have to keep an eye on him to make sure he was all right.

After

SHE FOUND A MIRACULOUS PARKING space at the end of the block.

"Fuck the bastards," said Johnny from the cramped back seat of the Mini Cooper, his crushed velvet-wrapped knees halfway up around his ears. "You don't need them. We can raise a glass to Dougie and Joseph down the pub instead."

"You have every right to be there," said Alfie from the passenger seat looking ravishing dressed in his best black suit. "They were your friends, too."

She checked her face in the mirror, an unnecessary habit given her skill with a brush and the special properties of her homemade makeup, but a comforting one nonetheless. The haircut Millicent had given her looked good: sharp and spiky the way she liked it. Out on the street a couple she recognized from drunken nights of partying at the club dressed in somber evening wear got out of a black taxi and headed toward the doors.

"No," she sighed. "I have to go. Adair will be there. I need to hit him up for more work."

The huge cashier's check was already dwindling thanks to their mounting pile of bills and a broken hot water boiler too complex for a witch to fix with any recipe or spell.

They each took a second after clambering out of the Mini to primp. She checked her pocket for her lipstick. Over the past week she'd only had it against her skin when completely necessary, a welcome break from the barrage of ambient Influence on her subtle senses.

For once there was actual security at the front door of the Cheyne Arts Club and invitations were more than just a formality. The cover story the hacks at Waterford, Wakefield, Winston, and Whorl had come up with had stayed close to the truth: five celebrated artists arrested on trumped-up indecency charges by an anti-gay task force within the Metropolitan Police resulting in two unexplained deaths and a cover up that committed the survivors to a mental hospital. The scandal was all over the papers and several prominent heads had rolled at Scotland Yard, resulting in a marked spike in media interest in the work of Sir Wilfred and his friends. The security guard, of course someone Alfie knew from the nightclub circuit, checked their names against the list and unhooked the velvet rope to let them in.

The crowd in the bar, usually all spirited drinkers, stood around in small and somber groups, clutching their drinks and talking in low voices. Gosha had been to a few memorials at the club. They started quietly, but by nightfall they would rev up to a boisterous celebration of the dearly departed. Adair, dressed in a broad-shouldered and wide-lapelled black suit with a black sequined pocket square, excused himself from the group he was talking to and came over to greet them.

"Mrs. Armitage," he said with a broad, open grin. "Such a pleasure to see you here on such a tragic occasion. I was never properly introduced to your companions."

"Oh, I'm so sorry. How rude of me." To her surprise, the ritual of social interaction made her feel less nervous. "Alfie Lester and John Suharto."

"Sigit Sigit Johnny!" said Adair, using Johnny's stage name, his eyes lighting up. "I thought it was you. I saw you and your band perform at Heaven. It was a great show."

"Aren't you sweet," said Johnny, holding Adair's hand far longer than a polite handshake required as he fluffed up the large man's pocket square. Adair seemed quite delighted by the attention. "Great suit."

Seated on one of the overstuffed leather couches by the doors to the garden, Sir Wilfred held court. He looked tired, the sharp edges of his personality softened, but not worn away. Andrew Mills and Richard Howell, at the center of their own groups, looked much the same.

"Sir Wilfred's looking well, considering," said Gosha.

"Yes, they're responding well to the therapy we've devised, as are all the survivors, I'm glad to say. Terrible business. Without you it could have been much worse."

A silence fell over them as they all contemplated the peril of the week before.

Across the room at the bar, Gosha caught sight of Miranda in conversation with one of Sir Wilfred's favorite models. Miranda glanced over at them. Gosha smiled, but her friend made no sign of recognition.

"Mrs. Armitage," said Adair, interrupting the litany of regret that began to crawl its way up from the back of Gosha's mind, "forgive me for talking business, but we have a few accounts the partners feel would benefit from your particular attention. Hopefully nothing as serious as this, but still well within your unique area of expertise. Perhaps you might come and see me tomorrow at the office? Say at about ten?"

"I'd be happy to."

Not only did she need the money, but she was desperate for an excuse to get out of the suddenly very crowded house. With Eleanor comatose in Gosha's bedroom, and the ladies a constant presence as they tried to help Rosamund, Gosha's other new lodger, recover from Dropnick's treatments, plus endless awkward questions about the new arrangements from the boys, her every waking moment was a constant kerfuffle.

"Enough business," said Johnny, threading one arm around Adair's. "Let's get this party started. Buy me a drink, big boy?"

Adair beamed and allowed Johnny to lead him to the bar.

"I'll get us drinks. Usual?" said Alfie and followed them.

"Gosha, dear!" Sir Wilfred called out.

Fifty pairs of eyes turned to look at her.

Great, she thought, wishing she had a glass of wine for fortification as she joined him.

To her shock, Sir Wilfred sprung up from his seat and wrapped his arms around her in a bear hug. He was world-renowned as a cold and prickly individual, and a dreadful misogynist. Gosha didn't think they'd ever so much as shaken hands before.

"Come and sit by me," he said as he plopped back down on the sofa, shooing away his neighbor, a playwright enjoying a revival of his first play at the National Theatre. "Oh, don't be a sour puss."

He patted Gosha's hand as she sat.

"I was just telling everyone how I would still be in that awful loony bin if hadn't been for you. It's a marvel I'm still alive. Julian, you should have her find out who that awful man is who keeps sending you those dirty letters."

A week ago, all these people had been looking at her like she smelled of rotting fish, but she couldn't blame them. God knows what lies George had been spreading around about her.

"It's a nightmare, Gosha," said Julian, leaning in with abject worry pantomimed in his every gesture. "I feel like I can't get away from him."

“And Melanie’s been distraught trying to get her grandmother’s jewelry back from her cousin,” said Sir Wilfred.

“It was in the will,” said Melanie, her back stiffening in high dudgeon. “And she’s claiming it’s nowhere to be found.”

“Come to the house one afternoon this week,” said Gosha, settling into familiar ground. “I’ll make a cup of tea and you can tell me all about it.”

Two drinks in, Gosha excused herself from the chattering attention of the barroom. Thanks to Sir Wilfred’s exuberant endorsement and an open bar, the members of the club were warming to her once again. It felt good, she thought as she splashed water on her face, to have a doorway to her old life before Craft opening up to her again.

“Can you forgive me,” came a voice from behind her.

Miranda.

“George told everyone the most terrible things about you. He said you’d been cheating on him for years, you were on drugs, you stole all his money. He even said you threatened to run away with the boys.”

She stepped into view of the mirror, a shock of blonde hair and dark eyeshadow against her pale and freckled skin. She looked good.

“I wanted to believe him. Everything that happened was just too ... strange. His horrendous stories were easier to believe. I even convinced myself all that mess with Emerson was a bad dream. But then I saw the look in Wilfred’s eyes when he first came back to the club and I knew. It wasn’t only the business with the police, was it?”

“No.” Gosha shook her head and turned to face her. “It wasn’t.”

“Can you forgive me for being such an awful friend?”

Gosha hadn’t been sure how she would feel if this moment ever came. She and Miranda had been so close. She’d done so much for her over the years. Her rejection when Gosha had needed her the most had seemed impossible to overcome, but tears welled up in her eyes. Miranda would always be close to her heart.

“Of course.”

They hugged, a long embrace to make up for the distance between them, but Gosha couldn’t really enjoy it. Weighing heavily in her pocket were the remaining cards of her telling deck. Upon her return from the Between they all turned black. The cards had begun to lighten as the days passed in the vaguest mottling of light and dark, like a photographic image developing in a chemical bath in her studio.

She dreaded what that image would turn out to be.

ACKNOWLEDGEMENTS

Thanks again to Sandy Blaine, Lisa Simon, and Erica DiCaro for being trusty readers and editors, and to Curtis Wallin for the cover and my mother, Barbara Hulanicki, for the interior illustration.

And thanks to Kris for always being there.

ABOUT W. V. FITZ-SIMON

W. V. FITZ-SIMON is author of the Witch of Cheyne Heath series of supernatural thrillers. His books combine occult traditions, otherworldly realms, New Wave synthpop, camp, humor, and adventure. He lives in New York City with his husband where he knits sweaters (slowly), plays board games (frequently), and teaches yoga (joyfully).

www.wvfitzsimon.com
witold@wvfitzsimon.com
www.facebook.com/wvfitzsimon
www.instagram.com/wvfitzsimon

GET A FREE SHORT STORY

Be the first to learn about deals and new releases from W. V. Fitz-Simon, get exclusive sneak peeks behind the scenes, and receive a free copy of the short story, By Dawn, A Witch, the secret history of the first Witch's Betrayal.

Sign up for the free newsletter today at:

www.wvfitzsimon.com/free-book/

Made in the USA
Las Vegas, NV
28 January 2022